AT MIDNIGHT
IN A FLAMING TOWN

Lorraine Bateman
with
Paul Cole

First published in 2011 by
Karnac Books Ltd
118 Finchley Road
London NW3 5HT

British Library Cataloguing in Publication Data

A C.I.P. for this book is available from the British Library

ISBN-13: 978-1-85575-859-9

Typeset by Vikatan Publishing Solutions (P) Ltd., Chennai, India

Printed in Great Britain

www.karnacbooks.com

To our parents

I HAVE A RENDEZVOUS WITH DEATH

I have a rendezvous with Death
At some disputed barricade,
When Spring comes back with rustling shade
And apple-blossoms fill the air—
I have a rendezvous with Death
When Spring brings back blue days and fair.

It may be he shall take my hand
And lead me into his dark land
And close my eyes and quench my breath—
It may be I shall pass him still.
I have a rendezvous with Death
On some scarred slope of battered hill,
When Spring comes round again this year
And the first meadow-flowers appear.

God knows 'twere better to be deep
Pillowed in silk and scented down,
Where love throbs out in blissful sleep,
Pulse nigh to pulse, and breath to breath,
Where hushed awakenings are dear …
But I've a rendezvous with Death
At midnight in some flaming town,
When Spring trips north again this year,
And I to my pledged word am true,
I shall not fail that rendezvous.

—Alan Seeger (1888–1916)

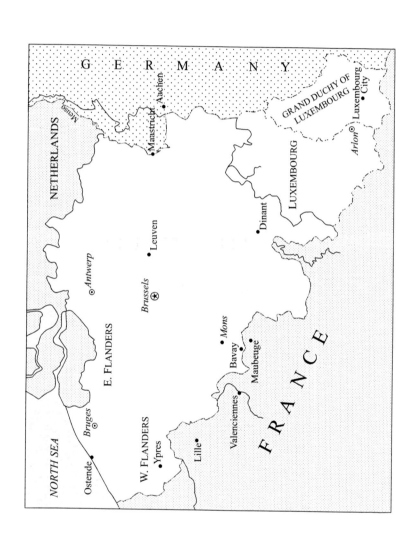

25TH AUGUST 1914

LEUVEN, BELGIUM

25th August 1914
Leuven, Belgium
Therese

Therese scrabbled to get away from him, tearing her fingernails on the stone floor. She writhed and twisted, but was trapped by her skirt beneath his knee. His breathing was heavy and his body and breath rank. The harder she fought the more there was for him to vanquish. Veni, vidi, vici. He came, he saw, and he would conquer. He pinned her down and his thickset fingers worked himself free from his uniform. He yanked his belt undone and pulled it in one movement through the loops of his trousers; the metallic sound of the buckle clattering on the floor was lost amid the cries and screams of women. She grabbed the belt and bit on it to withstand the pain and silence her screams, but she did not submit. In the final moments she was determined to find his eyes; she turned her head, held his glazed gaze, and tried to lance his soul with her look.

He finished quickly, fuelled by drink and domination. There was no movement from her. He looked down at the crumpled robes and for a moment saw them empty on the floor, as if discarded at the end of a day. He pulled himself backwards, up to his feet, and staggered to regain his balance. He almost forgot his belt. He bent to retrieve it, and wrenched it from her grasp. The heavy buckle caught in the folds of fabric released with his tug and was soon in place, on his waist, the words *"Gott mit uns"* (God with us) standing proudly engraved.

He was dressed and ready to regroup before many others; for him one was enough. He was more interested in food than another woman. Some would later boast of three or four conquests, depositing Prussian seed in each of their unwilling hosts. He moved away and saw another soldier climb onto her; it was easy for him, she lay still with those piercing eyes closed, her spirit broken. Her lips moved as she mumbled like the mad. Therese had retreated to prayer.

ONE MONTH EARLIER, 26TH JULY 1914

LEUVEN, BELGIUM

One month earlier, 26th July 1914
Leuven, Belgium
Russell

Having satisfied himself that the porter knew the address of his hotel, Russell left him at the railway station with his luggage, an American size tip in his pocket and the diversion of a trip across town. Russell had only travelled from Liege that morning so still managed a tidy, pressed look. His youthful vigour, long limbs, sun-tanned and handsome face created a stir when he passed people, but this was something he rarely noticed. Guidebook in hand, he strode towards the tram-cars, paid 12 cents and settled himself for the ride down Rue de la Station to the Grand Place. He could have walked, the temperature was moderate and it was no distance, but his seat on the tram made an instant connection, for him, with the town. He was in its flow, moving at the pace of the people.

With its silent commentary, his copy of Baedekers led his eyes to a monument of a revolutionary, then a bronze statue of a scholar, and offered details of architecture from pavement to rooftop. Russell swivelled around and ducked his head to spot the treasures, and received a few grunts from the man sitting next to him as he caught him with his elbow one time too many for him to let it silently pass.

"Pardon, excusez-moi," said Russell in French, tinged with his American accent; he had no Flemish to call upon. He received a grunt in response, but this had a more cordial tone: his apology had been accepted.

The highlight of Leuven was Russell's first destination. He was not disappointed when he alighted from the tram in front of the Hotel de Ville and the church of St. Pierre, in the central square. The Grand Place was indeed grand. He moved away from the disembarking passengers, and stood for a few minutes to absorb the scale of the impressive facades. It was not a market day, so there were no jostle of shoppers or mixtures of smells. The movement of people in the square looked choreographed: a matrix of unseen tracks were followed as walkers angled themselves, from their entrance on one side of the square, across the expanse, to their purposeful departure on another.

In no rush for detailed examination, Russell headed to a café and, with his pot of coffee ordered, soaked in the grandiosity of the medieval architecture; he knew that the majesty of the buildings was in the structure and external decoration. Russell had done his homework on Leuven or Louvain as it was also known and he was in the best café to admire the sights. Leuven was the last stop of his tour before Brussels and he had structured his visit, but first he wanted to enjoy the atmosphere, a drink, and some moments to catch up on the news. As he opened and began to peruse his copy of the daily paper, *L'Etoile Belge*, his attention was caught by the headline that the Serbian Army had mobilized against Austro-Hungary; he wondered what escalation would follow.

Trouble had been brewing in the Balkan area of the Austro-Hungarian Empire in recent years, with Serbia fighting its neighbours for more land, and encouraging nationalists to speak out against their imperial masters. It was a Serbian nationalist who had assassinated Archduke Franz Ferdinand on 28th June, the day Russell had set out on his European trip. He had kept a close eye on the news ever since; the murder of the heir to the throne would not be allowed to pass without punitive measures: of that, the politicians, and newspaper editors, it seemed, were sure. When Russell was in Liege, a couple of days before, the emperor, Franz Josef, issued his ultimatum to Serbia. It was designed to bring the Serbs into submission, and to hand over the murderers of his nephew. Instead the Serbians secured Russian support and both began to ready their armies. In response the Austro-Hungarians prepared for war, assured that Germany would protect their eastern flank from Russia.

Russell understood enough about international politics to know that brinkmanship was at play, but he assumed that diplomacy would still win out. The picture his newspaper painted was more pessimistic; it referred to the pact between Russia and France, which placed Germany between two adversaries. The German Army had started its own preparations to fight on two fronts. All were poised, but would one of them strike?

The latest telegram from his parents had urged him to get back to England; news that trouble was brewing in Europe had hit the headlines in the USA. He imagined their concerned breakfast conversations and wished they could picture him now, relaxed and enjoying the view in front of him. His parents would not appreciate that Belgium was neutral in these matters and, even though it might be in the thick of it, geographically speaking, it would not take sides; he was in one of the safest places in Europe. Even if he wanted to leave, it would be easier said than done. His tickets were pre-booked and pre-paid; a great value deal at the time, but with little flexibility for last minute changes, without extra cash, and of that he was short. At railway stations during the previous days, he had seen queues at ticket booths. There were some heated exchanges when homeward bound travellers put the infrastructure, and themselves, under stress to head west. There are always those who panic, but he was not one of them, and he enjoyed a rueful smile. Russell had been determined not to miss out on Leuven and his visit to the university: for him the European sister to the blue spires of Oxford.

Similar to Oxford University, with its numerous colleges, Leuven's academic history was just as prestigious. The university lay behind the Hotel de Ville, and currently out of Russell's sight in Rue de Namur. Usually when he set himself a timetable, he stuck to it. The university was on day two of his itinerary; but perhaps in response to the edginess that seemed increasingly to pervade these July days, he walked around, instead of up to, the Hotel de Ville, to the main building of the university. A medieval hall that housed the cloth market in centuries past, it was intricately decorated. Baedekers kept in step with his progress and delivered information when he scanned its pages, but his personal interest was with the library. He established his bearings there for his appointment the following day and then headed back to the Grand Place.

Russell followed closely the written descriptions through the large rooms of the town hall, and then attached himself to a group of tourists as they entered the church of St. Pierre. With its many ornate chapels and bell tower, all designs were for the glory of God, and to him, it seemed, for the intimidation of man. There was nothing soft or comfortable in the Gothic lines and the cool air. Although initially welcome when he stepped in from the street, the chill soon seeped through his jacket and skin, almost into his bones; he became conscious of his shivers. He left the church, and walked past some "sweet little houses", into Rue de Malines and a sun-filled street that warmed him. The transition was so swift and easily made that he never, in weeks to come, recalled his moment of discomfort, that a person with pre-cognition might have called dread.

His steps soon brought him to the church and convent of St. Gertrude. He had no more appetite for religious artifacts: they oppressed, rather than impressed, his spirit of wonder. A chapel man himself, he needed no symbolism to focus on his God, just solid wooden planks to surround and underpin his spiritual communion. Instead of entering the church Russell looked at, and into, the windows of the surrounding houses that formed part of the convent. They looked like every other building in this part of town, but Baedekers informed him that the blue door led to the schoolroom, the green one was used by the sick and behind the two white doors were housed some of the nuns of St. Gertrude. He could make out very little inside the rooms and soon felt embarrassed by his peering curiosity and moved on.

Rue de Malines crossed a couple of tributaries of the river Dyle that meandered alongside the street, north to south, and ended at the ramparts that encircled the city. Russell walked along the ramparts, stopping whenever he fancied, in sun or shade, to enjoy the vantage point and rooftop views of the town, home to 45,000 residents. He had no need to rush. During one of his stops he mentally retraced his steps through Europe, recalling the highlights of his tour, and his thoughts returned to Oxford and his studies.

When Russell arrived at Oxford the previous October, he had deposited his bags in his rooms at Merton College, and almost run to the Bodleian Library in his desire to inhale the historic air. He could recall the tingle of electricity that coursed through him the first time he handled historic documents, and imagined travelling

10

back through time. His Oxford. The intensity of his passion for the place made him call it his own. Not for him the familial rite of entry; he was an interloper from another continent who competed to prove himself worthy of attendance and his acceptance had made the national as well as local press in America. A Rhodes Scholarship was a known path to significance.

He could clearly remember the day when, a student in Washington, he was called to the provost's office. This was an invitation, or more accurately a summons, without precedence. So unusual was an audience with the senior college administrator he had to ask directions to the office, which took him to a corridor he had not known. Along the walls were details of the long history of his Georgetown University and, with time to kill, he lingered at some of the pictures of benefactors. He adjusted his tie and was ushered in.

The wood panelled walls of the provost's office stood in solid guard over the many conversations they held secret. The provost poured each of them glasses of water and had them both seated before Russell even considered how to announce himself.

"Let me get straight to the point, Mr Clarke, Russell, and tell you why I asked to see you. I want you to apply for a scholarship. It would bring honour to this university, be an example to your fellow students, and probably change your life. I know you can be successful."

Without seeking a response he went on.

"Hear me out, go away and think about it, and come back and give me your decision, perhaps after you have talked it over with your folks, and if they need to be convinced, bring them in to see me."

With his silence taken as agreement the provost launched into what was probably going to be one of the most momentous conversations of Russell's life; a turning point, fed by another's belief in him.

"The deal is the Rhodes Scholarship, named after an Englishman called Cecil Rhodes. Actually not after him, named by him. It's his vision and money that fund it, so it's really his legacy. It's an international award to study at the University of Oxford with all expenses paid."

He suddenly had Russell's full attention.

"Competition is tough for this, very tough. There are only 50 places worldwide each year."

Russell was a man of words, not numbers, so did not even attempt to get his mind around the odds that were represented by these statements, but he was not daunted by the thought of competition. If the provost said he was good enough, then Russell was ready for the effort.

"You'll need to prepare your application and Professor Atkins can tutor you on this. You have all the credentials scholastically, and your captaincy of the tennis team shows you as an enthusiastic sporty guy. I've heard you're quite popular too. You speak French and Spanish and your downtown internship with those Mexican immigrants will make a distinctive contribution. All you need is to work out your philosophy for your life and convince them of your worth in service to others, and what you want to study, of course. Do you know Atkins, he's our head of philosophy?"

Russell had almost staggered out of the room, dazed and disoriented. It was a surprise to have his achievements and activities so well known by another and to have them used to create, in one brushstroke, an image of himself that seemed fully formed. Throughout the 23 years of his life he had driven himself down each path of achievement, but had never stepped back and joined the dots to admire the result. Instead he was always more conscious of the next mountain to climb, and yet here he was, singled out, and expected to surpass his peers.

His parents had been delighted and were beyond proud when he won a place; Professor Atkins had groomed him well.

The scholarship had taken him to England and his summer tour to Europe. Now in Leuven, with a privileged ticket for the reading room, he had access to the priceless collection of medieval manuscripts in the library. He could not wait.

His hotel was easily found, in Place du Peuple, as was the dining room that he waited to enter at the time stated by the receptionist. There was a slight jostle as the crowd that had formed in the vestibule surged forward when the doors opened. He was in the middle of the restaurant before he had even begun to take in the room, propelled by the tide of guests. He looked around and did not know where to sit, but was rescued by the head waiter who directed him, by a movement of his head, to a table next to a window. The restaurant had 12 tables in all. The white tablecloths and napkins brought a starched freshness to a room that was otherwise a nondescript brown colour. Russell was not alone for long; he was joined by a couple, in their late twenties, he thought, also American. Russell quickly learnt they were on their honeymoon from the conversation that tumbled out of the newly-weds. He was charmed by the way their words bumped into each other and she sometimes corrected his. He liked the way they talked over each other and their need to have him listen, his quips or a question every now and then enough to set them off onto another memory that just had to be described.

"Tell him about Certosa di Pisa, honey."

"Those three-dimensional paintings ..."

"And amazing tiled floors that leapt up at us ..."

"We were on our way to Florence ..."

"From Pisa ..."

"We just stumbled upon it ..."

"It was empty of people ..."

"Awesome."

Their pride at their "off the beaten track" discovery could not have been greater if they had actually unearthed treasure at an archaeological dig.

"The paintings covered the walls ..."

"And ceilings ..."

"You felt like you could put your hand behind the figures ..."

"Geez, they were so old."

Russell did not want to steal their delight so kept quiet about his own visit, specifically to see the trompe d'oeil paintings in the 14th century Carthusian monastery in the town. He had planned his circuitous route from Florence to Lucca via this site, and they were correct, it was largely overlooked. The couple re-lived each moment and he could see they were storing their memories for future access. Russell was happy to provide the prompt.

They progressed through the initial formalities of their meal and placed their orders, the selection matching the budget, and Russell hoped, his palate. The newly-weds turned their attention to learn more about him. Every fact he proffered, to their questions, was matched by one of their own. They echoed his "I'm from Maine," with "We're from Iowa." His "I'm a history student, on a programme at Oxford University, England," with "We're teachers." Then followed, Russell felt, a somewhat defensive description of how their

13

schooling, in Iowa, was not as grand as Oxford, but they were sure they were going to make it good. Her "Weren't we already as we're on honeymoon in Europe," and his "You should've seen the size of our wedding," provided the introduction for her to describe their wedding, until they were almost through to dessert. Russell heard all the details; it was an easy interlude for him.

Introductions were not always easy for Russell. With his accomplishments and good looks, he stood out from the crowd, but he was not always at ease in company. His attempts to pare down answers about himself could make him seem aloof, awkward, and even slightly patronizing. It was too easy for a new acquaintance to assume he carried disdain for another's more mundane life, when this was far from his actual perspective.

To distract further conversation from their wedding, or more questions about himself, Russell drew out of his dinner companions their plans for the following day. He was able to pass on snippets of his experience to help them with their itinerary. When he described his planned days in the reading room of the university library, she, Mrs Felson, laughingly said: "You'll have to wash off the grey dust of ages past, before you come in for dinner."

Her husband said she sounded "quite the poet", and Mrs Felson seemed to melt at his compliment. Russell experienced his solitary distance from their entwined world when he withdrew for his coffee and they retired to their bedroom. He imagined that neither husband, nor wife, wanted too much time to elapse from compliment to embrace.

Russell breakfasted alone, ahead of many of the other guests, and enjoyed his Belgian pastry. He returned to the university and made his way to the library. With his student documents, and letters from his professor and the librarian at the Bodleian, all found to be in order, he was invited to step from the public corridors, into the inner sanctum of the reading-room. Russell was led to his assigned seat and glanced around while he waited for the manuscripts he had previously ordered. The room was magnificently decorated, with wood panels and exquisite carvings of a bygone age. Here time had stood still. He intended to savour every moment.

Along with the manuscripts came a pair of white gloves, the type worn by butlers and magicians. These were not to protect his hands, but to ensure he left no mark on the documents that crackled at his touch. His research project at Oxford was to determine the roots of jurisprudence by tracing the way law was created and developed throughout the medieval period. Today's legal documents had been the property of Burgundian dukes, and while his ability to make sense of the writing would be limited, the experience of seeing and touching them was one of reverence; Russell marvelled that they had kept safe and significant to this day.

Russell settled himself into a day of total absorption, and remained blissfully unaware of the increased tensions that ricocheted throughout Europe. He little realized that these manuscripts would never see the light of day again.

28th July 1914
Brussels
Marion

With matron away, Sister Wilkins had called a meeting for later in the day. Not even a declaration of war, it seemed to Marion as she tugged and tucked in the crisp and clean sheets, could upset the training routines. She put her hands to the small of her back as she righted herself, before she shuffled the pillows into their rigidly starched sheaths. She stood and admired her work. There was not a patient in sight, but the room of beds was pleasing with its regimented rows, stiff with anticipation. With time in hand she stood and gazed out of the window. She was lost in a reverie of dream-like thoughts when Clara, one of the domestics entered the room with a bucket and mop. She nodded when Marion stepped past her and out of the ward. They held no conversation; Clara's English was as poor as Marion's German. The best for them was when they both spoke French, but today they had nothing to say and too much to absorb.

The morning's newspaper contained the Austro-Hungarian declaration of war against Serbia along with a flurry of editorials opining what needed to happen to curb further aggression from other countries. Upset had been created and offence caused. All could and must be settled, Marion had read, before any further shots were fired.

Columnists in the national press still clung to Belgium's neutrality. This was not their war.

Marion paid more attention to news reports since she had left England. She tried to follow the politics of the country where she was living, much more than she had done at home, where such conversations always took place among the men, and she was not expected to comment. In fact, to do so was frowned upon in her circles and a woman could easily be snubbed and dubbed a suffragette if she voiced strong opinions about any subject. Marion secretly admired this feisty set of women who would not conform to the way the world determined they should be. In a quiet way she had mounted her own personal rebellion, to train at a school of nursing in Brussels which was run by an Englishwoman. This had not been part of her mother's plan, but Marion carried the maternal disappointment lightly. It was through a chance remark someone made to her father that she found herself selected, and on her way to Belgium in October 1913.

Excited about her adventure Marion arrived prepared to embrace the full experience of working and living abroad. She found that Brussels was not a difficult city to feel positive about; easy to get around, with wide tree-lined avenues, and cafés on almost every corner. She arrived on her first day with the list of items she had been directed to bring with her. This included her probationer's uniform, which she so admired. She wore it with pride and relief. For her it was a badge of honour, her statement of individuality, and a form of identity that required no words of explanation; her place in the world was understood. She would not stand in the shadow of a man's achievements for her status in life to be determined. She had rung the bell at 149 Rue de la Culture without the slightest feeling of trepidation, just excitement, and was greeted warmly by two students.

The school had been opened in 1907 and was now a well-established provider of qualified and apparently much sought-after nurses. Marion had signed on for five years, a length of time which horrified her mother, who saw her consigned to spinsterhood when released at the age of 27. Three of those years were for her training and then two were required to fulfil contracts on behalf of the school in local hospitals. Marion's escape from situations arranged by her mother and aunts, for her to admire eligible beaux, and in turn to be admired, had almost become necessary for her mental health. Her frustrations had built to a dangerous peak with her wishes relentlessly ignored. Perversely, she found the less interest she showed in the vetted men, the more they inclined towards her. When she did engage them in conversation they would concur with the "awfulness" of the set-ups and the expectations they were destined to meet.

In her mother's softest moments she had declared Marion ridiculous for not accepting a husband. She should trust that adequate freedoms would accompany the right match; she was being stubborn, and blind to the ways of the world, and what it cost to live. In her hardest moments, she just refused to speak, and would withdraw from Marion and the household with one of her headaches.

A favourite of her father's, Marion had welcomed his support and subtle influence on her mother. Marion knew he would have made a stand if he had evaluated one of the suitors as worthy of her, but luckily he shared her judgments. They discussed the young men and were in agreement about their lack of maturity; all appeared to be dutifully sitting in the passenger seat of their own lives, driven by parental expectations, rather than steering a course for themselves.

In recent years Marion's father had met an increasing number of the more entrepreneurial type of man. Marion knew he enjoyed their spark and could see their type of drive would keep pace with her energy, but they were considered too vulgar and grasping by her mother and perhaps she was right. Marion's drive was not for betterment in material ways: of such things she seemed quite oblivious. She simply wanted to be the best she could be and needed time to discover her own potential before she signed herself over to the control of another, as she saw it, and the constraints of a marriage.

Despite her father's support, Marion was aware that her refusal to step into the status quo created tensions in the family. Her father preferred a settled existence, and their life had been largely predictable and comfortable. His living as a country rector had been the gift of his cousin. Marion's family lived on the periphery of grandness. They were neighbours to her father's cousin, William Drake, lord of the local manor, JP and master of hounds. He was a landlord with extensive holdings, and a lineage that described him as the tenth generation to hold such titles and wealth. Her

19

branch of the family were by now the poorer relations, but through friendship, horsemanship, and location, they had maintained enough invitations to be aware of the social niceties that should govern their family by association. Like Austen's Bennet family their household was not wealthy enough for an entitled entrée to society, but they were considered too refined for her or her sisters to marry men from the local town. Luckily, as she had so often heard her mother say, all the girls had good looks and fine figures, not insignificant considerations when it came to negotiating a dowry.

William Drake's generosity in giving debut parties for her and her sisters' seasons had encouraged two men of good standing to step forward, and they were now her brothers-in-law, both Army officers. Unlike her sisters, Marion held on to her determination to be different. She was no bluestocking, practical rather than intellectual, and when she applied herself to studies, she learnt quickly. She had withstood her mother, and decried the marital measures of success so readily adopted by her sisters.

It had been through a congregational connection of her father's that the Brussels opportunity had materialized. Her interview had taken place in London, preceded by lunch in Piccadilly and followed by the tea rooms at Fortnum and Mason; all accompanied by her mother, who was determined to have some pleasure from the day.

"What do you know of nursing?"

This had been the opening question at her interview. It had caught Marion out; she had been ready to launch into the reasons why she wanted to train as a nurse. She took a few seconds to re-orientate herself and her answer.

"Nursing is an honourable calling and a profession in which the particular skills and graces of a woman can be best applied."

Marion was proud of this statement, crafted over many hours of preparation and was deflated with her interviewer's retort.

"Yes, very laudable, but what is it that nurses actually do? What conditions do they work in? In what ways do they need to think? What is the reality of this world you want to make your own, what can you tell me of that?"

The flood of questions was delivered with a more jaded than aggressive tone. Marion rose to the challenge, and talked in a detailed way of what she understood to be the expectations of the job of a nurse. She was soon in her element and in full flow.

The moment of triumph for Marion was when asked, "When can you start?"

With the formalities over Marion was delighted when her interviewer confided in her. She said she had spent the morning meeting girls who fell largely into two camps. One sort was the dreamy ones, who thought of nursing as glamorous, and leading to amorous advances in their lives. The second were those who favoured the freedom of a nurse's hostel over a garret, and considered the job the same as being in service in one of the big houses. She told Marion she was a perfect candidate for this fledgling profession that had yet to define clearly the entrance requirements.

Somehow the fact that she would be abroad added an acceptable level of glamour and mystique to the life she sought, and sat more comfortably with her mother when she declared Marion's plans to those whom she considered needed to know. The fact that Marion would be out of sight, and for many thereby out of mind, drew a halt to the gallop of odious comparisons made, and enjoyed, by those mothers who had all their daughters married. Her mother's ladies circle, even though part of their congregation, could be competitive under the cover of Christian concern.

Marion stopped to straighten her cap as she caught sight of herself in the mirror on the landing at the top of the stairs. Her dark brown hair would never lie flat, even when pulled back into a bun: tendrils always escaped onto her forehead and the back of her neck. She was tall, slim, and cut a fine figure in her blue cotton uniform dress, with white apron, white linen sleeves, and plain white cap. She gave herself a smile and continued down one flight of stairs, almost at a skip, her skirt held in one hand, and the other, to guide her, slipped along the dark wooden banister. She followed through the corridors that eventually took her into 147. The nursing school and clinic stretched through four houses that had been knocked together in ways that tracked budgets more than design. No floor layout was straightforward, and routes had to be learned to access rooms in the sequence that doorways and stairways made possible. Sometimes she gave up, and instead of weaving her way through inside, she would leave by a front door, and re-enter further down the street.

This was frowned upon, but not forbidden and was sometimes her only glimpse of the sun on days that were intensively timetabled.

All the houses shared the basement, for the use of laundry, storage, and service rooms, and the garrets were for the domestic staff. 149 was occupied by the matron, or *directrice*, as she was also called, and her two assistants, nursing sisters Wilkins and Jones. They had their private rooms, as well as offices and consulting rooms throughout the various floors. Next door, 147 housed a small operating theatre, and lecture and teaching rooms. 145 contained the patients' beds, divided into wards of five to ten beds each, and six private rooms. Number 143 was the largest, and was used as a hostel for the nurses. The houses were on the opposite side of Rue de la Culture to the medical institute, where major surgery, and their surgical training, took place. A project was underway for new facilities, but they were some way from completion.

There was little privacy afforded the probationers. 143 housed them all, Norwegian, Dutch, English, German, and French. Each nationality adopted a slightly different approach to the disciplines of the establishment, and high spirits always found their outlet. The students generally mixed well, but close friendships tended to be with fellow nationals. The intimacies and nuances of life were more easily shared in the same language, but they studied in both English and French and were taught Flemish.

This was Marion's first day after a run of night shifts. She felt sluggish and hoped she could maintain her attention in the meeting. The noise of voices in the room muffled to silence as Sister Wilkins started to talk.

"There is a growing air of disquiet around in Europe and we have received telegrams over the past few days, and more today, from some parents, who request we release you to go home. We can't anticipate what the politicians will conclude. These are anxious times, but we don't know how worried we should be, whether there will be difficulty ahead, or if this will be a storm in a teacup. I don't intend to make any decisions today, and will wait on the return of Matron Cavell. She's due back from England on the fourth of next month. Then we'll review the situation, but I don't want any of you to be unduly worried. If your circumstances are cause for personal concern, then do come and see me, and we'll work out what we can. Meanwhile, back to your duties and tomorrow's lectures will follow their planned schedule."

She repeated her pronouncements in French, but gave up trying to translate "storm in a teacup", and Marion could see she left the room slightly flustered.

It took a while for the room to clear, and the opportunity to share reactions was immediate. Regardless of the language in use, everyone had had their say by the time the room was emptied, the air warmed by the sentiments of solidarity against parental concerns. Marion doubted her parents had telegraphed.

It was later that evening before Marion gathered with some friends and fell into conversation again. Their talk played down the fears, and each stated their determination to stay. Marion's friend Gwen implied that efforts to create a drama were foolish when nothing was clear, a line that Marion thought to adopt in her next correspondence home.

"We have tests coming up, and are better served putting our efforts into our studies," Olga had stated, with Germanic brevity. The girls started to test each other for their anatomy paper. Mostly in their early twenties—Marion was typical at 22, they were too mature for schoolgirl giggles, but they did share some laughs at the diagrams of the male body.

Marion drifted off to bed earlier than most. Her body clock struggled with the change in shift and she lay awake longer than she usually did. Marion located the smallest flutter of what— excitement?—in her solar plexus. There had been something different about today: the meeting with Sister Wilkins was a change to routine, the backdrop of news, parental interference, all contributed to a sense of anticipation and slight unease, but before she could think further she fell into a deep sleep.

1st August 1914
Leuven
Russell

As Russell lay in bed, images from the week drifted in and out of focus. He felt a slight stiffness in his lower back, the result of days sitting on a wooden chair, bent forward over documents. He kicked off his sheet and blanket to do some stretching; his tennis coach came to mind. He bent both legs and together let the weight of his knees tip to each side until he felt the pull through his back. He contemplated more exercise and swung his legs off the bed: sit-ups would be next, but his feet on the floorboards put him off such exertions. He could move a rug to give him a softer base but he did not fancy putting his head down on the dark wool whose pattern disguised years of tread and no doubt dirt. He was a fit man used to physical routines, and the walk of a tourist, even though miles could be covered in a day, did little to raise his pulse. He wind-milled his arms and almost knocked the bedside lamp off the set of drawers next to his bed.

His room was small. It took very few steps for him to move to his sink and peer at his reflection in the brown age-spotted mirror. His ablutions were swift. Not one to pamper, he wasted neither time nor thought. While he shaved he recalled the conversation at dinner last night with Mr and Mrs Felson. He had noticed a tension between them: surely not a lovers' tiff?

They had all sat at the same table, at the same time with the same waiter and were presented with the same menu. The routine had comforted with its familiarity, and provided a moment of belonging for Russell on this transient trip. More used to one-night stops, he had surprised himself by looking forward to dining each evening with the newly-weds, Larry and Gail, now on first name terms. After the intensity of his long days in the reading room, to take a book to dinner did not hold its usual appeal. He was hungry for light relief as well as his meal. The menu did not absorb him for long. With limited choices he asked for the dishes he had not selected the evening before. He decided to avoid the house speciality of *moules*. "Better to be safe than sorry" once again separated him from a mouth-watering experience.

Russell asked them about their day.

"Oh, it was a swell day," Larry said.

Russell caught a quick look of surprise on Gail's face. What was going on here?

"We followed the tourist trail around the high spots, and could have done with your French a couple of times when we ran into a bit of a problem." Larry shrugged and smiled to make light of the situation.

"What type of problem?" Russell asked, and directed his look to Gail, who needed no more encouragement to reveal the truth of their day.

"We had a bad time. We've been robbed."

She paused to gulp in air, almost like dry sobs, and Larry silenced himself with a mouthful of bread roll.

"They wouldn't take our tickets, and not just ours, lots of people were turned away. They oughtn't do that, it was robbery; to see the sights they wanted cash, but we've already paid, and for all these."

Russell glanced at Larry, who continued to munch, as she rummaged in her handbag and produced a concertina book of tickets, which she slammed on the table, accompanied by "worthless, all worthless". At this moment, Russell became aware of a murmur of assent in the room. Gail's eruption had burst the bubble of unease that was present in the room, and similar experiences started to be voiced, with guests talking to each other across tables, no longer isolated by their own incidents of rejection.

26

Russell had been offered a similar package from his travel agent. All excursions and entrance fees paid in advance for a reasonable discount, and for the traveller, less fuss with the different coins and currency as they moved across borders. Russell had paid ahead for his train rides, but had wanted to maintain a vestige of freedom in the way that he explored the cities on his itinerary, so declined the offer of the excursion tickets, and this decision had served him well. To Russell, Larry appeared somewhat chastened by Gail's outburst, as if he bore the situation as his own fault. Perhaps, Russell mused, he was embarrassed to acknowledge publicly the tight budget they were on. To pay twice would not only be an injustice, it would not have been possible for him, and perhaps this was the same for them. They told him they had spent much of the day on the town ramparts, and faced the impenetrable barrier that is erected by inadequate funds. Russell knew from experience that this barrier was only ever visible from one side. Gail's "Honey it's not your fault," to Larry's silent appeal, seemed to leave him untouched, and to Russell's eye, unchanged. Larry's ego had been bruised, in a way that could only be understood by another man. Russell's nod to him acknowledged this.

They had gleaned, they told him, from smatterings of English that it was because of the threat of war; the Belgians had stopped accepting promissory notes from foreigners. Hard cash was the only currency they would take. Pre-paid tickets and travellers cheques held no value. Luckily the hotel collected all vouchers at registration, so their tenancy, and his, was secured, a fact Russell checked with reception at the end of their meal.

"Did the Belgians know something" they didn't know? Were the newspapers "holding back on the truth"? Why were the streets suddenly full of Belgian soldiers? Why had the stationmaster refused two travellers a trip to Liege? The room buzzed with questions and any suggested answers became facts by the time they had traversed the restaurant, table by table. "What'll we do?" hung limply in the air.

With so few funds, the options available to them were limited, so decision-making, at one level, it seemed to Russell, was easy. They all had to head home. He was on the final leg of his trip anyway, so this was no great upset for him, but he could see how perturbed Gail and Larry became as the scale of their honeymoon diminished.

They had agreed to meet again at breakfast. Although younger, Russell's capable air and linguistic skills seemed to put him in the

27

lead, and by the end of dinner, Gail had ceased to turn to Larry for answers. She said they would follow his advice in the morning.

Russell dabbed his face after his shave on the thin, stiff towel. His full head of light brown hair was matched in volume with the stubble he fought to remove from his chin, sometimes twice a day. He dressed and headed downstairs. Larry, who had on knee length scout's trousers, met him in reception and waited while Russell collected the daily newspaper to take into breakfast. The hotel reception area was already littered with suitcases and Russell almost tripped over twice.

With breakfasts ordered Russell looked at the newspaper and translated the headlines to Larry. Gail was finishing a postcard. Russell had not ventured an enquiry but Larry had told him, and the waiter when he ordered her breakfast: she would be down shortly.

The news in the paper was daunting for Russell to read. It looked like brinkmanship was over and the war machine ignited. Germany had heard that the Russian Army was on the move, so they swiftly declared themselves at war with Russia. The editorial, Russell told Larry, ventured the opinion that France would now declare war on Germany, and Belgium had better look smart to protect its borders from the crossfire. They had no time to comment on this before Gail arrived. Russell noticed her dejected spirit of the previous evening had gone, replaced with a more upbeat mood.

"What's in the papers?" she asked.

"Things are getting a little hot honey, it's right that we plan to leave," Larry replied.

"If I'm cutting short my honeymoon, it'd better be for a goddam war."

Russell could imagine her dining out on the thrill of her war story in years to come. There'd be more interest in these than descriptions of leaning towers and decorative churches. Gail thanked Larry for ordering her breakfast and began to eat her croissant. Russell folded the newspaper.

"What's our plan then?" Larry looked expectantly at Russell.

Russell took them through his thinking. He did not share his first thought that morning, to get up and go, and leave them to sort themselves out. He knew he would manage without great difficulty and did not particularly want to feel responsible for the dilemmas of others; but after years of Methodist indoctrination, this was his Samaritan test.

"I'll go to the railway station with our tickets and secure our ride to Brussels, while you get packed and ready for when I return. You have another night available to you at the hotel, so don't check out in case we need to stay until tomorrow. Hopefully there'll be time to take in some more sights today, if I aim for an afternoon train."

He paused, and they both nodded.

"In Brussels we'll make our way to the American legation. They'll be obliged to help you get home. No doubt they'll have had several enquiries by now, and will have plans worked out."

Larry stepped in the minute he stopped speaking.

"I'll come with you. I'm not one for being cooped up and Gail can pack more easily if I'm not under her feet, isn't that right, honey?"

The last words were addressed to Gail as a statement, not an enquiry, to which she could only nod mutely.

"Okay, let's meet in reception in 20 minutes." Russell rose from his seat and headed to his room to pack his own suitcase. He was still no further than reception when Larry and Gail walked out of the dining room a few minutes later. He had been intercepted by a couple of garrulous fellow countrymen. They seemed to think that someone else should organize what they kept calling their evacuation. They were the couple Russell had heard haranguing the reception staff the day before. They considered they had an inadequate number of clothes hangers in their room and were the sort of people that just shouted at problems. Mr and Mrs Becker, who introduced themselves as Jerry and Myrtle, were quick to latch onto Russell's plan.

When Russell returned to the hotel reception to collect Larry and Jerry, three more had joined their number and they set off to walk, rather than take the tram to the station. The morning air was still fresh. A temporary desk was set up inside the ticket hall manned by two harassed staff and a volunteer, who attempted an explanation in broken English to a perturbed tourist. Several people and a number of soldiers in Belgian uniform milled about. The volume of people steadily increased every few minutes with the arrival of separate individuals and small groups. Russell used very little of his French to explain their situation to the staff; their circumstances seemed to be implicitly known, as it affected so many. He did need his French to follow their explanations, and instructions, that he then passed on to his fellow travellers.

"The normal timetable has been abandoned because trains are taking Belgian troops to the eastern border with Germany. Our rides will be on trains when they return towards Brussels. They can't say when these will be coming through and whether they'll always make a stop; seats will be on a first come first served basis."

Russell ignored the grumbled murmurs and continued.

"They don't want us cluttering up the platform, they need to keep access clear for the soldiers and supplies, so we're to queue, outside the front of the station, to the left, away from the tram lines, and wait."

"What about our tickets?", "Why are there soldiers?", "Will they make us pay?", "Has the war started?", "What money will they take?", "What if it rains?", "Will Belgium fight?", "Will there be seats?", was the chorus of questions directed at him the minute he stopped.

"All pre-paid tickets will be honoured."

Russell delivered this good news and then stepped to one side behind Larry to shift the focus from himself. The men repeated his statements to each other, rehearsing the speech they would make to their wives back at the hotel. This was where they all soon headed, some with a quickened pace, intent on securing a place at the head of the queue when they returned to the station with luggage and spouse in tow.

Russell and Larry lagged behind.

"What do you make of it?" Larry asked.

"It seems a bit more ragged than I'd expected," Russell replied. "I'm tempted to try to get a train to Brussels this morning, rather than later in the day, but how do you feel about missing your sight-seeing?"

"To be straight with you, I don't have the cash to double pay for this trip. I'm worried how the shipping line will make out if things get worse. I've said nothing to Gail. No need to worry her, for now at least."

Russell agreed and they walked along in a companionable silence until they had to step to one side to allow a group of soldiers to pass.

"Makes me nervous to see them. Why do they have guns?" Larry asked. "I didn't think Belgium was going to fight".

"They're not," Russell replied. "They just want to make sure no one strays across their borders: this isn't their war."

Gail seemed to take the information about their imminent departure well and immediately had the idea that they should take some provisions. She would make some sandwiches, in case they had a long wait for the train, and Larry was dispatched with a list. Russell went to talk to the hotel manager to explain they were vacating their rooms but did not want to check out of the Felsons' room, just in case their journey to Brussels proved impossible, and they needed to return for the night. The Felsons' tickets covered them until midday the following day, but Russell's tenure was already over. The hotel manager was very accommodating and assured Russell that they would find a bed for him should he need somewhere that night.

Russell marvelled at the orchestration required to mobilize and supply an army; it had taken them two hours to pack and prepare what felt like a small picnic in the bag he now carried. They had walked to the station and joined the back of the queue, which was already quite long. For the first hour, people talked quietly to each other in their family pair or group; by the second hour conversations had started with neighbouring parties, and by the third the gathering had the look of a church picnic as food started to appear and was shared. There had been several false alarms when trains had been heard to approach, but so far none in the direction they wanted.

On the fourth hour Russell wandered into the ticket hall on the hunt for a scrap of information. He had held back from being part of the posse that every hour had interrogated the poor staff, who had no new information to pass on. He loitered by some locals who had just come away from the ticket counter, and they seemed to be certain that a train would be along within the hour. Somewhat cheered he returned to Gail and Larry. They were in the middle of describing their wedding to the people behind them in the queue. He knew they were about half-way through: he recognized the script from their first dinner conversation. How relaxed everything had seemed then. He smiled as he approached them, but did not want to announce his news in case it generated a stampede of enthusiasm, which would crush him should the train not materialize. But the train did arrive, 30 minutes later. With considerable decorum and manners they all boarded. Brussels was their next stop.

1st August 1914
Norfolk, England
Edith

Edith was frustrated. It was taking time to organize her return to Brussels and as each day passed the pressure on her not to return increased; and in her mother's eyes, the reasonableness of her intent to go diminished. Edith repeated well-worn phrases to her mother's suggestions that she stay at home. The political tensions in Europe mounted, and the more solid rationale seemed to support her mother, but Edith's stubbornness was insurmountable.

"It is not only my home now, mother, but I have responsibilities there. I can't leave my organization in the lurch; it would be unfair and unprofessional. The worse the situation develops, the more I'll be needed. I really must go as soon as my transport is confirmed. If there is to be fighting on the Continent, journeys will only become more difficult, if not impossible."

Her mother's warnings fell on deaf ears. She was a widow in her eighties, and too frail to withstand a determined Edith. When arguments were spent on both sides, they silently acknowledged the truth to themselves; this parting was going to be particularly difficult. Edith's father had died just weeks before the start of her annual vacation, a few years back. She carried guilt because she had missed his illness and death, and was now faced with the impact

33

that her departure would have on her mother. She was relieved that her mother would not be alone. Edith's sisters were close by and she had a live-in housekeeper now more like family than Edith, who had lived abroad for seven years.

Edith had been delighted when she first set out to Belgium, having secured the post as head of the Belgian School of Nursing. Her appointment had been a personal coup and largely rested on her ability to speak French; she was not considered to be outstanding management material by the London nursing fraternity. She just did not have glowing references and her implacable statements at interview had failed to generate any offers. She did have some supporters but the roles she sought were not in their gift. At 42 her gratitude was heartfelt when Dr Depage, a leading surgeon in Europe, appointed her as matron to the first training school for nurses in Belgium.

It was the iron will, self-discipline, and hard work that she brought to her role that delighted Dr Depage. He needed her single-minded drive and praised her as she cut a swathe through the "do-gooding" ladies' committees who enjoyed the hold they had on the purse strings of his clinic. The exchanges in the early days had become legends, fondly recalled as she and the ladies now enjoyed an *entente cordiale*; and Edith had results on her side. The reputation and number of student nurses had grown year on year and under Edith's financial control the school now made a modest profit.

Edith Cavell was serious by nature and nothing about her appearance softened her image. Of medium height and slightly built, she did not dominate through physical size; but with grey hair drawn back from a face that rarely smiled, and more introverted than sociable, she was a difficult woman to warm to, and she could intimidate. She used her persona to her advantage. Like many self-possessed people, Edith had an intimate group of people with whom she could relax and have some fun, and most of these were family and friends around Swardeston in Norfolk. Her farewells with this select group were mostly light and full of laughter, with no foreboding of what lay ahead.

The idyll on pony and trap at the start of her journey back to Brussels was soon forgotten when Edith found herself in a crowded and uncomfortable railway carriage and then on a choppy crossing to Ostend, which she found in chaos. She had been so duty-bound to return that it was not until she had travel time alone that she allowed herself to question what she might be stepping into. She still did not waver and was not daunted, in fact if anything she felt a thrill of excitement. She always liked the challenge and opportunity of the unexpected.

She had no experience of war, but had read much about it during her studies. The practice of nursing as she knew and taught it had largely come from Florence Nightingale's battle zone experiences, some 60 years ago, in the Crimea. Edith tried to recall the lectures she had received on the Geneva Convention. She knew it meant she should be safe; the neutrality of hospitals, medical staff, and wounded men was guaranteed. If they made an army aware of their status, and adopted the international sign of the Red Cross, her presence would be understood. Although she had followed the newspapers Edith had not entirely worked out who the potential enemy might be and how Belgium could be involved; it was all a bit of a mystery. She had probationers from several different countries, but could not fathom the possible implications. She was missing too many pieces of the jigsaw; it was one day at a time for now.

Unable to make any meaningful plan, she mused instead about her current intake and was drawn instinctively to reflect more on the British girls. She always knew these much better than the rest. The ease of corridor conversations in their mother tongue had built a rapport as her paths crossed with theirs, often several times in a day.

"Remind me nurse, where is your home in England?"

"In Winchester, ma'am."

"A beautiful city I understand."

"Yes, ma'am, but much more compact than Brussels. It'll seem small and pokey when I return, the avenues here are so wide and straight."

"When are you next home?"

"In six months, at the end of my first year exams."

"Do well."

Edith enjoyed the exchanges and was pleased that she was not stand-offish in the way that her matrons had often been. She would have been disappointed and hurt to hear of the fun that was taken out of her corridor interrogations, when the girls gathered at the end of their day. Particularly if she had been mocked by Marion Drake.

Edith liked Marion. She thought they were similar in their approach to a task: both gave matters serious consideration when required, and were always prompt, practical, and even anticipatory in their thoughts. But what she most liked about Marion was the warmth that she projected in an easy way that Edith envied. Edith knew such affection was within her too, but it always seemed to hide its face behind the practical. She was in this work to care for people and wanted no one to suffer, but she was more likely to tuck in a sheet with a precision fold than give a word of comfort. She liked to see Marion with patients, porters, and the people who gathered at their back door from the streets: she treated everyone with the same respect and as if she expected to like them all. Edith was not alone in her admiration. No one disliked Marion.

She recalled their first meeting. Marion had knocked on the door of her office at the appointed hour. Edith had already met the new intake of trainees, en masse, and given them an outline of her expectations. By the expression of her will she expected to impose order, and in large part did. Edith always followed through with a private meeting for each student nurse. Marion walked in, looking smart in her crisp uniform, with her dark hair tied back under her cap. She was taller than Edith: at about five foot seven inches, she was taller than most of the nurses. With an appropriate build for her height, she was nicely, and most important for Edith's professional eye, neatly proportioned. She was poised but there was nothing posed about her. What always struck others was her ability to seem totally at ease with herself, no fidgets or cautious glances or hesitant throat clearing coughs. Her lack of self-consciousness enabled those in her company to lose any awkwardness. Edith faced Marion as she sat down and felt herself relax behind the persona she presented to the world for so much of her working day.

"So, Marion, how are you settling in?"

"Very easily, thank you, matron. Being paired with a student who has been here a while has helped enormously. Brigid has shown me around, and answered questions I didn't even know I had, and all the girls are very friendly."

Marion paused, and looked directly at Edith. Her brown eyes softened as she smiled and continued.

"I can still get lost within the building. But I saw Sister Wilkins confused with her directions yesterday, so I won't be too tough on myself just yet. I'm so pleased to be here and can't wait for the lectures to start."

Marion's enthusiasm conveyed a genuine eagerness to Edith; so different from the triteness of some students' answers. Edith watched her reflect on each question before she spoke: she seemed determined to present an accurate picture of how she felt. Edith could see she felt settled but was relieved not to be swamped by emotional responses; it was as if Marion instinctively knew what Edith found acceptable.

"I'm pleased to hear it, Marion. We try to instill a sense of service to each other as well as to the patients, so it's good to hear when this works."

"I think you've done more than instill a duty, matron. The spirit that exists between the girls is wonderful. Newcomers feel it immediately and respond in kind. You must feel very proud of what you've created."

While struck at the time by Marion's comment, it had been on later reflection that Edith realized how rarely she received compliments about her achievements. Perhaps she didn't invite them, but Marion needed no invitation. From some such an observation would sound like flattery, but because Marion was direct, Edith was able to hear the acknowledgement without brushing it to one side. Her tendency was to diminish acknowledgements, which could create awkwardness.

"Thank you, Marion. Shall we look through your timetable to make sure you understand it, and I can answer your questions? After today, all aspects of your personal schedules will be handled by Sister Wilkins, but I want to be sure at the outset that all is clear."

Their conversation had moved onto the logistics and abbreviations of the theory and practice that sat within the schedule in front of them. Edith dismissed Marion at the end of their session and Marion stood up to leave. She turned back as she reached the door and said, with a smile, "Do let me know if I can be of help at any time, I'm not just here to learn," and she had closed the door to Edith's "Thank you".

Their paths had crossed with no greater frequency than any other in the community, but they always exchanged pleasantries and Marion would enquire how Edith was and then listen for the answer and sometimes comment if she looked tired. Edith dropped her shield with Marion, and opened the door for small intimacies of empathy, welcome moments for her.

Edith smiled as she came out of her reverie. Her journey to Brussels was taking longer than usual and had been less comfortable. Corridors and carriageways were full of bulky luggage and many people asked directions from others. Unlike her usual pattern of solitude, she had been in conversation with other travellers as news was exchanged. Expert and amateur opinions all focused on the questions that would determine Europe's fate. Would France fight the Germans? Would Great Britain defend France? Would Belgium stay neutral? Could the gathering momentum be stopped?

In the days it took for Edith to complete her journey the course of destiny towards war had been determined and a new map of international relations drawn. Of one thing she could be sure, the future was uncertain.

2nd August 1914
Brussels
Russell

After they arrived in Brussels, Russell, Larry, Gail and a crowd of others from the train made their way directly to the American legation. They almost had to force their way through the throng of people standing in the reception hall to find a member of the embassy, who when found had no answers to the multitude of questions fired at him in rapid succession. The staff, it appeared, was under-prepared.

In the circumstances Russell was impressed that within two hours they each had a voucher and the name of a hotel to go to, and for those with no cash, a promissory note underwritten by the legation, and signed by the secretary to the legation, Mr Hugh Gibson. Mr Gibson had to assure the doubters that his paper was not worthless and would be accepted in the city, before they would depart to put his words to the test. All these arrangements were being finalized when a new group of travellers arrived and distracted the staff, so Russell volunteered to write each of his party's details in a ledger, to lodge their accounts: an offer that Hugh had welcomed and then left him to it. Task finished, Russell had looked up to locate Mr Gibson to hand back the ledger, but instead found a queue of people who had been sent over for him to record their details too.

"Apologies for the liberty, Mister? …"

"Clarke, Russell Clarke."

"Hugh Gibson." Hugh shook Russell's hand.

"Thank you, Mr Clarke, Russell if I may? You helped me out of a tight spot. Not enough staff in the embassy to deal with all these people."

Russell had been filling in the ledger for almost an hour; Gail and Larry had left for their hotel with his promise to find them later.

"You did well, stepped right in, neat handwriting too. I'm much obliged."

"You're welcome, happy to help."

"So what's your situation?"

Hugh's interest in Russell's answer led them to have a drink together, followed by a casual dinner in a local restaurant at Hugh's invitation. This was after the last traveller had been lodged and, like all the others, been told to return the next day. Hugh was seven years older than Russell, single and, it became evident through their conversation, they shared interests in sport, travel, architecture, and history. Hugh had also studied history at college; he was from Los Angeles, California. He held Russell's position as a Rhodes Scholar in high regard.

"That could tip you right into diplomatic work," Hugh volunteered. "I had to jump through several hoops to get a foot in the door. This is a backwater; I'm cutting my teeth before I move on to a more testing territory, but it's a great posting to see Europe."

"It didn't look much like a backwater today," Russell said, "more like rising rapids. And what happens tomorrow when they all return?"

"The minister, Mr Whitlock, has been garnering resources today and we'll be more organized. But we could do with fellows like you. Do you have to leave or could you stay a few days and help out? My personal assistant is on his vacation. You could see behind the scenes; you never know it might tempt you into this type of work. What do you think?"

Once they had overcome Russell's concerns about not having appropriate clothes to work in, he agreed to attend a meeting arranged for the volunteers and staff at half past eight the following morning.

The briefing was opened by Mr Brand Whitlock, the American minister to Belgium.

"Let me begin by saying how grateful I am to all of you for your assistance at this difficult time. Whilst I know we can be proud of most of our fellow countrymen and how they disport themselves in times of trouble and uncertainty, there are always some that disappoint and test one's capacity for courtesy. I know that you will all rise above any tetchiness that might manifest itself."

Russell was sitting in the second row of chairs that formed an arc around the minister; there were 12 other people in attendance, all smartly dressed and Russell felt uncomfortable in his more casual clothes. The ministerial title conveyed formality to Russell, but Mr Whitlock had made his introductions by name rather than title, and appeared genuine in his thanks and personable in his approach.

"We find ourselves caught up in something of a maelstrom that's beyond our means to manage. Not much of import generally happens here but today we find ourselves with front row seats in the theatre of what might become war in Europe. Should matters escalate Germany will most likely want safe transit through Belgium for their army. They will want to steer clear of the heavily fortified border between themselves and France and Belgium is the back route for a quick march to Paris. We know the German army is massing at the Belgian border in the East and all are waiting on the next move. Tensions are running high and we need to help move our countrymen out. We have no instruction from Washington, so we've had to rely our own resources. Luckily I've just tapped into a rich vein of American residents in Brussels. They are well connected back home, and in London, and are prepared to step into the breach to assist Americans who need to return to America. We've formed a committee that will be chaired by Mr Heineman: some of you will know Daniel, and he has co-opted Mr Millard K. Shaler and Mr William Hulse. Another gentleman, Herbert H. Hoover—I believe he consults with governments on mining—is in London at present and he's prepared to involve himself in what will be known as the American Relief Fund."

Mr Whitlock paused to give an opportunity for comment on his pronouncements thus far. The names of Heineman, Shaler and Hulse were obviously known to the two in front of Russell who nodded to each other and repeated them like a mantra. Mr Whitlock continued:

"They'll raise money for this enterprise and will repatriate all Americans in Europe who need a ticket home. We'll no doubt have

41

more visitors today who'll require access to cash and accommodation until transportation can be requisitioned and their passage organized. Mr Heineman has identified and secured accommodation where we can direct people. News sheets will be routinely posted at each facility, with up to date information on travel arrangements. We anticipate a high number of our countrymen through our doors over the next few days or even weeks; we need to give them assurance, and the means to manage until transport is ready. Mr Gibson will now give you a more detailed brief on what we can tell people today and how we will organize ourselves. Thank you, ladies and gentlemen."

Hugh stepped forward to join Mr Whitlock. They shook hands and talked together for a moment, perhaps agreeing a final detail. The minister was the taller and slimmer of the two; with an aquiline nose and high forehead, the cut of his suit, and his confident air, he attracted attention. Hugh, by comparison looked more workmanlike to Russell, who watched him as he added a few notes to his papers before turning to address the company.

Croissants and pastries were served at the end of the meeting and Russell took the opportunity to introduce himself to a few of the others in the room. It became clear he was the outsider. The other volunteers were a fraternity of Americans who lived in Brussels, with close links to the embassy. Word had passed around already that he was a Rhodes Scholar, and many of their introductory remarks included congratulations to him.

"Thank you for joining in, Russell," Hugh had approached him. "We're about to open and we have people at the gate already. Prepare yourself for quite a day."

The legation was soon full of all types of people and situations: jockeys, clergymen, actors, musicians, physicians, and tourists of all kinds. Many had no money, and redundant coupons. All were hesitant and undecided as to what to do. Whether they should leave, and if so, how? Would matters worsen? Would it be safe to be on the sea? Some demanded protection and action and even cash from the minister, who braved a walk though the hall at different times of the day with palliative assurances.

A system to channel people soon had them queued according to their need. Hugh had placed Russell on the first desk that people approached. Russell's easy confidence had apparently impressed Hugh and his ability to assess a situation quickly and pacify frayed nerves made him effective in the front line. It was Russell's job to register the details of each party and the date and time of their arrival with him. The skill was to try and keep their stories to a minimum while he found out enough about their circumstances to direct them to another queue.

"Yes, hello, I'm travelling with my wife, we're touring together, but need to head home. Is it safe for us to go to the coast? Where might we stay? Our boat isn't due for another two weeks. Will it still come?" The man looked nervous and his wife glared at him as if, Russell thought, she held him personally responsible for their disrupted itinerary.

Russell directed them to the desk where a volunteer was logging details of travel arrangements.

"Good morning, I've just arrived from Germany. I'm a doctor and have lived there for ten years, but think it's the right time to return to America." Russell guessed that the man was in his early forties and he had almost lost his American accent. "The Germans are ready for war. I need to have papers to travel."

Russell directed him to the desk for passports.

"I demand to see the minister. I'm an American citizen and I know my rights. I want to have transport arranged back to America for my family. I need somewhere to stay, and some cash. Apparently my cheques are no longer good enough for this country. Just who do they think they are, and who do you think you are to stop me seeing the minister?" Truculent was the word that Russell had for this man before he had even opened his mouth; his face was set in a glowering frown, but Russell had not been prepared for the loudness of his voice.

Unlucky for him, but opportune for Russell, the minister was on one of his walkabouts and within earshot; he approached the desk, introduced himself and moved the man away from the desk. It took him only minutes to pacify and return him to Russell whereupon he gave his name and family details and joined the queue that Russell directed him to; he seemed happier after his desired audience.

Some people were very appreciative of the efforts made on their behalf and kept their requests to a minimum, conscious of the pressures being piled on by so many travellers. Others seemed oblivious to the melee they were in and launched into details of their experiences. It was as if Russell, a captive listener, was their reward for the patience they had shown while they waited in his queue, despite the fact that it was just such narratives that created the delays. Russell thought it a mistake to have seats in front of his desk, but to remove them might appear too discourteous. Sometimes he found their stories of such interest he had to remind himself not to ask too many questions and move them through. One such story had caught him when a rather glamorous lady, he thought in her fifties, approached his desk.

"They've taken my car, and I have too much luggage to move myself. Can you have someone fetch it from the front steps? It's the matching set to the left of the entrance. Such a bore."

The final words were uttered as she sat down and lit a cigarette.

"Who has taken your car?" Russell asked, absorbed by her story even before he had logged her name.

"The Belgian Army. Apparently some general needs it. They gave me a chit for it, but I can't remember where I put it, it's somewhere in my handbag. The problem is I'm on a road trip, and without the car I can't get anywhere. I never have understood trains, or perhaps trains have never gone in the direction I've wanted to take, and timetables are meaningless to me. I can't follow the same line across the page. You look capable of much more than me."

These last words were accompanied by a direct look from exquisitely lashed blue eyes. Even though lined with age, they still arrested Russell's attention.

"Well, let's secure your luggage first," Russell said.

He looked around for some assistance from embassy staff. Before he had spotted any, a man in the queue behind this damsel in distress volunteered his help. It only took him a few minutes to step outside, locate and move the luggage into a side room and return, during which time Russell took her name and directed her to the queue for the travel desk. Russell thanked the helpful man and then tried to contain a smile when he asked for the name of the lady he had assisted.

"Winters," Russell told him, "Miss Winters."

A few minutes later Russell heard introductions between the two as they stood together in the queue for travel arrangements. The flow of people continued throughout the day.

Russell was weary when he left the legation, with a promise extracted by Hugh for him to return the following day, but he felt more energized after a bath back at his hotel and the thought of dinner with Larry and Gail. Russell wanted to hear about their day in the city and he had his tales to tell.

"We aren't the only ones having problems with cash," Larry announced to Russell.

"Shopkeepers wouldn't take their own notes," Gail added.

"Everyone was using coins …"

"But they don't have enough …"

"But what happens when the money runs out?"

They both looked at Russell for an answer and then interrupted him before he could speak.

"We saw lots of Belgian soldiers …"

"They were in cafés or walking in the boulevards …"

"Nothing military was going on …"

"I think they were final walks with their loved ones before they leave. I would hate to say goodbye to you, Larry, if you were off to fight."

And with this her handkerchief was up to her face.

"But they are not off to fight," Larry said, with more edge than reassurance. "Belgium is neutral, it won't fight".

"Well, what exactly is all the fuss about then?" Gail asked. "Who is going to fight? Is this drama for real?" She looked somewhat embarrassed by her emotion and put her handkerchief away. They both looked to Russell and this time waited until he spoke.

"Well, the problem for Belgium", Russell said, "is they are the pig in the middle, geographically speaking. Germany might plan to march through Belgium and quash the French before the Russian Army is ready to attack them from the east. If Belgium let them through the French would view Belgium as on the side of Germany and against them. So Belgium would need to defend her borders and keep them out".

Russell paused as the waiter brought their starter of soup, and he buttered his bread roll.

"The German Army has apparently massed in large numbers to the north-east: this is where the Belgian soldiers are headed. If Belgium has to defend its neutrality, that's where the fight will be. I heard today that the Belgian Army has just about 100,000 soldiers and the Germans and French have millions. Belgium is small fry."

They all sipped their soup. Russell then added: "Belgium managed to avoid any involvement in the Franco-Prussian war 25 years ago, because the attack was directly across the French and German border. But France has fortified its border, so now it's considered impregnable. This is why the Belgian border is best for a fast German approach to Paris."

"But wouldn't it be suicide for the Belgians to fight," Gail said. "From what you say, they wouldn't stand a chance, surely they can see that?"

"Maybe they do," Russell said, "but no country wants to give up without a fight. The Belgians have fought for their independence before".

Russell checked himself for sounding like a history book.

"They wouldn't want to give that up by hiding behind shuttered windows and locked doors. Their fear would be that whoever marches in might never march out again."

A look passed between Gail and Larry. Russell realized they had just grasped the magnitude of the drama that they found themselves in. Larry's hand squeezed hers on the table.

"Don't worry honey, we'll be gone from here before any fighting starts, won't we Russell?"

Russell knew when reassurance was required.

"Of course you will. Belgium has some defences. There are several forts at Liege and Namur, and the river Meuse itself provides an effective barrier against an invasion. Belgium could at least keep the Germans delayed until their allies arrive."

"Who are they?" Larry and Gail asked in unison, startled that even more countries might be involved.

"Well, without going into all the reasons why, because I am not entirely sure myself, the British and French will support Belgium's defence against an attack from the Germans."

"That levels the odds a bit," Larry was keen to contribute.

"But would the British come?" Gail asked.

"The important thing", Russell said, "is to sort out our transportation home. It's not our battle to worry about".

"Thank goodness America is so far away," Gail said. "You're right, it's not our war".

Dinner conversation moved on to Russell's anecdotes from his day. It was their last meal together. Gail and Larry were informed of their departure the next morning and they were on their way by noon. Their honeymoon was over.

2nd August 1914
Brussels
Marion

"What's happening over there?" Gwen asked Marion as she pointed to a crowd of people. They were in the Parc Centrale, enjoying the beautiful weather while they watched the best, and the rest, of Brussels do the same. The park was criss-crossed with paths edged by manicured borders and lawns. Everything looked as it usually did but the feel of the day was different in many ways to their normal outing, the air heavy with anticipation. They had been alarmed, as they had walked along Avenue Louise, to see the national flags taken down from the flag-poles on the grand houses. Marion had stopped a man who carried several in his arms to ask the reason and was told that they were needed at the borders, to mark out Belgian soil. The streets were full of soldiers, not in formation, but with their families or loved ones. Their boots creaked with the newness of leather yet to be broken in. The park looked festive with balloons and rosettes in national colours on sale and carried and worn by many. Flower sellers out to capture the high spirits would start to sing the national anthem, and then sell their blooms to the crowd that would rapidly form and take over the verse.

The gathering that Gwen had pointed out had grown larger and louder, but these were not singing. Marion and Gwen moved nearer.

Angry voices were raised and they drew back when scuffles started. Marion's French was better than Gwen's and, a capable linguist, she had picked up some Flemish, so she turned translator to explain what the trouble was about.

"They're shouting about the prices that the food sellers want to charge: apparently they are double the usual price. One man has called them German lovers; he says no Belgian would turn against his own in this way if he loved his country. Another just spat on the hot potatoes. I think he aimed at the man but missed."

The crowd suddenly moved forward and surged into the carts, knocking them and the traders over. In the melee and scrambles that followed, many hands reached out for food and with pockets full the crowd moved swiftly away from the scene and dispersed. Marion stepped forward to see if anyone had been hurt, but her offers of assistance were brusquely brushed aside by one of the potato sellers. He righted himself, his ego and stall more battered than his body. The disgruntled crowd had rapidly disappeared and Marion and Gwen were almost amused to see a member of the Garde Civique head in the direction of the long gone scene when they made their way out of the park some 20 minutes later. He would find no perpetrators there.

At the gate, some horse riders were loitering. Their voices were solemn and one lady was in tears. Gwen, a horsewoman herself, took in the scene to see if someone had fallen and then realized what was missing, the horses. They soon learnt that afternoon rides had been interrupted by the Belgian militia who had handed out chits, taken over the reins and led the horses away to the military stables. The riders were distressed. The stylish among them looked diminished without their mounts, and uncomfortable as they moved off to walk down the avenue, the men slightly bandy-legged in riding trousers. One lady in the party required assistance, her boots, designed for riding, did not suit her feet for an afternoon stroll.

Almost reeling from the vignettes that had shattered the rhythm of their routine, Gwen and Marion stopped at the café that served afternoon tea and gave their usual order. They stacked their coins on the table to show they had the means to pay, their money quickly collected by their waiter. They heard him turn custom away when thirsty customers offered bank notes.

"Why aren't notes being accepted?" Gwen asked Marion.

"The cook told me it always happens when there's war. Gold and coins hold their value but notes become worthless."

"But there isn't a war."

"Yes, but there might be."

"So they're panicking?"

"Being careful."

"Being difficult, more like. Matron is due back today," Gwen said. "I hope she makes it before this war kicks off, if it does. I don't think Sister Wilkins can take the strain and Sister Jones could never cope. But what if she gets stuck somewhere?"

"I can't imagine that she will," Marion said. "There's no reason why she should. The trains are still running. It might just take her longer, that's all."

A newspaper boy interrupted their conversation when he walked into the café and shouted out a headline. On a normal day he would never have stepped into the establishment and would not have received any sort of acknowledgement by the clientele, but today there was a rush towards him led by the proprietor. Soon each table was poring over the late edition of *Le Soir*. Marion translated the gist of the main article for Gwen.

"The Germans have been called barbarians because they occupied Luxembourg yesterday, but the German minister in Brussels, Herr von Below is quoted as saying they will respect Belgium's neutrality; German troops won't cross into Belgian territory, so we have nothing to fear."

"That's if we believe him," Gwen said.

"Or what they choose to put in the newspaper," Marion agreed.

They did want to believe it and took the reassurance as a welcome respite from some of the tensions they had experienced in the day. They returned to the school in a cheerful mood and met Sister Wilkins as they crossed the hall. Marion told her of a fight they had witnessed in the park and handed her the evening copy of *Le Soir*.

"The German minister says Belgium will be left alone," Marion told her.

"We have nothing to worry about," Gwen added.

"Well, that news is welcome." Sister Wilkins scanned the headlines. "Perhaps everyone will settle down now and some of our nurses will return".

Ten nurses had left over the weekend. They had succumbed to orders from their parents to go back home, despite pleas from friends that they remain.

"Matron won't be pleased to hear of their leaving: it unbalances her books. She's just returned." Sister Wilkins tapped the ledger under her arm, "And wants to see the figures straight away".

"I'm sure matron will be delighted with all that you've managed in her absence. You couldn't ignore concerned parents, although most of us choose to, and if the girls return it will be because of how you made them feel about departing," Marion said.

"We teased them mercilessly," Gwen said.

"Thank you, Nurse Drake, I did my best," Sister Wilkins said. She tended to bristle where others might blush. "We can only do our best. Now don't let me keep you from getting ready for your evening shift, and I must go to matron".

They parted company and Marion marvelled at the memory for rotas that Sister Wilkins carried in her head. Marion was pleased matron was back; the school had not seemed the same without her. Despite the external uncertainties everyone had seemed more relaxed. None were lax in their work, but the slight anticipatory frisson that generally pervaded the corridors was missing. Marion preferred a slight edginess: it kept her alert. She readied herself for work.

Edith and Sister Wilkins completed their review of all the reports and ledgers. To Edith all seemed to be in order, apart from the departure of some of her probationers, which was disappointing. At the end of their meeting Sister Wilkins produced the copy of *Le Soir* that Marion had handed her earlier, and reiterated the view that Belgium would be safe from war. Edith was less sanguine. She had recently experienced the more hard-hitting messages in the British press, and doubted the optimism that always seemed to underpin reports by the Belgian editors. For some time the British newspapers had been full of Germany's ambitions. The country had a desire to increase its influence by economic, industrial, and military domination but was bordered by hostile countries in France and Russia, so had to be watchful. It was clear Germany's intent was to expand, and the only way to do this was to take territory from others. Newspapers in England, full of news of the mobilization of the German, Russian, and French armies, had not widely broadcast that reservists in many English counties had made their way to their regimental bases where canvas camps had materialized overnight. Edith had spotted some at Thetford from her train.

One of Edith's travelling companions on her journey from England had been an American journalist. He relished her questions and the fact that he had information or opinions to inform her views. Her education had been rapid, and she was now better equipped with a mental map of the political situation. She understood who was in the fight and why, although for her there could never be a satisfactory reason for taking a life. It was clear that German aspirations were too great to let the small matter of Belgium's neutrality get in their way. The journalist had stressed the Germans' need for speed. They had to take and secure Paris quickly, then turn back and face the Russians. The Belgians, he had said, wouldn't stand a chance of stopping them. These views jaundiced her opinion of the words in the newspaper that Sister Wilkins had flourished.

Edith thanked Sister Wilkins for her reports and for all her efforts in her absence. All that remained was for Edith to tour the establishment. Her habit was to go from top to bottom and with notebook in hand she set out on her own.

With an eye for dust and order Edith could find the flaws in a room or on a staircase in the blink of an eye. She paid as much attention to the back stairs as to the public areas. Her standards were not for show; they formed the backbone of the institution and at a personal level she really did care about the conditions for all in her employ. The only difference was in the treatment of the surgical areas. There, on top of the usual cleaning standards, everything was washed with surgical spirit. The smell would intermingle with ether on operating days and cause eyes and noses to water. She noted with pleasure that her list of things to mention was short and the anticipatory nervousness that had been with her since she had begun her return journey started to subside. She would soon be back in her stride.

By the time she came to inspect the wards it was evening and the light was not at its best for detailed examinations. With notebook closed she looked instead at patients' notes and watched the rhythm of the nurses as wards were settled down for the night. She came upon Marion sitting at the nurses' desk in the ward on the top floor. Only half the ward was in use; the most distant part was accessed through an archway and only used when they were at full capacity. Edith heard Marion's ward report. As ever it was succinct and efficient, with none of the stutters that could accompany delivery from some of the students. Edith was aware that she could intimidate, but usually found this to be to her advantage. Like a headmistress, she could use silence to encourage confessions and would often receive a tumble of misdemeanours that no amount of interrogation would have unearthed; most were of no significance.

Edith paused at the entrance to the annex of the ward and stepped through. She felt for the light switch and then took in the dimensions of the room. It had two garret style windows and currently held six beds, but if they were moved closer together, Edith could foresee this number doubled. Marion had followed her into the room.

"Can I help with anything?" Marion asked.

What she really meant was, what are you looking at, but knew it was not her place to be that direct.

"Yes Marion, perhaps you can. I have some thoughts and it would be useful to hear what you think."

Edith moved further into the room. She did not want to be overheard by any patients.

"On my return journey I was caught up in conversation with an American journalist, on his way over to report on the war. Not that he knew which border to aim for, but he had given himself a head start. He was convinced that large-scale war was imminent and that trouble would come our way. He felt sure the Germans would use Belgium as their route to France, despite the assurances in the newspaper today."

Edith paused to examine her reaction but Marion created no drama and asked, "What were the views in England?"

"Pretty much that a war would start with Germany against the Russians and the French, but with little appetite for us to get involved. The stock market took a big tumble last week and the bankers advised the government against us supporting the French. They said the cost would be too high."

Edith and Marion drifted towards one of the windows and stood side by side.

"The opposition, the Tories, say that national honour is at stake and we have no choice but to defend Belgium, should this be needed, but they were more ambiguous about support for the French. The newspapers inferred the government was playing for time, sending reminders to Germany to keep out of Belgium, but not an ultimatum. I saw that reservists had been recalled to their barracks: sometimes actions give clearer messages than words."

"I know what you mean," Marion said. "And sometimes newspapers print what they think people want to hear. Who knows what goes on behind closed doors?"

"The papers and newsreels had been full of the royal review of the Navy and I must say it was a splendid show. The majority of our fleet was gathered at Spithead and filled the sea for miles."

Although Marion had only been out of the country for under a year, Edith's talk of the British government and the Tories, the fleet and national pride felt surprisingly alien. Marion found it difficult to relate it to the insular world that so absorbed her. She felt more annoyed by its intrusion and the potential disruption, than threatened by the talk of war.

"The journalist was convinced the British would soon be across the channel to fight and he said something that made me pay attention."

Marion caught a slight frisson from Edith and wondered where this conversation was going to lead.

"It was almost a throw-away line, but he said any wounded British soldiers would be lucky to find a British nurse in Belgium, and "Just make sure you keep them out of the hands of the Germans"."

Edith's thoughts were ahead of Marion's who could not imagine wounded British soldiers in Brussels.

"If the British do come, we need to be ready for them," Edith said.

"What do you mean?"

"I would want us to be able to nurse soldiers of any nationality and that's what the sign of the Red Cross would make possible for us. We would be neutral, but if the Germans had taken over Brussels, I would want to shield our boys from them," and as her glance slid around the room Marion immediately understood.

"Could we hide some?" Marion asked herself as much as Edith.

"I don't know the answer to that but I think it's the question we should consider."

Marion was delighted to hear the conspiratorial "we" in Edith's response that included her in the enterprise and she readily stepped forward to volunteer.

"Would it be easier if I explored the building for you, although you, of course, know it much better than me?"

"Yes, it might," Edith said. "What we need are areas we could disguise, even corridors we could block off, as long as we don't disrupt the main flow of traffic through the buildings, to create spaces where we could secrete soldiers. The attic and basement might also offer some opportunities".

Edith had turned to look back at the room, and the archway to the rest of the ward.

"Yes, why don't you have a look around and then report back to me when you have some ideas. But let's keep this between you and me for now. You see, if we could put an old wardrobe in front of the entrance to this room, no one would know it was here. That's the sort of thing we need to think about."

"I'll make a note of any spare furniture that we could move too," Marion said. "I know there is quite a lot stacked in the basement of 143. Each new intake goes down and picks through things for their room and to swap some items".

"Good idea," Edith responded, "but I don't think there is any point in trying to spot opportunities within 143. That would be close to too many people and would become too obvious. The fewer people involved in this the better. I'll tell Sister Wilkins that you have an assignment for me so you can explore 149 without any problems. She has enough to trouble her at the moment, so don't worry if you bump into her, she won't give you a second thought. Thank you, Marion. I may be ridiculously premature and perhaps none of this will be necessary, but there is no harm in being prepared. We just don't know what's ahead of us".

Any anxiety Edith felt was belied by her practical stance, and she did nothing to encourage the expression of concerns, nor offer comfort. They returned to the ward and after a cursory check on the patients, Edith left them to Marion's care. Neither of them appreciated just how unsafe their conspiratorial conversation was to make them and just how soon the war would begin.

3rd August 1914
Brussels
Russell

What a difference a day makes, Russell thought as he followed Hugh up the staircase and along a wide corridor on the first floor. This was his first view of the grandeur of the American embassy. The floor covering was quality carpet, the curtains were heavy and rich with an embossed pattern, some walls were wood panelled and others decorated with wallpaper. The colour scheme was muted from a palette of light greens, beige, yellow, and cream. He had no idea where he was going or why; he had just responded to Hugh's request to follow him. Another volunteer had taken his place at the table, much to the surprise of a lady who was in full flow about her personal predicament. Hugh stopped outside a closed set of double doors and turned to Russell.

"We are expecting some visitors and I need you to take notes. Look as if you belong in the room, but you won't be introduced and please don't speak. Ready?" And he opened the door.

"Well done, Hugh. They've just arrived and are on their way up." The minister stood next to the unlit fireplace and nodded to Russell.

"Places, gentlemen, please."

Russell was directed to a chair at a small desk and to a notebook and pens. He had just checked the flow of ink when a knock at the door and the minister's "Enter" drew his attention to the door and in walked two uniformed Germans. The door was closed behind them. The four were obviously very well acquainted and shook hands with warm greetings, but when they drew back from each other an air of formality descended. Russell saw one of the Germans prepare to speak and picked up his pen, ready to transcribe. He later learnt this was Herr von Below, the German attaché to Belgium, and the man with him Herr von Strum, Hugh's equivalent at the German legation. Russell had not been briefed on what notes to take so decided to record, as best he could, all that was said. Herr von Below spoke in faultless English:

"It is with deep regret that I find myself here today to ask you to take over the representation of German interests in Belgium. We are now at war with Belgium and I, and my staff, are under instructions to leave today. We are to head home through the Netherlands and a train has been arranged."

It took all of Russell's self-control not to gasp as he took in the import of this request. The war had started.

"I must tell you", said the Minister Whitlock "that I received the same request from Monsieur Klobukowski, the French minister, earlier today. I am still waiting on a reply from Washington for the stand they want us to take. We're only a small staff here, and are swamped by our own nationals at present. There is a limit to what we can take on. Monsieur Klobukowski and Monsieur Fontarce have 30,000 French nationals in Brussels and many have knocked on the doors of their legation already"

Von Below seemed totally unprepared for this reply and was taken aback. The minister directed them all to seats and the German minister seemed to sag like the cushions he sat on. His assistant put his head in his hands, perhaps to hide the fact that he was close to tears. It became apparent that they were both exhausted; neither had slept, they said, since they had presented the German ultimatum to the Belgian prime minister, Monsieur de Broqueville, the evening before.

"Oh, why don't they get out of the way, these poor stupid Belgians, why don't they get out of the way? I know the German Army; it will go over Belgium like a steam-roller. It will be like laying a baby on the track before a locomotive. Why don't they get out of the way?"

This emotional explosion was uttered by von Strum. Although his thoughts probably echoed those of von Below, decorum required more constraint, and a rather awkward silence followed. Hugh stepped in and with a nod from the minister encouraged them to talk through all that had happened in the previous 24 hours.

It was clear that in this company, von Below knew that the conflicts in his role would be understood. As minister he was the local operator of his nation's agenda, his country's ambassador required to establish cordial local relationships, but he had no say in whether neighbours continued in fellowship or as foe. He had no face to save in this room; they were all puppets. Even now, his American peers waited on Washington. They all spent much of their professional time with hands and tongues professionally tied.

"I delivered the ultimatum to Monsieur de Broqueville as it had been despatched to me. I have a copy here if you wish to read it, and the reply. This is a sad day."

Hugh moved to collect the pieces of paper from him and gave them to the Minister Whitlock whose German was better than his. Russell strained to hear the contents as the minister dropped his voice whenever he was less sure of a translation. Von Below waited politely and then summarized for them all.

"Germany has no designs on Belgium, we just want to march through to France and all we ask is for neutrality from Belgium for our safe passage. If Belgium helps us in this way, we will pay for all that we use, and anything that we damage on our way through. But if Belgium opposes us, in any way, then they become an enemy and will have to face the consequences of this. My country gave them 12 hours to decide and they were prompt within the deadline. I understand the cabinet were in discussion all through the night."

The minister turned to the second piece of paper, a copy of the Belgian reply. This was easier for him to read and as he summarized for the room, he picked out parts of the statement.

"The Belgian government views the German request as a flagrant violation of international law and if they acquiesced they would sacrifice the honour of the nation and betray their duty towards Europe. Belgium, they informed the Germans, would remain neutral and independent and would repel, by all the means in their power, every attack upon their rights, whether that be by the French or the German armies."

The silence that followed the pronouncement was shattered by a knock at the door and the uninvited entrance of one of the legation staff. He had in his hand a telegram and a note, both of which he handed to Hugh, who upon reading them handed them to the minister and they both stood up in one synchronized movement.

"Well, gentlemen," said Minister Whitlock. "And to think we were all at dinner together, only last week".

Their German guests stood, so Russell did the same, but then sat down again to record the minister who continued to speak.

"This telegram from Washington instructs me to accept responsibility for any legations who make such a request as yours, but as I'm sure you'll appreciate, the amount I can do for any one country mustn't cut across another. We have to go now; we've been summoned to hear the king address Parliament. As soon as he's free Hugh will come and deal with your administration. We'll endeavour to make sure we don't delay your departure."

Von Below bowed his thanks to the minister which seemed heartfelt when he said:

"I'm sure the demands on you will be short term; there will be a German administration here within days. My concern is for the safety of all my fellow Germans: they will need safe passage back to Germany; in all humanity do help them please."

"We'll do our best," Hugh assured him, and he led them from the room. Minister Whitlock turned to Russell.

"Tell me, did you get all that down?"

"Yes, well, sort of," Russell said. "Enough to be able to write it out in full, if I sit with my notes quite soon."

"No need for that, if they are good enough to remind you, they'll work for me. Put them in the drawer and I'll collect them later. Now bring your notebook and pens, I want you to do the same when we go to hear the king. Hugh's assistant is away, but he tells me you're on a Rhodes Scholarship. Pleased to have you on board by the way. You'll have to stand behind Hugh and myself and won't see anything, but it's not done for me to write anything down in public and there's too much happening at the moment for me to recall it. My journal used to be an easy task to keep and quite a delight when I recorded meals enjoyed and country drives; all these official conversations are a different matter entirely."

They had moved out of the room towards the top of the staircase and both looked down upon the mass of people milling about in the vestibule. The minister turned around.

"We'll go out through the rear exit," and they retraced their steps.

They met Hugh who had returned to find them. Russell kept in step behind.

"Take Mr Clarke with you when you go to the German legation later Hugh. There can be quite a bit of administration and we don't want any misunderstandings about what we agree. He can take notes for you."

Hugh turned to look at Russell and winked, "You're having quite a memorable day Mr Clarke," and to himself, "this is quite a memorable day".

The minister's car, with American flag and driver, was ready for them at the back entrance. Russell sat in the front with the chauffeur and Hugh and the minister took up the back seats. The day was warm and sunny and soon all the windows were open. They heard the noise of the crowds before they turned the corner into the Rue Royale, their quickest route through the park to the Parliament buildings. It was only the status of the occupants and the flag they flew that gave them permission to drive along the route which was lined by flag-waving crowds, there to witness the cavalcade of the royal family as they made their way to the National Palace. The noise was immense. Russell felt like a royal himself, even though he had no part to play in this scene. He was at the heartbeat of national events, and a world away from the dusty historic documents he had studied just days before. He almost had to shake himself.

Russell's academic orientation had always been with the past. The histories of civilizations, particularly the development of social policies and legal frameworks, all designed to create harmony in communities and between communities. They were the codes that governed interactions, specified freedoms to act, and built mutual respect, yet here they were, after generations and layers of civilizing sophistication, on the brink of war. Good fences only make good neighbours if the intent of the neighbours is to remain on their side of the fence.

Russell's musings were interrupted by their arrival at the National Palace. The car arrived at the front of the building and stopped by the main entrance. They alighted as a car with a Union Jack pulled up behind them and Sir Francis Villiers, the British minister, greeted Mr Whitlock and Hugh and they all made their way into the building and up the red-carpeted, marble staircase to the House of the Senate. Russell could just make out the sound of the national anthem, *Brabanconne*, through an open window that faced the square he had stood in minutes before. At that time he had heard nothing above the cheers from the crowd. The throng of people was held back by the Garde Civique, and it was one of their uniformed bands that provided the music. It very aptly captured the sentiment of the moment, and distracted the excited crowd, intent on a sight of their king and queen.

Their party came to a halt at the top of the stairs while many handshakes and greetings were exchanged. None of these social niceties involved Russell so he took the opportunity to take in his surroundings. He had stopped next to a door that opened into the reading room. Normally quiet, today it housed many gentlemen, clustered to share the news and gossip of the day. Their talk sounded agitated to Russell. On the far wall he saw a large portrait of Leopold I and one of his queen, and Russell supposed that the numerous other portraits were presidents of the Senate. He looked out of a window at the compound of ministerial buildings at this northern end of the park; the sister buildings housed the ministries of railroads, post and telegraphs. Russell's focus returned to the room and his eyes brushed past paintings, colossal statues, and decorations that would normally cause him to pause and ponder their genesis. Today he was struck by the drama; the place buzzed.

"Come along," said the Minister Whitlock, who had turned to find him, "we need to find our places before it gets too tight," and led him into a gallery that looked down into the Great Hall or the Salle des Seances as it was locally called. All the galleries were crowded. Opposite to where Russell had entered sat the wives of the ministers and down below were their husbands and senators and members of the lower house of deputies, all dressed formally in black. Some were already seated and others stood in conversation. None of the foreign diplomatic corps had brought along their wives and their space was already limited and quite cramped. The minister positioned Russell in a place where he had a shelf to lean on to assist his note-taking, but he would have no view of the proceedings. He took the opportunity to stand and take in more of the room, which progressively filled with every minute that passed.

The room was laid out with a semi-circular pattern of seats, the walls lined with massive sculptured mahogany panels, each one forming the frame for large portraits of counts, warriors and legislators of Belgium. The rich gilt ceiling was decorated with the escutcheons of the nine provinces. Russell had just counted them when he heard the crowd outside burst into a mighty cheer: the royal party had arrived and he settled into his position. Russell had no view, and was later told by Hugh that the queen had entered the chamber first and sat on the throne to the left of the tribune. At her entrance the room erupted with applause, which she quietly acknowledged. As the members became still, the king, in field uniform, stepped into the room and onto the dais, and with a sheaf of notes started to read his address to the assembly. His attempts to be brief were thwarted. With every point he made, the room burst into frantic cheers that were then echoed by the crowd outside. He called on all factions within the country to put their differences aside and step forward to defend Belgium's independence against their common enemy. His supporters that day were French, Flemish, Walloons from the eastern region of Belgium, Catholics, Liberals, and Socialists. They all pledged the defence of Belgium at any cost, by death if need be.

The royal party left the hall to a standing ovation that continued for some minutes until the prime minister reached the podium and asked for order. He read the German ultimatum and Belgium's reply. Russell was relieved that he had already covered this ground at the earlier meeting because he found it difficult to take notes, his arm kept being knocked by the person pressed up against him, and his translation from French was slow. After reading the documents the prime minister made a short speech that earned him his own ovation as he stepped down from the dais. To everyone's surprise he returned, as if to provide an encore, which in effect he did.

"In the present crisis we have received whole-hearted support from the opposition; they have rallied to our side in the most impressive way to prepare the reply to Germany. In order to emphasize this union of all factions, the king has just signed a decree that appoints Monsieur Vandervelde as a minister of state." Monsieur Vandervelde, the leader of the opposition shouted "I accept!" above the roar of more applause and cheers.

Many took the opportunity to exchange greetings and comments on the situation as they made their way out of the Senate. Due to the number of people and blocked passageways, it was half an hour before Russell and Hugh emerged from the palace. The crowd had begun to disperse. They had seen the queen and royal children return to their palace at the other end of the park and the king had left to go to the general headquarters of the Army, in an unknown location. Despite the seriousness of the occasion spirits had remained high. None realized that the Germans had already breached their borders to the east of Liege early that morning.

Hugh indicated they would have some lunch before they headed back to their embassy and then on to the German legation, to take temporary responsibility for its interests. He seemed in no hurry for this chore.

When they returned to the American legation, the place was in tumult. The human traffic of previous days was now a constant flow with Americans in need of solace and assistance, but now the place was also full of Germans. Word was out that the Americans had taken over responsibility for German interests, so here the people came; they wanted safe passage to their homeland. Some were in real fear for their lives; they did not know what reprisals might come their way. Family groups huddled together around suitcases of hastily packed possessions, wide-eyed and alert to any anger that might be directed towards them. Hugh was aghast. His experience had not prepared him for this sudden movement of people nor their need for protection. Harmony had turned to hostility in the blink of an eye.

Russell was left alone when Hugh dashed off to make some phone calls, so he made himself useful and manned desks when others took their breaks. Hugh came to find Russell later and at about five o'clock they arrived at the German legation. On the way there Hugh told him of his conversations with the Garde Civique. They were now directing all German nationals to schools, convents, and civic buildings, and away from the American legation. The numbers of displaced Germans had risen rapidly, as had the hot-headedness in some groups of Belgian youths that gathered on street corners. They had started to shout abuse at some of the refugees.

By collecting the Germans together it was easier to guard them and provide provisions, but they became larger targets, should feelings get out of hand.

The Garde Civique proved to be valuable allies when Hugh and Russell reached the German legation. They forced a path through crowds of anxious Germans. By the time they left the building these people had been marched to the German consulate building that had been provisioned, as if for a siege, and were safe inside. A heavy detachment of the Garde still remained at the legation to form a protective shield, in case of trouble. Hugh was relieved to see this as he had just signed and sealed the protocol known as *La garde des clefs et des sceaux*, that made America responsible for the premises.

Inside they had found a mass of activity; staff intent on sealing archives and packing boxes rushed from room to room. A special train had been arranged to take all the diplomatic and consular staff to Holland, and they were working against a fast approaching deadline. Instructions were rattled off to Hugh, all of which Russell captured in his notebook and all seemed to require immediate attention. It was the confidently held view of the staff that the German Army would march into the city within three days, so his responsibilities would be short-lived but very significant for those Germans who needed to leave the country. They repeatedly told Hugh he had a humanitarian job to do; they were saddened by the circumstances of their departure, which were not of their making.

Hugh and Russell were both pleased to leave the building, until they stepped outside into a maelstrom of people. All were German and all seemingly upset that their access to the embassy was denied. The Garde actually had everything under control; it just took time for messages to pass through the clusters of people. Groups were formed up and moved off under guard towards one of the public buildings in the town; they would be held there until onward transport could be arranged. Transportation would be Hugh's first job to sort out the next day.

While Hugh talked to the senior garde, Russell's attention was caught by a group of young ladies. They stood a little way apart from the masses at the gate. He smiled a greeting in case they should look his way and he was surprised when two of them broke away from the others and walked towards him. They were both in nurses' uniforms and wore the insignia of the Red Cross.

Marion looked to Edith in anticipation of the questions they needed to ask. Edith spoke in French.

"I need to arrange transportation for my nurses. Can you help?"

Russell replied that he could. His accent gave him away as Edith's next question was to ask if he spoke English.

Russell, who in that moment had locked eyes with Marion, was very pleased that he did.

That Evening
3rd August 1914
Russell

It was one of those moments when time stood still. Words were unnecessary for Russell and Marion to fuse the connection that fired between them. Instead they both smiled.

"Russell Clarke, American, at your service."

He was about to shake hands, but it was Edith who stepped forward, not Marion.

"Edith Cavell, English, and director of a nursing school. My colleague is Nurse Drake," with a nod towards Marion, "and these", she said, as she turned to unblock the view of about 15 women, "are German students who require repatriation. I need to know where they can be taken and be chaperoned. Can you assist us?"

Russell was in the front line again, but this was not a request to pass on to another: he wanted to impress this pair—well, one of them at least. Even though they had not even spoken he did not want to break the link he felt with Nurse Drake.

"I'm sure that I can help, just give me a minute to ask some questions and I'll be straight back to you ma'am."

Russell had managed to tear his eyes away from Marion to direct his response to Edith, which was when he realized the age difference. Miss Cavell had grey hair and was a woman in her fifties, whereas he thought Nurse Drake was his age or perhaps a little younger. To his eye her physique was perfect and he liked her assured manner. With a parting smile he turned to join Hugh and the sergeant of the Garde who looked up as he approached. They had been examining a street map of the city.

"We've just planned the best routes to move all the Germans to the railway station tomorrow. The more they mass, the more likely we might run into trouble. Then all we need are some trains," Hugh said.

"I wonder if you can both help me for a moment. Apologies for the interruption," Russell said, not the least bit apologetically, "but where would you direct a group of young German student nurses, who need to be chaperoned? Are any of the convents taking in evacuees? Their director is English, and keen to know they'll be safe".

The sergeant nodded, and pointed to a place on the map.

"Here is good for women. It's not far from the railway station. They'll be secure, but not very comfortable."

Already sympathy towards German nationals was waning; they were the enemy who would be professionally dealt with, but nothing more. The sergeant continued:

"I'll give you two guards and will brief them on the best route. You'll have a 45 minute walk. Be ready in two minutes."

Russell was delighted with the assumption that he would accompany the group, even though his presence was superfluous for their safety. When Hugh pointed this out, he stretched the truth and said it was on his way to his own hotel, so was no trouble to see them settled. Hugh walked with Russell back to the nurses.

"I have a guard organized and a convent that will take the girls in overnight. I'll personally join the escort to see that all remain safe. It will take us about 45 minutes to walk there ..."

Russell's speech was interrupted by the arrival of the two guards.

"And it looks as if we're ready to leave now."

"Mr Gibson, secretary to the American legation," Hugh said as he introduced himself to Edith. "This young man is endorsed by me and will be as good as his word. I understand you are the English director of the nurses. Are you at the clinic in the Rue de la Culture? You have an outstanding reputation, and I'm delighted to meet you, but sorry it is in such difficult times".

"Miss Cavell," said Edith as she shook his outstretched hand. "Thank you, Mr Gibson, and to this young man for his assistance. Shall we be off?"

"There's no need for you to accompany them further, Miss Cavell. They'll be safely quartered until transportation is arranged for their departure. The convent is the wrong side of town for you. I myself will be walking back your way, if you'd allow me to accompany you."

"Thank you, Mr Gibson, you are most kind, but I have to report to their parents, so I really must see them safe."

"In that case", Hugh announced, "I'll join your party. A walk will do me good, as no doubt much of my night will see me working. Why don't you and I", he directed his comment to Edith, "walk at the front of the group with one of the guards and Russell, you walk at the back with the other guard. Everyone ready?"

Russell, who had stood in Hugh's shadow for most of the day, somewhat reluctantly held back as the group formed and started to move off. The girls seemed very keen to link arms so there was some jostling as they partnered each other and, like a school outing, moved along the pavement. Russell was surprised when he found himself in step with Marion. She had appeared at his side without any apparent manoeuvring and he was delighted. He had thought she'd depart with Hugh and Miss Cavell and leave him martyred to his task as escort. Now he had the walk he wanted.

"How difficult to be saying goodbye to friends in this way," Russell said.

"It must be much harder to say goodbye to someone who was going off to fight. I can't imagine what that would be like," Marion replied.

"Torturous, I'd imagine," Russell said.

"They're not all particular friends; I know some better than others, but the sad part is, they don't want to go. It's not our war and none of us want to take sides, but matron received notice today that all German nationals had to leave, so we have to obey instructions."

"That friends can become foes overnight seems ridiculous." Russell described the scene from earlier in the day when the German and American ministers had greeted each other as friends, before the realities of war crept in.

"But America and Germany aren't enemies, are they?" Marion stated more than asked.

"No," Russell said.

He found himself slightly miffed that Marion had taken the fact that he was witness to such a scene entirely in her stride. He was still stunned by his day, but then she was not to know that this was not routine for him.

"No, not enemies," he continued, "but a friendship can't be enjoyed when aggression is shown against parties who have been mutual friends. Even when it's one's job not to take sides".

Russell kicked himself, he sounded as if he was making a speech, but Marion did not seem to have noticed.

"What is your job?" she asked. She knew that the reciprocal question was redundant as she was in her uniform.

Russell paused and for a moment imagined her impressed with his role on the embassy staff. He had collected enough terminology and experiences in one day to dine out on for months, so he could carry it through this conversation, but as he opened his mouth he told the truth.

"Actually, I don't have a job."

"But I thought you worked with Mr Gibson."

"Well, I do, sort of, but it's only temporary and voluntary and totally happenstance."

Russell cast a glance across to Marion. They walked side by side and both watched their feet as they stepped up and down kerbstones. He had taken her arm a couple of times to cross some cobbled streets. She caught his eye and smiled.

"Sounds as if you have a story to tell, Mr Clarke. Do let me hear it."

"Well I, like many other Americans, was at the embassy as we attempted to find our way home when …"

Before he could get any further she touched his arm.

"I don't want to hear the end of the story, start at the beginning. Who are you, Mr Clarke?"

"If you call me Russell, I shall tell you."

"All right—Russell."

"And only if you'll tell me about yourself too."

"Yes of course, but no more conditions. Get started. Where were you born?"

"That far back, goodness." Russell had started to form an abridged tale of what had brought him to Europe. "If I start right back there I'll have only reached long pants by the time we arrive at the convent".

"Well, surely you would then see me back home," Marion said. She seemed totally in control of their exchange. "So that should take us through your teens at least".

"It was only in my twenties that life really started to get interesting, so you'll miss all the best bits," he said as he picked up on Marion's sparring, "and when would I hear about you?"

"I feel sure I can volunteer to see the girls onto the train tomorrow, so perhaps we could continue our exchange then; unless you've been reassigned from escort duties by then. Not that any of us know what tomorrow will bring."

Marion's words reminded Russell of the circumstances that surrounded their walk. He had momentarily forgotten the dire decisions of the day and the unknown consequences ahead. He was caught up in the intimacy that he could sense they both wanted to nurture and feed. It was the first time he had been conscious of such a strong mutual attraction, and the first time he had not felt self-conscious in the presence of a young woman. He wanted to talk and talk and he wanted her to do the same. But conversation was only one of the familiarities by which he would know her. Just to look at her told him so much.

He was captivated by her statuesque figure outlined in her uniform. Her movements did not seem constrained by the starched cotton, and her strides almost matched his. When she turned her head towards him he would catch a glimpse of her smile. Handsome rather than pretty, he thought her lovely. She had a purposeful air about her. This evening she was on a mission, but somehow he suspected her energy would be focused most of the time. She seemed at ease with him. It was definitely of her making that they walked alongside each other. She had brought them together while he had just been awestruck, although he had orchestrated the mobilization of the group, until Hugh had stepped in. And thank goodness he had, otherwise Russell would have been escorting Miss Cavell and not Marion. Each time he took her arm it almost took his breath away.

"Whatever tomorrow brings," Marion said, "I have a feeling I've found a new friend".

Marion's words conveyed all that needed to be said.

"Me too."

Russell felt he knew her.

"So, Russell, where were you born?"

"Oh, that old chestnut." Russell marvelled at the fact they had created a history of humour between them already. "Let's cross this road and then I'll begin".

He had been right, they had progressed no further than his junior years by the time they arrived at the convent. Marion had made it more of a conversation than a monologue with constant interruptions and questions. He had actually enjoyed talking about himself, and that was another first.

Russell was totally surprised when he saw the convent. He had expected it would be old, but the group had stopped in front of a newly built red brick building, a modern take on the Gothic style. They had turned off a main road, Rue Belliard, into Rue van Maerlant and Hugh had already knocked at the entrance door of the three-storey building when Russell and Marion approached. Adjoined to the residential building was a large steepled church and next to this a much older and smaller grey rendered chapel. It did not take long for Hugh to establish their welcome. They were not the first party to arrive at these doors that evening and within minutes Edith and Marion were caught up in farewells and the emotion of the moment.

"Looks like a new building," Russell said to Hugh.

They had moved next to each other.

"Yes, the garde told me they've only just moved in. It's the order of the Sisters of Perpetual Adoration. Not a new order but their previous home was purchased to make way for the new railway station. Nothing is sacred when it comes to progress."

"Were they all right about taking in these girls?" Russell asked, while he kept half an eye on Marion.

"They explained they had very little to offer apart from shelter, but they've made all their guests as welcome as they can. Apparently they have quite a few families inside already."

"Do you think there'll be any trouble from the locals?"

"Difficult to say," Hugh said. "I don't think so, but these are very strange times. Who knows what scores some people might want to settle. It's how we move them out of the country that concerns me. I must get onto this straight away. Which way are you walking now?"

"Your way, if you need some help; but perhaps we ought to accompany our two nurses back first."

"I think I drew the short straw," Hugh said. He had spotted Russell's glances towards Marion. "Is she as nice as she looks?"

"I think she is."

"She looks like an English rosebud," Hugh said, waxing more lyrical than literal as by now it was hard to make out any specific details in the dusk. "Yes, let's see them back and then return to the legation and see what's what. You can bed down there for a few hours if needs be."

Their walk to the convent had taken them to the south-east and beyond the central area of the city. Rather than retrace their steps they were able to cut across the myriad of streets that led out from the city centre like the spokes of a wheel, and walk around to the south. Once they had crossed Avenue Louise they knew they were almost back to the school, then with a turn north Russell and Hugh would soon be back at the legation. Russell and Marion had continued in conversation as they walked in step behind Hugh and Miss Cavell. They had laughed less and listened more intently, subdued by the proximity of their seniors in front.

"We're almost back," Marion said, "and at least I do now know what you are doing in Brussels".

Russell felt he had galloped through his high school and college years, compared with his expansive descriptions of the events and geography of his early life. But much of their earlier conversation had been prompted by Marion's questions. He was the first American she had ever spoken to, and she was as fascinated to hear about America as to hear about him. He loved the way she sounded, so refined compared to him.

"And I know nothing, apart from the obvious, about you. When can I see you again? You have to face my questions next."

They had nothing definite arranged by the time they turned into Rue de la Culture, but each was sure of the other's desire to meet again. Russell tried to create an opportunity to return when he and Hugh stood at the bottom of the steps to their building. He noted the door number.

"I can come and inform you when the girls are to leave, in case you want to see them off at the station," he said, but Hugh cut across any reply.

"No, that's not a good idea. The numbers to be repatriated have increased by the hour. There could be a bit of a scrimmage at the station and we'll want to keep the numbers of by-standers down, in case of trouble. Best you stay away."

Russell was disappointed. His plan to see Marion had been squashed and they had nothing else in hand.

"But", Hugh continued, "you could report to Miss Cavell when they've left. I'm sure she'd want to know when her responsibilities for her charges are over".

"That news would be most welcome," Edith said, "and perhaps, Mr Gibson, you might like to visit and have a tour of my establishment at some time in the future. I can see that you are busy right now. You have been most kind to us this evening. If such friendship could be extended across all nations, we would not be faced with the animosities that drive us into strife today. Thank you again for your courtesy".

"Yes, thank you," Marion added, with a nod and a smile to both of them, before she turned and followed Edith into number 149.

Russell and Hugh strode away in silence, both lost in their own thoughts, only interrupted when Hugh said, "She's a remarkable woman".

"Yes, she is," Russell sighed in return.

"Not Nurse Drake, you lovesick puppy: Miss Cavell. She's built the training school from scratch. She's a woman with a vision."

"And Marion is a vision," Russell said, playing into Hugh's view of his captivation with her.

"She's had very little direction, remarkable. Did Nurse Drake speak highly of her?"

"Oh yes," Russell lied; and he suddenly realized that Marion had not said anything about herself or her views at all, "very highly".

Hugh seemed pleased that his opinion of Miss Cavell was mirrored by one who worked with her.

Russell felt a pang of remorse that he had not learned anything about Marion. Never before had he spoken about himself so freely, and in a way that even to him made sense. He had been straightforward and not at all self-conscious. More than anything he wanted to be liked and respected by her. It would be when he wrestled with his bed sheets in the sweat-drenched early hours of the morning that another way he wanted her became clear.

The two men arrived at the legation and Hugh sent Russell off to the kitchens to rustle up some supper while he made his way to his office, the telephone, and his action list. It would be a long night.

4th August 1914
Brussels
Marion and Russell

Marion and Gwen had to change the beds. They found it quicker to work each bed as a pair, and so enjoyed their conversation neither of them was in a hurry to finish.

"What does he look like?" Gwen asked.

"Tall, dark, and handsome," Marion replied.

"Aren't they always?"

"He's tall, over six foot, and his hair is light brown and a bit wavy. My mother would say it needed some oil, but I like the natural look. Natural is a good word for him too. He moves freely, there's nothing stiff about him. He was a perfect gentleman, nice manners, but comfortable with me. Not like those men who mutter and blurt as if their tongues have been starched with their collars. I've suffered afternoon tea with too many like that."

"Handsome as well," Gwen sighed. "You've hit the jackpot".

"He has blue eyes, a broad smile, and perfect lips."

"You didn't kiss him? Tell me you didn't kiss him," Gwen shrieked.

"Ssh, of course I didn't. I just mean his lips look perfect, not too thick or too thin. He has to shave, unlike some of the milksops my mother tried to foist on me."

"What are his hands like? Can you imagine holding hands with him?"

"That, and a lot more," Marion laughed, and caught a pillow thrown at her by Gwen.

"His hands are strong and manly. He plays tennis and the piano; there's a gentleness about him too. As I keep telling you, he's perfect, my perfect man."

"I never thought I'd ever hear you say that, Marion Drake. You've been against the whole thought of men ever since I met you with your "I'm never going to marry" statements and the way you idolize matron. Now, the first American you meet and you have turned into putty. What did you talk about and when are you going to see him again? Will you need me as a gooseberry? Oh, and does he have any friends?"

Marion did her best to keep pace with Gwen's questions as she relived the conversation she had had with Russell. She had repeated it in her mind many times already and welcomed the opportunity to replay it out loud, each revisit embedding the facts and descriptions into her memory. She did not want to stop talking about him and Gwen was more than happy to play stooge.

"How old is he?" Gwen suddenly realized she had missed a fundamental fact.

"Twenty-three, nearly 24."

"Experienced?"

This time a pillow hit her.

"No, seriously, what do you think?"

Marion hugged the pillow that Gwen had thrown back to her, and thought about the question. She recalled the way he had confidently taken her arm at road crossings. There had been no awkwardness if ever their arms bumped when the pavement narrowed or they squeezed together to let others pass.

"Yes, I think so, but I don't think he's been in love."

"Perfect combination," Gwen said.

"Absolutely," Marion agreed.

They had both heard horror stories among their colleagues of furtive and inexperienced fumbles that resulted in little satisfaction, for the woman at least. Marion had never paid much attention to these late night confessions: she had no experience to contribute. And Gwen had been right, she had had little interest in men. Well, that was before: she was alive to them now—well, one specimen anyway.

Marion was astounded at just how alive her body felt. She only had to conjure up a picture of Russell in her mind and she could feel a hot flush go through her body.

Marion started to feel the conversation was getting a bit too gritty and she wanted to remain in a romantic haze.

"What time is our evening lecture?" Marion asked to distract Gwen from Russell.

"Starts in half an hour. Shall we walk the long way round and get a breath of fresh air?"

"Good idea. Let's get these beds finished quickly."

Russell had managed some sleep the night before. He had been of very little value to Hugh who had struggled through hours of conversations in his attempts to secure trains for the German nationals, so Hugh had sent him off to bed. Although tired, he was at the end of what he would always consider to be the most memorable day of his life, and sleep was elusive. To have been in the presence of history in the making was heady stuff and beyond his previous imaginings. He tried to take himself back to the minister's room and the exchange with the Germans. He tried to again hear the roar of the crowd as he processed down the avenue to see the king, but however much he tried to drag his attention to these scenes, all he could picture was Marion.

Never before had he felt so comfortable in the company of a woman, nor had he spoken so easily. He had been physically close to women before: it was one of his perks as captain of the tennis team to be assured of easy embraces. But to talk about himself so openly was to him, true intimacy. Until this moment he had never felt alone, but now he had met Marion, he felt their separation as a physical ache.

Marion excited him; he felt close to her, but it was more than that: he felt deeply connected with her. A beautiful woman, true, but it was the ease of their immediate companionship that most entranced him. Today he thought he'd learnt what it meant to love someone. Although knowing little about her he was sure of his feelings for her. What excited him too was how good he felt when with her: he could really be himself. This was the first time he appreciated the wonder of commitment to another. He wanted Marion in his life. He had never been more convinced of anything, and yet he did not understand where this certainty came from. His mother had always told him, "Some day you'll meet someone and you'll just know." Before, these words had held no meaning, but he believed them now. When sleep had eventually come, it was not a welcome escape, more an intrusion on his thoughts of Marion.

The next day Russell's task was to shadow Hugh, make notes and at times run errands within the building, or even just hold on to the telephone until the recipient of the call returned to the line to speak to Hugh. It was chaos; they had thousands of Germans who needed transport home. Understandably, easing the path for any German nationals did not feature high on anyone's list of priorities, apart from Hugh it seemed. By four o'clock in the afternoon Hugh was despondent and was showing signs of fatigue. He stood, stretched and said:

"I think I need to go and have a wash and brush-up and perhaps a nap, then try another approach. There are just no trains that can be made available, or I've failed to speak to the person who can send them here. I need a break. Can you have this notice copied and taken out to all the places on this list and posted downstairs? It will let the Germans and their temporary hosts know that they need to settle in for another night. I hope they all have enough food. The staff downstairs can organize the distribution: just leave it with them and then I suggest you take a break too. Let's meet back here in an hour."

Russell looked a picture of health next to Hugh who had the pasty look of one who spent too much time indoors. Hugh was thin, of medium height and although bookish in appearance had a vitality about him that set a fast pace. Russell was impressed by how seriously Hugh took his responsibilities, and how he so often found ways to inject humour into a conversation. He was a true professional. Listening to his diplomatic ways on the telephone that day had been a lesson for Russell in how to be tolerant in the face of obduracy. He did notice Hugh had doodled a few hangmen on his pad, but he always managed to bring a smile to his voice as he yet again explained his request for trains.

Russell was in the office to pass on Hugh's distribution request some minutes later when the minister walked into the room, with Hugh in slight disarray behind him.

"Stop that. Change of plan," Minister Whitlock said. He had their attention. "Four trains will arrive between eight o'clock and midnight. I've just had a telegraph. Hugh has done some great work today. Now we need to move these people. Upstairs in half an hour please, and organize some coffee and sandwiches please, we're in for quite a night," and with this pronouncement he departed, again followed by Hugh.

Russell assumed the task of procuring the food and drink from the kitchens. When he entered the minister's room and found it full of people, deep in conversation he immediately left again to organize more provisions. He gave the extended order to the kitchen staff and returned straight away: he did not want to miss out on the action. Only Hugh acknowledged his return with a nod of his head. Without an invitation to step into the group, and no obvious point of entry, he loitered near the window, quite self-conscious. All Russell could do was hope to glean an understanding of what had been determined as the conversation jumped from English to French, depending on the speaker. The uniforms and insignia helped him identify the seniority of the people present, but it was Hugh later who told him who they were. The head of the Gendarmerie and the Garde Civique, the burgomaster of Brussels and the minister of justice had all attended this hastily called summit, with their assistants. All were concerned to maintain public order and they wanted the Germans moved with as little fuss on the streets as possible; they thought under cover of dark was an advantage. The group split into two just as the refreshments arrived: the town dignitaries stayed with Minister Whitlock and the rest were assigned to Hugh. Several of them literally rolled up their sleeves and Hugh gestured for Russell to join his group.

A street map was laid out on the table. The station had been clearly marked, as had several buildings that were known to host displaced Germans.

"This is our problem," one of the burgomaster's assistants pointed to a central spot on the map. "We came through the Cirque Royal and it was already filled with people. Word seems to be out about the trains already: we need to avoid a rush to the station".

Russell was surprised by the immediacy and magnitude of the problem. He had thought they would decide on the order in which the evacuees would be taken from the buildings, but evidently there was a moving mass of people that needed to be directed and controlled, and quickly. Decisions were made fast. Clear-cut instructions were agreed. They all, apart from Russell it seemed, shared an understanding of what was needed.

"Keep a record please, Russell," Hugh said as he shoved a notebook in his hand.

Russell's panic was calmed when one of the assistants handed him a pen.

"It will need gardes at the station to keep people clear of the platform and orderly outside, and keep any excitable Belgians looking for trouble at a distance. Let's get them directed there quickly." The head of the Garde immediately picked up the telephone.

"We need a squad to go the Cirque Royal to contain the people there and not let them rush to the station. I suggest some town officials go there with the Garde to keep them informed, and hopefully reassured."

Another assistant peeled off to brief the burgomaster so that he could decide whose attendance would be best.

"We need gardes at every establishment that houses Germans. They are to keep them inside until we know we can manage their passage in a safe way."

"Leave that to me," the head of the Gendarmerie said. "My assistant will stay with you to brief me on further actions that are needed. I'll set up runners between each location so we can keep people informed." Just as he turned to leave, Hugh called after him.

"Don't underestimate your numbers for this job. It will only take a few people panicking to cause a stampede from those buildings. People won't want to be left behind."

"I think I know my job." The head of the Gendarmerie had 20 years on Hugh.

"Of course." Hugh was immediately apologetic and to placate him asked, "Before you leave, can you think of anything else we should do?"

In acceptance of the proffered apology, the gendarme replied, "I think you have it all covered. I assume you will coordinate from the railway station. Just make sure we know when you are there".

And with a parting shot, which seemed to surprise them all he said, "Why not see if we can get refreshments available for these people. They will have a long wait".

Russell, who had just begun to appreciate the scale of the mobilization of panic-stricken families, could not immediately accommodate the concept of serving queues of people cups of tea in the middle of the night.

"Good thought," Hugh said, and to the group, "How might we organize that?"

The minister of justice had heard this exchange and separated himself from Minister Whitlock.

"I will speak to my wife, she's chair of the Ladies Benevolent Committee and I'm sure they can sort out something. Vats of hot milk is their winter speciality. I'll telephone her when the garde is finished with the telephone. Safety must come first."

"Any other suggestions? Anything we have missed?" Hugh asked, and glanced at each of them.

Russell waited to see if anyone else was going to speak and when none did he offered a question.

"Do you think someone has told the staff at the railway about the trains? Only, when I was travelling from Leuven a few days ago they seemed to have no information at all at the station. They might need to call on more staff."

"Thank you, Russell," Hugh said. "We can brief them with what we know when we get down there, but no one will be collecting tickets from these passengers."

"Where will the trains take them?" enquired another in the group. The question seemed to stun them all and had not crossed Russell's mind. Away from here was as far as he had considered the matter.

Minister Whitlock, who appeared to have the skill to be in one conversation while he also tracked another, volunteered the answer.

"The trains will go to Esschen, on the Dutch border. From there the Dutch will orchestrate their transport to Germany. You seem to have all angles covered, gentlemen. Now we await the trains."

"That was admirable," Russell said to Hugh. He was not quite sure how praise from him would be received.

"That was the easy bit," Hugh said. "What happens on the streets is how tonight will be remembered, and we probably have a few tough weeks ahead. I hope we haven't put on you too much, but I'd like it if you could stick with me through the evening. There's an awful lot to coordinate and I'll need to keep the minister informed too. You in?"

Russell had entirely forgotten that he had a choice, so embroiled was he in the machinations of the day and now the plans for the mobilization.

"I'm in."

"And so are the British," Hugh said, and to Russell's confused look, "The war, the British have declared war against the Germans. Now we're in for a spat".

12th August 1914
Leuven
Therese

Therese had been woken in the night by a noise at her window. She had accommodated the tapping sound within her dream and had paid it no particular attention. It was only as it persisted and she was roused from sleep she realized its source. There was someone knocking on her window from the street. She did not know what to do.

Therese's life was governed by routine. In fact Therese's life was totally governed, not just her routine, and it had been that way since she had first walked into the convent of St. Gertrude as a postulant ten years earlier. Noises in the night and the need for independent action were so rare that her mind was almost paralyzed, but she sat up in bed and gingerly placed her feet on the cold stone floor. She had no idea of the time. She normally woke in response to the call to matins, timed for daybreak, but it was still dark and she fumbled to dress. Now that she had concentrated on the movement outside, she also heard voices and, she thought, some sobs; it made her hurry. Sisters Rose, Judith, and Esther walked past her room as Therese stepped out of her door. She almost knocked the candle out of Sister Rose's hand and all were startled. Therese stepped in behind them and they soon arrived at the main entrance to the street, and there was Mother Superior with Sister Paul. Therese could sense they were all on edge: a tension had pervaded the community since Mother Superior told them about the declaration of war a few days back.

The convent was in the town, but the separation of the nuns from the outside world was almost complete. They did not go out but did open their doors to the sick for whom they ran a clinic, and to children, for some classes they taught, but only a few of the nuns were involved in these activities. Most were devotional, and when not undertaking their chores, were secluded. It was rare for Mother Superior to bring details of external activities into the community. Usually when she led them in prayer her themes were generic and not named, as in "world leaders", "royal families", "world famine", but last week she had declared their local crisis. They were at war with Germany.

Sister Paul stepped forward, opened the door and their light spilled onto people outside. They looked a sorry group and their number quickly grew, the open door attracting clusters of people who had been targeting different houses in the street. They were bloodied, confused, and all seemed tired, in need of shelter; and they were invited in. Two of the sisters moved ahead and led them into the schoolroom, the largest space they had outside the cloistered domains. Therese counted 45 people into the room, the total that was sent to the kitchens for food and drink to be prepared. These people were displaced, hungry, and hurt, and needed food and shelter ahead of words of comfort.

Therese, who sometimes helped out in the clinic, was asked by Mother Superior to take the injured to the next room. Sister Paul had roused the sisters who ran the clinic. Therese asked no questions, she just shepherded any on whom she spotted blood or burns down the corridor. One girl in her late teens would not be separated from her mother. The mother shook and cried and the girl seemed to be in a trance; together they stumbled their way into the waiting room. Therese attempted to organize the dozen or so people into some sort of priority order for Sisters Mary and Ruth, who strode in and surveyed the scene. Therese was delighted to hand over her charges, but soon had plenty to do as she fetched hot water, found bandages, brought hot drinks, and held candles. Before long she anticipated what was needed rather than waiting for requests. Some patients wanted to talk of their woes and yet Therese found herself drawn to those few who looked as if they might never speak again, such was their shock.

By the time dawn arrived and the bells rang for matins most of their visitors were either asleep or sitting quietly in huddles. The sisters left them and walked to their chapel, but Therese found it difficult to shift her attention to the service. Her mind returned constantly to the horrors she had heard, and worse, the ones she was left to imagine. The girl and her mother were traumatized, but neither of them could or would speak of their experience. Therese eventually entered into a prayerful place, and brought each face to mind. She imagined a golden halo of light around each one; often words were not needed for prayer.

The kitchen and refectory buzzed with conversation that morning.

"Who are they?"

"Where are they from?"

"Where are the Germans?"

Those sisters who had not been disturbed in the night wanted to hear about their visitors, and those who had been involved were themselves disturbed and wanted to talk about what they had heard. The details they had gleaned were harrowing and as each sister volunteered the snippets she had been told, a picture started to form that had them shocked and shaken.

Many of the refugees had travelled from Hermee just to the east of Liege, although some came from the suburbs of Liege itself. The German Army had marched into Belgium as soon as their leaders had declared war, but the proclamations that they bore no aggression against the Belgians had lasted no time at all after they met the resistance of the Belgian Army. The proud Prussian brigades had not expected to be stopped by them. Repelled and pushed back they immediately retaliated on the civilian population.

"It was the fort at Pontisse that stopped them ..."

"They were heading for Liege ..."

"Our arms factory in Herstal was well protected by our Army ..."

"The Germans lost lots of men. Took them by surprise."

"They turned tail."

"They went through the villages and took out their frustrations."

"They were barbaric."

"In Hermee, soldiers pulled people out of their homes and torched the buildings. Nearly a dozen villagers were shot. They had nothing to defend themselves."

"Tens of people were taken by the Prussians to form a human shield. They stood them on the bridge across the Meuse to prevent Belgian artillery attacks."

"They raided the cellars and drank all their wine …"

"They were drunk …"

"They attacked the women and girls."

"Their commanders did nothing to stop them."

Therese could not take in that such inhumanity could exist from a civilized nation, from their neighbour. The war had come close and was real in a way that she hadn't thought possible.

Mother Superior's declaration that they were at war had been accompanied by re-assurances that Belgium's neutrality would be respected by the Germans, but these intentions had proved themselves to be lies. Therese felt a prickle of fear.

"What do you make of it all?" Sister Winifred asked her as they left the refectory to start on their chores in the laundry.

"If I hadn't seen the people with my own eyes I'm not sure I would have been able to believe the stories. I understand how doubting Thomas felt; but this is just unimaginable. Innocent people, whose only crime was to be in the wrong place, have had their lives and homes taken. That isn't war, it's murder."

"War or not", Sister Winifred said, "they've brought the troubles closer to us. How many more will knock on our door for food? We don't have unlimited supplies ourselves."

"The Lord will provide," Therese said somewhat sanctimoniously. She wanted to censure Sister Winifred for breaking the vow of poverty in her company. It was the hardest vow for Therese to keep and the toughest part of her training. She knew that Sister Winifred's thoughts were practical, but food was not theirs to possess, it was to use in God's service. Therese did not find it difficult to have no possessions, but the vow of poverty was about more than this: she had to lose her sense of self as an individual, and dismantle the concept of mine or me and step into a state of oneness with the community and God. All too easily she could slip into thoughts about herself;

just this morning in matins she had felt tired and wondered how she would manage through the activities of the day, because she had given up *her* sleep. Changes to routine were likely to throw up many challenges, she mused.

"And it will be our hands that willingly toil for Him," said Sister Winifred, somewhat piously Therese thought, and they smiled at each other. Therese nursed an anxiety that had yet to be voiced.

Both were in their mid-twenties. They had entered the convent within a year of each other, but there the similarities stopped. Therese was fine-boned with slim wrists and hands while Sister Winifred was stocky with short dumpy fingers. Their wimples framed faces that were in contrast: Therese's fair skin to Winifred's ruddy cheeks; Therese's arched, fair eyebrows to Winifred's heavy brow; Therese's engaging smile to Winifred's permanent frown. Therese was the taller of the two.

The laundry was the best place for them to be that day as the work was strenuous and required them to keep pace with each other. The physical rhythm they established soothed the jangled edge to their nerves. They pushed and pulled sheets through mangles, and felt the sun on them as they hung the items on the maze of washing lines that crossed the courtyard. It was a satisfying task.

The evening meal was usually held in silence, whilst a reader read from the Bible or other learned tomes. Therese liked it most when extracts from the Psalms were read. The simplicity of the messages that came through the poetry, imagery, and wisdom of the texts always soothed her; but not tonight. Although silence was maintained it was clear to her that the attention of the room was not on the words; everyone was absorbed in their own thoughts. The tales of the refugees had permeated the community and had unsettled the harmony that usually accompanied this special, almost companionable, part of the day. At a signal from Mother Superior, Sister Paul went to the reader and spoke to her quietly. The reader blessed and closed the Bible and Sister Paul stepped up to the lectern.

"Today has been a difficult day for many of us. It was to remove ourselves from the world and step into a union with God that we were called together in this community. Our work is to channel God through prayers, meditations, and thoughts for mankind's spiritual health and well-being, but today the Lord has brought us a different need. Our guests have brought the troubles of the world into our midst through their trauma and pain and we will be their Samaritan."

Sister Paul paused and many heads nodded at her words, but some were still.

"It is for us to examine our hearts to find the service He wants from each of us during what appears to be a time of great turbulence and need. For some it will mean deeper devotions, for others longer hours in the kitchens, gardens, or laundry, for others talking with our guests to help them, so that they do not lose their way at this time of strife. Examine His call for you tonight and we will speak tomorrow to arrange your roles."

Therese felt a release within her at these sentiments. The wisdom of asking each of them to reflect on their increased contribution reduced a pressure that had begun to build in her. She now realized that she didn't welcome disruption; for one thing it challenged her spirit of obedience. She might not like new requests that could be made of her and she dreaded her struggles to accept new direction; the vow of obedience was a constant challenge for her.

"We do not know, nor do we want to imagine, what lies ahead of us, but we are here to serve God's purpose, through whatever trials. The resources and facilities that have been made available to us will be stretched, but the Lord will provide."

Sister Winifred nudged Therese as Sister Paul finished and when Mother Superior then led them in prayer, the communion in the room felt restored. Their attention had returned to God's will and that was a unified place to be, but evening prayers felt sombre. The truths they had heard that day, man's ability to hate and destroy, were hard to shake off, and this was reflected in the prayers for protection and wisdom for the world. In her meditation Therese saw the mangle she had used in the laundry that day, but in this scene it sucked the world through its hungry jaws and reduced it to a squashed mess. She knew this meant they faced a time of terrible destruction and she prayed for this to end. The picture changed to a washing line on which hung a set of flags from different countries blowing gently together in the breeze and sunlight. Peace would come.

Heading to her room at the end of the day, Therese stopped by the schoolroom to see how the visitors had settled down for the night. She was shocked to see that their numbers had increased, at a glance she thought nearer to 60, and the mix had changed. There were more women and children; some of the men who had been there that morning appeared to have left. Therese heard that Mother Superior had arranged additional accommodation in the crypt of St. Pierre, which was large and close by. Being near men did not disturb Therese. The vow of chastity was the easiest of the vows for her to keep. She had had no sexual experience before she entered the convent, and had not the slightest inclination to fraternize with any of the local young men. It had just not been her way. Neither had she had any close girlfriends: she was a loner at heart. Her mother's concern, when she said she wanted to become a nun, was how she would cope with living in close proximity to others in the community, but Therese had not worried about this. The vow was about all relationships: the only affinity was to be between her and God and that was fine with her. Nothing would get in the way of her dialogue with the Almighty, of that she had been clear.

Therese left the room with no conversation, just nods and smiles with guests who caught her eye. It was enough. When she awoke to the call for matins the next morning she knew what her contribution was to be and went off in search of Sister Paul.

16th August 1914
Brussels
Russell

"I thought you'd forgotten about me," Marion said.

"And I thought I was never going to see you," Russell replied.

It was Sunday afternoon. Their walk in the park took almost the same paths that Marion and Gwen had followed two weeks before.

"I walked here on my last day off, with Gwen. I can't believe how much has changed since then, and yet in some ways nothing has changed. I can still walk in the park on my day off; it's almost as if there are parallel worlds. Sorry, I'm babbling, aren't I?"

Russell so enjoyed being with her and hearing her voice he would happily have had her "babble", as she called it, all afternoon.

"I still have to pinch myself," Russell said. "I think I've stepped into that parallel world entirely. Assisting Hugh and the minister through these extraordinary days has been, well, extraordinary, and not at all what my life is usually about".

"So what has been happening?" Marion asked. "I only know what I've picked up from the newspapers and from the people who arrive at our back door to ask for food, and believe me some of those stories are grim. What have you been doing?"

"Now that's not fair. You've thrown questions at me again. You promised that when we met again you would tell me about yourself, and that's what I want to hear about—you."

"Yes, I know, and you will, but I need to know the news first. I read in the newspaper that the German nationals left Brussels; apparently it took days. I didn't read of any, but was there trouble?"

"All right," Russell said, "I give in, I'll tell you all about it, but please, I have lots I want to ask you too".

"We have plenty of time," Marion said and they rewarded each other with beaming smiles, both delighted at this thought.

"It was like a military operation once the trains started to arrive. Hugh coordinated everyone's efforts until he could hand over to the consul-general, Mr Watts. He had been in France on vacation and it had taken him a while to get back. But it went on for several nights. The first night we moved about 5000 people, your nurses among them."

"Yes, matron received a note from Mr Gibson. He told us of their departure. We'd followed his advice and kept away from the station. That's a lot of people."

"The following night was about half that number, the one after about 1200, and the next about 400, and the last two nights 200 each. Every day we tried to keep track of the numbers. We weren't the only city that had German nationals to move and the military still wanted to use all the trains to transport troops to the border. Hugh was on the phone for hours. The railway timetable had been torn up, no one knew when trains would turn up, no schedule was followed. I wouldn't want to be a signalman, I can tell you."

"Its sounds chaotic," Marion said.

"Yes, and we also had Americans and British people to get to the Channel too. They proved to be the hardest to handle. Less patient than the Germans, some seemed to feel put upon by the situation and expected us to put things right. They certainly didn't like it if it looked as if we put the Germans' transport needs ahead of them. They didn't want to hear we couldn't direct the trains for their benefit."

Russell allowed himself to pause and Marion stayed quiet by his side. The story of the last week had lost something in the way he told it. It had been the most fraught and stressed time of Russell's life and yet here, in summary, it seemed sanitized and ordered. Hugh and he had shared moments of despair and frustration, and euphoria. They had suffered from lack of sleep, irregular meals, and no changes of clothing for days. Words seemed inadequate to describe his delight when he sank into a bath and then into a proper bed after four nights on a camp bed at the legation. It had been an exhausting time.

"People were so kind: the Belgians, I mean. Chocolate and biscuits were handed out to the queues, hot drinks were available and the gendarmes, who were there to protect the Germans from any trouble, played with the children or held some as they slept. It became a place for friendship, not hostility."

"A wonderful moment to be part of," Marion said. "It almost restores your faith in mankind, in the middle of all this madness".

"Yes, and those are the things to remember, not the fractious egos," Russell said.

"It sounds as if you and Mr Gibson worked well together," Marion said.

"Yup, we did, well actually all I did was whatever he asked me. I was largely his runner and note-taker. Hugh was the architect of everything. He has a great way with people; he assumes he'll get the best from everyone, and he does. Most people bend over backwards for him. He didn't have to bring the minister in once to call the shots. I've learnt from being alongside him. I'd make a better captain of the tennis team now, I can tell you."

"Why don't we sit here?" Marion asked.

They were level with an empty park bench. It was largely in the sun, but one end had some dappled shade from the tree that stood behind it.

"The weather has been so beautiful. I hadn't expected blue skies like this. I'd been warned to expect rain like we have in England," she continued.

"Yes, Hugh had told me this was unusually good weather," Russell said as he sat beside her, "and I must say the park looks beautiful. As do you".

The words slipped out and he blushed as he looked at her. She did look beautiful. She was wearing a cotton dress to just above her ankle, as was the fashion. The fabric was in muted shades of yellows and blues and one of the blues perfectly matched the jacket she carried. Her hair was tied loosely and clipped back at the sides, which he noticed accentuated her cheekbones and the line of her jaw.

Tendrils of her shoulder length hair curled onto her forehead and cheeks. The bodice and skirt of her dress created the same outline as her uniform, but he found her softer and more feminine today.

"Thank you," Marion took the compliment completely in her stride. "You look good too, although I think I prefer your hair natural rather than oiled".

Russell raised his hand to his head and ran his fingers along his sleeked down hair. He had been in two minds whether to oil his wavy locks, but Hugh had been clear that it must be done, to convey to Miss Drake the importance of the occasion.

"I'll remember that," Russell said, pleased she had spoken frankly. To move the focus away from himself and his hair, he continued:

"The problems we've dealt with at the legation are nothing compared to the battering the Belgian Army has taken. They've slowed down the German advance but the fear is that the last fort at Liege will fall today and that doesn't leave much in their path to stop the Germans. Have you thought about going back home?"

"No, yes, but no," Marion said. "What I mean is I have thought about it, but I've no plans to leave. I'm training to be a nurse and what better place is there for me to be than here. We've already had some Belgian soldiers into the clinic. They've had a brutal time".

" I see," Russell said, "but will you be safe?"

"Oh, yes. We have the Red Cross flags on the clinic and this is the last day I can be out without wearing my uniform. We're well protected."

"I know that Washington has briefed the minister to advise the ministers not to fight the Germans when they arrive in Brussels. They and he consider it better to accept their terms for a safe passage through the city, than have the German artillery do untold damage, not to mention the loss of life. The burgomaster still has to decide. There's no sign of the British Army and the French are already fighting in the east. No one can get here in time to help."

Russell was proud of having the inside track to what was going on.

"But", he asked, "if they do defend Brussels and there is fighting here, would you contemplate leaving?"

"You probably think I'm silly, but I haven't considered Brussels under attack. The battlefield always seems some distance away, but I guess it could happen. Let's hope and pray that it doesn't come to that. I like my independence here and don't want to return home, and matron is clear we have a job to do here. But what about you, when are you due to return to Oxford, can you still get back there?"

Russell had hoped to delay this part of their conversation to later in their day, so he attempted to divert the question.

"There you go asking me questions again. I want to hear about you. When does that opportunity come?"

"You're quite right," Marion conceded, "ask away, but do you mind if we walk?"

"Not at all." Russell rose from the seat and offered his arm. "Which way?"

Marion turned him towards the empty bandstand and they wandered, rather than strode, along paths that criss-crossed flower-beds.

"So, Miss Drake, tell me about you and your life, and like I did you have to start at the beginning. Where were you born?"

"Touché. It will all seem mundane compared to your American life, so when you start to get bored, nudge me onto something new."

"You couldn't bore me, of that I'm sure. Please begin."

At the point when Marion had introduced her wealthy uncle, as she called him, into the description of her family, they had to sit on another bench so she could clearly explain to him the hierarchy of British aristocracy, landed gentry, and disenfranchized brothers and cousins, before he had her incorrectly linked to royalty. Like most Americans, Russell was impressed with British titles. The more she delved into the societal norms that governed lives and determined status, the more relief Russell heard that she was away from it and all the more determined to stay in Brussels, regardless of the dangers.

"I don't want to go back there. I don't want to fit in; I would feel suffocated. Whatever happens here I shall stay as long as I am able."

Before Russell could speak, she continued, "Even if I'm sent back to England, I'll go to London and join in the war effort from there. And then who knows where I might be sent?" she ended triumphantly.

Russell could imagine Marion using this argument with her family. She was feisty and determined and he loved her frankness, but he was anxious for her safety—and worried that he would lose her. When Hugh had broached the subject of his departure with him that morning, he had a romantic notion that he and Marion could return to England together and continue seeing each other. She obviously had other ideas, and he did not seem to feature in them. Despite this notion being ridiculous after such a short acquaintance, he felt disappointed.

To cover his disquiet, he blurted out some information that he had picked up from Hugh that morning, but which was definitely not his place to share.

"The royal family and the government ministers are leaving Brussels tonight. They'll set themselves up at the coast. I don't exactly know where, probably Antwerp. They know they can't stop the Germans now."

"And you think I'm stupid to stay," Marion retorted.

"No, Marion, I don't think you're stupid. I just don't want to risk losing you." The words were out before Russell could censure himself.

Marion had looked as if she was readying for an argument, but his words and the softness with which they were spoken stopped her and instead she reached for his hand.

"And I don't want to be lost. Let's go and find some tea, and you can tell me about your plans."

Marion led them to the café she and Gwen frequented. Most of the tables were taken and they had to wait a few minutes for the waiter, who looked rushed, to clear the debris left by the previous customers. Russell produced a pile of coins and after some consultation gave their order.

"Hugh says I should leave with him when he travels to Antwerp next week. He'll be the runner between Brussels and the Belgian government; it will only be neutrals that can move around the country soon and he said I should leave before the Germans arrive. They're probably no more than a week away. It's odd but Oxford feels so remote to me now. You, me, here, us, this is real and yet this is where the madness is. Oxford, and the life I had mapped out for myself, suddenly feels fake; perhaps I've been travelling for too long and I've lost my bearings."

He stopped for fear that he had said too much.

"I know exactly what you mean, the world has turned topsy-turvy but we're supposed to keep ourselves steady. What life do, or should I say did, you see for yourself?"

"Completing my time at Oxford, receiving an invitation from an Ivy League university to do a doctorate and then into a professorship in medieval history, or even law."

"So you want to teach," Marion said.

"No, not really, but there would be some of that. I mainly want to research and write. But this sounds so alien to me now."

Marion blurted out, "Gwen said I changed the minute I met you, I might as well tell you".

An awkward moment followed that was interrupted by the waiter; he delivered their drinks and cakes and they both focused their attention on the service. The café had emptied so the waiter was able to give them more attention than in the earlier rush. He had positioned each cup and saucer and plate with measured precision and would have stayed in conversation with them, if either had given him an opening, but they were intent on each other.

"Perhaps", Marion picked up their thread, "we've both lost our bearings, because that's what happens when countries start to fight each other. Nothing can be relied upon to stay the same. We're on the brink of something ominous and can't see what's ahead; maybe if we can hold ourselves steady and ride the storm, we'll remember what's important to each of us." Marion looked at Russell, and sipped her drink.

"Yes, perhaps," Russell said, and Marion waited for him to fill the silence that grew between them.

"This may sound crazy," Russell said after a long pause, "but I think we've said too much. I just want to be in your company, to enjoy time with you. To relax, play tennis, take walks, and get to know you. I guess normally I'd only need to know that you wanted the same to be happy, but today, in these circumstances, that doesn't feel enough. We don't have the luxury of a carefree summer ahead of us, and I want you to know that you feel important to me. I already care about what happens to you. Explain that if you can".

Now it was Marion's turn to be silent for a moment.

"I can't explain it, but I know I want time with you too, and I've never wanted to care about any man. I wanted to remain a free spirit and never be bound to another. Maybe we are saying too much. You know that I am taken with you. That's enough," and with this it was her turn to blush.

"So, will you leave soon?" Marion covered her embarrassment.

"Yes, I have to. I have no means to stay and the scholarship to fulfil. I'll go in the embassy car with Hugh to Antwerp next week. I don't know which day that'll be, but I can come and say goodbye before I leave. And we can write each other."

"For as long as letters get through," Marion said.

"Perhaps we can get them through in the embassy post." Russell would make sure to ask Hugh about this.

"Well, it looks like we are finished here," Marion was prompted by the waiter clearing their table. "Perhaps we can take in some of the sights of Brussels together, before they get blown to smithereens".

Russell grimaced at the thought, but she told him to cheer up and took his hand to lead him into the street.

17th August 1914
Brussels
Marion

"One, two," and on the count of three Marion and Gwen moved the Belgian soldier onto his side. While Gwen held him steady, Marion lifted the bottom sheet and put a new one in its place; she tucked it as far under the soldier as her fingers, and his grunts, permitted. The counting and manoeuvre were repeated on the other side when Gwen pulled the underneath sheet through and tucked it in. They laid the soldier gently onto his back and changed the dressings on his wounds. The influx of casualties into the city had increased each day, as the German Army pushed more and more troops at the Belgian defence. The Belgians were in retreat and the outlook for Brussels grew more ominous every day.

When Gwen asked her whether she was going to stay, Marion recalled her conversation with Russell the day before.

"Yes I will, but I have to say I'm becoming a bit more anxious about it. Russell and I stumbled across some trenches, at the edge of the park. There was barbed wire over the top of them. I don't understand what they're supposed to stop, but someone obviously felt they were worth all the effort."

"I'm sure I heard some guns last night," Gwen said. "I don't mind assisting the wounded, but I don't fancy getting fired on myself".

"Neither do I, but we should be safe under the Red Cross banner."

"If they stop to look," Gwen retorted. "I've talked to some of the refugees from Liege and what they describe is truly monstrous. I'm sure one said a priest had been shot, but I might not have translated it correctly. But if they'll shoot a priest, and set fire to churches, I'm not so sure we will be safe".

"Are you saying you want to leave?" Marion felt shaken. She had heard tales herself of the dreadful things that had happened. Villages burnt to the ground; women and girls raped; men and boys shot. Everyone who passed through their kitchens had a tale of horror to tell. She did not know what to make of it. When she had mentioned some of the stories to Russell he had told her that such stories always abound at the start of wars.

"The enemy always takes on monstrous proportions; it's happened throughout history. The Prussians are a professional army," he had said, "and the Belgians are very aggrieved. There is bound to be exaggeration. The Belgians need bad stories to get their allies to hurry up and help them." She had allowed herself to feel reassured by his views, which she now shared with Gwen.

"I'm not sure that I can agree with him," Gwen said. "The family I met yesterday were really terrified; I'm sure it wasn't an act put on to get more food out of us".

"I can't imagine what becoming homeless would be like, and combined with the danger, I'm sure I'd be a wreck too," Marion said.

"Well, let's hope neither of us will be tested in that way. It might not be our choice whether we can stay anyway. Apparently we have to attend a meeting this evening. Who knows what we'll be told."

They walked to the next bed and Marion realized that Gwen had not answered her question about whether she wanted to stay, but she did not want to push her. It was a sombre feeling that pervaded the clinic and no doubt the rest of the city. Marion had not mentioned Russell's news that the minister's plan was to convince the burgomaster to concede Brussels without a fight. It was obvious that resistance would be futile and destructive, but the Belgians were in a strident mood and "surrender" did not fit within their lexicon. Rumours of the proximity of the British Army passed around like wildfire, but the stories they were close to Brussels were unfounded.

With or without violence, Brussels would soon be in German hands and evacuations would then be impossible. It was a sobering thought.

Marion found it difficult to lift her mood, even when Gwen, in an attempt to lighten them both, asked about her afternoon and evening with Russell. Marion had not returned until nine o'clock.

"We must have walked miles," Marion said in answer to Gwen's enquiry.

"I can imagine you did," Gwen said, "but spare me the sightseeing, do you still like him as much? Was he as you remembered him? What did you talk about? Will you see him again?"

In a moment of self-insight, Marion realized that her despondency was not from insecurity about her safety, but because she feared that the answer to the last question would be no.

"I don't know if I'll see him again. He has to return to England this week."

"But if you could, you would want to." Marion heard this as a question.

"Yes, I would. The more time I spend with him, the more I like him. He's comfortable and easy to be with, and we talk so easily I could spend hours with him."

"I'm relieved to hear it: you've mooned around like a lovesick cow for the last two weeks. I'm so pleased you weren't disappointed."

Marion did not tell Gwen, but she was relieved too. It had been such a change for her to have an interest in a man that even she had begun to doubt Russell was as good as she remembered. But he was, and her feelings were real: any doubts had been swept away within minutes of them meeting up.

"So what did you talk about?" Gwen prodded.

Marion's answer was interrupted by a fretful patient who, when examined, required pain relief. Gwen went to find one of the sisters to administer morphine. They were not yet signed off for this; it was in their curriculum for next term.

Marion was relieved. She was not ready for one of Gwen's dissections. She wanted to keep her time with Russell to herself, to savour their conversation and she certainly was not ready to tell Gwen about their kiss. She actually tingled at the memory.

101

"We have a tradition in America that at the end of an enjoyable day with a beautiful lady we are permitted to show our appreciation with a kiss."

"We have a tradition in England that young ladies should offer their kisses sparingly, and in particular, not with strangers," Marion had replied.

"Do I feel like a stranger to you?"

No you don't, Marion had thought. She had learnt more about him in two meetings than she had about anyone, even girlfriends who nearly always held something back. And it was not about the amount of information they had exchanged; it was more a sense that she knew the core of who he was. For a moment she doubted that she would be anything more than a passing fancy for him. She could see that he was on a special path, while she was, what?—pretty, but quite ordinary in her ambition. Unused to such uncertainties about herself, she was relieved when, as if he had read her thoughts, he continued:

"A kiss, particularly a first kiss, when given thoughtfully can seal and transform a friendship. This is the first time I've used this tradition in this way. And I'll not want it to be the last … with you," he had added hastily. "I see this as the start of something, not a parting gesture".

She had moved towards him and just before their lips met, she had said, "I think we're talking too much again." They had broken off from their first kiss laughing, but the second kiss had contained a stillness that she could step back into again whenever she closed her eyes. No, she was not ready to have Gwen share this moment; it would remain hers alone.

The groans of the patient interrupted her daydream and she gave him her full attention until Gwen, with Sister Wilkins in tow, came back into the ward. Marion excused herself from them and slipped away. She had a couple of hours assigned to orchestrate the movement of furniture that she and Edith had agreed.

Marion and Edith had spent an evening talking through the possible arrangements. Despite the proximity of the German Army it seemed more fantasy than reality that they would need to hide soldiers in their building, but a feeling of panic was sweeping through Brussels and many householders were already evacuating or burying their best china and silver in their back gardens. To do nothing felt wrong and they had wounded soldiers to consider.

"We have five wounded Belgian soldiers as patients, and two of them, Philip and Henri are weeks off walking out of here. Are the Army likely to move them or will they stay here?" Marion had asked Edith.

"Hard to say. I'm sure they'll want to take them if they can, to keep them away from the Germans. But the retreat seems chaotic: they may well have lost track of where the wounded are," Edith replied.

"Well, they're from the east, near Liege, so they can't go home to convalesce. We'll just have to keep them comfortable here." Marion opened her notebook to finalize the plans with Edith. "We could move them to the annex ward on the top floor".

"I'll discuss the matter with Dr Depage when I next see him. But if these boys become separated from their units, they will need our shelter. Let's go through your notes."

Marion found the two porters in the basement. They had started to move two of the wardrobes she had marked with chalk to the bottom of the stairs and were assessing angles when she joined them. She was pleased to see they had started the job without her. Marion was totally absorbed for the next two hours. She had made drawings of where each of the items was to be moved and these proved an invaluable help across the language divide, although the porters were very responsive to sign language. The main problems they experienced were on the staircases at the top level where the tight turns restricted their ability to manoeuvre the larger pieces of furniture. Marion was determined for her plans to work and, with her encouragement and their persistence, and the reassembly of a couple of the wardrobes, they succeeded.

Marion and Edith had a design for the top floor that cut off the ends of two corridors with large wardrobes. Into this enclosed passageway Marion placed mattresses, lamps, and two washstands. There was no room for bed frames, but she thought that mattresses would be comfort enough. A third wardrobe had been positioned to cover the entrance to the ward where Edith and Marion had first discussed the preparations for British soldiers. This hid the annex into which Marion squeezed four more beds and two mattresses. Marion stood in the void and imagined it full of wounded soldiers, then made a list of the medical and nursing equipment that would be needed in the occupied room. There was a fireplace that could be used to heat water, but she would need an iron stand to place the pot over the fire.

It was the porters who drew her attention to the time, when they said they had to finish for the day. She thanked them and then had to hurry to the meeting called by Edith. Luckily she was not the last one into the room. A group of nurses arrived just after her from a lecture. Marion had no time to find Gwen; she sat herself in the first unoccupied seat she spotted. It was only as she settled herself that she realized how dirty and dusty she was, and was pleased she did not have to account for the state she was in to Gwen.

Matron welcomed them all to the meeting and after some preliminaries revealed the reason for calling them together.

"I have been informed today that the British minister is to leave Brussels for Antwerp and his offices have advised that all fellow countrymen, and by that they mean women too of course, should do the same. They can provide no further protection for us and I was warned that the Germans are only days away from the city. Transport will be available for any and all that wish to leave. Departure will be at ten o'clock tomorrow morning from the British embassy." She paused and a murmur of voices rose in the room, but this stopped the moment she continued to talk.

"I and Sisters Jones and Wilkins will stay and perform our duties in the best way we can, under the banner of the Red Cross. This means we will nurse the wounded from all nationalities, which will include Germans, a fact that you must take into consideration when you decide on your plans. I am aware of the stories from the refugees, and recognize it can be hard to separate emotions from one's professional charge, but this we must be able to do. We face testing times. I can and will do my best but I cannot guarantee anyone their safety. Each person will need to make and stand by their own decision. All who leave will be welcomed back when this travesty is behind us. I am going to hand over to Sister Wilkins who will take you through all the necessary arrangements. I will be in my office if anyone wishes to see me."

And with this she left the room. Sister Wilkins, very wisely Marion thought, said, "I will leave you for half an hour to think things through, and when I return I will go through all the arrangements with those who have decided to leave." Mayhem followed, with everyone talking at once.

Marion looked around for Gwen. She was waving an envelope at her from across the room; Marion made her way over to her.

"What is it?" Marion asked. "Have you received instructions from home?"

"No, this is for you. I've looked everywhere for you. Where have you been?"

"Oh, I just had some things to sort out."

"You're filthy. If I hadn't spoken to him myself I would accuse you of an assignation in the basement with your dream man."

"What do you mean you spoke to him? Russell? Where? When? What have I missed?"

"You missed your man. He came to say goodbye. Sister Wilkins and I found him at the front door. He asked for you and I was sent to find you, but no one knew where you were. Sister Wilkins very kindly gave him a pen and paper and he wrote you a note. He took his time; I think he hoped you would appear. Where were you?"

"Never mind that," Marion brushed her question aside. "When was this, when is he leaving?"

"It was about half an hour after you left me with sister and the morphine injection. She let me give it, you know, under her supervision. You can see the patient relax in front of your eyes when it hits their bloodstream: it's remarkable stuff. I found the vein myself …"

"Gwen, please," Marion silenced her.

"He has gone, Marion. He said Mr Gibson had been summoned to Antwerp and he had no choice but to go now. But here's his note."

Marion took the small envelope and put it in her skirt pocket. She was distressed and frustrated by the news of his visit and departure and of her own absence, practically the only time she had not been traceable in the building since she arrived. Fate, if that is what it was, played cruel games at times.

"If it's any comfort, Marion, he looked upset not to see you, and if you don't mind me saying, he really is a dreamboat. No wonder you've changed your mind about men. I think he could've captivated Sister Wilkins too. You lucky thing, he looked smitten to me."

"Where's the luck when he's gone?" Marion muttered.

"You've just been offered a one-way ticket home, go and join him. Pack your things and you can knock on his door in Oxford before the weekend. That's an easy decision to make."

"Give me a minute, I can't believe I missed him," Marion said.

"Well, you've got 25 minutes to make up your mind before Sister Wilkins returns. I know what I'm doing: I shall be on my way home tomorrow."

"Really?"

"Yes, I can't get those horrific stories out of my mind. It was a priest that was shot and two women I met today had been attacked, probably raped. These Prussians are monsters. I won't stay and nor, I hope, will you."

"I think I'll get some air. I need to clear my head."

Marion rose and left the room. She went down the stairs and out of the front door and sat on the top step. There was enough light in the summer evening for her to read his note, and her hands shook as she opened it.

My Dear Marion,

I am so sorry to have to write this note and not see you to say goodbye. I met your friend Gwen, but she couldn't find you.

As I feared, it is a sudden departure with Hugh. I only wish I could take you to safety with me. If you have the chance to leave and return to England, please do. It's going to get very hot around here. The Germans will probably be in Brussels on Thursday. Come and find me in Oxford, ask for me at Merton College.

If you can't get away, or even if you don't want to, I want you to know that you will be in my thoughts and in my heart. I will write to you, and look forward to the next time I see you.

Remember how we sealed our friendship.

Yours forever, Russell.

Marion tried to steady herself. She was in a spin; jumbled thoughts churned in her mind. She could not separate them: Russell or independence, personal safety or nursing, love over purpose. She could see the merits in every point of view. She had met the most wonderful man and yet she faced a once in a lifetime situation in the clinic. She wanted both and resented the fact that she was forced to choose. But choose she must. Marion stood up, tried to brush some of the dirt off her uniform and stepped into the house to join the others. She started for the stairs and met Edith, just as she crossed the hall. They both paused and looked at each other. Edith gave a slight nod of her head as if in dismissal, and Marion felt the release of her decision made. She ran up the stairs.

19th August 1914
Leuven
Therese

The news was getting worse. The last of the 12 fortresses that protected Liege had fallen, and day-by-day the Belgian Army had retreated, ineffectual in its efforts to stop the invaders. But at least the Germans suffered for each advance. Therese had heard that the headquarters of the Army, with King Albert, had departed Leuven the previous day. Although a rearguard defence was left behind, in reality the town's security departed with the generals, as did many of the residents, their belongings piled high on carts. There was a restless spirit in the convent: the Germans were coming.

Therese had fully embraced her work as record keeper, the role she had described and volunteered herself for to Sister Paul.

"So much has happened to these refugees, so much that is wrong. The authorities will need to know of their hardships. I'll spend time with them and write them down."

Her words had poured out to Sister Paul, not in a way to convince, but as they came. Sister Paul saw her mission and was not about to step in her way.

"Sister Therese, what a gift you'll bring to these people, to be heard. By all means write down what they say, but most helpfully you can support them in their fear and grief and pass God's blessings to them."

Therese had nodded at Sister Paul's permissive and reverent words and saw the wisdom in them, but her zeal was for making the record. The vision she had in her meditation before she slept was of a courtroom where people were held to account for their actions. This was not in a heavenly realm, but was here on earth, man-to-man and people were angry. She had not seen herself in the room, but knew she had a part to play.

Three notebooks were already filled and Therese set off for the schoolroom with a fourth in her hand. She had built a clear picture of the initial German advance on Liege and the defenders' retreat. Villagers to the east of Liege had shut themselves into their houses as the invaders had marched through. Relieved to see the last of them they had not expected them to return, but return they had, in disarray, and angry with the resistance they had experienced. One man had described the devastating events in his village; it took him a long time with his many pauses.

"We hid in our cellar when the first soldiers approached. All our neighbours did the same, to keep out of sight. We had no weapons … they'd all been taken and locked away by the mayor. He didn't want any hotheads bringing trouble down on us. The ground shook as they marched … dust fell on us … we stayed there until they'd gone …."

"It was early morning and the animals called to be fed, but they had to wait."

"It seemed to take an eternity for them to pass, but it was probably only a few hours. Mid-morning, when it was quiet, we came out …. All was as we left it. Some cried from relief."

"Neighbours even hugged each other."

The man had seemed most surprised about this public display, and stopped until she had written it down.

"We went about our business for the day …."

"Most were in their homes that evening when the trouble started …. But I wasn't."

"That's the only reason I'm here today …."

Therese waited; she had learnt not to prompt people or push their pace of recollection. Each relived the moments and then made her a witness to them with their descriptions.

"My wife and I had eaten. I left the house to go and set some traps. Rabbits are good at this time of the year. I was on my way back when ... when I heard glass breaking and men shouting. There'd been distant gunfire and explosions all day .... I was already jumpy."

"I stepped back into the woods and waited."

The man put his head in his hands; the recollection and responsibility for his actions lay heavily with him.

"I saw houses set alight and heard shouts, screams, and gunshots .... I was paralyzed."

"Villagers ran to the woods, towards me and I called out to them." "The Germans are back, they'll kill us all," one shouted. He rushed past me into the gloom of the trees. I was petrified ...."

"I didn't follow them, and hoped my wife would run. But she didn't."

"I was about to go and fetch her when a group of soldiers came close to the woods. There were a dozen or so and they had four women with them ... or they could have been girls."

"The soldiers pushed them around; the girls cried and pleaded, but they were raped. Some men ... perhaps their fathers ... rushed out from the houses. But they were easy targets for the soldiers' bullets, and no help for the girls. The soldiers laughed as they fell".

Therese tried to write down every word he said. Emotion made it hard for his words to flow at any speed, so she had moments to catch up. She felt the power of the confessional as he told of his fear, his weakness, and thoughts for his own safety before his wife. Therese felt too inadequate to mete out forgiveness, and soon realized that this man would never forgive himself.

"More of the village was set on fire: the sky was red. The screaming and shots went on a long time .... Soldiers started to leave the village, back towards the east; they staggered along the road, bread and bottles in hand. Two of them tried to take a cow with them .... Another walked past and shot it ... they all laughed."

"My life was destroyed in front of my eyes. I hid under a bush and then ...", he almost whispered, "I fell asleep".

The man seemed to shrivel in front of Therese. He had made a choice and now faced a future without his wife. She had died without his protection, alone, without him by her side.

"I don't know how long I slept ... when I woke the flames were still high in the sky .... From the silence I guessed the soldiers had gone, but whether they had or not, I knew I had to go back .... She was dead ... my wife ... she was dead. She looked untouched apart from her neck; it was almost cut through .... She lay outside our home, what was left of it, but no man had touched her, of that I was sure ... and grateful."

"I can give you my name: that's all that's left of my life."

Therese had noticed how uncomfortable he was each time she had seen him eat or drink, and he did not look at anyone directly. He seemed too burdened to be thankful for his own survival. She said nothing. Therese was determined to be methodical in her records and noted down his name and on a plan of the village had him put a cross where his house had stood. The piece of paper had seven crosses on it already, still not enough for each grave that had been filled that night.

"People came out from the woods ... some were wounded, all shocked. We knew we had to leave .... The Germans would be back; we were their enemy now. People collected all they could from the houses .... Some of us moved the dead to the churchyard. The priest made a list of their names. The burials were only makeshift .... I must go back to finish it."

He stood up. Therese thought he intended to leave, but he sat himself down again.

"Animals were set free. People formed into groups as dawn approached."

"I decided to head off alone .... I didn't care where I went. I stumbled upon two women: they'd survived the attacks by the soldiers. They'd almost crawled their way to the woods: they'd been badly beaten. We travelled together and made our way here, to Leuven ... doesn't seem like we can run far from these Germans though, does it?"

Therese had shaken her head. "No, they come closer each day, but hopefully we'll be safe here".

Even as she said this she had felt no comfort behind the words and unconsciously her hand went to the wooden crucifix around her neck. The man stayed only two days. Therese did not see him depart. She doubted he would ever settle his restless spirit, and she held him daily in her prayers.

While the name of the village and the people might change, this story had become all too familiar to Therese. The German advance

112

had turned Belgium into a battlefield. The Germans resented the fight presented by the Belgian Army and their revenge knew no bounds. To one mayor the Germans justified their reprisals as self-defence against *franc tireurs*, telling him they had been shot at by some of his townspeople. They directed all the men out onto the streets, and shot half of them. Therese had been told repeatedly that all guns were handed in to avoid such butchery. These so-called *guerilla* fighters did not exist; as far as Therese could see they had no fire power. The mayor's son was one of those executed.

A young girl and her mother refused to speak to her. They had arrived with the first influx of refugees, but were too traumatized to talk. The defensiveness around rape was high. Therese often experienced reticence; even when she listened to fathers' reports, none wanted their daughters' names put forward for the record. If the rape was not recorded it could be forgotten and the girl could have a future. No prospective husband would want a girl who had been taken in this way. Such events remained shrouded in secrecy by all concerned, and no doubt history would be rewritten with episodes erased. The thought saddened Therese.

Neighbours were different. They felt no loyalty to protect reputations and wanted the truth to be known; the soldiers had been uncontrolled savages.

"They started on the first house in the village and carried on until all were wrecked, and they drank every bottle they found. People were killed after they'd opened their cellars. Many died as their homes were torched, or were shot when they tried to escape. I saw three girls taken into a house and soldiers were in and out, no doubt taking their turns. Only one of the girls survived. I've seen her here, poor thing; I don't think she's spoken since. Her father and brother were shot, but her mother's here too. For once my age and wrinkles spared me, but I don't want to live with these memories."

The witness, an almost toothless woman, gave Therese names and locations of the deeds and scenes that had seared themselves into her mind.

"It plays on my mind, I still feel the fear, it makes me shake, but now I've told it I can try to forget."

Therese captured her testimony like a courtroom scribe and the burden shifted from the woman to the pages of the book. And that was Therese's mission: to make sure the stories were heard and archived.

Nothing could erase their memories, but the incessant replay in their minds could stop when the detail had been captured.

In her meditation, three days into the interviews, Therese's vision had been of people clinging on to rocks in a river that was in full flow. It hurt them to hold on; their hands were cut and they were exhausted. Into this picture came her own voice that said to each one, "Talk, let go, grieve." She had watched them release their holds and been taken by the river into a calm lake. Therese had not spoken of this to anyone, but she held the picture in her mind and it gave her comfort as she listened to the refugees.

She appreciated that they all needed release from their experiences; solace was not to be found in silence for these people. Once one woman started telling Therese what had happened, she could not stop shouting. Spittle showered from her mouth as hatred towards the soldiers that had killed her husband and daughter spewed out of her. She hit her fists against the wall and it took Sisters Mary and Ruth from the clinic to help restrain her. Once the fight left her she cried for hours, gut-wrenching sobs that had her gasping for breath. Therese sat with her until she fell into sleep, though her whimpers continued for a long while.

Sister Paul called her into conversation on their way to their evening meal.

"How is your work, sister?"

"It's going well. I know it's the right thing for me to do, even though there are more practical things that need attention."

Therese was aware she was defending her calling, but Sister Paul smiled.

"I have no doubts, Therese, and there are many hands for the practical work. I've seen that you can remain detached; you seek out the detail and yet you don't withdraw from the horrors. Many of the sisters can't face the stories and would stop them and move straight to prayer. But sometimes that can sit like a heavy blanket, rather than heal. You must continue. Bring your notebooks to matins tomorrow: we can pray for their relief the grief. We want them to feel God's love."

"I will, Sister Paul, and I'm sure they feel God's presence in everything that's done for them here. My concern is for those whose anger and pain has already turned them away from Him. We won't meet those people; they won't come to us for sanctuary."

"We can hold them in our prayerful thoughts, sister, and draw them into His light."

It was prayer that had determined Therese's future and had led her into a devotional life. No road to Damascus experience, nor miraculous answer to prayer, had convinced her of her God. She would say she had been born with an awareness of His presence. She had talked to Him for as long as she could remember and, most importantly, she felt, she had listened to Him and for Him. The conversation in her family seemed like noise to her and she had kept herself as separate as she could; invariably someone would be sent out to find her at mealtimes. God's thoughts came to her in pictures, in scenes, and one came once that transformed her life and led her to the convent. She had discussed prayer with Sister Paul at her first interview and Therese still felt the communion between them.

No further words were needed, and they walked in prayerful silence to their meal.

20th August 1914
Brussels
Marion

It was Thursday evening and Marion felt lonely; Gwen had left the day after Russell, as had many of the student nurses. Some had headed home, but the majority of the local probationers had gone to the Belgian front with the Red Cross. She missed her friends and their chatter, and she missed Russell. But it was more than this that had her feeling alone; Brussels was now cut off. The German Army had entered the city that morning and an air of oppression had settled on the streets, like a blanket that suffocated and stilled the will. The city had been notified of the planned entry, and all firearms had been handed in including those of the Garde Civique.

The Germans had arrived with a fanfare of marching bands and nationalistic songs. Many Belgians put up their shutters and stayed indoors in their desire to convey a snub, but the noise and the numbers of soldiers were a spectacle and many were drawn to watch. They lined the streets in silence, too overawed or scared to jeer. Marion, Edith, and Sister Wilkins, who Marion had recently been given permission to address as Elizabeth, had chosen a place to watch the occupiers arrive. They felt quite safe in their nurses' uniforms.

The bulk of the Army was to pass through Brussels, and stay no more than three days. An administration would take over the Hotel de Ville, and a small force was to be stationed at the railway stations and another at the Grand Place. This was the information that had been announced publicly when the city was told of the peaceful takeover.

Marion's first sight of the invaders was of rows of lancers on horseback, followed by artillery and large field guns and then the infantry. The noise of the wheels on the road was quite thunderous and the ground vibrated as more and more soldiers marched or rode by. The horses' hooves struggled on the cobbled road, and Marion gasped as one slipped and fell in front of her. In what looked like a well-practised routine a soldier immediately put a coarse cloth underneath the horse's head and another man positioned one under the front feet, so that the horse would have grip as they helped it right itself. They were so quick it hardly created any delay to the procession. And what a procession it had been.

"There are so many," Marion whispered to Edith.

They had stood for over an hour, mesmerized by the sights; just when they tired of row upon row of greenish-grey uniformed soldiers, they were entertained by the look of the supply carts that had everything, including the kitchen sink, hanging off their sides. Smoke poured from the chimneys of these mobile kitchens and the smells from the vats of soup had been most appetizing.

"What do they have on their chests?" Marion pointed with a motion of her head at some officers who rode by. They wore what Edith declared were electric searchlights attached to their chests with leads that connected to a battery that poked out of their saddlebags.

"We could use those in our operating room." Edith made a mental note to mention them to Dr Depage.

It had been quite an industry on the move. One or two of the large motor trucks were fitted out as cobblers' shops and despite the motion a dozen shoemakers pounded away at men's boots. Some soldiers rode on the running board while their footwear was seen to, and then hopped off and rejoined the ranks. Each foot soldier had an extra pair of boots that hung from the knapsack he carried.

Marion studied the soldiers as they passed. It was difficult to spot anything individual about them as they marched in formation;

their heels drummed to a precise beat. They looked young to her, surprisingly short and stolid with shaven heads, but with no animation on their faces; their eyes stared straight ahead. Only the officers on horseback displayed a more distinct individual style and to Marion they appeared haughty, leaving her in no doubt who was in charge.

Very little conversation had passed between Edith, Elizabeth, and Marion. Aghast at the magnitude of the army, each had been subdued when they returned to the clinic some hours later. Marion had excused herself from their company and taken herself to her room. She had lain on her bed and cried.

"Why was I so stubborn as to stay here?" she berated herself; Gwen had done her best to change her mind, but she had become entrenched and would not listen. "To think I could be on my way to Oxford now, with a surprise visit to Russell. Instead all he will receive is a letter, if Gwen remembers to post it for me." Marion groaned with despair.

"What's going to happen to us here?" Marion asked her room, where every other bed was now empty. The sights of the day had daunted Marion. The threat of real danger had started to permeate and she feared for herself for the first time. Her mood lifted when she caught herself humming the hymn, *The Lord's My Shepherd*, and she laughed. "In times of trouble, girl, you know where to turn," but however much she mocked herself, the words and the memories of hymns sung with her family brought her comfort.

She had no desire to study. Her programme of lectures and exams were all suspended, and without this momentum she found she lacked motivation to open her books. She enjoyed the practical side of nursing, away from the classroom. The interaction with patients, with their unexpected wounds and moods made her feel that her decisions and care could contribute to their comfort. She was good on her feet, so far never flustered and able to think her way through to an appropriate action.

Marion had not appreciated how accustomed she had become to the sanitized world of the operating theatre and the wards. Most patients were in her care after surgery and she would make them comfortable and dress their neat incisions. The wounds she had seen over the last week were very different to this; soldiers were brought in straight from the battlefield, weary, dirty, dehydrated, with parts of their body torn open and gashes full of dirt or pieces of their uniform. Despite a few hesitant starts her confidence had grown and she felt more able to cut their clothes from them, find and clean their wounds, and assess when she needed to draw the doctor's attention to a patient as he made his rounds. Since the Belgian Army had retreated there had been fewer casualties. Most of their military patients had left before the Germans arrived, but the two with the worst wounds had remained. Philip and Henri had been moved into the annex ward that morning and removed from their register of patients. Dr Depage had warned Edith to expect an inspection by the German administration within days. The first place they would look for soldiers would be in the hospitals and clinics. The negotiations to spare Brussels had its sacrifices. Any soldiers in the vicinity were to report to the town hall within three days of the Germans' arrival; they would then become prisoners of war and sent to Germany.

Dr Depage had brought an acquaintance with him when he visited Edith the evening before. Marion had been invited to join them.

"Can I introduce Prince Reginald de Croy."

Edith and Marion had both bobbed a curtsey as they had shaken hands and been introduced.

"Please, it is an ancient title only, I am not a royal; there are no protocols with me." He had a pleasant smile and Marion had felt at ease with him, and he proved to be true to his word. He was mannered in the casual way that aristocrats can be; Marion was reminded of her uncle.

"Prince Reginald has a chateau to the south-west of Brussels, right near the border with France, and close to Mons. You may have heard of Mons, it's quite an industrial area ..."

Dr Depage was interrupted by Prince Reginald, "And very near the Forest of Mormal, beautiful countryside."

Dr Depage smiled and continued.

"I'm sure the prince can tell you himself of the reason behind his visit to Brussels, but it is important we are brief as he must be out of the city before the Germans arrive tomorrow and we have many calls to make."

The conversation had been brief and after the men departed Edith and Marion had discussed the visit. Despite downplaying his status the prince was well connected with the Belgian government and had, like his father, been attached to the Belgian embassy in London. He was in Brussels to establish informal communication links that could be maintained during the German occupation. He had heard of many wounded Belgian soldiers who had been separated from their units and he wanted to ensure they had a route back to the Army when fit. During his visit he was enlisting guides and safe houses, hence his introduction to Edith and the clinic.

"So the password will always be "Yorc"?" Marion asked Edith.

"Yes, Croy in reverse. What a charming man. I'm sure this business will be secure in his hands. Dr Depage will tell us how we contact a guide when Philip and Henri are ready to leave. It feels much better than them having to hand themselves over to the Germans."

"It was good to hear that our Army has arrived," Marion said. "He said they were massing near Mons and getting ready for a battle. They'll push the Germans back soon, and they'll be leaving Brussels as soon as they've arrived. Just you wait".

"Did he say his sister's name was Marie, Princess Marie, that is?" Edith asked.

"Yes," said Marion, "and she's made their home into a Red Cross hospital, to assist the British and French if needed, but like us, I'm sure, they'll have to take in German wounded too. I do hope none come here".

"We must remain impartial at all times."

"I know, and we'll all do our best, but they can't expect to be welcomed, can they."

And there had been no welcome on the streets of Brussels that day.

After her tears Marion felt restless and low; it amazed her to think that just a week ago, she had been excited about the thought of when she would next see Russell. The anticipation had been wonderful, and now here she was, on her own, with no freedom to walk the city as she and Russell had done. Marion was unaccustomed to feeling sorry for herself, and was ill at ease with the indulgence. She missed Russell, but he had returned to safety. What must it be like, she thought, to have your loved one go into the Army, and into battle? How could anyone live with the anxiety that this would provoke, and still function? The burden must be unbearable. Marion shifted her thoughts from herself to the Belgian people she knew, and counted the number who had male members of their family away from home; she realized what little laughter she had heard in recent weeks. Although deeply sympathetic, she also recognized how separated she was from the locals' experience of the war. She had felt fear and would, no doubt, share in the hardships as shortages increased beyond inconvenience, but she was not plumbed into the heartbeat of the nation and would not endure each loss in the same way. This disconnection left her flat; Marion was driven by her passions and she wanted to feel involved.

What would her father say? she mused. Marion's father, Bernard, was adept when wise words were needed; she waited until she could hear his voice and chuckled when it arrived.

"What's the best you can bring to this moment, Marion?"

She pictured him sitting at his desk and her standing in the doorway of his study; she would have stopped by with a grumble or grief at something and he would let her have her say, then put his question: it never failed to stop her in her tracks. Thoughts of her father also brought back the scene of their last private conversation before she left for Belgium, again in his study.

"Well, my dear Marion, you have attained your freedom and are on your way to your adventure. I hope it delivers all that you seek, and surpasses the life you have fought so hard to escape. I know you don't think much of our life here, but I want you to remember this, there will always be a home here for you and no problem is ever too big for you to bring home. Now come and hug your father."

The memory brought tears to Marion's eyes, but these were not tears of self-pity, they were of love. He was such a special man. She had no doubts that he would like Russell. She could imagine conversations that would easily spark off between them. Her father was always interested in exploring the opinions of young men. He used them to calibrate his own thoughts, always concerned that his judgment was balanced and had not become stuck in the prejudicial domain of the elderly.

So, young lady, Marion said to herself, what's the best I can bring to this moment? She lay and pondered but her mind drifted back to Russell. She had written a letter for Gwen to take, with her promise of early posting when she arrived in England. Marion had tried to be intimate with her words, but the voice of doubt had deafened her. She feared that once he returned to Oxford, to the intellectuals who more closely matched his mind and aptitudes, she would be easily forgotten. She might just hold a place in his memories of those magical days, when he experienced the workings of diplomacy at first hand. They had been heady days for him, and for her too. She remembered their kiss.

A knock at her door was not as welcome an interruption as it would have been when she was in her earlier melancholy. Marion jumped up and opened her door to Clara, one of the domestic helps. She handed her a note. It was an invitation from matron to join her, Sister Wilkins, and two other nurses for supper that evening. Marion readily accepted and immediately felt a surge of motivation return. She was part of a team, not on her own, and one of the gifts she could bring was to support Edith. The pressure to run the establishment must sit heavily in these conditions and she was not another passenger to be carried. The fact that she was not burdened by the grief or anxiety of losing someone in the war meant that her energy should know no bounds and she would put this to the best possible use. She smiled as she imagined her father's approval: this was the daughter he would recognize.

The supper was informal, in Edith's sitting room. They had no need of a fire, and they soon settled into easy conversation. The first topic, as at all mealtimes, was about the food. Never fancy, it had also never been austere, but it was clear from the soup and bread that had been served, followed by a small amount of cheese, that good food was now harder to achieve on their budget. Edith was notorious for her financial controls, but Marion learnt through their chatter that it was the lack of available goods that determined their menu, rather than the cost. The German Army had progressed across the country and driven the farming folk ahead of them and off the fields. In their fear, crops had been abandoned or trampled or purloined by the German soldiers. They left people with worthless chits of paper for future recompense. Marion had translated one such note for a family of refugees, but she had not appreciated the scale of this devastation, nor that it would impact so immediately on their own provisions.

Their talk shifted to the steady influx of refugees and the question of who would pay for medical treatment they extended to any who arrived injured at their door. They had each attended to minor injuries, but the condition of some recently had been severe, with burns that needed significant medical attention. Most of the injured were directed to the city hospitals and even some private homes that flew the flag of the Red Cross. Despite the war, Edith still carried responsibility for the financial viability of the school and the clinic, but as the conversation continued she heard the discomfort of the nurses when they had turned away distressed people in need.

"I'll find out what more we can do," she promised the room, "but for now do all that you can without admitting more refugee patients into our beds. We must put the soldiers first, and these can all be accounted for".

Then the topic was the occupation itself and here the conversation became anecdotal, with official notices recited and the threat of reprisals recounted.

"The riding of bicycles has been banned and any bicycle found will be confiscated."

"The telegraph system is shut down so no one knows what's happening to us here, apart from what the Germans tell them."

"*Le Soir* has been stopped. I suppose there will only be a German newspaper available now."

"The story about the poison in the water supply was only a rumour."

"Thank heavens for that, but unfortunately so was the story that the British Army are close."

Marion's attention shifted from one exchange to another, surprised there were so many nuggets of information to share. Their conversation mimicked her mother's ladies meetings, at which local gossip was exchanged and magnified. They were certainly not short of newsworthy topics and Marion began to feel stimulation from the drama that was unfolding.

"I heard that 50 million francs was paid to the Germans to guarantee the safety of Brussels." The room gasped at this pronouncement made by Sister Wilkins. The figure was a fortune.

"Where did you hear that?" they chorused.

"I overheard it when I was at the bank. It wasn't idle talk. It was two gentlemen: they were very businesslike in their conversation. One of them called it blackmail, but the other supposed it was the spoils of war."

"It's certainly robbery, whatever title it's given," Edith announced.

Marion was shocked; from her conversation with Russell she had presumed that it would have been a gentleman's agreement that had been reached, not a financial settlement. What price for a life she pondered, and then realized she had spoken aloud as she saw she had everyone's attention in the room. She shrugged her shoulders and repeated her question, "What price for a life?" and was then sorry; her question subdued the room and their banter. Even though the subjects were serious, their evening had been fun.

Edith used the moment of silence.

"I need to remind you all to abide by the curfew and be in by nine o'clock. I would prefer no one ventured out on their own at any time of day or evening, even if you think it might just be for a quick errand."

Marion was sure she spotted a look pass between Edith and Sister Wilkins and felt that a reprimand had been delivered. The evening had now sobered and when Edith rose from her chair everyone followed suit and soon made their way to their beds.

"Marion, why don't you come and bunk up in our room? We don't like to think of you on that floor on your own."

Marion was delighted with the invitation from the two nurses.

"I certainly will tonight, thank you. I had enough of my own company earlier. It will be much brighter with you two. I'll get ready and come down."

Relieved that there would be no more soul-searching or loneliness for her that night, Marion hurried her ablutions and joined the others. She belonged again.

23rd August 1914
Mons, Belgium
Private Culloch,
British Expeditionary Force

Bill Culloch stared at the horse; he knew the animal had but seconds to live, and that he should move, but he was transfixed by the huge uncomprehending eye that stared at him. One foreleg had been blasted off, the other was twisted at an impossible angle and the creature had been thrown upside down against the bank, by the side of the road. Its head rested on the road not six inches from his boot.

The air was full of dust and his ears still rang from the explosions. Just moments before, along the road ahead of his platoon, an ammunition limber had been hit by a German shell. More had rained down nearby in the fields on either side. The gun and horses that followed had panicked and ploughed into the chaos.

The road had high banks with thick hedgerows on the top; it was narrow with no room to manoeuvre. The energy of the shell and the exploding ammunition was confined by the ancient roadway and had blasted forward and back down the lane. Fortunately, a sharp bend, behind the doomed artillerymen, had shielded Culloch's group from the full effect of the multiple blasts; even so they had been close enough to feel the shock wave.

They were a platoon of the 1st Gordon Highlanders assigned to escort a Royal Horse Artillery field battery. Half a mile to the north and east Culloch could hear thunderous gunfire where the rest of their battalion along with other units of the British Expeditionary Force valiantly fought an outnumbered battle against the German invasion force in Belgium.

Two in the platoon were new to the Army. Both were as nervous as kittens and useless as far as Culloch and his colleagues were concerned. The rest of them were reservists or serving professionals and many had seen action abroad in the Boer War. At 30 Culloch was an old-timer.

"Culloch, move you bastard. Gray, you too; get up there and keep watch while I deal with this."

Culloch realized his sergeant had shouted at him, and was pointing up the road. His ears cleared and his faculties began to return. He saw that some of the men had moved towards the injured; others gawped uselessly at the debris of fallen men and horses. Sounds slowly entered his consciousness. One man who had been flung against the bank was moaning, and another, his lower body trapped under a dead horse, screamed and screamed. Blood, whether human, animal, or both seeped onto the road.

Culloch was glad to leave the scene and move on. Gray, one of the fresh recruits, jogged after him. Beyond the bulk of the destroyed horse team two dead men lay across each other in the middle of the road. They had been on the front two pairs of the gun carriage horses when the shell had hit. The impact had driven the rest of the team backwards but these two riders had been catapulted out of their saddles and crashed into the road surface ahead. Whether it was the explosion or the violent fall that killed them was irrelevant now; they lay in an embrace of broken limbs and tattered uniforms and looked, to Culloch, as if their bodies had been tied together and fired from one great cannon.

Culloch told Gray to keep watch ahead and he moved towards the bodies. With the instinctive reactions of his criminal youth from the meanest of Glasgow's streets he made a show of feeling the pulse of each corpse while he slipped one soldier's watch into his pocket; there was nothing on either wrist of the other man. A further pretence to check them over for signs of life left him with one gold coin and several francs. The sound of a horseman's approach caused him to jerk upwards from the dead men and interrupted a more thorough search. Gray, to his credit, had raised his rifle. Their commander,

Second Lieutenant Hamilton came round the bend. Hamilton had lost his cap and, as if to match that, Culloch noticed his usual composure had slipped.

The panic in Hamilton's eyes, as he faced an aimed weapon, was rapidly displaced by anger when he saw that it was held by one of his own men.

"Put that down you bloody idiot." Hamilton brought his horse to a stop in front of the two soldiers, "Where's Sergeant Cobbett?"

Hamilton raised his eyes and expected to find his dependable NCO behind the two men; his mouth gaped as he registered the killing ground. He had seen many dead soldiers and horses that day but nothing so intimate and personal as his own troop.

Cobbett appeared from the carnage, and approached the lieutenant.

"Four dead sir, including these two," he pointed at the two bodies between them. "Three more wounded: one won't last long I reckon. All the horses are down too."

The sergeant's self-possession and control helped Hamilton; he ran a hand through his hair and felt dust and grime lodged there.

"Thank you, sergeant. There's two more teams behind me; the front lines have pulled back in retreat, us too. They should be along soon. You'll have to turn around and move out."

"Beg pardon, sir," Cobbett said, "those teams won't get down this road, it's blocked with carts and dead horses."

Hamilton snapped back, "Well get them moved, man, we've lost one gun already and I'll be damned if I'll get blamed for losing the lot."

He dismounted, handed the reins of his exhausted and nervous horse to Gray, and walked towards his unit. Several soldiers were comforting the wounded horsemen with gruff reassurances. Their words sounded hollow but Hamilton could see why this felt the right thing to do, regardless of whether their mumbled prayers were for the wounded or to thank God it was not them that had been hit. He watched a soldier put a bullet into the head of each of the three horses that had not been killed outright. The man was crying.

The rest of the platoon was jolted into action when Hamilton and Cobbett clambered over the mass of broken carts and started shouting orders.

Hamilton knew, with the battlefield fractured, German patrols could be expected anywhere. He ordered one more man, Duncanson, to join Culloch and Gray. These three were to keep a lookout and guard the backs of their colleagues while the rest cleared the lane for the expected artillery teams.

By now, one of the wounded artillerymen had died and two men were ordered to lift his body and the other corpses away from the road. The least severely wounded men were also moved and Hamilton ordered one man to stay with the casualties; it was clear to all this was for form's sake as they were very badly wounded.

The men, Hamilton, and Cobbett tried to clear a path wide enough to take the gun carriages but the dead horses and the broken carriages were difficult to haul up the steep roadside banks. There were curses as splinters from jagged wood caught at fingers and palms. When an angled pile of debris became too large and slipped back down the bank, frustration rose among the sweating men.

Hamilton strained to pull on a carriage wheel but was distracted when Culloch appeared accompanied by a captain from the Royal Scots Fusiliers. Hamilton knew the Scots had been fighting alongside his own Gordons, out on the right flank.

The officer introduced himself as Captain William Campbell. He and his men had fended off German infantry throughout the day, and no doubt, thought Hamilton, while under intense bombardment. The remains of his company, now some 70 men, Campbell told him, were behind him. They were out of water, had little food beyond some emergency rations and had been ordered south to regroup with the rest of their battalion, or at least what might remain of it. The man looked exhausted and kept his conversation to the barest facts. His face was streaked with dust and his voice was not much above a whisper. Through the hard day's fighting he had shouted himself hoarse. He still had some miles to cover that day.

Hamilton had no option but to stop his work while Campbell led his group of battered infantrymen through the carnage. Like so many men in this expeditionary army they had marched to Mons in new and ill-fitting boots. Most had feet so swollen they dared not take their boots off and now they stumbled forward, few able to bear weight equally on both feet. Despite this and the obvious battle fatigue, Hamilton saw defiance on their faces. They were in retreat but not defeated.

The company slipped, slid, and marched over and around the obstacles in the road. Campbell stood with Hamilton and confirmed that, from what he had gathered, the fight had become confused and fragmented; some units still fought while others were in retreat. When the last of his ragged group had passed, Campbell offered Hamilton, his junior in rank, a handshake. Somehow, in these surroundings it seemed more appropriate than the salute Hamilton had been about to make. Campbell advised him not to delay and went on his way.

Not long after Hamilton heard the sound of hoof beats and the rumble of wheels. Gray ran up to him.

"Guns are 'ere, sir, both of 'em."

The lieutenant followed Gray, and the rest of the unit resumed their efforts to haul debris off the roadway. The gun team had arrived breathless but intact. The lead rider dismounted; he was a competent NCO that Hamilton had come to trust in the short time they had been together.

"Glad to see you, Edwards."

There was a pause before Edwards slowly turned his gaze away from the scene in front of him to look at Hamilton.

"Do you think you can ride the teams through this?" Hamilton waved his arm vaguely down the lane.

By now some of the dead horses had been pushed against the roadside and used as props to stop the shattered parts of the gun carriages from rolling back down the banks. Despite the platoon's best efforts, the way remained far from clear and the passage of the Royal Scots had made progress even more difficult. The wood that they had trampled and splintered was easier to shift, but soldiers had also walked right over the dead horses, and through the bloody remains of unidentifiable organs, glistening innards, and flesh. Edwards shook his head at once.

"No, sir, the only way we can is to unhitch the horses and lead them through one by one: they're not happy, you can see. We'll have to manhandle the guns ourselves."

When Hamilton looked at the horses he grasped the man's meaning. The leading pair had recovered their breath after their recent dash but had now seen and smelt the dead horses in the cramped road space ahead: their eyes rolled and they were jittery.

Hamilton nodded his assent; he wanted movement. Edwards and Cobbett picked out half a dozen men who claimed to be familiar with horses and together with the artillerymen they led and pushed one frightened animal after another through the mire, several of the skittish beasts rearing up dangerously.

When the six-horse team was safely through, the men pushed and pulled the gun carriage down the lane. This proved to be the hardest task. Soldiers slipped and fell into the foul mess under their feet. Pulling on ropes did not work and wheels had to be turned by hand; it was a gruesome task.

By the time the first team was through it was early evening. Hamilton was aware that every minute increased their likely isolation from the main British force; the men seemed to feel his concern and carried on without flagging. It took more than 20 minutes to lead through all six horses of the second team, and it left one man with a dislocated knee from a hoof kick; Hamilton now had another wounded soldier unable to make his own way.

The last part of their work was to bring through the final gun carriage. All this time Culloch, Gray, and Duncanson had remained up the lane guarding the backs of their sweating colleagues. Gray turned to watch Hamilton, who with half a dozen men walked up to the 13-pounder; the tired group positioned itself around the gun for a concerted effort. With the heavy work and the strain of the delays Hamilton's fuse was short.

"You," he snapped at Gray, "what the hell are you looking at? You're supposed to be watching for Germans, not gawping like an idiot. Keep your bloody eyes on the road. And where are the other two?"

"Aye, sir, sorry sir." Gray was red in the face; he stood to attention and then remembered the question. "They're roun' the corner, sir, told me to stay back 'ere and tell 'em when it's time to go."

Hamilton snorted and stalked past him. There was a long curve in the road and once round it he came across Culloch and Duncanson. The noise of his approach, with Gray in tow, had given the two men some warning but they did not have enough time to disguise the fact they had been sitting on the verge passing the time of day; around them there was the familiar hint of pipe smoke.

"You stupid lazy sods," snarled their officer, "I told you to keep a proper watch. Do you think this is a bloody picnic? I should have you on a charge right now. What do you think the rest of us have been doing while you've been sitting on your useless backsides? You know better than this. One of you should have been up in the damn field so you can see properly. What's the use in you all being down here in the road? You can't see further than the next corner."

He broke off. His voice had risen through this diatribe but he realized now was not the time and place to make any further issue: more important matters called him. He gave the two men a look that conveyed disgust and turned on his heel to join the rest of his men and their efforts.

Culloch was put out. To be bawled at by a superior did not bother him at all, but he could see Hamilton had been working hard, and if an officer had been reduced to dirtying his hands then the rest of the platoon must have slaved away all afternoon as well. Normally, to miss heavy work would be a cause for self-congratulation and an envious ribbing from the others, but this was not peacetime. He did not want it known that he had been careless with his mates' safety: the boys would get him for that.

Culloch scowled at Gray who had remained with them rather than follow Hamilton. "What are you lookin' at, milksop?" He was glad to have an outlet for his annoyance. "What's 'appening back there, how long before we get out of 'ere?"

The youngster Gray still seemed frightened and confused. He stared at Culloch.

"Forget it, Bill, he's fuckin' useless." Duncanson turned away and seemed to dismiss both Gray's presence and value. Gray looked close to tears. Culloch scowled at Gray.

Culloch and Duncanson agreed that Culloch, the lighter of the two, would climb up the bank and stand in the field; this would give him a good view of the lane that twisted through the fields, and the surrounding area. He scaled the steep bank, and over the hedge at the top. The thorny branches lacerated his hands and legs; the flesh exposed by his kilt was bloodied. He tumbled into the field, hauled himself upright and cursed at the pain. He looked down at Duncanson who grinned up at him. Culloch was about to mouth an insult when his attention was caught. The sun was behind him; he could see the slag-heaps that dominated the landscape to his left and the lane they were on as it snaked its way to the east of Mons. Culloch was immobile for the seconds it took his mind to register what he could see. The tops of a dozen or more lances, with small triangular flags, were advancing along the road towards them. Over the hedgerows he glimpsed the *pickelhauben* headgear of the riders, not the cloth cap of their cavalry; their trotting motion told him they would soon be on them.

"Huns!" Culloch shouted and frantically pointed towards the lance spikes. Due to the twists in the road he indicated across Duncanson's shoulder rather than directly down the lane but his friend registered the threat and checked his rifle.

Culloch pulled his own Lee-Enfield off his shoulder as hoof beats became audible; only one more bend and the horsemen would be on them: there was no time to warn Hamilton and the others. Culloch saw Duncanson raise his rifle and heard him shout at Gray to do the same. Culloch suddenly felt exposed and vulnerable. He would be outlined on the skyline; he ducked behind the hedge and heard a whoop of triumph from the leading German riders; they had spotted their quarry. Culloch peeked over the top of the hedge.

Duncanson had time to fire one round before they were on and over him. Culloch saw his friend tumble under a horse. Whether his bullet hit a man or not was impossible to tell, but no rider or horse fell as they pushed forward. Gray was next in their path and he was already running back to the platoon. The sight of the back of a fleeing man seemed to spur on the cavalrymen. The young Scotsman did not have a chance as a lance entered his spine and erupted from his breastbone, his body was then trampled under the enemy horses. Two abreast the Germans rounded the corner. Culloch watched them pass and then raised himself up and fired into the back of the last rider, who fell backwards off his horse without a sound. He watched them disappear from sight and tried to keep abreast of the cavalrymen as he struggled over recently ploughed ground, behind the hedgerow.

Hamilton and the men were still struggling with the second gun when they heard the first shot. The officer's first reaction was to pull out his revolver and turn towards the threat. The rest of the men stopped their work at the sound of the cries and shots. Some of the more experienced soldiers looked for their rifles but before they could reach them the first horsemen appeared round the corner. Lances were lowered and the enemy surged forward.

134

Without hesitation Hamilton stepped forward away from the gun carriage and, with his revolver held in front of him, moved towards the cavalry bearing down on him. Culloch saw him fire off three quick shots, hitting one of the leading horses whose legs collapsed under it. The dead animal's momentum flattened Hamilton, killing him instantly, and flung its rider ten feet ahead. The German's cry was cut short when he landed squarely on the mouth of the stranded British gun, the man folded round the metal of the barrel, his backbone snapped. The dead horse followed behind him and crashed into the carriage. The German horses and riders closest behind had no time and no room to react before they also crashed into the carriage that suddenly blocked their passage. Culloch watched four British soldiers nearest the gun carriage, including Sergeant Cobbett, engulfed by the impact.

Edwards was at the rear of the group. Evidently he had been organizing the departure of the one surviving gun team, for Culloch could just see them moving off, away from the conflict. Now Edwards and the half dozen soldiers that remained rounded the corner, rifles at the ready. For the second time that day the lane had become a jumbled mess of men, horses, and gun carriage; British and Germans had been thrown together, dead and injured. Behind the blockage, the German horsemen milled around as they looked for a way through.

"Open fire," Culloch heard Edwards shout.

His men raised their weapons and let loose at the Germans; hemmed in by the high banks they were easy targets at this short range. The four riders in front were quickly brought down, together with two of their horses. The remaining two horsemen turned their mounts in the tight space and fled to the protection of the nearest bend in the road.

With the immediate threat gone, Culloch watched Edwards hurry his men from the scene, no doubt sure the enemy would soon be back. Two men, too badly injured to leave with them, were left propped on the road bank with water bottles. Culloch slumped behind the hedge. He had seen Duncanson and Gray fall, and watched German cavalry overcome the rest of his platoon, and he had failed to warn them of the charge heading their way. On reflection it had been stupid to shoot the last German: this could have drawn attention to himself. Surviving a brutal and impoverished childhood had left him with a fierce sense of self-preservation; he had no tribal temperament and little sense of duty. If it had not been his only choice he would never have joined the Army. He moved, but not to join Edwards; instead he headed across the field, away from the nearest sounds of battle. He scurried along, keeping his head low, as fast as possible.

24th August 1914
Mons
Private Samuel Elliott,
British Expeditionary Force

Samuel Elliott returned to consciousness and experienced an unusual confusion; he had no idea where he was, and felt pain all over his body. One ache came to the fore, a deep throb in his skull that made him wince and screw his eyelids tight together. He felt grime and dirt on his face and could taste mud mixed with blood in his mouth. He tried to wipe his face but his arm was trapped against his side. Something heavy pinned him down. He could move his other arm though and he reached up to wipe his face. It was crusted in a mask of dried earth. He rubbed and then opened his eyes, blinking all the while in an effort to keep out the dirt.

A moment's panic that he had lost his eyesight, and then he realized he was looking up at a night sky with tree branches only a few inches above his face. Where was he? Now the answer to his question came and memories and emotions flooded in.

Samuel was a soldier in the 4th Middlesex Regiment. They had marched to Mons and been ordered to build defensive firing positions close to the canal bridge. His position had not been envied. Many of the soldiers could take advantage of the pit-heads and broken landscape to dig in, but his platoon had moved forward and their trenches were little more than rabbit scrapes a few feet deep.

There had been a sapling in front of him and its roots had made it difficult to dig, but he had been grateful for a little extra cover when the fierce battle had started suddenly.

German infantry had emerged from pine trees in front of them, about a third of a mile away and had moved in solid ranks towards the British. At first Samuel had stared at this open target, but then he had opened fire along with the rest of his battalion. They had supports on which to rest their rifles and at that range they could not miss the rows of walking men who were thickly clustered together. The dead piled up. Many of the Germans crouched down and used their own dead and wounded as cover; their haphazard return fire was ineffectual against almost invisible defenders. Samuel's rifle barrel was too hot to touch; he fired and fired again. He and the four soldiers alongside him laughed as their initial fear evaporated.

Then the German artillery found their mark and shells had rained down in their area. He saw a similar position near him blasted away; one moment there had been half a dozen soldiers shooting, then an explosion close enough to make him duck. When he looked a moment later there were no more heads to be seen. Smoke enveloped the area and earth and stones rained down. Piercing screams could be heard that sounded more animal than human; then they stopped as suddenly as they had started.

He and the men with him fired at whatever targets they could see. The Germans had fragmented into groups of men and the scene became confused. When there was a lull in the firing he had taken the opportunity to drink from his canteen and find more ammunition; at that moment shells landed around their position, and that was where the flashbacks ended.

It was a body on him that was holding him down. He reached upwards with his free hand and grabbed some of the foliage in front of him. The sapling that had stood in front of their small dug-out had blown over and was just above him. He held onto a handful of thin branches and tugged himself from under the corpse using the horizontal tree for support as he tried to lever himself out of the bottom of the hole.

He sat up, grimacing with pain, and noticed his hearing was still intact. Strange he hadn't thought of that immediately but he could hear voices; not close, and not British as far as he could tell; he suppressed an instinctive reaction to call out. He cautiously moved onto all fours to make standing up easier. There was a sharp pain in his stomach, though whether muscular or more serious he could not tell; his forehead thudded and his throat was bone dry. After a long pause he pushed with his hands and tried to stand; his right leg collapsed under him, and he retched as dizziness overcame him.

Samuel could see little, but he needed water so felt his way around the remains of his little shelter; nothing was as he remembered it. He thought he knew where they had left their rations and water bottles but recoiled when his hand touched a dead face. He had to leave. He crawled up over the lip of the dug-out and raising his head to find his bearings he saw pinpricks of moving lights and not far away the sound of voices. He started to crawl away from the voices, favouring his left leg for leverage. His right was hot and, worryingly, felt wet. He lay flat every so often to recover his breath. With his eyes used to the dark he could see the outline of bodies around him. Every so often he passed close to one of the corpses, and noted that they were all British; this meant that the Germans had recovered their own already which made his survival all the more miraculous. Mercifully he found a half-full canteen of water near one body and downed its contents. This restored his senses somewhat.

Half crawling and stumbling he headed towards the town of Mons, silhouetted against the night sky; he had no idea where his own army might be located. On the way he found a discarded pack and retrieved two tins of bully beef and one of hard biscuits. He thought about taking a rifle that was beside a body but it was too heavy to lift in his weakened state. Instead he took off the bayonet and slipped it into his belt. Every so often he froze when voices were close, but finally he reached the outskirts of the town. It loomed up in a ghostly mixture of pit-heads, buildings, and slag-heaps.

He took a side passage beside some houses and found himself in an alleyway that passed small back yards. He was well down the narrow path when he heard footsteps headed in his direction. He stopped, and put a hand on the alley wall to steady himself. He picked up some voices; it sounded like two or three men, their talk loud, guttural, and brusque. German soldiers.

Hands up and surrender, or carry on? The wall was only about five feet high and that made the decision for him. He grunted with the effort as he heaved himself over and he fell, heavily, into a cobbled yard. He curled up against the brickwork and tried to stifle his breathing as boots clumped nearer and then stopped close to where he had stood a moment before. He held his breath and waited. After a moment of laughter Samuel heard the soldiers relieve themselves against the brick wall. Two sets of footsteps started to walk away before the third had finished his stream of urine; this caused more jocularity when he ran to catch them up.

The soldiers' footsteps faded but Samuel remained huddled into the base of the wall; he had fallen onto his wounded leg, and this was now the primary focus of his pain. Unwilling to climb the wall just yet he looked around and saw he was in the yard of a small, darkened, and silent terraced house. There were two outbuildings; the smaller one he guessed from the smell was the privy. Alongside this was a slightly larger shed; on his hands and knees in case any more soldiers should walk along and peer over the wall, he crawled towards it. He stretched to unlatch the door, crawled in and pulled the door shut behind him. Some moonlight shone through cracks in the woodwork but he could not make out the contents inside; he felt tools on the walls hanging from hooks, and in one corner there were several filled sacks made of rough material. He slumped onto the wooden floor, leaned against the sacking, and groaned.

The sanctuary felt womb-like, but the apparent peace and safety only emphasized his desperate plight and the unreal experiences of the last 24 hours. The anxiety he had felt subsided a little but the pain in his leg had intensified. His head still hurt, he was bruised all over and, worst of all, Samuel felt isolated and alone with no idea of what to do next. His thoughts went to his home, his pregnant wife, and then to the men in his platoon, all, as far as he knew, dead. His situation overwhelmed him and tears started, and then a shudder broke through his body; sobs surfaced from deep inside so unexpectedly he was helpless to contain this unmanly reaction. He only stopped loud howls by biting on his sleeve. On it went until exhaustion claimed him and he curled up and slept.

Samuel awoke with the words "Must get back", "Must get back", "Must get back" echoing in his head like a mantra. He hurt all over and his eyes felt swollen. With surprise he recognized the sensation from a distant childhood, when he would wake from a tearful sleep that followed a punishment or a lost pet. But the release of tension had settled him, and he felt more confident.

Light came through a small skylight and cracks between the wooden panels. He saw glass jars arrayed on shelves above him and winced and groaned as he levered himself upright and leant against the flimsy wooden walls for support. The contents of the nearest jar looked like a dark jam; he unclipped the catch, plunged in his fingers and licked off a globule of a fruit preserve he could not identify. The sweetness gave him a surge of energy and he wolfed down most of it.

He weighed up his options. He could walk out onto the streets and hand himself over to the first German he saw. Now that it was daytime and yesterday's battle fever should have receded, he felt the odds were good that he would be respectfully treated and not shot on sight. The other possibility was to wait for nightfall, and try to find his army. The uncertainties of facing the enemy he had so recently been killing, set against the comfortable familiarities of his own army, decided the case and he determined to see out the day in hiding.

He turned his attention to his most pressing injury. There was a long bloodstained tear along one leg. He tried to remove his trousers to investigate further but the material was glued to the wound with dried blood; he decided to leave it as it was, and hope he reached help soon.

He could move all his limbs and though movement brought pain from many parts he concluded nothing was broken. His stomach hurt but the source felt superficial rather than internal. There was blood mixed in with the dirt on his forehead where he guessed he had been knocked unconscious, and that had caused his headache. Overall, he concluded, only his leg needed real attention.

Samuel studied his refuge again and noticed half a dozen bottles in one corner. He prized the top off one with the bayonet, sniffed the contents to ensure it did not contain paraffin or the like and then sipped from the neck. It was a fruit drink, bubbly, sweet, and alcoholic; he did not risk drinking much: alcohol had never featured in his family and it was water he needed.

Hanging on the back of the shed door was an old winter overcoat, apparently discarded, smelling mouldy and damp. Samuel did not hesitate to try it on; it fitted well enough. Alongside the jars of preserves he found some hard cheeses wrapped in cloth; he put two bundles in the coat pockets to take with him, as well as another jar of jam.

The implements he had felt the night before were land workers' tools. A short one had a handle with a grooved blade; he decided to keep this on him to replace the unwieldy and conspicuous bayonet. He sat down, leaned back against the sacks and waited for the day to pass. He tried to ignore the deep pain in his leg and alternated small bites of cheese with sips from the bottle he had opened; nothing in his comfortable past had prepared him for this.

Samuel had joined the Middlesex Territorials at 18, his interest in the Army stirred by family talk of his grandfather who had died a sergeant in the Crimean War. It had been an impetuous decision on Samuel's part, something of a young man's need to disassociate himself from his paternal model, for even though Samuel had followed his father, working as a clerk at the same bank, he had always felt life could give him something more, and his years of training with the Territorials helped with that belief. Through his cousins he met Rose, an only child. In truth she was not especially attractive in looks but with a lively spark in her manner she contrasted dramatically with all the other females in his limited circle of friends and family.

Marriage had followed and the two had moved in with her parents. The initial intention was as a temporary arrangement but Rose's father had benefitted from his profession as an engineer on the new underground railway workings. Within two years they were all living together in a house large enough to give both couples privacy, with a maid and a housekeeper to cover most chores.

Thoughts of home made Samuel feel peacefully detached from his current plight and he steered his daydream towards recent memories.

He had just recalled the day after his 26th birthday when his wife told him he was to be a father, when he was jolted by voices, and they were close. He peered through one of the cracks and saw two soldiers by the open back door of the house; they had a pile of bottles at their feet. One of them pointed at the shed and the shorter of the two walked across the yard towards him. Samuel was paralyzed. The soldier started to undo the flies of his trousers and lifted his head as he smelt the air; his nose led him to the privy next door to the shed and Samuel listened to the man strain. There was nowhere for Samuel to hide so he readied himself to surrender. As quietly as he could he struggled to his feet and with his weight on his good leg raised his arms and faced the door.

The soldier left the privy and rattled the latch on the shed door but was distracted from opening it by a shout from the direction of the house; his steps immediately retreated. Samuel was frozen to the spot, the only movement was a stream of his own urine that escaped and ran down his leg. It was some time before he dared move and he collapsed back to the floor and remained on edge for the rest of the day, though luckily he had no more visitors.

By dusk his leg had stiffened up and it was a struggle to stand. He unclipped the latch on the door, peered out and checked that all was quiet. He reasoned that as the advance parties had been in and presumably through the town it was certain that the German supply chain and administration staff would not be far behind them; there seemed no reason to hesitate and he was impatient to move.

He moved back towards the wall, his only way out of the yard as the wooden door to the alleyway was chained and bolted shut. He favoured his uninjured leg and resolved to find something he could use for a crutch. Samuel listened and then peered over the wall and looked down the alleyway; it was empty and he pulled himself over the brickwork. He tried not to land on his wounded leg, but his ungainly landing made him topple over and the impact of the drop caused him to gasp at the sharp pain he felt. He fought the temptation to lie there, and staggered upright and limped to the end of the passageway.

He headed in what he thought was a southerly direction, with just enough moonlight to guide him. He only saw lights in a couple of windows and assumed most of the town's residents had fled. Every so often he heard voices and the sound of cartwheels on cobbles, sometimes accompanied by hoof beats. Most footsteps sounded unmistakably military and each time he thought his path might merge with another's he took evasive action and pulled himself back into the dark shelter of a building or wall before easing himself along and away when the noises diminished.

Stop, pause, listen, then look and if all clear, move on to the next sheltered spot. Even his leg felt a bit more comfortable as activity loosened up his limbs. For a Londoner the pit-heads and slag-heaps dotted around a town had been a fascinating novelty at first sight, and now Samuel could use these high fixtures as beacons to guide him southwards.

The built-up areas of Mons soon ended; there was more space between houses, some of which looked grand and manorial. The more lowly homes looked rural, with signs that their occupants had kept poultry and pigs. Occasionally a dog barked as he slipped past, but no one came out to investigate. He reached farmland and across two fields he could make out a black wall of trees which held out the hope of a safe haven.

He hurried as best he could, though was forced to be more cautious when once he missed his footing on the uneven ground and yet again fell heavily on his wounded leg; a fresh wave of pain caused him to hiss between his teeth as he struggled to his feet and carried on.

Samuel staggered into the woods and felt his way past the first trunks in front of him. After only ten feet or so he judged he had come as far as he could and lowered his back against a tree, panting hard and completely exhausted. Within a minute he had started to doze and just had time to slide himself sideways onto the earth before his eyes closed.

How long he slept he had no idea, but he awoke in daylight, his head on the woodland floor; he was damp and cold. He opened his eyes and found he was looking at a pair of boots. He groaned and struggled to push himself upright. The unknown person who stood in front of him took one step back and waited.

25th August 1914
Leuven
Therese

The city had been under occupation for six days. The German soldiers marched in on the evening of 19th August, only hours after the Belgian Army had departed. Therese had not been aware of their arrival until the following day when she was awakened by a persistent hammering on the door of the convent. The reason for the interruption was given at breakfast when Mother Superior herself read out a proclamation that had been handed over by the soldiers who had knocked at doors along their street.

"We are to conform to a curfew; no one is to be on the streets after eight o'clock in the evening. We are not to lock our doors to the streets and at night they must be left open. Curtains are not to be drawn and lights are to be left lit."

Mother Superior lifted her head and looked around the room.

"I am sure you are asking yourselves the questions I voiced, but rest assured the Germans consider themselves a higher order than that of the Church or our Lord whom we serve; we are to obey them. The only exception that has been made is that we are not required to have any soldiers billeted with us, but they will expect us to provide food for one of their makeshift barracks."

Gasps and murmured voices filled the room. These women who had separated themselves from the world would not be viewed as different by the new administration in control. They had thought themselves sanctified and secure behind locked doors, neutral in their lack of direct association with the world and beneath the sign of the Cross, but there was no dignity in the way they had been included in these proclamations. Therese felt shocked. What Mother Superior failed to share with the whole community was the fact that the soldiers took several of the refugees away with them. Therese had seen this happen and had felt a tension within her ever since, that no amount of meditation had relieved.

The refugees had joined a group of people on the streets that were to be held hostage by the soldiers to guarantee the conduct of the citizens. Therese doubted that the citizens required such tactics. Those who had remained in the town were already subdued and fearful: the stories of atrocities in other towns and villages had spread.

"Sister Paul will orchestrate some changes in accommodation to bring all sisters into the cloistered rooms. This will mean double or sometimes triple sharing in rooms, but I don't want any sisters to be in rooms exposed to the streets. I know that you will all embrace this change while it is required," intoned Mother Superior, while she smiled her most benevolent smile.

Therese would have preferred to stay where she was. Despite the dangers from the street, her room was her sanctuary, the place she talked aloud with God, the place in which she could be in complete silence. Sharing her space would be difficult, but even as she thought this she felt God's challenge. Her room was not a space for her to possess; she had given up possessions and this realization humbled her. Not once had any of the refugees complained about the loss of their own possessions, and they had no guaranteed roof over their heads. She had become too comfortable and satisfied; God was shaking her world to ensure she stayed focused on Him.

The move of rooms was managed with no fuss, but also with no warmth in any welcome; in her case, three now slept in the space of one sister before. Therese spent time with the refugees in the schoolroom rather than return to her new room in the evenings. There were always new faces and new stories to capture as visitors passed through, but what she craved was her quiet time with God. She started to feel crowded and it made her feel physically

146

unbalanced. She consciously slowed all her conversations down as if in recognition that it would take longer for each word to find a place to settle within her head. Her speed of writing had quickened and by now seven notebooks had been filled. She had written her records on the unused side of the pages in the cook's old housekeeping ledgers; each finished tome was locked in a drawer in Mother Superior's office: the day of reckoning was ahead.

As well as her books, Therese fed all the local information she gleaned through to Mother Superior and Sister Paul: the arrival of the German First Army and their departure a few days later; the increased concentration of soldiers billeted in the town and temporary barracks; the taking of hostages and the billboard proclamations that demanded obedience. Posters announced the ruthless intent of the Germans; if they found even a single weapon the owner would be executed, neighbours evicted, and neighbourhoods destroyed. The fact that such reprisals were known to be no idle threat kept all indoors.

The atmosphere within the convent was subdued, with nerves jangled by the closer proximity of their living arrangements, but they felt in no immediate danger from their oppressors. Daily routines continued, but Therese had noticed a reduction in the food that was available to them as they stretched their rations to include refugees and the demand for meals from the soldiers. Kitchen staff reported it was difficult to buy supplies and visits from local farmers who used to bring vegetables to them had abruptly stopped.

All the nuns were at their evening meal when they heard gunshots ring out at quite close quarters. There were many shots, ragged gunfire, not an orchestrated volley; each found its echo in the return fire.

"What can have happened?" Therese asked.

"Perhaps the British have arrived, or the French, and this will all be over soon," spoke one of the sisters in reply.

At this suggestion of hope many of the nuns made the sign of the Cross as if in anticipation of an answer to prayer. Therese doubted this very deeply but kept her thoughts to herself. She thought it more likely that the shots were a sign of reprisals being meted out. She knew, perhaps in more detail than they, what these invaders were capable of: at the slightest irritation they would destroy.

147

A sense of foreboding had grown in her each day. In each of her meditations for the last week a particular scene had played out, and however much she had tried to clear her thoughts, it had persisted. The picture that came into her mind was of her looking at the crucifix in the church of St. Pierre. It stood high behind the altar and had the figure of Christ impaled and anguished in painted ceramic relief. In the scene Therese imagined Him in the minutes before His death when He felt separated from God and burdened by the sins of the world, and she was examining her heart for the deeds or thoughts that she should seek His forgiveness for, when flames started to lick at His feet and soon engulfed and destroyed Him. As the flames hid Him from her sight she would hear a voice. His voice and His words were always the same. "You may not see me, but know that I am with you." Words of comfort, but they held no comfort for her. It was His destruction that sat heavily with her.

Sister Paul called for their attention.

"Sisters, we can hear shooting and don't know what that means, but we must endeavour to keep ourselves and those in our care safe. I ask that all remain cloistered after supper. We will not assemble in the chapel this evening. I also ask the sisters who have assisted the refugees to accompany me to the schoolroom and medical centre to see what help is needed; but be warned, our doors will be open to the streets."

Therese felt not a moment's hesitation and responded to Sister Paul's request. The only thing she did before she followed her to the schoolroom was to take the latest notebook to Mother Superior's office to be locked away. She was the last nun to walk from the cloistered side of the convent before the gates were locked behind her.

Sister Paul was attempting to bring some order to the chaotic scene that met Therese when she walked into the schoolroom. There was a mass of people, many that she did not recognize, and some very obviously in need of medical care. Although she had heard the gunshots, she had so far been sheltered from what was happening outside. Only now did she become aware of the sound of glass breaking and shouting. In a repeat of the time when the first refugees arrived, people were corralled and queues established for medical attention. Those seeking shelter formed their own huddles and tried to take up as little of the space as possible. Two women told Therese that it was as if the soldiers had suddenly gone mad. They had started to shoot at random and kick in people's doors; they were firing into rooms and torching buildings and, as people escaped the flames, shooting at them. They were working their way towards the town centre from their barracks, collecting more soldiers from their billets along the way and ransacking homes. Stolen belongings were being piled onto carts that followed the soldiers' progress down the streets.

This roomful of people had run ahead of the soldiers and Sister Paul had directed the men on towards the crypt of St. Pierre. Therese went to the door to look into the street and saw a tidal wave of people run past in the direction of St. Pierre and the Grand Place. From their panic it was obvious that the soldiers were close behind and she went to find Sister Paul.

"Should I lock the doors, Sister Paul?" Therese asked.

"No, we must put up no resistance and hopefully they will ignore us. In fact make sure the doors are open and that you can be seen. I will join you at the far door." Sister Paul turned to the two nuns who were tending the injured: "I will shut this door so that you can continue undisturbed."

She and Therese took up their self-appointed posts by the entrances. They did not have long to wait before a couple of German soldiers tumbled into the room off the street. The two people they pushed ahead of them, almost as shields, fell at Therese's feet from the momentum of their shoves. The soldiers looked at the room full of people and one locked eyes with Therese who clutched her crucifix. Without a word to each other, both soldiers turned and went back out of the door, but instead of moving on they remained outside and waved the soldiers past as more and more of them poured down the street, some carrying flaming torches. If it had not had such hostile intent, Therese thought, it could almost have passed as a night of revelry.

The relief in the room was palpable as the immediate danger passed their doors. Therese herself felt quite weak when the fear that had coursed through her started to subside; not that she knew they were out of trouble. The threat had gone but so had the soldiers from their doors, their guardian angels.

Therese and Sister Paul turned their attention back to the room and its occupants. Therese could see these were not country people like their first refugees: these people seemed refined and genteel.

149

She introduced herself and met the wives of academics from the university, professional people used to a world dominated by respect and reason, but on this night they had no voice. There were servants who kept close to their mistresses, forming a unit that was solid in its support. This German aggression had taken everyone by surprise. They told Therese there had not even been insolence on the streets, just immediate acquiescence, if not acceptance, of the instructions they had received since the start of the occupation. Again, Therese wondered what had happened to wreak this storm of violence, and when would it end?

A woman with burns walked in. She looked dazed and unaware that the skirt of her dress still smouldered. Therese addressed this immediately and then led her through to the sisters in the medical room. Therese stayed and assisted with dressings and conversation as people's wounds were tended.

More people with burns arrived, and the smell of the fires came in with them. The stories of the destruction that accompanied them became increasingly unbelievable, and a gasp went around the room. And people started to weep when they heard the soldiers had torched the university and the library. Therese herself was no scholar but did not know how such barbarism could be contemplated. A shudder went through her. She imagined spirits released from the ancient books, into the smoke or laying in ashes in the gutter.

The sky was alight with sparks, smoke, and flames. She heard the roar and crackle when she looked out into the street and stumbled back into the room as a man ran past her shouting "St. Pierre, St. Pierre, it's alight." The words hit her like a physical punch. Her vision, the picture she had carried for so many days, the crucifix on fire, it had happened, and she instinctively knew that worse was to follow. She fought hard not to vomit as she felt her body repel this thought, but could not stop herself sinking to the floor.

It was Sister Paul who helped her to her feet.

"You are distressed my child, return to the cloister and get some rest."

"St. Pierre is on fire, the soldiers have torched it," Therese almost shouted this at Sister Paul.

The church was only 100 yards from the convent and close to St. Gertrude, their church. Sister Paul almost staggered as Therese had done, and tears came to her eyes.

"I must tell Mother Superior at once. Can you keep a watch at the door. The fire could easily spread down the street to us. We must stay alert. Ask some of those sheltered here to help you. We might need to be ready to leave."

"Sister Paul, if we have to evacuate can I ask you to collect my notebooks from Mother Superior's room. We must take them with us."

"Mother Superior will decide what we must take, but I will remind her. Send word through to the cloisters if fire approaches. *Pax vobiscum*, my child."

"And with you," Therese said automatically, though these were the least peaceful circumstances she had ever experienced.

Sister Paul departed and Therese asked two volunteers to stand by the doors and watch the skyline for flames. Thankfully the wind had blown smoke from the flaming buildings away from them, and no sparks were landing near. Therese found herself mesmerized by the smoke that swirled in the night sky, lit by the glow of the burning buildings. It was the sound of more glass breaking nearby that brought her attention back to her immediate surroundings.

A group of soldiers had turned into the street. They did not have the look of organized troops, more of a disorderly mob. They were breaking windows with their rifle butts and pushing their way into the homes. Many already had bottles in their hands and it seemed that wine and beer was the booty they sought. From the way they moved, Therese could tell that they were drunk as they bounced off walls to keep themselves upright. And then the screams started.

Therese had seen three soldiers go into one house and then had heard what seemed like two women screaming. The sound was awful to hear, but what was even worse was when it stopped, suddenly. More soldiers arrived and they became louder and more aggressive in their actions. Therese decided it was time to bolt the doors and pray that they would be ignored, as they had been earlier in the evening. She turned to douse their lights and then moved to close the doors. She succeeded with one of the two but the second was abruptly pushed back against her and soldiers tumbled in.

Therese never regained her footing. Each time she tried to raise herself she was knocked down. Bodies seemed to fall in all directions. She was dazed from a knock to her head and had no idea whether this was from a fist or a boot, or another body as it flailed to right itself. The women who had sought refuge found themselves attacked. Screams were silenced by punches or kicks. The soldiers were intent on collecting their spoils. This was their war, their enemy, and their right to conquer.

Therese had no time to think and no defence. A soldier who had grabbed her was heavy, strong, and determined. All she could do was make his task as difficult as possible. She fought to get away from him, but he had her trapped and with a few grunts he took her. In the moment that she felt his hand on her flesh she knew what it was to hate. She saw in her mind the picture of the burning crucifix and the anguish on Christ's face as He burned, and she focused on this. Both of them separated from their God in their darkest hour. Father forgive them, had been His words, but hers, as she fixed her attacker with a piercing glare, directed him to rot in hell.

The futility of her resistance sapped her strength and as the soldier left her, she could not move. The next attack swiftly followed, but by this time Therese had entered into the sanctuary of prayer. "Thy will be done" were the words she repeated to herself and as silence returned to the room when the last soldier left she heard "I am with you" and her spirit was stilled, as pain seared through her body.

29th August 1914
Brussels
Marion

"Thank you, Marion, now please sit down. If you don't mind my comment, you look fatigued, you both look fatigued," Hugh said, as he included Edith in his observation.

Marion had been on her feet to pass a cup of tea to Hugh Gibson. The secretary from the American legation had sent a note around the day before to ask if he might avail himself of the invitation that Edith had offered earlier in the month. Edith had asked Marion if she would like to join them and she had been thrilled to accept. To be in Hugh's company brought her one step closer to Russell; although fanciful, she almost felt he was in the room with them.

"In the spirit of such observations, Mr Gibson, you also look fatigued; we're all working hard, I suppose, and in difficult times," Edith said.

They were correct; Marion was exhausted. She realized as she sat down and picked up her tea that this was her first break, apart from to eat and sleep, in days. Refugees had flooded into Brussels from Leuven, and they, like every establishment in the city, had opened their doors to the injured.

"I hope I don't add to your pressures with my visit today," Hugh said. "I feel I've been in a maelstrom and the thought of a visit to you

153

here stood out like an oasis. No one knows I'm here, so I'm free of responsibility for the moment, but I'm conscious that I'm interrupting your duties."

"You're a welcome guest, Mr Gibson, and provide an opportunity for us to stop work for an hour; you've created an oasis for us too. But no doubt with our questions, you'll find you're working still. Can I ask, what news do you have from outside Brussels? We've heard nothing, have we Marion? We can't get English newspapers, they've been banned, and the censorship makes *Le Soir* a poor read."

They and the citizens of Brussels had lost freedoms that they had not even appreciated existed until the German pronouncements took them away. The instructions were prolific and conveyed menace. A steely intolerance underpinned the new bureaucracy that was steadily being put in place, and the Germans had only been in the city for a few days.

"We've heard some of the news of Leuven, but it sounded unbelievable; is it true, the burning, shootings, and looting"? Marion asked.

"I'd meant less local news than Leuven," Edith said, quite tersely thought Marion, and she felt chastened, "but Mr Gibson, what can you tell us of the situation there? I hope it's not as bad as the stories we've been told."

"It's probably worse, I fear." Hugh replaced his cup in the saucer and put it onto the table beside him.

"If I hadn't seen it with my own eyes, I don't think I would have believed any record of the event," he said.

"What were you doing there? How did you get there?" Marion was on the edge of her seat and was reminded of etiquette by Edith, who raised a finger to her own lips as a sign to quieten her.

Hugh smiled at Marion so she did not feel admonished and he settled into his tale.

"I went yesterday, and am back safe as you can see, so there is no need for anxiety. I travelled under the American flag and my destination was the American College in Leuven, to check on their safety. I have to say I wanted to see the place at first hand too. Like you, the stories I had heard were terrible. It became quite an expedition: the Mexican and Swedish chargés d'affaires wanted to come along, and another colleague from the legation. We set off after lunch in the embassy car and made good progress until at the first outpost, this side of Leuven, our papers were examined. We were told to go no further as there was fighting in the town. Ahead was a great column of grey smoke and we could hear the muffled sound of shots. Down a little street we could see dozens of white flags which had been hung out of windows in a childish kind of way of averting trouble."

"I thought that was the universal sign of surrender," Marion said. She was indignant that such an act would be viewed as naïve or childish. "What else could these people do to protect themselves?"

"You're quite correct, Marion, and to admonish me. I've spent too long in the company of jaded men; it's just that any defensive attempts seem feeble in the face of this army."

"Please continue," Edith said, with a nod of encouragement to him.

"We talked to the soldiers and asked them what had happened. The refugees who came to our legation reported that the Germans had mistakenly started to fire on themselves and then took out their rage against the town; but these soldiers had a story about the son of the burgomaster shooting one of their officers. We asked every group of soldiers that we met and each had a different story. Who knows if the truth will ever be known?"

"They're bound to say they were fired on first, but even that doesn't defend what they've done to innocent people. It makes my blood boil." Marion had interrupted his flow for the third time.

"Marion, please," Edith said. "Let Mr Gibson talk."

Hugh did not seem at all put out by Marion's manner, or her interruptions; he took it as another opportunity to send a smile her way. For the next 30 uninterrupted minutes Hugh spoke of his visit; he described dead bodies and debris from houses, blackened buildings, drunken soldiers, and smoke that continued to pour out of the library and St. Pierre. A commander had told him his orders were to raze the town to the ground and have the people of Belgium respect the might of Germany. Hugh held them spellbound with his descriptions and by the end Marion's face was wet with tears and Edith was pale and tight-lipped.

Marion wanted to ask Hugh what he had said to the commander; surely it was Hugh's job to tell him what he was doing was wrong? But Hugh offered nothing of his reactions. Marion wanted to hear some righteous anger expressed on behalf of the Belgians.

Who upheld morality in these situations? And what was the point of Hugh being there if he did nothing to stop them? But she stayed quiet.

"It's difficult to hear of the calculation behind the destruction," Edith said. "One can better imagine it in the heat of battle, but this is wanton savagery."

Marion did soften towards him a little when she then noticed Hugh was still shaken.

"Our journey from the town was particularly harrowing. The volume of human traffic made our progress slow. There was fear on all their faces. We passed townspeople, peasants, priests and nuns; the whole thing was a nightmare."

Hugh sank into himself with these final words. Marion had to resist her instinct to reach out and touch his arm: she was sure Edith would have considered this an impropriety. Instead she busied herself. She removed the tea cosy and poured each of them a new cup of now lukewarm tea.

"I can see that you're troubled by all that you've seen," offered Edith with a "thank you" to Marion for her freshly filled cup. "Thank goodness Brussels was spared this fate and that we can welcome the evacuees. Their spirits are quite broken and now I can quite understand why. We'll do all we can for them, but the impact on our supplies is a serious problem. Is there any news on where we might find more food and provisions?"

Hugh seemed to welcome the diversion from the horrors of Leuven and picked up on Edith's question about food.

"The city has a severe problem: in fact estimates are that we'll be out of food within three weeks; the poor are close to starving now. Most of the shops have their shutters up and all the big factories are closed. The importation of food, even from outlying districts, has stopped. This season's harvest has been wasted, and the Germans even had the nerve to arrest citizens of Belgium, by the hundreds, and transport them to Germany to harvest their own crops."

"What's to be done, Mr Gibson, do the Germans have a responsibility to feed us as they are keeping us captive?"

"No, it seems they don't, Miss Cavell. They're not supposed to use our supplies of food without proper requisition or recompense, but at the moment they seem to be making up the rules to suit themselves. They clearly have the upper hand."

"But you're neutral," Marion broke in, "they have no fight with you. Surely you can tell them we need food, and that it must be found?"

Hugh smiled at Marion. He could just picture Marion banging on the desk of von Below, as she demanded his attention on this issue.

"The way of politics is rarely a straight line, Marion. We Americans have neutrality yes, but we also lack any direct leverage. The Germans will not listen to us at the moment so we need to help ourselves."

"What does that mean?" Marion felt fogged by his political response. "Surely this is urgent enough to get anyone's attention?"

"Officials here are reacting to what happens day by day. The Belgian Army and government still intend to defend Belgium, and they are too busy fighting to sort out what people need. The Germans don't want to stay here, they want to reach Paris and to know they can turn their back on Belgium and still be safe; they didn't set out with the occupation of Belgium in mind. We've all been caught unprepared."

"Meanwhile we run out of food," Marion said.

"We do have the attention of some significant people in London." Hugh attempted to relieve the tension he felt was building in Marion. "At the outbreak of war we assisted some 100,000 Americans to get back home via London, and that took some orchestration I can tell you."

"I know. Russell, I mean, Mr Clarke, told me about it. How is he? Have you heard from him?" Marion was unable to contain herself any longer.

"No, and Russell was a great help. But most importantly we had a Mr Hoover in London with the assistance of two American industrialists, Mr Kellogg and Mr Eastman. They coordinated the funding and transportation of thousands of travellers. They're only now winding down their operation and I hope to convince them that they have a new cause to take on, the feeding of seven million people."

"Are you in contact with London?" Marion asked.

"No, which is why I will have to take a trip there, and soon. We've just had word that there is traffic between Ostend and Folkestone, so that will be my route. I have to go via Antwerp and brief the Belgian government and the queen on all that has happened here. Perhaps

I can bring you the British news on my return. But I really must be going now." Hugh rose to leave.

"Thank you so much for your visit, Mr Gibson. Although not cheery in any way, your news has brought us up to date. We'll manage ourselves sensibly until your return, and yes", Edith said, "we'd be delighted if you can bring us news of England when you next visit."

"Talking of England, I know it's short notice, as I leave tomorrow morning at 11, but if you or any of your students have letters they want to send to family I can take them in the diplomatic bag."

"Now that is a gift for us all, thank you," Edith said. "I'll spread the word."

"Perhaps Nurse Drake could bring them around to the legation tomorrow. If you come at 10.30, they'll be safely packed. Don't worry about postage; I can take care of that in London. My best wishes to you both." He reached out to shake Edith's outstretched hand.

"I'll show you out." Marion opened the door.

They walked down the staircase in silence, across the hallway and to the open street. A group of German soldiers walked past them as they stood at the top of the steps.

"I shall never get used to seeing them here," Marion said.

"You're a brave girl to stay when you had the chance to leave," Hugh said as he shook her by the hand.

If, in that moment he had offered her a ride to London, she would have accepted, and arrived the next day at the legation with her bags as well as everyone's letters. How different her life would be. But no offer came. Instead, Hugh put on his hat, touched the brim as he said goodbye and she watched him walk down the street. When he had turned the corner she went to her room to start the longest series of letters she had ever written.

9th September 1914
Leuven
Therese

Therese awoke, and for the first time since the attack she could feel that her body had recovered a little. She stretched each limb and, while tentative with her movements, did not feel the pain that had caused her to groan or grimace on previous mornings. The scabs on her face had improved dramatically in the last week, but her skin would be marked where the flagstones had rubbed the skin off her face as she had been repeatedly pushed onto them. She had been battered and bruised but no bones had been broken; even so all she wanted to do was rest. She continued to lie in bed and let her thoughts wander back over the past few weeks. Was that all it was since the attack? Sometimes she felt it was a lifetime ago. She had yet to reconnect with the person she was before that night, but Sister Paul said to give this time.

Sister Paul had been the face she had recognized after the attack, but it was the noises that she registered first. As if from a great distance away she started to hear groans and then sobs and then the scraping sound of bodies as they dragged themselves across the floor. She had been unable to move, not because she was pinned down but she just could not find her body. She could see a hand close to her face and she tried to move her fingers, but her brain could not connect with the action: nothing moved.

Sister Paul seemed to know what to do. She remembered being carried, and despite the gentleness, heard herself cry out, but she could not locate the source of the pain. The sound as the gates to the cloister clanged shut behind them registered with her; she was safe, back in the inner sanctum, like a return to the womb and that was the image she held onto. She knew that she had a body, but she could not communicate with it. She was aware of her surroundings and what was said, but had no way of speaking.

"She has passed through the veil, but will return when she's ready," Sister Paul explained to one of the nuns who was concerned that Therese did not speak. "We must keep her warm, fed, and safe until she returns, but first let's bathe her and tend to her wounds."

Therese remembered the delight of the bathtub as she sank into the warm water; it was so deep that she floated. She had not enjoyed such a sensation since she had last swum with her brother. They had floated on their backs, looking at the branches of a tree on the riverbank dance to a slight breeze as they caught the rays of sun.

"You won't do this when you are a nun," he had said. "They'll have you trussed up all the time. You might never see daylight again."

"But I'll see God's glory in other ways and find new delights."

She almost giggled at the thought of how sanctimonious she had sounded, and a startled look from Sister Agnes made her think that perhaps she actually had giggled. She enjoyed her weightlessness and was not ready to be lifted out, dried, and wounds dressed, but she was under their management and she had no will to resist. She was packed with cloth between her legs. She couldn't remember where she was in her cycle, but she presumed the warm water had started a bleed. It had been luxurious to be bathed. Ablutions were normally hurried affairs, with cold water and eyes closed. It was easier this way than to wash with clothes on, the traditional way employed by the older nuns. But here she was, naked. Fresh linens were brought and although she tried to help them to dress her she heard them say she was like a rag doll as they put her to bed.

She had no idea how long it was since the attack. It seemed that sisters took it in turns to sit and tend her and change her dressings.

It was at these times that she was conscious of where she was; otherwise she was in blissful oblivion, as if she was suspended in nothingness. She did not sleep, pray, think, or speak; it seemed too far for words to travel from her brain to her mouth and they gave up along the way. It was on a day when Sister Paul came to feed her that this changed.

"Our Lord has shown me the journey you are on and has asked me to take you by the hand and lead you back to us and then we can walk together."

She took Therese by the hand.

"I am going to move the covers and help you sit up."

She pushed the covers back, sat her up and swivelled her round so that her legs came over the edge of the bed and then placed her feet on the ground; she kept her own hands on Therese's feet.

"I want you to look at my hands on your feet; feel the warmth come through from my hands and now you can wiggle your toes." And she was right, she could.

"Now I want you to stand on your feet. I'll help you stand, but I want you to feel your weight through your feet to the ground." And she did.

"I want you to close your eyes. In front of your eyes is a gossamer light curtain and there's an opening in it. Reach out your hand for the opening and push it to one side. Hold it there while you step through." She moved forward.

"You can open your eyes now, Therese. You are back with us." Therese looked at her, and then started to cry. Cry was not really the right word, she sobbed, gut wrenching sobs that came up from her pelvis and out through her heaving chest. They both fell to their knees and Sister Paul prayed; then spoke:

"We will both be blessed, Therese. Hold still and you will feel a shower of golden rays rain down on both of us. Lift up your face and let it run through your head and down your back and be absorbed by all your limbs and your body, and listen, listen for God."

Therese's breathing became steady. She closed her eyes and imagined showers of sunlight pierce through her body; she listened and she knew she heard Him.

"I am with you, Therese. I am always with you."

She slept for hours after this.

After stretching, Therese rose, washed, dressed, and was ready for when Sister Paul arrived. Her world had shrunk to the size of the room she had been resting in, but today Sister Paul was taking her for a walk to the chapel. She was not yet ready to meet and mix with the other nuns, but after their private prayers she and Sister Paul were going to talk. Today she felt ready for this.

The convent felt eerie, Therese thought. Used to it being quiet, at first the silence had not fully penetrated, but as she focused she felt that the air held no breath at all; it made her shiver. Perhaps thinking this was from the cold, Sister Paul stepped out at a brisker pace and Therese was pleased to soon arrive at the chapel. Everywhere there was dust: everywhere, in the sunlight, on the seats, in the altar cloth, on the flagstones. On closer inspection Therese saw it was not dust, but ash, and she could taste smoke in the air; startled, she looked at Sister Paul.

"All in good time, Therese. Let's pray first and then we can talk." And that is what they did.

"Our town turned into Sodom and Gomorrah the night you were attacked. The Germans torched and plundered. It continued for days. They evacuated the town and destroyed as many homes as they could. St. Pierre went up in flames and many lost their lives in the crypt. Most of the devastation has been to the other side of the Grand Place, so our buildings have been saved but many of the sisters have left. We don't have enough supplies to feed great numbers. They've moved to a convent near Brussels, safely so I hope."

Sister Paul paused; she did not want to rush Therese back into the reality she had evaded for several weeks, but Therese gave her a nod to continue.

"The ash is from the library; it burnt for days and sent a column of smoke up to the heavens. But we were blessed by the winds, and that they didn't torch us, although they did damage enough. Our community is no more, and you my sister, so badly hurt."

"What about the others, what happened to the other women?"

"You were the only one of our community who was attacked, but many of the refugees suffered as you did. We moved you back into the convent straight away, and the others we nursed in the schoolroom. But the next morning troops returned and put them all out onto the street and told them to leave the town. Any that fell in the road were shot."

Tears poured down Sister Paul's face as she relived the scenes.

"I cannot think that hell will be worse than this. It was as if God turned his back on all of us."

Therese was shocked by the anger in Sister Paul. Perhaps it was harder to feel God's hand in situations when others are harmed. Therese knew herself to be a victim, but she had never felt spurned by God. Somewhere in her consciousness she had remembered the words from her vision of the burning crucifix, "Even when you cannot see me, know that I am there."

"He is always with us, Sister Paul, it's just that we can't always see Him; and we don't understand His will."

"These are the words I should say to you, child, and here you are saying them to me. Perhaps my prayers for the well-being of your soul have been heard; God was with you through the veil and you've brought Him back with you. Let's sit here and talk."

They had reached one of the inner courtyards. Normally a place where the sounds of the town could be faintly picked up in the background, but all was silent around them. The holocaust was spent.

"I fought hard, Sister Paul, but my sin is I fought for myself. I gave no thought to the others around me. I didn't want the soldier to touch me. I am God's and will be no other's. I was determined but too weak. My spiritual lessons are nearly always about obedience and it took time for me to succumb to God's will. I didn't understand why this was happening to me, but I had to accept that it was. When I gave in and said, Thy will be done, it hurt less and I felt myself in God's presence, a place I didn't want to leave."

"It is not a sin to defend yourself from harm, Therese, nor to think of just yourself in such circumstances. It was a violent attack and, I can assure you, not sent by God. The ways of the world can be very wicked and the forces at play were not God's messengers. The reason we are separated from the world as nuns is to enable us to stay open to God, to channel His energy to where it is needed. If we had to protect ourselves from the world and its ways every day, we wouldn't be able to stay open to prayer."

"Then if it wasn't a lesson about obedience, why did it happen to me?"

"Bad things happen but it's how we choose to respond to what happens where God's hand can be seen. There are rich blessings for you, Therese, if you can stay in His gaze; it's a cold, ugly world without Him."

A silence fell between the two women, companionable and contemplative.

Therese recalled her first meeting with Sister Paul.

"So my dear," Sister Paul had said with a beaming smile. "God has brought you to us. Do you know why?"

Therese had knocked on the door of the convent at a prearranged time. She sat between her parents, book-ended by bristling resentment, after being ushered into a room with three chairs along one side of a table and Sister Paul on the other. Her father's attention seemed fixed on rolling his cap as tightly as he could manage, while her mother gripped her hand. Therese had beamed back.

"She thinks she knows," her mother interjected. "Perhaps you can tell if what she says makes sense? I think she's wasted in here; she can be of use at home and in our village. She reads and writes very well."

"She does," said her father who had lifted his head to Sister Paul, and then dropped it again.

"Therese?" Sister Paul looked at her.

"Well, Mother Superior ..."

"Excuse me, my dear, but I am not Mother Superior. I am Sister Paul and I watch over the novitiates, the probationers." She directed each word to each parent who had looked towards her as she interrupted Therese. "Do continue."

"Well, Sister Paul, I just have to pray," Therese said with no hesitation.

"All the time ..." her father said.

"Instead of chores ..." her mother added.

"As soon as she could speak ..." her father continued.

"She misses meals, that we work hard to provide ...." Her mother was in her stride.

"We can't afford to bring her here and that's the truth ..." her father confirmed.

"They don't take you in for nothing. I've told her." Her mother let go of her hand.

"So perhaps best we leave." Her father rose from the chair, and he was mirrored in his action by Sister Paul and her mother. Therese was stunned and stayed in her chair, unable to raise herself. Going? She could not believe it.

"Yes, I agree," Sister Paul said. "Perhaps you would like to leave now and I'll continue to talk to Therese about her calling. Would it be difficult for you to return in three days' time for us to discuss her future? Have you travelled far?"

"Far enough so that no work has been done today," her mother retorted.

"Would it suit you better if she was here a week before you return?" Sister Paul asked.

"Whatever you say," her father appeared to accept he had been outmanoeuvred. "We'll be here to take her home next week."

"That's agreed then, we'll meet again in a week's time." Sister Paul rang a hand bell and directed the nun who appeared to escort Therese's parents to the street. She walked with them to the door.

"You have been wonderful parents to bring Therese to us today. Our children are only in our safe-keeping until the Almighty shows each their path. You are the bows from which your children, as arrows, are sent forth." Sister Paul spoke in the tone of voice she adopted for reverent moments.

Therese's parents glowed at her lofty words and sentiments.

"The prophets hold such wisdom for us," Sister Paul said. "Those words are not mine, although I would love to own them."

She bowed to them and stayed bowed until they had left the room; she shut the door.

"Now, Therese, you were about to tell me why you want to become a nun."

Therese had never enjoyed such freedom in a conversation before this one with Sister Paul; she had found someone who spoke her language.

"I don't know that I do want to become a nun. Imagine what my father would say if he heard me say this; he'd have me back out working the fields immediately. I am not a shirker, I worked hard learning to read and write, but only so that I could learn more about God; He's the only person I've really ever talked to."

"And what do you talk about, Therese?"

"Do you know what I mean when I say we talk without words?"

Sister Paul gave an encouraging smile.

"I tried to describe it to my brother. He was the only one in my family who wanted to understand, or perhaps the others had no need to. I was different, and that was enough for them. I'll miss him."

"What did you tell him?"

"I told him I could always see where the sunlight was, even on a dark wet day, and when I stood in the sun's rays I would be talking to God, my heart would be singing, and sometimes I would be still and listen; we felt about the same things and it helped God to know that I cared. I don't think I care much for people. They can get in the way. They talk too much, and try to control too much and want too much of me. I just want to be left alone with God. My family is too big."

"The family here in the convent is large, Therese. Have you thought about that?"

"Not really," said Therese. "Here I see the space between people. You're not here for yourselves, but for God; you belong together but not to each other. You don't have to care for me, that's God's job; you all stay true to Him and His light shines on all of you."

"Why have you come to us, Therese? How did you know to come here?"

"It was in my vision."

"Vision, that's a big word," Sister Paul said.

"The priest gave it to me. I called it a picture. He told father he had to bring me, and as you saw, father did."

"Describe your picture to me, Therese. I'd love to hear about it."

Therese had loved Sister Paul since that day.

Therese turned and smiled at Sister Paul. "I'm feeling tired now and ready for a rest. Would you mind if I returned to my room?"

"Not at all, Therese. You've taken in a lot today. Enjoy your rest and we can talk some more later."

Therese lay on her bed and tried to absorb the news that Sister Paul had told her. The town ransacked, most of the nuns sent away, St. Pierre in ashes, and herself raped. She curled up on her bed and felt sunlight bounce on her face and pillow. She fell into a light sleep and as she dreamt she learnt just how different her life was going to be.

17th September 1914
St. Waast, near Mons
Isabelle

It had been nearly a month since Isabelle had found her first soldier. She had almost stumbled on him while the British soldier slept under some trees. When he stirred she had put her finger to her lips to keep him quiet, then knelt beside him. She spoke in English.

"You're British?"

"Yes." Samuel sat up and rested back against the tree.

"Can you walk?"

"I think so."

"Then we must move; you're not safe here."

She watched Samuel wince as he manoeuvred himself to his feet. He looked stiff and she saw blood on his right trouser leg, not that there was much of the fabric left in places; she could see his leg caused him pain.

"Take my arm, I can see you are wounded. We have some miles to cover. Shall we go?"

It had been a tiring journey and she had been fatigued, but not by the distance she had walked. Eight miles was not difficult for her. What had made the trip strenuous was the soldier, who had leant on her all the way, and the anxious moments when they had to hide and wait for German soldiers to pass. Isabelle was fit and strong, a fact belied by her almost waif-like figure. Of average height and with blonde hair that she wore tied back, Isabelle had a face that caught people's attention. Her lips were luscious, deep red and full and her blue eyes bright and alert. Her smile always made her look as if she held a secret.

The soldier, Samuel Elliott, had been in pain from his leg injury and could only manage a slow pace. They were both weary when they had arrived at her friend Jacqueline's house and Samuel was drenched with sweat. Jacqueline sent for the local doctor.

Isabelle's oldest friend, Jacqueline Laurent lived next door to her mother's house. Jacqueline's brother Martin was the local brewer but he was away in the Army and Jacqueline was doing her best to run the small premises with the help of one elderly retainer.

When the British Army had retreated from Mons some of the British soldiers had passed through their village, usually in ordered, though battered, units. These were followed later by small, bedraggled groups, and sometimes solitary soldiers. The villagers had thrust provisions into the exhausted men's hands, and when the stream had subsided they found they had six injured men on their hands, soldiers who were deemed unable to keep up with their companions and had, in effect, been abandoned. Samuel Elliott had joined them.

Jacqueline had taken the wounded into her house and had nursed them, assisted by Isabelle and occasional visits from Dr Aubry from the nearby town of Bavay. The doctor was one of the fortunate few allowed by the incoming German authorities to keep his motor car. They had requisitioned nearly all cars and even bicycles. Few locals had cars in any case and the majority hid their bicycles, leaving out a couple of old rusty ones in the village for the Germans to take.

Back to stay with her mother for the summer holiday, Isabelle had been caught up with the German advance through her home region. Now events had developed in a fashion that exhilarated her and presented more adventure than she could have ever imagined in her previously well-ordered life.

That life was happy, quiet and on the surface, conventional; born and raised in the small village of St. Waast, close to the Belgian border with France, her father had been the local doctor until his sudden death six years before. A popular man, his death from an infection had saddened the local people for miles around. He had been a liberal man and recognized the latent talents of his only child, so from the age of 12 Isabelle had attended a prestigious school in Lille, where she had excelled. She was now in a teaching post at the same establishment and quite often fulfilled the role of companion to the headmaster, Henri, a widower and 20 years her senior. He reminded her of her father. He was tender and kind towards her and she had found herself reciprocating his affection. He made her feel safe, but as she now faced these dangerous circumstances she felt herself revitalized and younger than in the life she had been living of late. She was only 22 and now she felt suffocated by the thought of another evening in Henri's study.

The first German soldiers into the village had treated the inhabitants roughly. They took what food and drink they could find and destroyed or spoilt what they could not carry with them. Matters calmed a little when their officers arrived and more orderly searches of the simple buildings were conducted. Fortunately Jacqueline and Isabelle had had the good sense to make a crude red cross from cloth and they had hung this from one of the top windows of their improvised nursing home. A German captain had carefully inspected the injured British soldiers to ensure their wounds were genuine; he had cut away dressings and caused much resentment, as well as pain, to the casualties. Once he had satisfied himself that there were no fit men within the group, the German leader left, and soon after, his band of men moved out of the village. They were an advance patrol under orders to probe forward at speed.

Two weeks after Samuel's arrival, a Scottish soldier was delivered to the house. A local farmer had sheltered him in his barn; he had picked up word of the girls' work, and did not know what else to do with his foreign visitor. The newcomer had no injuries so they hid him within the brewery building and away from the other men. The soldier, who gave his name as Culloch, was more taciturn and reserved than the men in the house, but he seemed grateful enough for shelter and food.

St. Waast was not on a major route but sightings of Germans had become common in the surrounding area, and occasionally soldiers, carts, and motor vehicles moved through the village. Soldiers nailed up posters that announced decrees for the civilian population, and threatened increasingly dire consequences for those who harboured weapons of any sort or sheltered and aided enemy combatants. The latest had announced the death penalty for any inhabitants who did not declare the presence of any soldiers.

Culloch was soon followed by another arrival, this time a courteous officer who introduced himself as Lieutenant Baxter. He arrived late one evening, brought along by Michel Petit, a young man from the village who was deemed too simple to be in the Army. His mother no longer wanted the responsibility of a fugitive on her premises. What had begun as a diversion from the village routine had now turned distinctly perilous. Isabelle's mother was terrified, and not just for the girls but for the whole village. News of reprisals filtered through regularly. Vieux-Mesnil had been torched by German soldiers, and this was after they had shot several women and children. Apparently two French soldiers had shot at a German patrol from an attic window in the village.

Isabelle had been about to leave Jacqueline's house when Lieutenant Baxter arrived; he was dirty and tired, but otherwise fit and well. They sat in the kitchen while Jacqueline made him a drink of hot milk laced with brandy, and some bread. Baxter told Isabelle his story and she translated parts of it for Jacqueline's benefit.

He had been trapped behind enemy lines north of Mauberge. Isabelle knew this had recently fallen to the Germans after a siege. Although ten miles away, she and her mother had listened to the artillery fire when the battle had raged. Baxter had hidden in a ditch for a few days. It was alongside the main supply route for the Germans and had been a busy route. Only when forced out by a lack of water and rations had he risked a midnight dash. He had blundered through the countryside until he found shelter at an isolated farmhouse; the farmer had brought him to the village and the Petits had taken him in.

Isabelle wondered if he would know any of the soldiers they had with them.

"What's your unit called?"

"I belong to the Dragoon Guards," he said. "Cavalry." When he saw their baffled faces he rocked back and forth on his chair and

170

clicked his tongue against the roof of his mouth. After a pause both girls began to laugh, and he joined in too.

Their smiles remained when their laughter stopped and Isabelle and Baxter appraised each other with a long look. Isabelle liked the man's eyes. They were brown and looked at her directly, but with warm friendliness. She saw no sign of the cautious, often hesitant and slightly furtive glances she was used to from the other British soldiers. This man Baxter was different. She assumed his poise came from being an officer; he was relaxed, despite his uncertain predicament. She guessed him to be in his mid-twenties. She tried to visualize him in clean clothes and without a dirty face. It was hard to tell how good-looking he was. His features all looked nicely proportioned, but it was his eyes that held her attention and she was not shy in returning his gaze. There was nothing sinister or predatory here; he seemed delighted with what he saw. She liked him instantly. She bit into her bottom lip as she held his eyes and laughed again as he had to clear his throat. She had practised that look with Henri in the classroom. She smiled at him again before she looked away.

"Can you take Lieutenant Baxter to join Mr Culloch, Isabelle?"

"Of course." Isabelle rose from her chair. "We have to hide you separately from the soldiers that are wounded. It's on my way out."

Isabelle led Baxter across the yard to the brewery building. They were in darkness, but she knew the way well and linked arms with him to stop him stumbling into barrels and other obstacles. She was delighted when this casual contact sent a pleasurable shiver up her spine. She had not thought of the low beams though and they had to stop when he cracked his head for the second time against wood. After this they continued with her leading him by the hand and he walking with his knees bent and his head down until they reached the tool storage room at the back of the building. She opened the door and heard straw rustle as Culloch woke up in some confusion.

"Mr Culloch, it's me, Isabelle. I have someone else to sleep here, Lieutenant Baxter."

"Pleased to meet you, sir." Culloch's voice sounded as if he was at their feet, and there was no warmth in his tone.

Even in the darkness and with so little said, Isabelle could sense the instant tension between the two men. She had thought Culloch

171

would welcome the opportunity to have company, but she realized that she didn't understand the ways of the Army.

"I'll bring you some food tomorrow: it will only be bread and cheese. And a rug if I can find one; we have no more blankets. Is there anything else you need?"

"Actually there is one thing, mademoiselle. Is it possible to have some paper and a pencil, or a pen?"

Baxter was close to her in the dark, and had almost whispered his request in her ear; her neck had tingled when she felt his breath. She knew she had flushed and was pleased that neither soldier could see it.

"Yes, I'll bring some tomorrow. You won't be able to send letters though, if that's what you were thinking, the post has been stopped."

"That's what I expected," Baxter said. "No, I need to keep some notes."

Culloch spat out a cough. Isabelle said goodnight and shut the door behind her. Once home and in bed she found sleep evaded her. She had been bold with Baxter and felt energized and comfortable with her new-found confidence. Always diffident with the local men, she had been flattered by Henri's attentions at the school, and comfortable with his undemanding moments in private. But that was before she had met a man whom she found attractive, and this one, Baxter, she did. To share a look and a smile with him felt the most natural thing in the world and not at all forward. She was excited at the thought of seeing him the next day, and the next and the next.

The following morning a deputation from the village left Isabelle and Jacqueline in no doubt: they had to move their guests out of St. Waast.

"Do you think we must go to Bavay?" Jacqueline asked that evening.

Bavay was the nearest town of any size, and contained a Red Cross hospital with French and British soldiers as patients; some were still too unfit to be moved into captivity by the Germans.

"And surrender our friends to the Germans?" Isabelle replied. "Only if there's no other option. I'd like to speak to the de Croys first. They run a hospital at their chateau and I know they've had British wounded there. They'll tell us the best thing to do."

The Chateau de Bellignies was in the village of the same name, two miles from St. Waast. The Princess Marie de Croy lived there with Prince Reginald, one of her two brothers. The most senior of the community's nobility, the de Croys were the most respected family in the area; further, they had strong British connections. Not only had their father, and then Reginald, served at the Belgian embassy in London, but their grandmother, who also lived at the chateau, was herself English.

"Good idea," Jacqueline said. "We must go to see them tomorrow. Now, we've got bread to bake."

To make bread for themselves and the soldiers was yet another task the girls had been forced to undertake when the village baker, like so many men, had left to join the Army.

In the morning, after they had fed and attended to the soldiers, the two friends set off for Bellignies.

"I've never spoken to the princess or her brother," Jacqueline confided as the chateau's medieval tower came into view.

Jacqueline sounded anxious and Isabelle had to remind herself that her friend only lived a rustic life, whereas she had spent most of her time in the huge town of Lille from her early teenage years.

"Don't worry, I've only seen the prince once or twice, years ago, but the princess knew me well when I was a girl; my father was the family's doctor. When I knew her she was gentle and kind, and her brother is supposed to be the same, but he's been away for years. Leave me to do the talking until you're happy enough to speak."

The girls walked up to the house and asked the maid who answered the door if they could speak to one of the de Croys. Soon afterwards a gentleman appeared from the side of the house. It looked as if he had been walking in the gardens.

"You wish to see me, young ladies? I am Reginald de Croy."

He was not a handsome man, though about him was the indefinable aura of high social status. He smiled in a welcoming fashion.

Isabelle told the prince their story and asked for his advice. He told them to wait a moment while he spoke to his sister; it was ten

173

minutes before he returned to the girls who had sat themselves on the doorsteps.

"Excuse the delay, my sister Marie and I had much to discuss: we have to be careful. We've treated many wounded here, mostly British, and some injured Germans; my sister goes to Bavay to help at the hospital there as well. The trouble is, our chateau has been used as a German headquarters a number of times since the invasion and we never know when a new group of officers will come calling to bother us with some new demands. It's too risky for us to hide the number of men you have for now, but don't worry, we have an idea for a safe place to take them; I'll send you word as soon as I can."

He bade them farewell and the girls thanked him and returned home. That evening Isabelle, the English speaker of the pair, told the soldiers the plan to move them soon. All the wounded had recovered enough to walk, although a fast march would not be possible and Samuel would need a rudimentary crutch made from a broom. She had taken time over her conversation with Baxter.

The second day after their visit to the chateau, Isabelle was surprised to have the prince himself knock on Jacqueline's door.

"I've come to see your soldiers. I want to take a note of their details to pass on to London. I have a way of sending some mail and messages through; but first, ladies, if you don't mind, a little word with you."

He smiled and put his fingers to his lips to indicate he had a secret to reveal. The girls invited him in. Isabelle was amused to see Jacqueline swept up with his conspiratorial style; evidently she had quite forgotten her previous reservations and now conversed with the aristocrat easily.

"We'll take the men to the Forest of Mormal," the prince confided.

The forest was a huge wooded area five miles from St. Waast. Isabelle could see its attraction as an excellent place for soldiers to hide. Her concerns about their care were answered by the prince's next words.

"Dr Jacquemart and I visited some of the gamekeepers and woodsmen. They are quite happy to take on your men; they already know of several hidden in the woods. We've promised to pay them for food, and we can move them tonight. How does that sound?"

Jacqueline nodded and Isabelle followed suit.

"I admire you young ladies very much for what you have done. And if you wish, there is still a lot you can contribute."

"Yes sir," Isabelle said, without even a look in the direction of Jacqueline, but her friend was close behind with her assent.

The prince explained how useful they could be with visits to the men to repair clothes and take extra provisions and also assist in directing any more fugitives into the woods. German searches had become more frequent and methodical, intent on finding more of the many soldiers abandoned throughout the villages and countryside. The men needed to be moved before they were flushed out and their hosts punished. Whenever he could he was moving British soldiers on to safe houses in Brussels and then into Holland, but this was a tricky business.

That night, under cover of dark, Isabelle and Jacqueline led the soldiers, who could only move slowly and often needed supporting, across the fields to the Chateau of Bellignies. At the gardener's cottage, as arranged, they met the prince and his sister. Princess Marie directed the men to a pile of clothing for them to select items for outdoor life in the forest. Samuel still had the tatty overcoat he had taken from the outhouse in Mons; others were soon in similar garb and it became hard to distinguish between them.

The prince and his gardener, Joseph, were to guide the men to the forest, and Isabelle and Jacqueline were returning home. Goodbyes were said and thanks offered by the men. The moment moved them all. To lessen the intensity, Isabelle told them they would visit them in the forest, so it was adieu and not farewell. The last to address her was Baxter.

"Are you sure, Isabelle, that we'll see you again?" It was the first time Baxter had spoken her name. "I hope that we do, but you must keep yourself safe. You've taken too many risks for us already."

Baxter held her handshake while he spoke and fixed her with a look that reached beyond that of a polite acquaintance; he smiled, squeezed and then released her hand.

Isabelle did not trust herself to speak: she nodded and smiled and raised her released hand to her lips, a gesture he saw before he turned and followed the men.

Isabelle and Jacqueline stood together in silence as they watched the group depart. Culloch was the only one not to have said thank you or goodbye.

"You have done good work, ladies. These soldiers have much to thank you for. Now be careful on your return."

Isabelle had forgotten the princess was still beside them. They parted company with warm farewells and turned down the drive and towards St. Waast. They had only taken a few steps when Isabelle was startled by a metallic scraping sound behind them. She spun around. Fear of having been discovered was her first thought, but against the lights of the chateau she could just make out the shape of an elderly woman. She was raking the drive.

"Is she deranged?" Isabelle pointed out the source of the noise to Jacqueline.

"No, she's clever," Jacqueline said. "She's removing all trace of the boots in the gravel."

Isabelle shuddered: the realization that this was no game, that these dangers were real, that Baxter had meant his words about her safety, suddenly hit home and she felt quite weak at the knees and almost stumbled.

"Come on. Let's get home." Jacqueline linked her arm with Isabelle's and they stepped into the dark.

3rd October 1914
Brussels
Russell

Russell put on the light to see the time. It was only half past four in the morning, some hours to go before it was a sensible or sociable time to rise. He knew that he was beyond any further sleep and let his mind wander back through the whirlwind of the last weeks since he was last in Brussels. He needed to distract himself; he was only hours away from seeing Marion and found it hard to lie still.

He thought he had been close to seeing her shortly after he had arrived back in Oxford but it was wishful thinking when the porter told him he had a lady visitor. He could only think that it was her but it was her friend Gwen. He remembered the visit well.

"Hello, do you remember me from Brussels? I'm a colleague and nursing friend of Marion Drake, Gwen Fincham."

"Yes, of course I do," he had said while he tried to mask his disappointment. He gave up the attempt, "I'm sorry, I thought you might be her. I'm not used to having lady visitors and I could think of no one else."

"You must be disappointed then, but I do bring news of her. That's why I'm here, I have a letter for you."

"Is she back in England? Did you travel together? Is she all right?"

"No, no, yes," Gwen laughed. "At least she was all right last time I saw her, but she stayed in Brussels. A lot has happened over the last few days, so we can only hope and pray that she remains safe."

"Oh, dammit, I hoped she'd leave. Sorry to use such language in front of you, and I've forgotten my manners. Come into my meagre rooms and I'll show you how I've perfected the British custom of making tea. It's really good to see you, thank you for taking the time to find me. Do you live far from here?"

They settled with their tea and some biscuits and Gwen told him of her journey back, and of Marion's resolve to stay.

"I think if you'd been there, she would've come away, but without you duty won through. I know she was torn and I'm sure she tells you of her decision in her letter." She handed it over with a flourish.

How he controlled himself not to ignore Gwen and tear open the envelope was a credit to his mannered upbringing.

"What will you do now you're back?"

"I'll try at a London hospital: they need volunteers, I'm sure they'll welcome someone with training. Matron gave me a reference and Sister Wilkins a document of the syllabus I've covered. The ideal is to train still while I work for them, but it all seems a bit chaotic at the moment; I'll have to go and talk to them. I want to have something arranged before my mother has me join her ladies circle, knitting socks or rolling bandages."

"I can imagine, that sounds pretty dire to me."

"I enjoyed such freedom in Brussels and will not return to the chaperoned world of my parents. I'm sure that's what convinced Marion to stay, although she likes to talk of duty and other lofty virtues. I was more concerned with what I'd be eating: the soup had become very thin by the time I left."

Russell sensed a competitive edge to Gwen and this was swiftly reinforced by an invitation that followed.

"Whilst I'm at home for the next couple of weeks we could meet up and I could show you some of the local sights. We can't tell Marion about it though as no post is getting through. It would be our secret." Gwen laughed, to diminish the impact of the betrayal.

Russell laughed too. "I had all my jaunts this summer. I'm afraid it's head down and hard work from here for me. And I do write to

Marion, every day; even though they can't be posted, she can read them one day."

The door of opportunity clanged shut for Gwen and she raised herself from her chair. She shook his outstretched hand and the look that passed between them was direct. She had tried and failed, but the glint in his eye conveyed that he did not mind the attempt.

"I've posted Marion's letters to her family, so they'll know of her decision. Her mother won't be pleased. Marion told me of the war of wills that exists between the two of them; I decided not to deliver that news by hand in case she shot the messenger."

"I'm so grateful to you for you bringing Marion's letter, it's too easy for post to get lost at the college. Leave me your address so we can keep in contact: you never know, either one of us may get some news through from Brussels."

Russell now smiled at the memory of Gwen's visit. He had left out the invitation she had extended to him from his daily letter to Marion; he did not want to introduce any friction into their friendship. His letters to Marion were in a bundle next to the bed, along with correspondence for her from her family; he had collected these letters himself. Marion's letter to him had contained her family address and on their behalf she had extended Drake family hospitality to him should he find himself in their area. He had used this to contact them when he knew of his return to Brussels. They had been most hospitable.

"So, tell me, Mr Clarke, what is it you say you'll be doing in Brussels?" Marion's father asked.

"Mr Drake, please call me Russell. I've been asked to help with the efforts to feed the Belgian people."

"America to the rescue," piped in Mrs Drake, but Russell was unable to interpret the tone. "We're concerned about Marion, the reports in the newspapers are dreadful; the Germans have done such terrible things, we've no idea if she is safe."

"We do," Mr Drake said. "She told us so in her letter: she said Brussels had surrendered to the Germans, so no harm would befall them."

"How can we take their words for anything? Look what they did in Leuven, deplorable," Mrs Drake continued.

Russell blanched at the mention of Leuven. He scanned the newspapers each day and had read articles on the German atrocities in Belgium. He had wondered if reports had been exaggerated. Each country had to take a position to feed the fervour of the population against the enemy; how else was Kitchener going to secure the numbers he needed for his new army? But when he had read about the vandalism of the city he loved and that the library had been torched, he had actually cried. He had written about it quite openly in his daily letter to Marion, and although he could not adequately put into words the grief he felt about the loss of the manuscripts, it had touched him in a way that deaths of the people did not.

"I am sure it must be safe there, otherwise I wouldn't have been recruited to return, but they are short of food."

"We have Belgians here in the village, refugees; there were too many in London, so they've been sent to the Home Counties. My ladies knit for them, those that aren't knitting socks for the soldiers, that is; some wool can be too harsh for one's fingers." Mrs Drake rubbed her imagined blisters. "I know they are God's children," she said as she looked at her husband, "but I'm still not entirely sure why it's us that they have turned to for help, and now the Americans will be feeding them. We've our own poor that need assistance. Will there ever be enough to go around?"

Mr Drake, with a practised air, smiled at his wife and then ignored her comments and directed himself to Russell.

"How does one feed a nation that has no food of its own? What a task, and in such circumstances. I'll be interested to hear how this is managed; who's in charge of the operation?"

"I actually know very little at the moment, Mr Drake. It was my friend … well, an acquaintance, when I was in Brussels who contacted me: Hugh Gibson, he's the secretary of the American legation. Mind you, by the time I left he'd picked up the keys of so many embassies, I'm sure he wonders who he does represent. It was a chaotic time."

Russell enjoyed his afternoon with Mr Drake who was interested to hear about Russell's experiences in Brussels, particularly the conversations he had been privy to with the minister and the king at Parliament. Mrs Drake soon lost interest, and busied herself with organizing a high tea when it became apparent her husband would like him to stay.

Over crumpets and cake Mrs Drake interrupted them: "I know you came to collect letters for Marion, but her sisters and I thought of a few things that she might like and her father put in some newspapers. Can you take it all with you?"

He had brought them all. Thoughts of Marion had crowded his head for weeks, and today he would see her. He knew he had a day of work ahead of him first, but he would try to get a message to her so they would meet that evening. He sat with Hugh at breakfast.

"It was Hoover's idea to get a Rhodes Scholar to help so I dug around a bit and came across your name. You'd made yourself so useful before, I thought you'd be just the chap we needed. Delighted you could come but sorry to upset your studies. Were they okay about it at the college?"

"You've no idea how sure they were. Mr Hoover is a big name within the scholarship programme and when his letter arrived, they couldn't pack me off quick enough. I had a hero's send-off and will be welcomed back with open arms, but I still have no idea what I'm here to do."

"Good of you to come back when you're blind to the task, but some how I thought you might like to return when you realized Nurse Drake had stayed. Am I wrong?"

"No, you are entirely right," Russell laughed. "I've no defence, I'm smitten. Have you seen her? How is she? I hope to see her this evening."

"Yes, I saw her a few weeks back. I had afternoon tea with Miss Cavell and Marion joined us. She asked after you but ..." Hugh hastily cut off further questions from Russell, "we need to knuckle down to the business in hand; I need to brief you so that we make you useful as soon as possible."

Hugh gave him the background to the newly established Commission for the Relief of Belgium. Russell was astounded to hear that the British had proved difficult and blocked the passage of the food.

"That's where you come in," Hugh said. "It will be your job to account for all imported food and provisions and make sure it stays out of German hands. It's the only way the British will allow it through."

181

Russell had been so caught up with his return to Marion that he had not really thought about what work he might be assigned to. He was daunted by the conversation.

"How can I make it so the Germans don't take the food? That's an impossible task. I'd have to be everywhere."

"No, it just has to be tracked through the books, counted in and counted out through the distribution centres. If any numbers are down then you'll have to investigate but the civic officers will be your agents on location and they'll know what's happening. They have no intention of supplying the German Army: they've suffered enough by their hands already. You'll soon get in the swing of it, I'm sure."

"Will we be working together?"

"Not directly, no, but we'll be here in the same offices. You'll be our working member of the commission. Mr. Whitlock, the minister will obviously be a prominent member, but he can't address the day-to-day matters. There's a full briefing meeting with him at four o'clock today."

"What are you working on at the moment?" Russell asked Hugh.

"I'm part of a panel that has to review the alleged contraventions of the Hague agreement. If the Belgians can't beat the Germans in battle, they are determined to kill them with words. *The Rights of Nations and the Laws and Customs of War* are tomes I am becoming increasingly familiar with."

"Is that the sign of a civilized society, that we have rules for warfare? I can't quite get my mind around that," Russell said.

"Another time for that debate." Hugh rose from the table. "There's a wagonload of papers for you on the desk next to mine, and don't forget the meeting at four o'clock. I might suggest you see your Nurse Drake at lunchtime today. I'm not sure you'll surface again after the briefing, these really are desperate times. Pierre can run a message around for you; I'll send him along. Oh, and good to have you back."

Russell found paper and an envelope and had his note written before Pierre knocked and walked in. He scribbled the address on the envelope and asked Pierre to wait for the reply. Then he found his office and set to work.

3rd October 1914
Brussels
Marion

"I can't believe they'd shoot so many people. One would have been enough to make their point and put the fear of God into everybody. How can they be so cold-blooded? How can soldiers pull a trigger on innocent people?"

Marion thumped the pillow of the bed she was making and Sister Wilkins stood at the window and listened to her rant. News had slowly filtered through to Brussels about a massacre in Dinant. It had taken place at the same time as the fires at Leuven, but Dinant was further to the east and word and evacuees had taken much longer to arrive, and to be believed.

"It's the same story over and over again," Sister Wilkins said. "The Germans say the civilians fired on them."

"Even if that's true it doesn't excuse mass executions, does it," Marion retorted.

"Believe me, I'm not defending them. Their cruelty seems to know no bounds."

"Where is Dinant?" Marion asked. "Why pick on that place? Those poor people, I can't bear to think of what they've been through." Marion sat on the bed she had just made, and ignored the creases she made as she slumped back onto the pillow. "I'm glad we haven't

183

any German soldiers as patients. I don't think I could bring myself to help any of them."

"We have to stay neutral." Sister Wilkins adopted a slightly censorious tone, but Marion was not in the mood to be chastened.

"I heard they put 100 men and boys against a wall and shot them; they set fire to people in their homes; another mass of people were shot outside the magistrate's house, and that included women and children. Children, what do they know about war? What monsters are these to shoot children?"

Marion felt tears start to run down her face. She sat up and gulped in air.

"Try not to upset yourself, Marion, I know it is unimaginable that such things can happen, and just because the Germans are annoyed their plans have been messed up."

"I know, I know." Marion straightened the bed and wiped her face. "Why don't they turn around and march back home? What gives them the right to think that they can take whatever they want, lives, food, property? Their arrogance and inhumanity appal me. I hate them."

Sister Wilkins latched onto the mention of food to divert Marion from another tirade.

"It's time for our coffee and briefing, even though the biscuits these days can be rather cheerless."

At the briefing Edith announced that they would resume their training and that lectures would start up again within a couple of days. Marion was delighted with the news and chuckled at the thought of how Gwen would view her enthusiasm. They had always bemoaned the hours of lectures they had to sit through, both preferring the practical side of the work, but Marion had begun to realize she was often quite bored these days. The clinic had been very quiet after the departure of the refugees. They had no military personnel from any nation to tend and Marion's days had become flat, empty, and long.

After the initial upset when the Germans had marched into Brussels, the city had quickly settled into a new rhythm. It was different. Many shops and businesses were closed and most people on the streets were out of work or homeless. When Marion went out she noticed the absence of young men. Any man of fighting age had been shipped off to Germany, they had thought to prisoner of war camps, but rumours abounded that they were made to work in factories and fields in Germany, while their own businesses and farms were wasted. Although the cafés stayed open, Belgians left if German soldiers arrived to be served. Marion noticed that people huddled together and spoke very quietly, constantly checking that their conversations were not overheard; with reports of spies exposing contraventions, paranoia was rife.

Marion loved to hear of rebellions, like the singing of the Belgian national anthem at night. It had been banned, but a practice developed where the family in one house would sing the first line, the next household the second line and so on down the street; because no one household had broken the rule and sung the whole anthem, no family could be punished. She giggled when she heard it at night. Marion copied the Belgians who would cross the road rather than pass soldiers in the street, and when greetings were offered they were not returned. Soldiers were billeted in private houses throughout the city, and with their privacy invaded the Belgians made no pretence of social niceties; these guests were unwelcome and Marion shared their scorn and disdain.

The clinic had been visited, two weeks earlier, by two German administrators. The number of rooms and beds had been noted, but so far they had not been allocated any military lodgers. Marion accompanied them on their tour and was delighted when the rooms she had blocked off with wardrobes were not noticed; not that any purpose for their secret use had presented itself. After the initial excitement of the war, Marion confessed to herself that life had become dull, so dull that a lecture series suddenly fired her with enthusiasm.

A feeling of isolation had settled on them all at the clinic, with very few letters from home. She had had none. She was confident that Gwen would have posted her letters for her, and Hugh the same. In fact she wouldn't be surprised if Gwen had delivered her letter to Russell by hand. Even though a dear friend, she could understand Gwen offering to play host to Russell as a way of spending time with him. He really did have universal appeal, and Gwen had warned her of losing him if she stayed in Brussels; she really had been a fool.

Marion stayed behind in the room after the briefing finished and the others had left. There was no pressing need to return to the wards so she chatted to the orderly and helped to clear the coffee cups. This was how she picked up most of her local knowledge, not that there was any good news these days. She heard her name called and went to the reception hall to see why.

"Marion, this man has a note for you and says he's instructed to wait on a reply."

Her colleague Nancy appeared to have met the man on the doorstep as she was on her way out.

"Hello, I'm Marion Drake, is that who you're looking for?"

"Yes, I have a note for you," and he handed over an envelope.

"Thank you," Marion replied, and put the letter in her pocket.

"I've been asked to take a reply, so would you mind if I waited?"

"No, of course not. Excuse me a moment and I'll see what it says. Who's it from?" She looked at him as she opened the envelope and pulled out a single piece of paper.

"Mr Clarke," he said at the same moment as she saw Russell's name at the bottom of the page. She gasped.

"Is he here?"

"Yes miss, he's at the legation. That's where I've come from and I must return promptly."

"Oh, I'm sorry, yes I won't delay you. Let me read this and find some notepaper for a reply."

She turned away and read the invitation in Russell's handwriting to meet for lunch that day. Today? Today! He really was here! How could that be when she had thought him in Oxford, and what was he doing here? The questions tumbled through her mind and she could not think straight. Could he call for her at one o'clock? He would only have two hours, but really hoped he could see her. He apologized for the short notice and would understand if it was not possible. Not possible? Not possible was not an option for Marion; she could not believe he was in Brussels.

Sister Wilkins looked startled when Marion almost fell into her office.

"He's back. Could I be excused duties until this afternoon, so that I can meet him for lunch? I'll be back for three o'clock and can make up the time. Do you have a piece of paper I can use and a pen? I have to send a reply."

"Who's back? Where are you going?" Sister Wilkins automatically rummaged for a pen and a piece of paper; she handed them to Marion.

"Russell, Mr Clarke, the American, my American, from the embassy. He's here and has asked me to lunch; I had no idea, it's such a surprise."

"Well, a delightful one by the looks of it. It's fine for you to go. It's not as if we are rushed off our feet."

"Oh thank you so much."

Marion's attention turned to the note she had to write and she wasted no time at all. Within minutes she was back in the hall handing her reply to Pierre with her thanks.

"I can make the appointment with Mr Russell at one o'clock."

"I'll take your message to him straight away, miss."

Marion looked at the time. She had two hours to get ready and the way her hands were shaking she would need every minute that was available to her. She almost ran to her room.

He was late and every minute after one o'clock stretched her nerves; they had become increasingly taut in the previous two hours. She started to pace backwards and forwards across the hall and had just decided to wait on the front steps when the doorbell rang and he was there.

"Sorry I'm late, I was caught by Hugh as I was leaving. He sends his regards by the way. It's great to see you, thank you for coming to lunch."

"You're talking too much," she said as she grabbed the lapels of his jacket and pulled him towards her for a kiss, then took his arm, walked down the steps and let him lead her along the street to the restaurant Hugh had recommended.

"I can't believe you're here," she said. "What are you doing here?"

"You didn't get my letter, did you?" Russell said when Marion paused to take a breath.

"I haven't had any correspondence for months."

"Well, I can change that immediately." Russell laughed with delight as he passed a package across to Marion.

"What's this?"

"Letters from your family."

"My family, what are you doing with them?"

Russell laughed; they'd reached the restaurant.

"I'll tell you when we've ordered. Are you hungry?"

"You'll soon learn not to ask that question around here." Marion allowed herself to be seated and they both listened to the meal choices of the day. Food was now so restricted that menus were not used; the proprietors used the freedom to charge the German soldiers a higher price than the locals. Their selections made, Russell started to address the bombardment of questions thrown at him by Marion.

"Gwen came to see me and gave me your letter."

"I'm sure she did."

Russell side-stepped the innuendo. "It was so thoughtful of you to give me the address of your folks. When I knew I was to come back I contacted them and said I'd collect any letters they had for you. What I've given you is the tip of the iceberg."

"More letters?" Marion felt the weight of the package he'd handed over.

"No, I think that's all the letters, but I have a suitcase of items packed by your sisters and mother, things they thought you might be short of; I've no idea what's in it, but I'll ask Pierre to bring it round to you later today."

Tears had sprung into Marion's eyes; the mention of her family brought them close but at the same time emphasized the miles between them.

"How are they? Who did you see? Did you meet my father?"

"Not your sisters, but your parents and they seemed very well. I thoroughly enjoyed my visit; your father and I could've enjoyed further conversation. He is a delightful man."

"The same delight was not there with my mother, I'm sure, or did she succumb to your charms?"

"Now how would I know that? She was very polite and hospitable and I'm sure I outstayed my welcome."

"Did she ask about your parents?"

"Yes she did, and about my studies and what I'd been doing in Brussels."

"If she asked about your parents, that wasn't out of politeness; she would've been assessing your suitability."

"Suitability for what?"

"As a suitor, for me; any acquaintance of mine would have to be vetted by my mother. Did she seem satisfied with your answers?"

"I really don't know, Marion. I know your father tried to divert her attention a few times, but really, I didn't mind their questions.

I want them to know me, and to be with them made you feel closer. I loved every minute of my visit and I love you too."

Marion shut her mouth. She had been about to launch into a tirade about what an embarrassment her mother could be and had been, many times in the past, when she registered what he had said. She reached her hand out to him across the table and they only let go to make room for the plates when they arrived.

The meal seemed to be over in an instant and they were both reluctant to leave the restaurant, but she understood that he had an important meeting that afternoon. Marion was in quite a daze. The suddenness of his invitation and arrival still had her in a state of shock. She had not taken in half of what he had told her; it was enough for her to hear his voice, touch him and know that his heart sang in the same way as hers. The rush of happiness when he said he would be working in Brussels showed her just how lonely she had been. He held her in close against him as they walked arm in arm back towards the clinic.

Marion had no appetite that evening so she skipped supper, and read and reread the letters Russell had passed on from her family. She wanted to tell the others about the news from home, but knew to be sensitive. She would have been very envious if roles had been reversed. She imagined Russell sitting with her father and was thrilled to find a postscript on the letter from him where he had written *I very much like your young man; give this one a chance M, love Papa.*

Russell's self-assured confidence and easy manners would delight her father, but might have slightly thrown her mother who liked to keep the upper hand in social settings. She would not have been able to wrong-foot him and he would not have looked to her for the assurance that other bashful beaux had sought. For her mother to have served tea to an American would create a stir at her next coffee morning and a welcome distraction from the knitting and bandage rolling that she referred to in her letter.

Despite the good cheer contained within all their letters she was not blind to their concerns for her and her situation, so misplaced when that morning the only thing she had feared was dying from boredom. That had changed with the arrival of Russell. She felt

189

heady from his declaration of love, however rashly that might have been said in the excitement of their reunion. The lectures timetabled for the following days held less appeal than when they had been announced; her attention now was on when she could next see Russell.

Give this one a chance, her father had written, and she promised him and herself that she would.

22nd October 1914
Forest of Mormal
Isabelle

Isabelle and Jacqueline were on their way to the Forest of Mormal; it was her turn to walk while Jacqueline drove a small cart, pulled by a donkey. The small beast could only manage the extra weight of one person. This basic means of transport had come from the de Croy estate. The princess had loaded the cart with provisions of fruit, vegetables, and a little meat, all covered by a thick layer of brushwood. In their old clothes the girls could easily pass as peasants and blend in with the forest inhabitants.

The small village of Englefontaine was just inside the boundary of the forest. It had been arranged for them to meet with the baker who would take them on to where the soldiers were camped, and help them with the supplies. Isabelle was pleased to walk and waved Jacqueline aside when it was her turn on the carriage; she was excited with the thought of seeing Lieutenant James Baxter again, and only wished that the donkey would move at a faster pace.

Baxter and the men had stayed close to the village at first, but recently, as German patrols increased in the area, they had been forced deeper into the forest. Their numbers had now swelled to 20 largely due to the efforts of the two girls, who had scoured the villages for soldiers.

Isabelle came to the forest as often as she could to see the British men, and more especially James. Somehow she always managed to find time alone with him. She had wondered whether this was engineered by him, or whether his men, and indeed Jacqueline, sensed an undercurrent between her and James and kept their distance for this reason. There was no doubt that a bond had developed between Isabelle and the English officer; she found him charming and loved the way laughter came so easily to both of them. She was strongly attracted to him. She did not doubt that she was being seduced by the glamour of a good-looking foreigner and the excitement of the situation, but she liked their risqué banter.

This was the first time the girls had visited the British soldiers since they had moved camp; they needed the elderly baker to lead them to the new hiding place. It was late morning when they arrived, and he had finished his main work of the day. He had time and bread to spare.

The donkey and cart had to be left in the village; the forest paths were too narrow to let them pass, so the provisions were loaded into a selection of bags and baskets provided by the man's wife. They followed him along a number of trails that became progressively overgrown and they laboured hard with the bags they carried. Just as Isabelle felt her arms were going to give out their guide stopped, put down his load, and they all rested. He looked strong and stocky, with bandy legs. What hair he had left on his head grew in strange tufts, and his smile displayed an assortment of missing teeth.

"Almost there ladies, one more path to go, but it's the hardest." He shouldered his bags, turned around and set off again. Isabelle and Jacqueline bent down to collect their bags and when they straightened up the man had disappeared. The undergrowth was high all around them. Isabelle looked at Jacqueline and saw the same surprise she felt in her friend's features; both girls started to laugh and lost control in the hysterical way that can escalate between friends. They had dropped the sacks and baskets and were holding onto each other when the baker stepped out of the bushes to one side of them. His amiability had been replaced by anger.

"Please, ladies, quiet," he hissed at them. "You are too loud, this hooting is dangerous, and will be heard from far away. You risk everything. Are you children, for God's sake? Now pick up your things and follow me."

The girls obeyed immediately; Isabelle reddened with guilt and embarrassment. This time they watched carefully as the baker led them onto a track that could scarcely be seen; once they were through he arranged the foliage to conceal the opening.

After five minutes of hard-going down a path that wound in and out of the trees, he stopped and reached out and pulled a piece of twine that Isabelle saw was twisted among the branches; they waited. Over his shoulder Isabelle saw movement in the gloom ahead; a man was threading his way through the trees towards them. At a dozen paces they could clearly make out a soldier in British uniform, and he carried a rifle.

"Stay where you are please," he stated firmly. Isabelle peered at him and exclaimed with delight, "Samuel, it's us, Isabelle and Jacqueline, we've found you again, thank heavens."

Samuel Elliott smiled back at her. "Nice to see you again, miss, both of you. I thought I heard some shouting a short while ago and was worried there was some trouble coming this way. Was everything all right?"

"Yes, sorry Samuel, Jacqueline and I were stupid, but we'll be more careful in future. How are you all, and James?"

"The lieutenant is fine, miss, and doing a grand job considering what little we've got, especially now we've had to move further away from the village. He keeps everyone busy and has a couple of sergeants to help him, good ones luckily, not like some I've had. We've just finished building a large dug-out; but food is more difficult to get now: we rely on people like Monsieur Leon here," and he nodded a respectful greeting to the baker.

"Follow me, and I'll show you our new base camp. I'll just tell them friends are on the way."

Samuel went over to the twine and pulled on it three times, then bent to pick up some of the girls' bags. He paused.

"Oh, er, ladies, look, the thing is, do you remember the one of us called Culloch, Bill Culloch?"

"Of course," Isabelle said.

"Well, he's got himself into a bit of trouble ..."

"Have the Germans caught him?"

Samuel did not respond to her question. He looked awkward, and carried on.

"With all of us actually, and, well ..." he tailed off.

Jacqueline had picked up her friend's concern and looked to her for a translation.

"The thing is, Lieutenant Baxter has been a really good officer, and I'm not just saying that because you like him. Oh, er, beg pardon, miss." Isabelle knew she had blushed, but she waved for him to continue.

"Anyway, we've all been hard at it since we came into these woods, well organized you see, and that makes the difference. We've made a dug-out, and hidden it well. We have three men on alert all the time, and there's careful patrolling. The discipline's been good, and no grumbling. When we came here the lieutenant said no one was to leave without permission, and certainly not go back to the village. We all agreed that was only right, but it was a shame because everyone there was very good to us and we had a grand time when we were in the huts. Hardly wanted for anything. I reckon they would've shared everything with us if it came to it. Now, Bill Culloch, I guess he missed it too much, because one of our guards caught him as he tried to creep back into the camp one night. He stank of drink and it was obvious where he'd been; didn't even try to deny it either. He just glared at us all, and believe me, everyone was mad at him. He wasn't much liked in the first place and now he'd put us all in danger. Well, some of the lads reckoned he should be shot, but the lieutenant did things properly and held a sort of court martial, and that's why you'll see him tied to a tree."

"What do you mean?" Isabelle asked.

"That's his punishment, miss. He's been tied to a tree, for a day, with no food, and he's gagged in case he plays up. Had to be a severe punishment, the lads wouldn't have put up with less. Quite a few thought he got off far too light, considering the risk. If he'd been caught he's just the sort who would tell where we all were, for a few favours. Afraid he's not been much liked, miss. Well, now you know, we'll get on."

Isabelle quickly explained to Jacqueline what she had been told, and they had picked up their bags to follow Samuel when they were joined by another soldier. He appeared from the undergrowth, presumably to check on Samuel's whereabouts. Monsieur Leon, the baker, followed the party.

It took them another ten minutes to reach the base and on the way yet another string had been pulled to warn another sentry of their approach. The system was impressive, Isabelle thought, and it thrilled her to see this proof of James's professional ability. She was thinking of James when she nearly bumped into another soldier, only this one was fixed rigid and staring malevolently at her. She brought her hand up to her mouth to stifle a scream of surprise. Jacqueline, who was following close behind, bumped into her, which pushed her onto him. It was Culloch with his hands behind his back, bound to a tree trunk, his mouth gagged with a leather strap. She recoiled and pulled herself away and with a few more strides entered the small clearing that was currently home for the soldiers. There were half a dozen of them in front of her, including James who was talking to one of his sergeants, a middle-aged man. James turned as the small party approached and smiled broadly at them, though his eyes were focused on Isabelle.

"Isabelle, Jacqueline, hello, and Monsieur Leon, it's so nice to see you again. I hope you were careful, we know the Germans are sweeping the forest more thoroughly now. Here, let me take those."

He came up to the girls and helped them with their bags. In the process his hand made contact with Isabelle's and he gave it a small squeeze, a gesture unseen by the others. For Isabelle that one moment of intimacy had huge meaning: she knew their desire was mutual. James showed the two girls around the area. The dug-out had just been finished and had room for up to 20 men with the entrance cleverly disguised by a bramble and brushwood screen attached to some thick branches. They only had five rifles between them, and less than 60 rounds of ammunition; fighting their way out of an ambush was clearly impossible. Their first priority was to remain hidden and avoid contact with anyone except for the few villagers who still provided them with food.

Isabelle was amazed to see that the men were clean and tidy though inevitably some clothing now needed repair, so Jacqueline and Isabelle settled down to the task. James sat next to Isabelle and they talked while she worked at the garments. They were both sitting on an old overcoat, near the dug-out on the edge of the clearing; Jacqueline was with a small group to the other side of the entrance. Every so often a soldier would appear from the woods and speak to the sergeant and then move off again. Isabelle could see that the patrol routine was well established; little wonder Culloch's exploits had caused resentment.

The conversation flowed easily with James and she enjoyed the looks they exchanged; they seemed to hold more meaning than their words, but she did find out quite a bit about him. He was the only son of middle class parents; his father was a horse breeder, a profession James said he would like to follow after his army career. In too short a time, they heard Monsieur Leon clearing his throat to gain their attention; he was anxious to leave. James smiled at Isabelle and she tried to smile back, but regret at having to leave made her lips tremble. He turned to face her and she moved to kiss him: their lips made contact as if they had been lovers for years. As quickly as they touched they drew back and both turned their heads to see if anyone had seen them. No one had, so they kissed again.

Isabelle felt giddy with the heat that swept through her; she opened her mouth to invite further intimacy and James held the back of her neck as he put pressure on her lips. They were lost in each other, but their union was suddenly shattered by gunfire and in an instant James had gone.

22nd October 1914
Leuven
Therese

She could not escape the fact that she was pregnant. She had recognized the symptoms she had been experiencing over the last month or so, familiar from watching her sister and mother at home. Two years older than Therese, and with a brother in-between, she and her sister had been close in years, but not in nature nor as friends. Nicole had been her father's favourite. She was always sitting on his lap and being petted by him, but Therese had never let him near her. She had learnt to adopt a prayerful repose whenever she had sensed his predatory gaze and this had kept him at a distance. Her sister was expecting her second child when Therese had joined the convent. The father of her children had never been named.

It was while Therese had mimicked being in God's thrall that she actually found herself in true communion with Him. What had begun as a sham, to shame and distance her father, had turned into her own salvation and vocation. Her connections and conversations with her family lessened; she spent more time away from the house and from them and, when there, in silence. They had pandered to her whims and ways and had allowed her to continue to learn from books, rather than work in their fields. She had always done her fair share of household chores and helped to prepare food for their meals, but her hands were the softest of them all. They were proud of her learning, but it drove a further wedge of separation between them all; she had been different.

But now, now she was the same. She had felt herself elevated, above the needs of the flesh, a pure channel for God's charity and love; but she was no longer pure, she was soiled, and spoiled. Why had this happened? Had she held herself in too high regard that she had to be humbled? Was it a façade that she was untouchable, God's own, and this was the penalty for such pride? However harsh a view Therese tried to take of her circumstances, to see this as a punishment, she was unable to hold this view for long. Her God was a forgiving God. He did not mete out punishment, He taught through gentle nudges and reminders. He had told her in her vision to believe that He was with her, even when she could not see Him in the usual way; this was certainly an unusual situation, but however hard she tried she could not feel upset that there was a baby growing within her. He—and she was sure it was a boy—was a new soul and she was the vessel chosen to bear him into the world. Not her choice, but that was the way it was, and not for her to question or doubt.

Therese had not spoken about her condition, but she sensed that Sister Paul knew. Her habit was shapeless so no bump showed and any growth could stay hidden for months, but Sister Paul was a confidante in waiting.

"Sister Paul, could I have some time with you today?" Therese asked as they met at breakfast. It was hard not to meet, there were so few of them in the community now.

"Yes, come along with me now, dear. Perhaps we can talk as we fold the sheets."

Therese did not know where to start with the conversation so they began to work together in the laundry room in a companionable silence. It was Sister Paul who broke it.

"Therese, it has been lovely to see you heal and repair after your ordeal. You still receive God's blessings and it's wonderful that you've stayed open to them; too many people fold in on themselves in times of trouble. God still needs the invitation to stay present; it's wonderful to witness your faith. Was there something concerning you?"

Thankfully, after such glowing accolades, thought Therese, she had no concerns about her faith. She'd hate to disappoint and add to Sister Paul's worries.

"I'm pregnant," she said at the moment in their dance with the sheets when they had both stepped up close to each other. She handed over the ends of the sheet she had held and stooped to collect the folded sides; she stepped back to pull out the creases and both held the tension, then she handed her ends back to Sister Paul, who took the weight and managed the final folds on her own.

"Shall we go to my office or the garden?"

"I'd prefer the garden." Therese and Sister Paul left the chores to find a seat under the boughs of a tree. Therese sat and rested her arms on her stomach, on the baby; she suddenly felt fiercely protective. Now that her secret had been voiced, she felt he was exposed.

"I've known for some weeks, but many babies are lost early on; my mother lost several, but I feel this one will stay."

Therese saw the question in Sister Paul's demeanour and continued.

"I'm all right, physically. I've had some sickness, but inside me, my head, my heart, I'm all right. I am honoured to be a vessel for a soul, this life. I feel no separation from God, no punishment in this. If truth be told, I feel quite joyful."

She stopped, a frown had appeared on Sister Paul's face.

"I'd not expected to hear those words. Oh, don't misunderstand me, I had thought to hear you were in this condition and I'm pleased that you've told me, but I had not anticipated such an acceptance of your condition, and certainly not joy. This situation is such a departure from our devotional life and is fraught with difficulties. I had certainly not expected to hear talk of joy."

Through prayerful meditation, Therese had been able to separate the thought of the child within her from the violence of the rape, but she had not explained this to Sister Paul. It was understandable that Sister Paul could not appreciate her joyfulness. She tried to explain.

"In my mind the two events are unconnected. The attack is separate from the life within me. I had no choice but to succumb to the violent will that was waged against me, but at midnight, in a flaming town, life was seeded within me, and I feel God's blessing in this."

"How can you speak of God's blessing after such a violation; nothing that comes from this is from God. The Devil was abroad that night," Sister Paul almost hissed with indignation. "Your purity has been destroyed, your body has betrayed your vows; you must keep your innocence and reject every part of this."

Therese felt shocked, chastened, and censured. She had been about to describe her vision to Sister Paul. It had brought her such comfort, but with a flash of insight she realized she must keep quiet.

The vision had come a few weeks after the attack. In it she had seen St. Pierre's alight and had watched as the flames and smoke writhed and danced against the night sky. As she watched, the smoke had taken the shape of a big mallet and it had beaten down on her with the words "My will", "My will" repeated over and over. The smoke had then disappeared and the dancing flames had formed into an arc, and one end of the arc had headed towards her and touched down on her, like a fork of lightening. She had felt a bolt of energy surge through her and when she awoke she knew she was going to have a baby. Sickness every morning had soon followed, but her spirit had felt enlivened.

Therese looked at Sister Paul; they were in uncharted waters, but it was apparent to Therese that there was a set of expectations about how she should react. She pictured the help that would be available to her if she had presented herself as a broken spirit, instead of repulsion from Sister Paul at her expression of joy.

"I have spoken to the bishop. He returned to Leuven last week," Sister Paul said. "He had met with Mother Superior, who is safe and well with the rest of our community, near Brussels. They discussed just this eventuality and decisions have been made. Now don't worry my dear, you will not be sent home."

"Sent home" screamed in Therese's head. Sent home, the thought hadn't crossed her mind and a look of horror must have passed across her face.

"The Church will stand by you," Sister Paul continued, "and will assist you to renew your vows. Now that is a blessing that will come from this. The bishop himself will hear your avowals and will cleanse you, but this will be after the event. You are to stay here for your pregnancy. There are only a few of us here so your condition can largely remain unnoticed; we ask that you speak of it to no one other than myself. A few weeks before your time you'll go to

200

Brussels, to a private clinic for the birth, and then to a closed order to prepare for your cleansing."

"The child, what will happen to the child?" Therese whispered.

"The progeny will be taken to an orphanage and will be no concern of yours."

So well rehearsed, Therese thought, the speech and arrangements were thought through and organized, but instead of feeling relief she felt suffocated and stood up to take in a large breath of air. Sister Paul looked surprised.

"Are you feeling all right, Therese, you look rather pale?"

"I think if you'll excuse me, I'll go and lie down."

"If you must. We can continue our conversation later. I'll come and find you."

Therese nodded her head and left Sister Paul before she was required to say anything else; she could not trust herself to speak. Her mind was in a complete whirl and she needed time alone to order her thoughts. She felt immense relief when she reached her room, shut her door and threw herself on the bed. She sank into her turmoil.

The nature of the conversation with Sister Paul had taken Therese by surprise. She had spent a lot of time alone recently, and thought herself resolved on many aspects of the attack and the subsequent consequence, her baby. She put her hand on her body where he lay, determined that he should feel welcomed. It had struck her that Sister Paul could not even refer to him as a baby or a child and had strongly implied he was the Devil's spawn. She knew this was wrong and that her baby was innocent, God's creature, even though born of violence.

Should she feel angry about the abuse she had experienced? Perhaps she should but she could not find the anger in her. She was a faceless victim of war; the spoils always went to the victor. The attack had nothing to do with her, she just happened to be in the wrong place at the wrong time, or perhaps, if this was God's will, then the right place at the right time. Either way, she had nothing to apologize for, and her mind did not need to be cleansed, nor vows renewed. She had never felt as close to God as she had over the past few weeks: she felt in step with Him and His will. She was indignant, that was the word. Discussed and decided upon in absentia, and she was to remain as absent as possible. She was an embarrassment; the thought jolted her and she sat up: they really had discussed whether to send her home. These were her people now, her family, but it was as if she had broken a rule, stepped out of line and it was they who would tell her what she needed to do to fit back in. She was familiar with obedience, so why did she have a problem with their plans?

Therese had handed over her independence when she took her vows. She had given her will and sense of self to God and to the community. She should accept everything they organized on her behalf, and actually, as she reflected, she could accept all that was arranged for her. Her concern rested with the baby. She felt she had a duty of care for this child that went beyond just bringing him into the world; he deserved more than the loveless existence of a Church orphanage. She had taught orphans and could see how starved of affection they were. They could not look the world in the eye. She promised him a better life and drifted into sleep with that thought on her mind.

Therese felt refreshed after her sleep. She opened her eyes and watched a shaft of sunlight come in through the window and onto her body, just where the baby lay. She put her hands onto her stomach to feel the warmth of the rays and felt a sense of peace; all would be well, she just had to trust in God. She had a smile on her face when Sister Paul entered the room.

"Are you feeling rested my child?"

"Yes, Sister Paul. I feel much better, much better indeed."

"Good, that's good. We don't want your health to suffer during this time."

"True, but we also don't need to make a fuss over this do we. I'll continue in my normal way and assume that no one will notice anything is amiss." Therese wanted to diminish the size of the problem she represented to Sister Paul, the bishop, and any other involved parties; the less they concerned themselves with her, the more freedom and flexibility she would find.

"Splendid, and I will accompany you when you go to Brussels."

"Oh, there'll be no need for that; this small matter will be quite straightforward for me to manage."

"It's a long time since you were out in the world, Therese, and me too for that matter. We'll take advice as we near your time. Who knows what the situation will be then. Hopefully this war will be over and we can put the whole of this episode behind us."

"Did the bishop say anything of the progress of the war, and what of the refugees?"

Sister Paul seemed to welcome the opportunity to turn the conversation away from Therese.

"Yes, he said circumstances were difficult in Brussels. All telegraph connections were down and post stopped, so it was difficult to have contact with anyone outside the country, but he'd heard that many thousands of refugees had made it across to England. Whether any were from Leuven I couldn't say; he seemed to think that most people who escaped from here had gone to Brussels, but food was in short supply. He said news of the fires in Leuven had caused an international outrage; journalists from abroad had taken pictures and told of the devastation. The bishop himself is on a committee to represent the troubles inflicted on Belgium by the German Army."

"He must have my notebooks; are they still in Mother Superior's office, or did she take them with her?"

"I don't know, but they're august men on the committee and I'm sure they'll find all the information they need. It's not our place to meddle in the ways of the world, and certainly not where the bishop is concerned."

For the second time that day Therese felt diminished by Sister Paul, and yet the vision of the information she had collected and its importance was still clear to her. The day of reckoning would come and the stories she had written down would convince any court. Of that she was certain. She felt at odds with Sister Paul and wondered why they were so out of step with each other, when usually they were so close.

Sister Paul had understood her calling instantly when, during their first interview Therese had described her conversations with God whenever she stood in the shafts of sunlight. It had been the shafts of golden light that beamed down onto the convent that had shown Therese where God wanted her to be. Radiance had filled the room, and both their faces on that occasion, but it was not present between them today.

The world and its ways had penetrated her sanctuary and her body. Therese yearned for the time when she could once again be a channel, purely for God. Man's determination had stepped between her and God just as her wilfulness made her stand separate from Sister Paul. Her spiritual energy was sapped and she longed for solitude and His light.

22nd October 1914
Forest of Mormal
Isabelle

Isabelle saw James and the sergeant reach an entrance to a path on the other side of the clearing at exactly the same time, but it was James who disappeared into the bushes first. He had moved so fast Isabelle could still feel the imprint of his lips on hers when he had disappeared. Isabelle and Jacqueline were quickly bundled into the dug-out where they sat with some of the men and Monsieur Leon. He was soon snoring in the corner, but luckily not too loudly. There were a few grumbles when Culloch was brought in, still bound and gagged, and he sat with his back to everyone else. The gunfire sounded muffled through the screen of the dug-out and although it seemed to be a distance away, Isabelle was anxious for James. It was some time before he and the rest of the men, apart from those left on guard, joined them. It was a German patrol in the woods, and James thought they had found a camp that some French soldiers had made about three-quarters of a mile away. His patrols had spotted the French a few days before, but they had not approached them and all now saw the wisdom of this separation.

James left his sergeant to brief his men further and he shuffled across to Isabelle and Jacqueline and told them they had to wait until nightfall before it would be safe to leave. He sat next to Isabelle and after a few shifts of weight she felt the pressure of his thigh which she returned. Isabelle understood that James could show no sign of their new-found intimacy in front of the others, but from time to time she caught his eye in the little light that was available in the makeshift bunker and the look he gave her made her flush; she was numb and uncomfortable but was determined not to move and lose the contact that they had. It was a long wait, only interrupted by a change in the guard: each one had less to say in answer to the sergeant's questions and after three clear reports, James declared it was safe for them to leave.

By now it was dark and movements were clumsy, their bodies stiff and cold; Isabelle was tired and would have preferred to settle down to sleep rather than struggle through the forest in the night, but Monsieur Leon was determined that they should leave. There was no private parting for Isabelle and James, but he did put his mouth close to her ear and whispered her name: it was enough for her.

Monsieur Leon led them back to the village by an even more tortuous route in order to circle far away from the direction of where the shooting had been, but at least this time their loads were light; nevertheless the girls were exhausted and near to collapse when they reached Englefontaine. Showing the resilience typical of his peasant stock the baker went to fire up his oven, while Isabelle and Jacqueline fell together into the one spare bed in the rooms he and his wife used above the bakery. After just a few hours' sleep they continued back to Bellignies with the donkey and cart; Isabelle felt wearier than ever before. The events and tensions of the previous long day had drained them. They were filthy and bloodied from scratches on their faces and hands from the night-time trek through the woods.

Their first stop at the chateau was the stables, where the donkey was led away by the gardener, who seemed to turn his hand to any task; their second was the kitchen. They were half-way through a milky cup of coffee and a fresh loaf of bread when Prince Reginald came in and sat with them.

"You look as if you've had quite an ordeal, ladies. I hope you're not badly hurt."

"We'll be fine after a bath and a good night's sleep," Isabelle assured him.

"What happened? My sister was concerned at your delay. I only heard of it when I returned from Brussels this morning. She calls you the girl guides, and I hear you have been all over the countryside, unearthing fugitives, truly remarkable. How were Baxter and the men?"

Isabelle and Jacqueline described all the events in the forest the previous day. The prince became agitated when he heard of the German patrol so close to them and the hardship that had followed for them.

"Enough, ladies, that's enough now, you must stop. You've been brave and selfless, but the situation has become far more dangerous, the risks are too great. What concerns me is how long the men in the forest can last. I knew the Germans were sweeping deeper into the woods and I'd hoped they would have given up by now; but every time they find another soldier they seem to increase their efforts. I must insist you keep away from there now, and no more searching for stray soldiers; everyone must be more careful, there's no point in taking unnecessary risks."

"But what about our British friends?" Isabelle blurted out. "They need our help." The thought of not being able to visit James, not to know if she would ever see him again, was too hard for her to bear and tears started down her face. She was too tired to wipe them away.

"There will still be local villagers who can take them supplies." His attempt to reassure her only drove a bigger wedge between her and James and her tears turned to sobs.

"I make sure they get paid for the food they take, and we won't let them take risks. They can arrange to leave the provisions at an agreed point for the soldiers to collect." He stopped when he saw his words made no difference to her anguish and he handed her his handkerchief instead. "You have both been under strain, it's right that you stop."

"We will feel stronger after a rest." Jacqueline walked around the table to Isabelle. "Come on Izz, let's get ourselves back for that bath and bed." Isabelle had contained her emotions enough to say goodbye and thank the prince for his hospitality, but the tears continued down her face for their walk to the village. They had no conversation apart from when Jacqueline said, "You love him, James, you're in love, aren't you?" Isabelle had not been able to reply.

The prince had been right to curtail the girls' activities and to be concerned for the British soldiers; the Germans began a methodical sweep of the forest with tracker dogs and with sentries posted on major tracks. Luckily their search plan appeared to have started in the north-west quadrant away from the location of Baxter and his men, and poor weather hampered their progress, but it was now only a matter of time before they would be found.

After the constant activity of the past few months, it was strange for Isabelle, even something of a let-down, to find herself idle. She had heard from Henri that the school still remained closed, but hoped to reopen before Christmas. She felt somewhat discarded. But the uncertainty over when she might see James again was the hardest thing to cope with. Since her return from the forest she had twice snapped at her mother, something she had never done before, and for which she felt ashamed.

She had taken to calling in at the chateau every few days to see Marie de Croy; if the princess was at home she was always made welcome. The de Croys were the most informed people in the community. Reginald was often away in the larger towns and cities, and both brother and sister had connections through every stratum of local society, from their own labourers up to the town mayors. Isabelle sensed that the princess did not tell her everything she knew, but she always came away with a new piece of information that reassured her that James and the men were still secure. It was enough to hold her steady. On one visit though, the news was different.

1st November 1914
Brussels
Marion

It was the start of a new month and for Marion it felt like the beginning of the most momentous period of her life so far; she was in love and the man she loved was back in the same city. There was nothing unrequited about these feelings; he loved her too. Bursts of energy surged through her, and she wanted to laugh out loud; she was happy and it showed.

To sit still in the lectures that day had been difficult, and there was no chance that she would be able to settle to her books that evening as she was due to see him the next day. It was just as well Edith had invited her to supper in her room that evening with Sister Wilkins; their conversation would force her to concentrate. She really missed Gwen as she was the person to delight with about Russell; with her encouragement, Marion's flights of fancy would have soared. There was no resistance in Marion now to the notion of love and marriage, but she tried to restrain her mind from rushing herself down the aisle.

Marion required little preparation for her supper. A brush through her hair and she was on her way. A knock announced her before she walked into Edith's sitting room, but she was the first there. There was a fire in the grate and its glow warmed the look of a room that was otherwise quite austere. Nothing unnecessary was to be seen and everything had its place. She sat herself in the smallest of the armchairs and watched the flames dance while she waited, which was not for long. She heard Edith's and Elizabeth's voices as they approached the door and she stood up as they entered; with greetings over they brought her into their conversation.

"We were discussing our concerns about the shortage of coal, Marion, a dull subject, but it's the tedium of life that holds our attention at the moment," Edith said. "We must make the most of each fire."

"I've heard that the mines are being worked again, but the coal isn't reaching Brussels," Elizabeth said.

"At least miners will receive wages; they must be some of the few men that are. But who will do the work?" Marion asked. "I thought all the Belgian men had been sent to Germany to work in their factories."

"Perhaps the Germans see the need to keep some industry alive, and they want to keep the trains on the move. They're still moving enormous guns along the tracks, or perhaps they're called cannons, I'm not sure, but I saw some yesterday; they were so heavy the ground trembled," Edith said as she stoked the fire.

"Now Antwerp's fallen the Germans will push themselves further into France," Elizabeth said.

Marion had nothing further to add. She only had a scanty knowledge of the battlefront, and when their conversation took another turn she realized that neither Edith nor Elizabeth knew more themselves.

"We can only hope if the trains run that food supplies reach us," Elizabeth said.

"I think a lot is being done to support us with food. Russell, Mr Clarke, my American friend, has returned to Brussels to work on just this thing. He's only just started, but I'll let you know more as I hear it. I was delighted to hear that our plight is known. Sometimes I feel so cut off, I think we've been forgotten."

"That is good news. He looked a very nice young man. You're delighted with his return too?" Elizabeth winked at Marion.

"Oh yes," and then with a look in Edith's direction, Marion continued, "He met my parents when he was in England and they enjoyed his company. I was very lucky, he brought some letters from them, and my father gave his approval of our friendship."

Marion felt sure she saw the almost imperceptible release of tension in Edith's face with the mention of her parents' knowledge and approval of Russell. She had shifted the responsibility for her wellbeing in this regard back to her parents, and Edith could now enter the conversation as a friend, rather than as a guardian.

"I look forward to meeting him," Edith said. "Perhaps he could accompany Mr Gibson on a visit here, although we haven't seen him for quite a time; these are such busy times for some."

Marion thought that Edith looked tired, unless it was the effect on her face of weight loss. They'd all shed a few pounds, nothing of any great concern, but Edith never carried any excess and looked a little gaunt.

Their conversation was interrupted by one of the kitchen staff with a trolley on which sat their supper of bread, cheese, and pickles.

"I've heard there are very few doctors available for the hospitals in Brussels. Luckily for us", Edith said, "Dr Depage is not of the age to go to one of the field hospitals, so he will continue here at the clinic, but his patient list has all but stopped. No one can afford the fees here at the moment, and for emergencies they can go to the general hospital. I've been asked to send more of our nurses, even if only trainees, to support the public hospitals. They can't pay our normal rate, but it might be better to secure some income through this route; every franc counts. I'll raise it at our briefing tomorrow and see if any want to sign up."

"Won't that disrupt the lecture series if some attend and some don't?" Elizabeth queried.

"We'll have to see how many volunteer", Edith said, "before we decide the impact on the training."

"I think you'll find that many will volunteer. I'd certainly be interested. It's all good practical experience, and", Marion added, "it has been rather quiet. But I know the start of the lectures again has been very popular too."

They were interrupted by a knock on the door by one of the orderlies who said there was a man in reception. Marion could not help herself and was on her feet before he had continued to say that the visitor had asked for Madame Cavell and had been sent by

Dr Depage. Marion was embarrassed by her presumption that it was Russell, but the two other women just laughed.

"Not tonight, Josephine," Edith said to Marion as she followed the orderly out of the room.

"You seem quite taken with this American gentleman, Marion," Elizabeth said. "I'd quite thought you were independent and wanted to avoid such encumbrances. Mind you, that was before you met him, and I'm not sure anyone could resist him; if you don't mind me saying he is a handsome young man."

"I quite agree, and anyway we both work, so who's to say that can't continue."

"Well, babies generally put paid to that," Elizabeth said.

"Babies! I thought I'd rushed ahead in my mind about him, but I've never travelled that distance." They were both laughing when Edith walked back into the room with her guest who she introduced as Mr Capaiu.

It was clear to all that Mr Capaiu was on edge and as if to explain this, he apologized that he was in a hurry. He needed to return home ahead of the curfew. This they all understood, now familiar with the curtailment of their civil freedoms and some people being shot for even small infringements of the prohibitions. The Germans had lost patience.

Edith spoke on his behalf. "Mr Capaiu has two patients that he would like to bring to the clinic and I have agreed to take them in. Dr Depage thought that we might be sympathetic to their needs and I find that I am. Half an hour after Mr Capaiu leaves they will arrive at our back door and I'll make them safe on our premises, and if you both choose, that is all that you need to know. I shall see Mr Capaiu out."

Marion and Elizabeth looked at each other.

"I rather fear she may be doing something rash," Elizabeth said. "And I'm not sure I should support it."

"What do you mean?"

"If the patients can't be admitted through the front door then I don't think they should be admitted at all. Edith may be about to put us all at risk."

"Perhaps it's best that you remain at a distance, Elizabeth. I'll stay here and see what I can do to help; it's too late to make her change her mind, it seems she has pledged her assistance to Mr Capaiu."

We mustn't forget it was Dr Depage who directed him here, and I'm sure he wouldn't invite trouble upon us."

"It's time I finished my evening with you anyway. I still have some numbers to run through for Edith tomorrow. If we release trainees to the general hospital, we still have to make it pay. Do you want to be part of Edith's goings-on? I'm sure she expects her room to be empty when she returns: she almost dismissed us."

"I'm happy to wait and see what she needs; it's probably nothing and our imaginations have run away with us."

"Imaginative or not," Elizabeth said, "people have been shot for hiding Belgian soldiers. Edith knows this, but she is still more likely to be patriotic than sensible. If these patients are soldiers coming onto the premises, my final word on this is be very careful and tell no one. No one can be trusted these days when there's a price tag on such information. Take care, my dear."

Without another word she left Marion and climbed the stairs to her own rooms on the floor above. Marion heard her door shut as Edith walked back in.

"I'm pleased to see you're here, Marion, and that Sister Wilkins isn't; this isn't for her constitution, and I would rather she remain ignorant of the facts. We'll find the right time to tell her what it was about."

"Is it about Yorc?" Marion remembered the password Prince Reginald had left them with.

"Yes, it's as we thought and have made preparation for. There are British soldiers, separated from the rest of the British Army, who want to return to England, and two such are in Brussels this evening. They're in need of a shelter, and one of nursing care. We have much to do, but this is an ideal time for them to arrive as none of the kitchen staff are on duty and we can take them up the back staircase to the room you arranged on the top floor."

"Oh, yes, of course, we must help them." Marion struggled to take in the information and step into Edith's practical outlook.

"I'll go to the kitchen to boil some hot water and watch the back door for their arrival. Why don't you go up and freshen the room. Can you move the wardrobe on your own? If not I'm sure one of these men can assist. I understand that only one of them is injured."

"Yes, I'm sure I can manage. It doesn't need to be moved far. The room is already equipped. I'd left everything there, but had given up on any thoughts of it being used, the fighting had moved so far away from here."

"These men have been in hiding for some months, in the Mons area, I believe. I'm sure many kindnesses have been shown to them by the Belgians, so it's not for us to turn our back on our own." Marion saw Edith glance up to the ceiling as she said these words, as if trying to convey her conviction to Elizabeth in the room above.

"Of course not." Marion was now entirely caught up with the moment. "But Elizabeth did warn me that we need to be very careful and not trust anyone with this news. There's a value on such information so we must be careful."

"And now we must be quick and quiet. They'll be here very soon. I'll bring them to you upstairs as soon as they arrive."

Marion turned to leave the room.

"Marion," Edith almost whispered, and Marion turned back to her. "Thank you, my dear, this is important work, but I know it is dangerous, so please stay alert."

Marion nodded and left.

Marion only had a few minutes to herself in the secret annex to the top ward when Edith arrived followed by two men. Apparently they had approached the back door as soon as they saw Edith turn on the light so she had yet to boil the water. She returned downstairs to do this and asked Marion to settle the men in.

Both men looked exhausted and not particularly clean. They refused to go near the beds until they had washed themselves. Marion had lit the fire in the grate and put water to boil in the iron pot. It had stood there for a few months but it was not water they were going to drink; it did not need to boil, just be warm enough to take off their grime. Introductions were made.

"Hello, I am Colonel Beecham and this is Sergeant Meachin. I know I speak for both of us when I say how grateful we are that you have taken us in."

"Oh, really you must save your thanks for Edith, Madame Cavell, it was her decision to assist; she is the director in charge here."

"Then we will thank her too. Actually would you mind if I sat down? I don't want to upset the bed. It's the first one I've seen since I left England."

214

"The beds are for you, so please, do use them."

Marion stepped forward and helped the colonel to sit. It was then that she noticed his roughly bandaged foot.

"So you're the injured party. Do you mind if I take a look?"

"Please do, but Meachin has an injury too."

"But yours is worse, sir, it's you that needs the nurse. Mine is just a scratch that wants a clean," and Meachin pointed to a crusted mass on his hairline that ran down the side of his face.

"Well, as I'm here, let me start with you, colonel." Marion knelt at his feet and was cutting off his bandage when Edith returned. The bandage was crusted with mud and blood and was hard work to cut through. She tried not to place any pressure on his foot but whenever this happened she heard the colonel draw in his breath, though he made no sound of complaint. Edith handed him a hot drink and suggested to Marion that they soak his whole foot, with the bandages on, in a pot of warm water.

"They might come off more easily then, and the foot will need to be washed anyway."

"The whole of us needs a good wash," Colonel Beecham said. "I don't want to touch those sheets as I am now."

"I've put on some water to heat," Marion said. "It's almost ready."

"Marion and I will return to the kitchen to fetch you some food. It will take us a little while to warm some soup, so I suggest you use this time to remove your clothes and give yourselves a wash. You'll find some nightshirts in the cupboard. Leave your clothes in a pile near the door and we can wash and salvage what we can of those later. When you are ready, perhaps Sergeant Meachin can help you with a pot of water and you can soak your foot. We need to take a look at this tonight, and you too sergeant, so leave that wound for our attention: I don't want you to start a bleed again."

Edith raised her hand to stop them as they started to thank her. "Later gentlemen, for now we all have plenty to attend to." And she and Marion turned and left the room.

Edith and Marion left them for half an hour while they prepared supper. They also set a tray for breakfast and then added some more food for lunch.

"We won't be able to prepare food again until tomorrow evening," Edith said. "There are too many people around during the day and it would invite questions."

As she said this Marion saw that the enormity of what she had taken on had occurred to Edith. For the first time ever she saw Edith flustered.

"We must tell them to keep quiet. We have to remove the dirty water and we must clean their clothes."

Before she could continue Marion interrupted her. "Edith, you are right about everything, but one step at a time. Take the supper tray to them, and I'll make sure the kitchen is left tidy before I join you. I'll bring their food for tomorrow up with me."

When Marion returned to the room, the men had eaten their meal and Edith was stoking the fire. Their clothes were in a neat pile near the door, just as Edith had directed. Marion put the tray of food on top of the cupboard that contained the medical supplies. She opened this cupboard and took out some antiseptic lotion, fresh bandages, and some lint cloth, placed a towel on the floor next to Colonel Beecham and asked him to lift his foot out of the pot where it had been soaking. This had been a good suggestion; the water had loosened the bandage so Marion was able to unwind it without putting pressure on his injury.

"I took some shrapnel in my foot, and I think there's still some in there," Colonel Beecham explained. "It's become harder to walk on, so I'm not sure what you'll find. There's no odour: I asked Meachin to smell it the other day."

Marion knew that by the mention of smell, he meant gangrene, and she was apprehensive. With the bandages removed she could see that his foot was a mess; his sock had become embedded in the wounds and his foot was badly discoloured. Edith was cleaning Sergeant Meachin's wound but she came over to take a look when Marion called her.

"Clean it as best as you can, Marion, but just on the surface, and put a loose dressing on it. I think we'll invite Dr Depage to come and look: this may need surgery."

Her last words were addressed to the British officer.

"I'm in your hands, madam."

"Now you must rest and we'll bring the doctor as soon as we can. There is food enough for you tomorrow. I must ask you to keep quiet; we need to keep your presence secret. We'll pull the wardrobe across the entrance as we leave. There is a pot in the corner for your toilet. Until tomorrow, gentlemen."

Marion took the dirty water out with her and she and Edith returned the wardrobe to its position against the wall and across the opening.

"Come to my rooms first thing tomorrow morning, Marion. I will need to send a message to Dr Depage and it might be safest to use you."

Marion fell onto her bed exhausted. It was well after midnight and three hours after their guests had arrived but sleep evaded her. She was now harbouring fugitives, and the consequences of this were deadly serious. She could only imagine the trouble they would be in if she and Edith were caught. A knot was forming in her diaphragm and she could already feel a tightening in her shoulders as tension started to settle in her body. She tried to pull her face into a smile at the thought of seeing Russell the next day, but the muscles of her face felt taut and her smile forced. What had she got herself into?

3rd November 1914
Brussels
Russell

"I shook hands with him, Marion, and he thanked me for all my efforts and hard work, and he used my name; admittedly Hugh had just whispered it in his ear, but still, he wanted to make sure he was being personal. What a man."

"Who did you say he was?" Marion asked.

"Hoover, Herbert Hoover. He's the mastermind behind the work to feed the Belgians, to feed us here. It all makes sense when he talks, and sounds so simple, but believe me it isn't."

"Who does he work for? Where's the food coming from?"

The questions poured out of Marion and that was one of the things he adored about her, her curiosity. He laughed and brought her to a stop in the street; they had been walking to their favourite café and had reached its door.

"In we go," he said as he steered her to a seat. "I'll tell you all I know, but I have to say I've only just started to understand the scale of the operation myself."

They ordered their drinks and for a moment he watched her as she settled herself into her chair. She shrugged off her coat and shook her hair after she removed her hat. She was still in uniform, one of the rules she had to adhere to when out in the city, and he was pleased to know it kept her safe. She caught him watching her, but he felt no embarrassment and his look continued to linger. He took in the slight flush to her cheeks from their walk in the cold air and her slightly damp hair that curled onto her face. She wriggled her shoulders as she made herself comfortable, but she did not lean back against her chair, and to his attentive eye she seemed less relaxed than usual.

"You look wonderful, as ever," he said and reached across the table and took her hand.

"I'd rather not be in my uniform," she said as she ran her free hand down the front of her apron. "A girl doesn't feel at her best in her work clothes. This apron is so stiff, but it's the red cross on it that's so important."

"This gal looks all right to me," he said, and received a smile in return.

"So", he asked, "what have you been doing? It feels ages since I've seen you. I must apologize for cancelling yesterday. I was caught up with all the arrangements for Hoover's visit. Behind the scenes, of course. Hugh and Mr Whitlock were his hosts, but I have had to keep them up to date with all that has happened in the regions; I've been burning the midnight oil. Sorry, sorry, I asked you what you've been doing and then kept talking. Please tell me, how have you been? I'm so pleased you could make it today instead."

"Yes, it suited me better actually. Yesterday was a busy day."

Russell was enjoying looking at Marion when he realized she had stopped talking. He was not used to prompting her to talk; she normally volunteered as much as he did.

"Have you had more patients? No one sneaking in the back door, not wanting to pay?"

"What on earth do you mean?" Marion pulled her hand from his.

Russell had never heard such a sharp retort from her before; he leant back in his chair and looked at her quizzically.

"I didn't mean anything by it. I thought you'd mentioned the problem of helping refugees who had no money to pay."

"Oh yes, of course, I mean, no we haven't. It's been very quiet in the clinic."

"One minute you're busy, next minute it's all quiet. Come on, tell me what you've been up to?"

"Up to! Nothing. Why? Nothing, of course. What could I be up to?"

Russell was startled.

"Hey, I didn't mean nothing by it. It's just an expression, perhaps it's an American phrase."

"No, of course it isn't, I know the expression. Look, shall we order, then you can tell me all about this important visitor you've had. My lectures don't make for an interesting conversation."

Russell was still not sure why his question had solicited such a charged response and was happy to have the distraction of dealing with the waiter. He had never felt out of step with Marion before, but this conversation was not going well. He wondered if she had been more upset by his cancellation the day before than she had said. He had felt genuinely bad about it, but had been given no choice in the matter; Hugh had been very clear where he needed him to be.

Russell laughed to lighten the moment. "I can't deny it, I've enjoyed myself so much. I'm so pleased I came, it's a fabulous opportunity; I never imagined myself involved in such a humanitarian programme, and to feed so many people, it makes my dusty research seem pretty meaningless now."

"That's just because you are caught up with the moment. When you go back to it, you'll find your interest restored. I didn't think I'd ever enjoy lectures as much as I am at the moment, it just depends what else there is to distract you."

"Maybe, maybe you're right, or maybe it's the time for me to rethink my future."

"But there's no need to rush that, is there? You're not supposed to be going back to Oxford yet, are you? You've only just arrived."

"No, no rush, but I do find myself thinking about it; Oxford seems so distant and this feels so real."

"I know what you mean, but we are so cut off here, it is as if someone has drawn a curtain between us and the rest of the world, and with communication severed it is hard to feel that our old lives are real; my family feels a world away."

"And they felt that separation when I was with them. I hope their letters were good to read." Russell took hold of her hand again.

"Yes, thank you, that was quite a bundle, and my father did manage to add how much he'd enjoyed your company—apparently I'll have to explain myself to him if ever I lose my interest in you."

"Lose your interest? I thought you'd lost your heart. Please tell me that you feel the same as I do." Russell put the back of one hand to his forehead and the other over his heart as he mimed the pose of a forlorn lover that would not have been out of place in a silent movie.

"Stop it, don't embarrass me."

Russell was pleased to see the glimmer of a smile.

"Tell me more about your VIP's visit and your work. I still don't really have an idea of what you're doing. How are you feeding the multitudes?"

Russell needed no further encouragement to distil the picture that had gradually emerged for him. He loved the fact that he did not need to edit or simplify when he talked to Marion; she picked up the threads in his conversation easily and he found his explanations to her helpful for him. It made him realize how much he had absorbed and the unique perspectives he had had exposure to.

"Hoover is not even a politician, he's a mining engineer. He happened to be in London at the start of the war and it was down to his efforts that all the Americans were repatriated."

"Not just down to him, surely? You played your part, remember."

"I was just a small cog in a big wheel, which is what I'll be this time too. It's this man's vision and his ability to galvanize people into action that's so impressive. He has taken on the responsibility to feed the Belgians, and I don't doubt that he'll achieve it."

"But how? Where do you start such a task and what are you doing? What is your job?"

"Your father asked me the same question. At least I have more of an idea now. From what I've discovered so far it was Brand Whitlock, our, sorry my, minister and Villobar, the Spanish minister who started it; they knew Belgium was running out of food fast. Hoover was just about to break up the team that had repatriated the stranded Americans; instead he volunteered his network in London and America to help."

"It's good to hear that the world out there knows about us. Perhaps we're not as cut off as we feel."

"Hoover created an organization, the Commission for the Relief of Belgium, and it's run by him from London. He has a chairman in Belgium, a gentleman called Emile Franqui: he coordinates the regional network of councils through which the food is distributed."

"And where do you fit in?"

"I'm getting to that bit. The problem was your British government. They stopped the food; they wouldn't let it into Belgium."

"What? What do you mean? Of course they didn't."

"Oh yes they did, and before you defend them, they did know of the shortages."

"That's ridiculous. It can't be true."

"It's true, I heard it from Hoover."

"They wouldn't want to starve us."

"No, not the Belgians, but they do want to starve the German Army. They were concerned the food would go to the soldiers. Hoover had to collect assurances from the German high command that no food brought into Belgium, through the CRB—that's our project name—would be requisitioned by them; but the British still wouldn't accept it. They held food ships at their docks, wouldn't release them."

"Why would they accept the word of these monsters? I wouldn't trust them either."

"So this is where I fit in."

"You? You convinced the British?"

"No, I wasn't involved with your government. Hoover came to an arrangement with the British that we Americans would account for the distribution of the food; and that's my job. I'll have a couple of Americans assigned to each region and I will coordinate the audits from here, in Brussels, and report to Mr Whitlock. The Belgians already have a great system for local administration, and they'll use this to decide where the provisions will go. We'll collect the promissory notes as well as count the stocks in and out; the Germans won't allow money to pass out of the country, so the food can't be paid for now."

"Paid for? I thought this was charity. The Belgians have no money, the Germans have taken it all. Have you heard how much they demanded not to put their guns on Brussels? Fifty million francs; it was blackmail."

"The spoils of war."

"The spoils of war! How can you be so glib? You need to watch out, Russell, your indifference sounds callous. You have to care when people are wronged. It's just not acceptable. People are more important than your precious paper and none of your political words mean a jot."

223

Russell felt a sting in what she said and assumed she meant his pain at the destruction of the library at Leuven. He had made clear in his letters he had given her how much that had hurt him. He had never seen her so agitated.

"Not all the food has to be paid for: much will be donated, but the transport costs are high. Loans have been secured from the British and French governments and from Belgian interests abroad."

"That sounds like profiteering to me. Everyone will be making money out of Belgium's hardships. Is that what you're saying, the British will benefit financially?"

"I didn't mean it to sound like that. I meant the British are helping. Two British shipping companies have donated their services without taking any commission on the cargo; everything will be ferried into Rotterdam and passed across the Dutch border. It's an amazing effort to mobilize producers, ships, financiers, and the public. Apparently at conservative estimates it's going to cost one million dollars a month to secure the food stocks and the American people are rallying to the call."

"Oh, I'm delighted." Marion's irony was not wasted on him. "The Americans are the heroes and the British the beasts."

A cold divide, like the Atlantic, sat between them.

"That isn't what I said." Russell had begun to feel exasperated. Whichever way the conversation turned he found himself wrong-footed. He struggled to know how to move their conversation onto more neutral territory. In the end it was Marion who intervened. She even attempted a smile.

"What food is coming in? It's so long since I cooked for myself I can hardly remember what basics are needed."

"From the lists I've seen so far it's flour—they want to make sure people can make bread, bacon and lard, rice and I think it was dried peas."

"That really is basic," Marion said.

"I'm sure the list will extend: this is just the start, and don't forget people will have local vegetables and fruit. It was only the main crops that were lost in this year's harvest."

"But the Germans just help themselves to whatever they want; they have no care about the hardship they create. Yesterday evening I was forced off the pavement onto the road when some soldiers refused to make room for me to pass. They just laughed at me."

"Why were you out in the evening?"

"Since when did I need your permission to go out?"

Russell had been anxious about the scene she described and he fired his question at her and then watched her bristle.

"I can look after myself."

"If they're the monsters you say they are, you need to take more care."

"If? If? One day you'll believe how bad they are."

"Don't make me out to be bad because I am trying to stay balanced."

"Balanced? Is that how you see it? There is no balance here. The Germans are trampling Belgium into the ground."

"Look, Hugh is part of an inquiry into the so-called atrocities. He's listened to hours of statements from victims and witnesses and bishops, priests, and burgomasters. There's a lot of truth telling going on, but the story is always different from both sides. There are always two sides to a story."

"And one of those sides is the truth and one isn't. I can see which side you believe, with your 'so-called' atrocities. They burnt your library: you thought that was an atrocity, or have you forgotten about that? Why don't you believe the Belgians?"

"To be honest, it's irrelevant what I believe. What anyone believes isn't going to make one iota of difference. The Germans are convinced that civilians fired on them and the Belgians are convinced that they didn't."

"It's not irrelevant to me, and anyway regardless of who fired and who didn't, what they've done is monstrous. Unforgiveable."

"That's war, Marion, that's what happens, people get hurt."

"Don't you dare talk down to me."

"I'm not, I'm just being realistic."

"Realistic? You should meet some of the victims, then you'll know what's real."

"Look, let's not argue. We get little enough time together. Let's get back …"

"To what? Fun and laughter?" Marion interrupted him. "I thought we were being realistic. The reality is we feel differently about this, rather I feel and you don't."

"Now that's not fair, Marion, of course I feel."

"Do you? You sound very rational to me about it all, and I disagree with your views."

"History has shown us that …"

"And now you're lecturing me. This isn't about history and theories. I'm talking about you knowing the difference between what is right and wrong. How can I have fun and laugh with someone who has no humanity."

"Hold on there, lady. You have no right to pass that judgment on me."

"I have every right to speak my mind. You have become too removed, sitting in your neutral zone and handing out favours." Marion rose and put on her hat. "You will never silence me."

"At least we don't make enemies and allow people to starve," Russell stood up too.

"You may not make enemies, but is silence comfortable when it blankets the truth? You carry on with your good works, Mr Clarke, and feel satisfied. It's my country that's losing lives for this cause." She moved to the door.

"Oh, so that's what this is about, is it? The only honourable thing to do is to fight."

Before Marion had formed her reply, the waiter had confronted Russell with their bill. Marion slipped out of the door and when Russell reached the street it was empty.

3rd November 1914
Bellignies
Isabelle

"Our British friends will have to move out of the forest, my dear," the princess said when she and Isabelle were sitting in her study. "They have to move again, even though they are so well hidden; the forest has become too dangerous, it's only a matter of time now before they are discovered, and getting food to them has become much harder. This cold weather has been tough on them and it seems that several of them are now quite ill; there are simply too many of them. I'm afraid it might have been easier if they had stayed in small numbers."

"I'll take the risk, I can take food and medicines to them. Please let me go. I hate to think of them suffering. Do you know who is ill?"

"No, I don't know any names. Is there someone in particular you are concerned about?"

"No, yes, well, all of them, of course, but Lieutenant Baxter is so good with the men, I'd hate to think of him unwell: they rely on him so much."

"Yes, the officer, the dashing cavalry man. Just like my father: he stole my mother's heart very easily. But no, you can't go. It is simply too dangerous, and worst of all, you might lead the Germans to them."

"It's so hard to do nothing; there must be something I can do."

"Maybe there is, or will be soon. Be patient, my dear."

The next time they met Isabelle was given a task.

"The men have to surrender, it's the only way they'll survive this winter." Marie de Croy made her emphatic statement after greeting Isabelle.

"The Germans shoot soldiers. They can't surrender. To give up after all their efforts, it's too dreadful to think about. Can't we hide them somewhere else?" Isabelle failed to hide her distress.

"We have hidden a few men here at the chateau, mostly officers. The Germans do seem keen to shoot officers. And we've been able to get a few through to Brussels. There is an escape line that Reginald has linked up. It's much easier to hide in such a large city, and there are many routes on to Holland; but we can't move 20 men in one go, nor can we ask anybody around here to consider hiding such a large group. People are too nervous, and rightly so."

Isabelle and Marie sat in silence. It was failure to surrender and was not a thought that Isabelle could countenance. She became concerned the more Marie spoke.

"What concerns us is how they can surrender in the safest way. If they walked out of the woods now there's always the chance the Germans might just shoot them. They've done that to others they found and captured. At the very least the Germans would make life very hard for the peasants living closest to where they are found; they'll know that some would have given help: the repercussions are bound to be severe. I wouldn't be surprised if they destroyed at least one of the forest villages as a warning to others; they'll want revenge, of that I'm sure. We've heard enough reports of that kind of thing already."

Isabelle thought of the baker and his wife as she digested Marie's words.

"We could hide Lieutenant Baxter and perhaps his sergeants here at the chateau, and try to get them through to Brussels; we are managing to move men in ones and twos. You know our tower?"

Isabelle nodded. The chateau was dominated by a round tower with a large conical top to it. It was the outstanding landmark of the area. Marie gave a conspiratorial smile to Isabelle and put her fingers to her lips before she continued.

"It dates from the Middle Ages. A few years ago we found a disused staircase in the wall by a downstairs window. The top had been closed, but my brother and Jules have opened it up. The stairs don't go anywhere now but there is a small space after one flight where a person or two can hide. Jules has disguised the entrance to look like a cupboard, but the panelling can be pulled back; it's really quite ingenious. I'll take you and show you. It's the one hiding place we can risk in the chateau. Now, you must keep that to yourself, my dear, and don't even tell Jacqueline. But we could hide one or two men until it's the right time to move them on. Reginald takes care of that side of things."

Isabelle was so relieved that James would not be handed over to the Germans. He would be safe. She hugged this thought to herself while concentrating on Marie's plan.

"If we can get the rest of the men to Bavay, it's not too far, and the hospital there is run by the French Red Cross. There's a good chance their surrender can be arranged without local recriminations. There'll be some tough questions, I'm sure, but they can't shoot that number, and in a hospital. Getting them safely out of the woods is difficult, but not impossible. It would need to be at night of course: the Germans don't move much after dark, they rely on the curfew."

"It's too far to Bavay in one night, from the forest." Isabelle knew her journey times well.

"Then we'll need to hide them here for a night or two. We need to make sure they are presentable for surrender as well."

"What do you mean, presentable for surrender?" Isabelle asked.

"Uniforms, they must be in their uniforms. If they surrender dressed as civilians they could be shot as spies, and the Germans would want to know who had given them the clothes. Then there'd be more reprisals."

"But they don't all have uniforms, what can we do about that?"

"We will have to sew, and quickly. Jacqueline can help, and my gardener's wife no doubt. Ask around in the villages for British Army coats: people will have hidden them away; so many were abandoned when they retreated in such a hurry in the summer. We need an army coat for each man; we may have to make some trousers, and those things they wind round the bottom of their legs."

"Puttees."

"Yes, puttees, anything that makes them look British and military. The clothes don't have to look perfect of course, just the right sort of shape and material. We'll have to make a big effort to bring in some extra meat and bread for the time of their arrival. They'll all be hungry by now: I know their food rations have been smaller. Hopefully they've caught some forest food."

"I'll be happy to help."

Isabelle was keen to be involved and was delighted to be busy again. For the next few days she spread the word about the army clothes and extra provisions, excited by the thought of seeing James soon. She fantasized about them travelling to Brussels together, perhaps as man and wife, a great disguise for a soldier and precious time for them. Isabelle borrowed the donkey and cart to transport the coats and extra provisions she had collected to the chateau. One morning she had found four coats under the bush by her back door, her job made easy by local kindness.

"Reginald and Jules will collect the men tomorrow night. They'll be cramped, but it's only for a short while: we'll put them in the attic of the barn behind the gardener's cottage. Lieutenant Baxter can be hidden in the chateau. He'll be with us for longer until papers can be arranged and we can move him on to Brussels."

Marie briefed Isabelle while they sat and sewed. Elaine, the gardener's wife was with them. She was fast and skilled with her hands and Isabelle followed her lead with the garments.

"Would it help if I travelled with him to Brussels? We could pose as man and wife: the Germans wouldn't expect that."

"If the Germans got a sniff of you young lovers, they'd whisk your man off to Germany to work in their fields. It isn't safe for any young man to be abroad. No, the lieutenant will have to disguise his youth."

Isabelle's dreams were crushed in an instant.

"We do have a request for your help, but you need to think carefully about it because the risks are high."

Marie outlined the plan to take the men to Bavay in two nights' time. Reginald had told the local mayor of their plans, so the hospital would be expecting the soldiers, but they wanted her to guide them.

"Jules can go with you, but he wouldn't think as quickly as you if you experienced difficulties. Think about it and let me know."

"Of course I'll take them. I know a route that will keep us away from the roads. You know I want to help."

"I know your mother was upset the last time you were away overnight, stuck in the forest. Why don't you come and stay here for a few days, then she won't need to know what you're doing. A social visit should cause her no anxiety."

Isabelle's mind jumped straight to James rather than her mother: to be under the same roof as he was, the thought made her tingle.

"That's a very generous thought. I'll bring some of my things over tomorrow."

The men arrived at about three o'clock in the morning. The princess and Isabelle had retired to their rooms, but sleep had evaded both of them. A tap on her door alerted Isabelle and she followed Marie down to the kitchen to find James wolfing down a huge amount of bread and ham.

"Isabelle." He jumped up when he saw her and she stepped towards him, but both were restrained by decorum and instead of the embrace she so badly wanted they shook hands.

"Isabelle, when the lieutenant has finished his meal, take him to the tower. I'm sure he is in need of some good rest. I'll go and check that there is enough for the other men."

"But Marie, let me do that, I can go out to the barn," Isabelle offered.

"No. I'm sure Reginald will have everything under control. I'm just fussing; you stay here."

The minute she left the room they were in each other's arms, holding tight. Their kiss, when their lips met was gentle. He spoke first.

"It's so good to see you. You look so well. The thought of holding you has helped me through many a cold night."

"You have lost so much weight."

Isabelle was shocked to notice how thin he had become. His eyes looked sunken into their sockets and his face was drawn. He looked more sinewy than muscular and she could feel the tendons on the back of his hand when she held it to lead him to the table.

"Come on back to the table, you must eat."

He did as he was told, but he ate at a slower pace than before. She made him a hot drink and he managed to eat and drink without ever once breaking the grip he had on her hand. She brought his hand to her lips.

"I am so glad you are safe, and that we can keep you safe. Have they told you of the plans to help you reach Brussels? Perhaps I can join you. They won't let us travel together, but I could meet you there. What do you think?"

"I think you are beautiful."

He lent over to kiss her again. This time there was more pressure applied and the kiss lasted for a long time before they came up for air.

"I'm not going to Brussels," James said.

"Oh, have the plans changed, which city instead? I can make my way there, wherever, I'm sure."

"I am going to surrender with my men."

"What? Why? Why would you do this?"

"Because they are good men and they need a leader and I can't abandon them now, certainly not to look out for myself."

Isabelle's heart sank.

"Do you remember Culloch? The weasel-faced Scotsman who we tied to the tree; he was trouble from the start. When he heard that we had to surrender he made off into the forest, but he took with him the last of our food. The boys will kill him if they ever see him again."

"I can understand he doesn't want to surrender. He might have more chance to get back to your army on his own."

"Oh, that one won't be heading in that direction I'm sure. He's a skiver, really shifty, no one trusted him"

Isabelle did not appreciate the diversion about Culloch and brought the conversation back to him and his decision, but however much she pleaded and probed, it was clear his mind was made up and duty would dictate his actions. As much as she feared for him, and resented the choice that seemed to carry such a high risk, she understood it, and grudgingly admired his stand.

"That doesn't give us much time." Isabelle drew him towards her, and you need some rest. Bring the rest of the food with you and I'll take you to your quarters; you are not sleeping with your men tonight."

232

At breakfast Marie was full of preparations.

"We have paper and pencils for the men to write letters. Perhaps you", she looked at James and Isabelle, "can write for those who need help. We need military details listed, and everyone to fit into uniforms and be fed as much as they can manage to eat. We don't know when you'll get your next meal. Can you keep your men quiet today? Apart from natural calls, they need to keep out of sight; we never know when a German patrol might visit."

"Yes, they understand the risks. Now Culloch has left, there isn't a bad apple among them."

"Isabelle, when Reginald returns he'll take you to Bavay to meet the mayor, Monsieur Mercier, to make sure arrangements are in place at the hospital, and so that you know where to go. You'll have to return on your own; Reginald has to go on to Brussels."

Reginald was short of time; after introducing her to Monsieur Mercier he had to leave them to their conversation and tour. The mayor walked her through the streets to show her the best route to the hospital, avoiding the main thoroughfares that the Germans patrolled. He told her that he had been distressed at the prospect of handing over British soldiers to the Germans but that he appreciated, for a group of this number, there was now no other option. The Red Cross officials at the hospital had been briefed to lodge the men overnight; the following day he would report their presence to the German commandant in the town.

"Then we are all in God's hands; let's hope Herr Hoffman is not in a bad mood."

When Isabelle returned to Bellignies she went to the barn to help with letter writing. The men all looked more gaunt than she remembered, and three clearly had a fever. It pleased her to see Samuel Elliott was well and still cheerful.

"We don't want the lieutenant to surrender, miss, but he won't hear of not going with us; perhaps you can make him change his mind?"

"I've tried, Samuel, but his mind is made up. He won't put his safety ahead of yours, he made that clear to me, and believe me, I begged."

"He's a stubborn one, for sure, but the men have a high regard for him."

Isabelle stopped herself from saying that she did too.

"He's an honourable man, Samuel, he'll always be true to his word."

Will he, she thought, will he be true to the things he had whispered to her the night before in their intimate moments, or had they both created a fantasy that wouldn't survive the ravages of war and separation? She knew that memories of the hours they spent together before dawn would stay with her forever. Their passion had made her feel young and alive and she did not begrudge him a minute of what she had given him.

The next time she saw James was at supper. Marie excused herself from the table and the room. They were to rendezvous at the barn in two hours' time and she had suggested rest for them before they set out. Isabelle and James knew these would be their last moments and she was keen to return with him to the privacy of the tower, but instead he took her into the lounge. They sat together in one armchair. Isabelle curled into James' arms, their faces together and hands entwined, but spoke very little; she even dozed until he whispered it was time to leave.

"I will think of you every day," was his final private promise.

"And I will pray for your safety," her last words to him.

At midnight they headed off towards Bavay. Isabelle led, with James a good 20 yards behind, in case she was challenged by a German sentry. Then followed the rest of the soldiers. All moved quietly. Jules brought up the rear to make sure no one was left behind and to take over as a guide if Isabelle was apprehended. They saw no one.

Once they reached Bavay they moved through the streets, keeping to the dark shadows, towards one of the small gates at the rear of the hospital. There they gathered while Isabelle went forward to make sure it was unlocked. She pushed the gate open and saw two lit candles in the window opposite, the signal that all was clear. She tapped on the window and returned to the men.

She nodded to James. He stood next to her as his men went into the hospital grounds. He made sure they were all accounted for. Isabelle smiled at them as they passed; most muttered their thanks and Samuel Elliott tried to shake her hand, but impulsively she kissed him on both cheeks and whispered, "Good luck, Samuel, and look after Lieutenant Baxter, won't you?"

"You can depend on it, Miss Isabelle, and thank you." And he was gone through the gateway.

James shook hands with Jules, gave Isabelle a quick kiss and before she could say anything, he was gone.

Isabelle spent the whole of her walk back with Jules mouthing the few prayers she could remember, over and over again. She went straight to bed when she arrived back at the chateau.

Isabelle, left to sleep, was amazed to find it was noon when she awoke. Her limbs seemed to weigh twice as much as usual; she felt her fatigue as she made her way downstairs. Reginald was back from Brussels and he and Marie were sitting in the kitchen: their faces looked grave and they gave her bad news. The Germans had arrested the mayor of Bavay and had threatened to shoot him. The prisoners had been led away from the hospital but no one knew where they had been taken. Isabelle felt her stomach heave; she reached across the table for Marie's hand, and all three sat silent, engulfed by their concern.

3rd November 1914
Brussels
Marion

What had she been thinking to walk out on him like that? Once she had reached the street and turned in the direction of the clinic, she had felt it more awkward to turn around than continue. She had felt angry, really angry and in that moment all her angst had been directed at him. She had marched herself up the street to a litany of complaints about him that sang out in her head.

"How dare he doubt the testimonies of the refugees; how convenient for him to label their stories as propaganda; the spoils of war, only a man could find that term acceptable; what is right is never irrelevant; truth has to be upheld; the Germans are monsters; just because he's protected from their antagonism, he can't see it; why doesn't he step into the shoes of some of the people I've met; he's smug and self-satisfied; who is this man, does he believe in anything?"

He had not caught up with her; she had let herself into the clinic, gone to her room, and flung herself on her bed. She had been trying to account for herself and this turn of events ever since. How had it happened? She groaned as she thought of what her father had written: *Give this one a chance M*; and now she had thrown it all away. For what? What had caused her to flare up? She had to admit it was all of her doing; she had put the bite into their conversation, and it was she who had flounced out.

"You will do that one time too many, young lady," her mother had once said when she had returned to apologize after her haughty departure from a room. "Not everyone will be as forgiving as me," her mother had concluded.

Russell had been full of himself with all his high flying politics and VIP visits and she did want to listen, but if truth be told, she thought that what she had been doing was much more exciting and, yes, that was it, she was frustrated that she could not tell him about it. She could not tell anyone, yet it was ready to burst out of her. She was tightly coiled with the tension, and she was scared. She also felt uncomfortable with the duplicity that her silence contained. She had secrets from him and that put her on edge. In a perverse way she wanted him to know that she was holding something back. She wanted to be sure that he could read her and she would be unable to hide anything from him, but when he had asked why she had been out, with a sub-text she had heard of "without him", she had felt a resentment flare within her. She was not under his control. Her resistance to a man's possessiveness had taken her down the path to sabotage. She had picked her fight with the confidence of one who felt they owned the moral high ground: he was lacking in humanity and she was the person who had heart; while the British fought, the Americans hid behind smooth words and good deeds; it just wasn't good enough.

Marion lay on her bed and the fight started to seep out of her. She was actually tired and had to acknowledge that fatigue always affected her levels of tolerance. The last three days had been full of intrigue and risks; she was living a double life and her hours had been long. She had looked forward to seeing Russell for days, but had not fully realized the toll on her until she had stepped out with him.

Edith had sent her to find Dr Depage the morning after Beecham and Meachin had arrived, but he was already on his way to the clinic, and they met on the street. Their concerns, about the colonel's foot, were well-founded, and Dr Depage asked them to prepare for him to operate later that afternoon. Marion had just been about to cancel Russell when his note arrived postponing their meeting until the following day. It suited them both.

With Edith and Marion in attendance, Dr Depage had removed rotten sock and pieces of shrapnel, and had cut away flesh that had started to decompose on the colonel's foot.

"Another week and this would have been an amputation," he had said, almost triumphantly. Marion would have liked to have watched Dr Depage more closely but it was her job to hold the colonel's shoulders and keep him still if he started to move around. She herself felt quite drowsy with the smell of the ether that pervaded the room. Dr Depage closed the wounds, which Marion dressed under Edith's supervision.

"These dressings must be changed daily and plenty of iodine applied. I want to make sure the infection doesn't return. As many vegetables as you can find will help him restore his strength. If you see or smell an infection come and fetch me."

"How should I account for this operation, Dr Depage? I will have no fees to put against the costs," Edith asked.

"Um, I suggest you start a separate record for such accounts. We'll have to look at how we balance the books at audit time. Now how do we get this patient back upstairs? He'll be coming round from the ether soon."

"We're alone in this building at the moment so we can use the lift. Sergeant Meachin can help us move the colonel into the ward when we're on the floor; there's no room to take the trolley into the annex," Marion said.

Dr Depage raised his hand.

"Don't tell me any more. It's best I know as little as possible. I don't need to remind you of the risks you are taking. I have no doubt that you've saved this man's foot and very probably his life, but stay alert to the danger you are in."

Marion felt herself bristle at his comments. The man who had directed this problem to their door now implied they had been foolhardy to be involved. Maybe he had done nothing more than divert the request from his own door, and had not expected them to accept, but how could they have refused? Marion kept her thoughts to herself and Edith did not seem perturbed.

Sergeant Meachin did assist them to put the colonel onto his bed. He seemed pleased to have him back in the room. Marion saw him wipe away a tear when the colonel roused after the operation. Marion stayed with them until the early evening to ensure there were no bad effects from the anaesthetic, which often caused nausea. Sergeant Meachin told her the details of their months in hiding.

"I was knocked unconscious by the hit on my head. It was the second day of fighting at Mons and it hadn't gone well. We'd just had the order to retreat, but the next I remember was when I woke up under a hedge; someone must have dragged me there. Whoever it was probably saved my life. I wandered around and found a Red Cross post and the doctor dressed my wound, but it kept bleeding for days. I'm with the Cheshires. The medic told me that some of my battalion had been taken to a convent in Witheries, so I joined them there; that's where I met up with the colonel and we somehow stuck together."

"That was some months ago," Marion said. "We read about the trouble at Mons in *The Times*."

"*The Times*, the colonel would love to see a paper; I'm not one for much reading myself."

"Oh, I'm not sure that we still have the paper. They're rare and expensive; a copy circulates for weeks around the city. I'll talk to matron and see what we have."

"Yes, we've been in hiding for months but never in such comfort as this."

"I can imagine the convent was sparse, but at least you were safe."

"Only for a short time. We had to leave. It weren't safe when the Hun started to search for British soldiers. I was paired with the colonel and we hid in the loft of a shed in a widow's garden for two months. She brought food each evening. She took some risks. She burned our uniforms and helped us disguise ourselves; the colonel grew his beard, and he wore her late husband's black hat and floppy tie: he looked like a real Belgian. I put padding in the back of a jacket to look like a hunchback. It kept my back warm too."

Marion interrupted Meachin with a hand gesture when she heard the colonel moan; he was drowsy and had moved himself on the bed, and had obviously felt the pain of his foot. He became still and Meachin resumed.

"Someone tipped off the Hun we was in the village and they raided houses and searched outbuildings; it wasn't safe for us, or her, so she arranged for us to leave. One night two Catholic sisters from Witheries came and took us to another convent; from there we went to Mons, right into the heart of German operations and we hid for a few days in the basement of the house of a photographer, a Monsieur Dervaire. He prepared a set of papers for each of us and handed us over to Mr Capaiu. We had three attempts to reach Brussels over the past week, but the patrols were too heavy. During one I fell off a cart and that started my head bleeding again."

"But where were the British Army? Why couldn't you get back with them? Weren't they fighting nearby?"

"Oh yes, we could often hear the fighting, but we didn't know where they were. We just knew that between us and them was the whole of the German Army, and they were shooting soldiers on sight. We knew we had to lay low until we could make our way back to Holland. I was glad I was with the colonel. I was scared they'd think I'd deserted. But he said we were doing the right thing, and he's been desperate to get back to his men."

"Well, you both need to rest up before you can set out again. The colonel's foot was a mess, but I'm sure it will start to heal now. Dr Depage is a good surgeon."

After a day inside, Marion stepped out of the building and onto the street. She fancied a quick walk around the block to clear her lungs from the smell of ether, but after an altercation with some soldiers who barred her path, she went up the steps just along the street and let herself in to her accommodation and went to her room. It was her mention of this that had fed her argument with Russell.

Marion established a routine to care for the men. She attended to them early in the morning and late in the evening to ensure that she attracted no attention. She was helped in this by the fact that many of the trainees had been assigned to various of the hospitals in the city, so no one could keep track of anyone's where abouts with any certainty, as all were on different shifts, but the staff were the ones she had to be alert to. She had almost been caught carrying a slop bucket that morning, on her way to emptying it. Edith had taken responsibility for the men's food. She introduced a daily stock check of their supplies, a good reason for her to spend more time in the kitchen and larders. The men were delighted to have regular meals; they did not mind what it was or whether it was hot or cold, and they kept their room clean and tidy.

241

"I like to keep busy, miss," Meachin had said to her. "I can sew, you know. If you bring our clothes back to me with some thread, I can do some mending."

Marion gave him their clothes in a neat and washed pile with needles, pins, and threads, for Meachin to do some mending. He was delighted.

"Thank you, miss, I hate having idle hands. Can I help you with the colonel? You just tell me what needs to be done and I can do it."

"Why don't you watch me as I change the dressing, just in case I can't get up to you one day."

Meachin paid close attention to all her preparations and the way she went about removing the soiled dressing, cleaning the wound, and putting on the fresh bandages. She did not wash the wound, just made sure it had a good covering of iodine. The wound looked good, no fresh blood and no sign of infection and the swelling had already diminished.

"It feels comfortable already," the colonel said, "and I feel marvellous after a good night's sleep and a day's rest. Mustn't get too comfortable though, we'll be on our way soon."

"Oh no, surely not. You must wait a while for your foot to heal. You couldn't walk far yet. The wound would open up."

"Don't want to outstay our welcome, y'know. It's a risky business for you to have us here." The colonel let Marion lift his foot onto a pillow as he relaxed back on the bed. He still looked slightly grey.

"Well, you can't go anywhere until Mr Capaiu lets us know who your guide is. We'll have to wait on him."

"We are much obliged to everyone, so good of you all to help." The colonel closed his eyes and Marion collected together all her medical paraphernalia.

"Is your head wound all right now, Sergeant Meachin?" Marion asked, just before closing the cupboard door of the medical supplies.

"Oh, yes, not a bother. Only needed two stitches. I'd forgotten they were there."

"Madame Cavell will be here soon with your supper and supplies for tomorrow. I'll be back in the morning with some fresh water."

"Thank you, miss. And a good night to you."

These thanks were offered by Meachin, as the colonel was already asleep.

On her own again, Marion's thoughts returned to the disaster of the day, her tantrum with Russell. She could forgive herself her intolerance: she had been under pressure. But without the full picture, would he forgive her?

Marion had been so deep in her thoughts that she was startled when there was a knock on the door and even more surprised to see Edith enter the room.

"Am I interrupting?" Edith asked.

"Yes," Marion replied, "and I'm pleased that you are; my thoughts are quite dark and I'd rather not be left with them for much longer."

"I've just come from the men. They seem to be doing well. Do you mind if I sit down?"

"No, of course, please do, this chair is best."

Edith turned to close the door and sat in the chair indicated by Marion.

"I feel quite exhausted," Edith said, "after all the rushing around and surreptitious moves of the last couple of days. My nerves have been quite on edge."

"I know what you mean," Marion said. "And it's helpful for me to hear it from you. I've just ruined my afternoon with Russell by feeling out of sorts. I picked a fight with him."

"Oh my dear, I am sorry to hear that, but we have been under a great deal of pressure, and I'm sure we'll both carry this for a while until we get more used to it. I no longer feel concern for our soldiers' health. The colonel's recovery is well underway."

"Yes, the wound looked good when I dressed it this evening."

"I thought I saw you return earlier today. I hadn't expected you back until early evening. Was it a big upset with Mr Clarke?"

"Yes, it was rather. It was unfair of me to take out my tension on him. He has his own pressures too; he's working very hard and has the burden of feeding the nation on his shoulders. My world must seem very tame to him."

"You didn't tell him about our visitors?"

"No, not a word, but that made me feel uncomfortable; I don't want a relationship with secrets."

"These aren't really secrets between the two of you, just confidences that you have to keep with another. If he knew, it would only give him cause to worry and I'm sure you don't want to add to his burdens."

"No, you're right and that's really helpful; to think of it as a confidence with another, and not me deceiving him. Thank you. But now I'm being ill-mannered with you. Was there something you wanted to see me about?"

"Well, we've had our special visitors for three days now, and we may well have more soldiers come to us. I wanted us to think about what we need to do to safeguard them and ourselves. What have we learnt?"

Marion and Edith spent the next hour generating lists and ideas, their conversation interspersed with snippets of chats they had enjoyed with the colonel or Sergeant Meachin. They created a regime that could be executed by either of them and that would involve no other person in the clinic, and they congratulated each other on the service and care they had provided so far.

"It's a small part to play in this awful war," Edith said.

"But an important one for each person that we help," Marion said. "They must be so desperate to be home, and for the likes of Colonel Beecham to be back with his troops. To help them on their way is an honour."

Marion's spirits were lifted by Edith's visit. She now needed to think about an apology to Russell, and hoped that their rift was repairable. An hour later she sealed an envelope with her note inside. Tomorrow, she would give it to him tomorrow.

4th November 1914
Brussels
Russell

"And where are you off to, young lady?"

Russell had just been heading up the steps to the clinic when Marion had opened the door to come out. She was taken by surprise and looked startled, and slipped the note she had been carrying into her pocket.

"I'm sorry, sorry," Russell said. "Its none of my business and I only meant it as a fun phrase, not a real question. Where you go is your own business and not mine, so please don't take offence. I didn't mean anything by it."

Russell stood in front of her, a note in one hand and a bunch of flowers in the other.

"I think you're talking too much," Marion said, and walked down the steps and kissed him.

"I am so sorry about yesterday," Russell said as he surfaced from the kiss. "I must have sounded like an insufferable sap. Thank you for keeping me honest. I hope you always will, that is, if you haven't given up on me entirely."

"Not entirely." Marion collected the flowers and buried her face in them to smell their fragrance and hide her smile.

"I had a good chat with Hugh and he put me straight on a few things. I'd lost sight of what really matters behind the pose. He is a passionate man."

Marion recalled the tears she had seen in Hugh's eyes when he had described the horrors of Leuven to her and Edith.

"Yes, the matters here concern him deeply," Marion said. "But you've hardly been here, you can't expect to feel the same as he does, and I shouldn't expect it of you either."

"Oh, but you must, I need you to keep my feet on the ground; it's too easy to repeat the rhetoric that surrounds me at the legation. Those men are so eloquent that it's impossible to disagree, and even if I did they would find a way to accommodate my point of view to keep everyone in the room amenable. As Hugh says, that's diplomacy."

"And you want to be a diplomat?"

"No, I don't think I do, but that warrants a longer conversation on another day. I have to be back at the embassy real soon, but I wanted to make sure you had my apology."

"Thank you, apology accepted." Marion planted another kiss on him, but did not fill the silence with any remorse of her own.

"I guess I'd better get going." Russell said. "Where were you heading? Can we walk along a bit together?"

"Oh, nowhere," Marion said. "Just out for a breath of fresh air. But I must go and put these flowers in water."

"Well, I'm pleased we spoke, and that you're okay with me. All forgiven?"

"All forgiven. See you soon?"

"As soon as I, sorry, we, can arrange to," Russell had replied as they parted.

Russell hated the fact that he seemed to be seeking reassurance from Marion, but despite her words and kisses he still was not sure of her. For one thing he had expected her to take some responsibility for their disagreement: it was she who had walked out after all. But she showed no chagrin. Perhaps Hugh had been right, he should have left his apology for a while longer. He had bumped into Hugh when he returned to the embassy after his row with Marion.

"Well done, Russell, Hoover was impressed. He'll send some more men over to go into the regions; they're coming from the Rockefeller Institute. He suggests they spend two days with you here before going into the field so that you can brief them and make sure they are equipped with all the right passes. I heard the minister sing your praises too," Hugh continued. "You inspire confidence, and that's a great asset to have."

"Thank you," Russell said, but it was almost a mumble. He wanted Hugh to leave him alone. He was not in the mood for company, and Hugh's compliments, although well meant, actually made him feel worse about himself. How could he shine with these people, and yet leave Marion with such a low opinion of him? Never in his life had a woman walked out on him. He had wanted to do it plenty of times in reverse, mostly from boredom rather than through a clash. A relaxed coffee, lingering looks, and then what had happened? What had made it turn?

"Are you all right, Russell? Is something on your mind? You know you can talk to me any time about your project; I keep pretty close to what's going on even though I'm not directly involved. Looks as if this inquiry I'm on is coming to a close soon: can't say that I won't be sorry; it's mighty dull."

"Mighty dull! How can you say it's dull when so many dreadful things have supposedly happened to people? The last word I'd expect to hear is dull."

Hugh looked surprised at Russell's outburst.

"What's bitten you?"

"Oh nothing; it's just war, isn't it, bad things happen."

"Yes, bad things happen."

"And I suppose you're not interested because when the talking is over nothing will change; right and wrong won't be apportioned, no one will be held to account, another few rules will be added to the book of warfare and signed by all parties at the end of this fracas."

Hugh rubbed his hands over his eyes. "When did you become a cynic, and who said I wasn't interested?"

"You did, just now, you said it was dull."

"I didn't mean dull because I wasn't interested: the proceedings are dull. It's a court of law and the procedural red tape ties you down for hours before any witness even speaks. These people have been broken. I'm amazed some of them turn up: some can hardly speak, no animation to their statements; an outburst of anger is rare but welcome when it comes. Those Germans are smug."

"But it's pointless, isn't it. The truth doesn't matter, it will make no difference."

"The truth is the point, the truth is always the point. The statements are the saddest things I've ever heard. The Germans have thrown away the rulebook; these people have been wronged and their subjugation will continue until this is acknowledged, and apologized for, but these Germans have no contrition, they'll answer to no one."

"How can you participate in this sham?"

"Excuse me, this is no sham; you insult the testimonies that have been heart-rending to hear, and you insult me. Whether the statements influence an outcome now or not, they are down on record and can't be denied. They will be there for history to see. It's that thought that holds me in my seat each day."

For the second time that day Russell felt he had been led into a trap, and he had seen neither of them coming.

"But you said it was dull. I thought that meant you didn't care. I didn't think it was a politician's job to care."

"You assume a lot, Russell. Of course I care; but it's not done to wear one's heart on one's sleeve, particularly not as a diplomat and not when a neutral in a war zone, but you must always know where your heart is located. If you lose your sense of the truth, you'll never do anything but blow with the strongest wind. Don't mean to lecture, but a passion for justice, truth, and not forgetting sound administration, is what gets me out of bed each morning. And the thought of a good breakfast of course."

"Nurse Drake called me callous and indifferent and scoffed at our neutrality."

"Yes, she has strong opinions. She was frustrated with me when I told her about Leuven. I'm sure she thought I should have stopped the destruction, and believe me, I would have loved to have been able to. She was ready to thump the table with von Below given half a chance. To be neutral in our jobs only means we don't take sides publicly; diplomacy means we seek to sustain dialogues, but a passion to uphold our beliefs, that's what has to underpin all our actions."

"Yes, I saw the feisty side of her today." Russell moved the conversation back to his overriding concern.

"So it's a woman behind your mumps is it?"

"Yes, it is. I wish we'd had this conversation before. I might have avoided a big upset if we had."

"Anything I can help you sort out?"

"I think you've helped already, I have some serious thinking to do."

Hugh looked quizzical.

"I need to be sure of what I think about the rights and wrongs of this situation. Being glib is going to take me nowhere with her."

"Ah, I see. Finding your true north."

"And then I have to hope that Nurse Drake and I are facing in the same direction."

"Good luck. I've never met a woman who had a sense of direction at all."

Hugh stopped Russell who had started to remonstrate.

"Only joking. Cheap shot, I know. She really does have your passions up today. You two will kiss and make up, I'm sure. See you for drinks at six. The minister is hosting as a thank you to all of us. Try and be gracious with him: start practising diplomacy."

"Yes of course I will."

Russell stood and put his hand out to Hugh, "Thank you, I think you've, very diplomatically, just told me not to be such a bozo, and perhaps I know now where my apology to Marion needs to start."

"Never rush an apology, simmering softens up the pot you know."

"Enough wisdom for one day; if you don't watch out I'll start respecting you and then where would we be?"

They laughed, shook hands, and parted.

Russell walked back to the embassy, relieved of the flowers and his apology, both of which Marion had accepted with equal warmth. There had been a way back for him, but as he reflected he realized it had been him that had made every gesture of reconciliation. Not entirely true, and he smiled as he remembered her kisses, but that had been her only offering. He accepted he had been crass, but it was *she* who had bitten at him, *and* flounced off and had not explained herself, and had been on edge the whole time, before he had opened his undiplomatic mouth. Something was going on with her and it made him feel uneasy. Evasive, that was the word. He felt she was being evasive and he was perplexed. What did she have to hide from him? Feisty he could manage, but he did not want them to have secrets from each other, and she was holding something back. This time he would follow Hugh's advice and let it simmer, but he would not take his eye off the pot.

14th November 1914
Brussels
Marion

Marion was tense. She was unused to sitting in a café on her own and felt conspicuous. She was conscious of every action, each stir of her cup and bite of her biscuit. She had not wanted any refreshment and found it hard to swallow, but she had to buy herself time in the café and try to blend in. Blend in! She could not look any more obvious in her nurse's uniform. She had wanted to wear her own clothes, but Edith would not hear of it: she may be noticeable, but the Germans wouldn't touch her, and anyway she did need to be found by the person she was meeting, so at least it would make it easy for him to find her.

Since Gwen's departure all of her café visits had been with Russell. She never gave her surroundings a thought when she entered a place with him. They would always be in the middle of a conversation and would be interrupted by the waiter to take their order, rather than looking to attract his attention for service. Today was different. She had almost been hesitant to enter and had then been unsure where to sit. She wanted to be facing the door so that she could be easily spotted, but not in the centre of the tables, where everyone would look at her. She caught several glances and returned them with a slight nod of her head, the Belgian way.

She had begun to relax a little as the café started to fill and her presence was less prominent, until her concern became that she would be joined at her table, but not by the person she was to meet. She sipped her coffee slowly to avoid being presented with her bill and waited. He was late. She slipped into thoughts of Russell. They had met twice since their row and his apologetic gesture of flowers. She felt guilty about this. She still had not acknowledged her poor behaviour and as time went by it became lame to think of doing so. He had never mentioned it again, but it was still sitting between them and it created a draught where once the air was warm. She knew she was on edge when she was with him, and had been since the colonel and Meachin had arrived. More soldiers had come to the clinic since then, but Russell seemed oblivious to her anxieties. Perhaps she was a better actress than she thought, and the smiles that she forced through her tense muscles appeared natural to him. She didn't like to think that she could deceive him so easily, or maybe he just didn't pay close attention to her. She could tell instantly if he was out of kilter in any way and a few questions would always have him reveal a concern. But that was it, wasn't it? She couldn't reveal what was going on, what she was involved in; she had to keep silent. Lives depended on it.

Today she was meeting the guide who was taking the colonel and Meachin on to the next stage of their journey. Mr Capaiu had visited the evening before to pass on the details of the arrangements and the address of the café. It was not one that she had been to before, but with its dark wooden chairs and linen-covered tables, yellowed walls and smell of coffee, elderly slow moving waiters, as all the young men had gone, and black-hatted and jacketed clientele, she could be in any of the numerous cafés in the city. He was suddenly in front of her and sat down. They smiled the smile of friends in greeting and he ordered for himself and her again.

"Has anyone come in behind me?" He asked her without looking round himself.

"No, no one. Two people just left," Marion said. "I take it …"
Marion was interrupted:

"No names," he sharply stated.

"I take it you're the person I'm due to meet," Marion tried again.

"The weather in Yorc is dry," he said.

The man was unshaven and not smartly dressed for the city, but carried it off with a Bohemian more than a dishevelled air. She thought him to be about 60, but he was sprightly. When he removed his hat he was mostly grey and thin on top.

"You were easy to spot," he said, and this time his smile seemed genuine and the one she returned was more relaxed.

"Yes, the uniform always stands out. I have to hope my face is forgettable," Marion said.

"It's a face I'd remember if I was 30 years younger," and the man reached across and patted her hand. "Don't look shocked, it's all for show," and he gave her a wink.

Show or not Marion began to feel he was taking liberties and drew her hands down onto her lap.

"You need to give me some information. I need to know where to deliver my guests." Marion steered their conversation towards its purpose.

"There's time for that; we have our coffee to enjoy." He certainly did not seem in any rush, so she sat back in her chair. The man went on:

"You have two that are ready."

"We have more than two, but …"

"I can only move two tomorrow," he interrupted her.

"Yes, I'm aware of that. Mr …"

"No names," he snapped at her.

"No, of course, I'm sorry. I knew it was only two, this time, for tomorrow." Marion was struggling with knowing what she could and could not say and he was so quick with his interruptions. She waited.

"No uniforms and they must look old. They'll blend in best in the country as peasant folk, so no city garb." He looked at Marion and she nodded to show that she understood him.

"Good if they can bring some food and money."

"But Mr … sorry," Marion continued before he could interrupt her, "I was told they wouldn't need to pay the guides, that would be dealt with separately."

"Yes it will, but they need some money for their own provisions."

"Yes, of course. We'll see to it." Marion began to wish she could make notes, particularly when he then gave her three locations to remember.

"We'll pick you up at one of them, you just won't know which. Spend no more than five minutes at each rendezvous. If no one approaches you, move to the next and then back home if no contact is made. If this happens try again the following day at the same time. Be at the first address at half past six. Any questions?"

"It all sounds pretty straightforward," Marion said. "But what if there are soldiers around, what happens then?"

"Nothing will happen, there'll be no pick-up. But make sure you don't walk with the men. Have them follow in the street behind you and don't you stop if the soldiers stop them. You must look like you are alone. It's their bad luck if they get stopped."

"Oh, we have papers for them. They …" he was quick again as he cut across her.

"Enough." She was silenced.

He beckoned over to the waiter and ordered another coffee for himself.

"I'll see to the bill," he told her, "but you leave now and I'll finish my coffee. Until the next time."

"Yes, of course, I see." Marion always felt she was one step behind him, but she stood and left as he had directed. Out on the streets she was surprised to see life going on as usual; for her all sense of what was normal had been temporarily suspended. She set off back to the clinic.

"He didn't tell me his name," Marion reported back to Edith, "just the details of where to meet. It's the nurse's uniform that they will look out for."

"So it could be you or me with the men?" Edith asked.

"Yes, I suppose it could, but I had assumed I would be taking them. You do too much already."

"Well, we will be having more than one handover, so we can work it out between us." Edith did look tired.

"I was due to be meeting Russell tomorrow evening, but I can easily postpone him. Let me take the men tomorrow. I feel responsible as I took the briefing. I'd hate it if I've forgotten something important. Agreed?"

Edith nodded.

"Thank you, Marion, but no risks. The men know they are on their own when they are on the streets. You must step away if there is any sign of trouble."

"Yes, I promise. I'm not up for any heroics."

Marion wrote a note to be delivered to Russell later that day. She apologized for the short notice but said that it was unavoidable, and perhaps at the weekend could be a better time. One of the porters would deliver her note to the embassy on his way home.

Marion and Edith saw the colonel and Meachin together to brief them about their departure and give them their clothes, papers, money, and food for their onward journey. They were under instructions to have as much rest as they could for the next 24 hours: no one really knew what was ahead for them. There were now five soldiers in hiding at the clinic and they had begun to play card games until late into the night.

"No cards for us tonight then, madam." The colonel had chuckled as he said this to Edith. His foot was healing nicely but he still walked with a limp, the better for making him look aged and infirm when on the streets. Meachin had not shaved for over a week and with a makeshift hunchback and bedraggled hair managed a somewhat deranged look, vacant at best. This was helpful, as he spoke no French. They seemed keen to be leaving and excited with the news of their departure. It appeared to Marion she was the only one that carried any feeling of anxiety, but perhaps they hid it well and certainly gave it no voice in her presence.

After a restless night and a day of routine activities that had demanded little of her attention, Marion, Meachin, and the colonel left the clinic from the back door at quarter past six, 15 minutes ahead of their first rendezvous time. They arrived early having met no one on the street and waited in the shadows. Marion was just about to indicate that they move on to the next address when two men arrived.

"The weather in Yorc is dry. Same time, here, tomorrow for two more. Which of you has the bad foot?"

Marion had been startled by their silent approach. She saw the colonel raise his hand in response to the question. She had forgotten he was fluent in French.

"You, with me. We will go by boat, fishing boat. The other will walk with the guide."

"What's happening, sir?" Meachin had stepped forward.

"We are going separately, it seems. I am to travel by boat and you are walking cross- country. See you back in Blighty."

"I'd rather we stayed together, sir."

"Me too, Meachin, but we are in their hands. God be with you."

"Ssh," one of the guides silenced them and pointed across the square. Three people had come out of one of the buildings. Marion watched them as they continued their conversation for a few minutes and then two moved away together. The third walked across the square towards the group. Marion took a step backwards into the shadow and found she was on her own. The colonel and Meachin had melted away with their guides.

But I didn't say goodbye, was her first thought, closely followed by a wave of relief that her responsibility had been handed over. She was free to walk back to the clinic without looking over her shoulder. She went straight to Edith upon her return. The Yorc escape line was established.

20th November 1914
Isabelle

The first two weeks since Baxter's departure had passed in a daze for Isabelle, but now the need for action pressed down on her. She had spent as much of her time as she could at Bellignies in the days after the men surrendered. She had struggled to believe that the British had all been taken out to the woods and been shot, but it had taken Prince Reginald two weeks to find out the truth, and to bury the mayor of Bavay. The mayor's captivity had lasted for three days and then he had been killed by firing squad. The whole area was in shock and mourning.

"The soldiers have been taken to Germany."

"Where to? How do you know?" Isabelle and Princess Marie both asked their questions at the same time and Prince Reginald held up his hands to quieten them.

"Darmstadt, apparently. I heard from some railway workers. The Germans still need them to operate the points."

"Darmstadt," the princess and Isabelle repeated in unison, swiftly followed by Isabelle saying "He's alive," and the princess "They're alive."

"Yes they are, alive and safe for the duration of the war, although I'm not sure what the conditions will be like for them. I have sent a message to London already. Hopefully they can send someone to check on them. There are rules for prisoners of war but I don't think the Germans follow the conventions any more."

"If they did they wouldn't have shot the mayor," Marie said for him.

"Precisely."

"He's alive," Isabelle repeated, and without thinking placed her hand on her belly. She was pregnant. She had known within days of making love with James. The changes to her body had been marked. She had started to grow breasts, a development that had escaped her passage through puberty, and she had a glow. Her mother had commented on how well she looked just that morning. She had been reading a letter that had arrived from Henri. It had taken three weeks to reach her and goodness knows through how many hands it had passed. His letter had contained two proposals and it was the second of these that came into her mind when she heard the news that the soldiers had survived their arrest. He had asked her to marry him.

The prince rose to his feet and excused himself. Isabelle stood too, but Marie suggested she stay a while. They walked through to the lounge and Isabelle sat in the armchair that she and James had shared during their last few hours together.

"What are you going to do?" Marie asked Isabelle when they were both settled.

"I am going to return to the school. I had a letter from Henri today. He wants me back there to help him to run it."

"I meant about Baxter."

"What can I do? He's in German hands. I'm just so pleased to know he is alive," Isabelle said.

"And the baby. You're going to have a baby, aren't you?"

"Yes, yes I am."

"Lieutenant Baxter's?"

"Yes, of course."

"I feel it's my, our, fault. We pushed you together, we have all taken advantage of your willingness to help, and now he has used you."

"No one has used me," Isabelle said, "no one, least of all him. If the truth be known it was me that seduced him. He was too much of a gentleman to lay a hand on me and certainly never an unwanted hand."

"It's early for you, the first few weeks, but I could tell. Your face has filled out. Has your mother said anything, or Jacqueline?"

"My mother said she thought I looked well this morning, but for me to be expecting a baby is so far away from what she would anticipate, it just wouldn't cross her mind. And I've been avoiding Jacqueline."

"I'm sorry that I have intruded into your personal matters, but I feel responsible. I quite envied you your romance with a dashing officer, but I should have insisted on more propriety."

"It is kind of you to say so, but the problem is entirely of my own making. I set my cap at him and got him, and I will never forget the exhilaration of that. He said he will think of me every day, and perhaps he will. Perhaps thoughts of me will bring him some comfort in his captivity. I certainly have a reminder of him." Isabelle looked down at her body as she spoke.

"I hope you consider me a friend, Isabelle, and don't think that I am intruding. But what are you going to do? You can't return to the school pregnant. It would be a scandal, as it will be if you stay here in the village."

"Yes, thank you, I do consider you a friend, and I am thinking of a plan."

"Let me call for some tea, and then you can tell me, if you'd like to of course."

"I am going to return to Lille, to the school I teach at. Henri, the headmaster has just asked me to marry him. He's a widower, and I'd never thought he would marry again. We've been close friends and he suggests we can run the school together."

"But what about your condition? And what about Lieutenant Baxter?"

"If I leave now—I received Henri's letter this morning—and we marry straight away, he will think the baby is his. His marriage was childless and I know Henri would like a child before he is too old. He'll be so proud the mathematics won't be a consideration. And that's if I carry this one. It's such early days I may lose it anyway."

"Then why rush all this, Isabelle? This war will be over soon and James will be free. You and he could be together as a real family."

"He made no promises about coming back," Isabelle said.

"But that doesn't mean he won't. He looked pretty struck by you to me."

"This was just an adventure. One of those rare moments when opportunity and chemistry collide. When this war is over he plans to train horses on his father's estate. He comes from wealthy stock, and I am no more than a country filly."

"I don't think you believe that, Isabelle. And regardless, if he knew of the child he would honour his responsibilities."

"That's the last thing I would want, his sense of duty directed to me."

"Well, I don't think this is a decision to be rushed," Marie said. "Marriage to Henri may feel like a safe option, but it is the rest of your life you will be committing." They sat in silence for a few minutes.

"There is another way," Marie went on. "Let me help you. I could send you to my family in England. You could tell your mother I have found you work there and she need never know about your child. You and James can then meet up after the war."

"There is no me and James, Marie. That's just a fantasy, a lovely thought, but fantasy nonetheless. In other circumstances, normal circumstances, James wouldn't have considered me and I wouldn't have seen myself worthy of him. It's better that I keep the memory of him and the excitement of our times together, to myself. I have to be practical."

"But to make such a definite move to marry Henri, it closes down any hope for you and James."

"Believe me, Marie, I'd love to live the fantasy of James returning on his charger and us all living happily ever after, but life isn't like that. It might be for people who live in chateaux, but not for village girls like me."

"My life must seem charmed to you, Isabelle, but I've had my share of disappointments in life. I wish I'd had your courage when I was young."

"What do you mean?"

"To grasp what you wanted, if only for a moment. I was strangled by protocols and lost the man I loved. My family considered him of too low birth. But you are not like a village girl, Isabelle. You could hold your own in any salon. You are well read, and have proved yourself brave and more capable than many. This war is not all bad news. There will be opportunities that present themselves for women through all this disruption and men will recognize these qualities that you dismiss about yourself. The stuffiness of the past will smother the returning soldiers and they will rebel against the strictures that society will try and pin them with."

"And you think James will step across the class borders? I wouldn't want him to. I wouldn't want to place any burden of responsibility onto him. When he has won his freedom, I will want him to keep it. No, this is of my making and I must sort myself out. Your offer is very kind, more than kind, but I can't accept it. And anyway, I couldn't disappear from my mother's life in that way, it would be too hard on her."

"Well, Isabelle, I can see you are determined and I can only admire you for that. But what am I to say to Lieutenant Baxter on the day when he comes back to find you? Tell me that."

"That I returned to teach in Lille, and that you think you heard that I had married."

"So, it will be my job to break his heart," Marie said. "I think I will say no more than you returned to Lille."

"Whatever you think is best," Isabelle said. "But I don't expect him to come knocking on your door."

"When will you leave?"

"As soon as I can secure my papers for travel. I am going to Bavay tomorrow."

"Perhaps there is something we can do after all. Reginald has to go to Paris at the end of the week. You could travel as his assistant to get across the border and then make your own way to Lille. He can get the papers endorsed quite quickly."

"Now that is a worry taken from me. Thank you. The sooner I can return to Henri, the better the chance of my plan working. Thank you for your help and counsel, Marie. You have proved yourself to be a true friend."

"It has been your wisdom, not mine, Isabelle. I still hold such a romantic notion of love. It escaped me, but I do so want it to be real for you. But you have a sensible head on your shoulders. I am sure everything will work out for you."

"I shall call the baby Jacques, if it's a boy, and Jacqueline if a girl."

"If Henri agrees," Marie said.

261

"He will," Isabelle said, "he will."

Three days later Isabelle set off with the prince on her return journey to Lille. Her mother had been sad to see her leave, but Jacqueline promised to look after her. Few words had passed between Jacqueline and Isabelle, but few had been needed. Jacqueline had seemed to understand and had not questioned any of Isabelle's decisions. Isabelle left her childhood home knowing that she would be married within the month.

FIVE MONTHS LATER

SPRING, 1915

23rd April 1915
Brussels
Marion

The German search party had about a dozen soldiers in it. They poured into the building, up staircases, along corridors and barged their way into rooms and wards. The good thing was, they made so much noise no other warning system was required to ensure the British soldiers retreated to their safe and hidden places to wait out the visit.

Marion was on edge; she had just had an argument with Private Culloch and was flushed and agitated. She busied herself by stripping and remaking the beds on an empty ward so that her unsettled state would go unnoticed. She punched the pillows and remembered their exchange with each blow. He was insufferable. Edith must move him out. He put too much and too many at risk with no thought for anyone but himself. She hated the way he stood so close to her, whether to intimidate or invite intimacy. The warmth of his alcoholic breath on her face made her want to retch. He revolted her and she felt unsafe when he was near.

This was the second search of the clinic in the last month; each time the soldiers had gone away empty-handed, but Edith and Marion's nerves were frayed. They were obviously under suspicion and the threat of exposure weighed down on them.

"I think we must close our doors, for a while at least," Edith said to her after the German soldiers departed that morning.

"But where will they go? The men need our help. We just need to be careful and not let in people like Culloch; I'm sure he's the one that attracts their attention: he goes out every night," Marion said.

"Yes, he is an odious man; he refuses to adhere to any instruction, quite the maverick," Edith agreed.

"Maverick? Selfish, I'd say."

"I heard you in an argument with him. There's really no point, he's not one to listen. We must move him on as quickly as we can. I'll send a message up the line that our doors are closed, we can take in no more men, at least not until this heat is off. We have over a dozen here already: it's too many."

"I'll make contact with the safe houses," Marion said, "and get the men moved out over the next few nights. We need to prepare for the maternity cases that are due here anyway, and they'll need attention round the clock. We have enough to do. This pressure isn't good for either of us."

"You're right, we will be busy, and remind me to brief you on a patient that I would like you to attend to personally when she arrives: she's due in the next few weeks."

"Is she for the maternity ward?"

"Yes. All good experience for you, Marion."

Marion had been due to see Russell that evening, but it was more important that she escort the men to the safe houses. From there they would meet their guides and start the next stage of their hazardous journey. She knew the risks had increased for everyone. The borders had younger guards now and they were less amenable to bribes. One guide had told her the Germans now electrified the border fences between Belgium and Holland so they were much more difficult to cross. The guides pushed rubber tyres into the fences and then fed men through the centre to avoid the voltage charge, but spotlights and machine-guns made border crossings a dangerous venture. She was always devastated to hear of deaths at this final stage of their escape when freedom was so close.

Marion sent a message to Russell at the legation that she could not see him as planned, and would be busy for the next few evenings; she apologized for disappointing him. He never made an issue of changes to arrangements, and she looked forward to a time soon when there was no need for secrets. The last six months had been a strain.

Marion set off early in the evening with one of the men. They left from the rear of the building and walked along some alleyways before they emerged onto the street behind the clinic. She always took the arm of each man she escorted, but rather than pass as a courting couple the men, in hat and coat, would try to imitate the shuffle of an older person, young men being targets to be stopped and arrested.

Marion was alert to other people on the streets and whether they were followed. She glanced around surreptitiously before she turned each corner. She twice walked the length of the street that housed the safe house to ensure no one was in sight, before approaching the door. Madame Francoise let them in immediately she knocked.

"Bring me more tonight. I have a guide here tomorrow: we can move them out. There is a fisherman's boat that will travel to Antwerp. We can fit seven on this. We need to clear them out, the Germans are too close to us at the moment". Madame Francoise spoke so quickly Marion had to concentrate to understand her French.

"Have you had them here?" Marion asked. "They were at the clinic today for another search, but found nothing. We are to shut our doors, Edith says, for a while at least."

"You people take extraordinary risks for us," the soldier said in schoolboy French, "and I haven't thanked you enough."

"Our thanks are when you arrive home safe, that's enough for us. It's the least we can do to help you, you fight for us," Madame Francoise said. "Come with me, I'm afraid it's the cellar for the night, but it's dry." The soldier understood her gestures and nodded.

"If it's all clear, I'll bring more tonight, but I'll wait until later," Marion said.

"Not too late: don't forget the curfew, although it is at nine o'clock now. You don't want to be in trouble for that."

"No, I'll watch myself," and she left from the back of the property.

"I need six more to be ready in an hour." Marion spoke to the sergeant who was their most senior soldier at that time. His looks reminded her a little of Sergeant Meachin, the first soldier they had helped. They had heard at Christmas that he had made it safely back to England but the colonel had been caught and put in a prisoner of war camp. "We have transport arranged, so perhaps the least fit to travel should come first this time. You'll leave Brussels tomorrow morning by boat. There is a bag in the bottom of the wardrobe in your room. It looks like it's full of brown cloth. It's your disguise to get you to the safe house; you'll be dressed as monks."

This idea had been Edith's and it had worked well on several occasions, but Marion still took the precaution of using the back entrance. The six arrived without incident at Madame Francoise's house. The men stripped off the monks' habits and Marion folded them into a sack to take back to the clinic. It was heavy when she lifted it and she debated whether to split the load, but thought with some rests she could manage. She was always visible in her nurse's uniform, but looked about cautiously when she entered the street. She was about ten minutes from the clinic, when she physically bumped into two German officers and dropped the sack, which one of them stooped to pick up.

"This is heavy for you to carry," he said in French.

"I can manage," Marion said, and stretched out for it. "It's blankets from the hospital, they need to be washed."

"Where are you taking them, do you have far to go?"

"To the clinic on the Rue de la Culture, it's not far. Please give them to me, I can take them."

"We will help you, we know where you mean. It is run by a Britisher woman," said the other officer. They turned and walked, one each side of her.

"Yes, Madame Cavell is the director. I am one of her trainees."

"Are you British also?"

"Yes, I am."

"So we can practise our English?"

"Yes," Marion said, switching from French.

"There are not many of the British in Brussels," said the officer who carried the sack.

"No," Marion said, "most went home last year."

"And why did you stay? Are you a spy?"

"No spy would answer that question," said the other officer, and they both laughed.

"You can see I'm a nurse. Perhaps you are a spy, your English is good for a German soldier," Marion said.

"We both studied in London before this war called us home. We could have met you in Trafalgar Square and had a drink in different times."

"Perhaps we could," Marion said, "but that was before we became enemies."

"Ridiculous, isn't it. Why would I ever want to fight someone as pretty as you?"

"This is the clinic. Can I have the blankets?" She reached out to take them.

"Quite right. You are like my sister. She wouldn't make friends with the enemy either. Here is your sack, and take some advice: don't walk out alone, not all my fellow countrymen are gentlemen and a girl like you is a temptation."

Marion took the sack and headed into the clinic. She rested against the door that she closed behind her and tried to steady herself. Her legs felt weak. It was an incidental encounter with a little light banter, but it sat on top of a stressful day and made her realize just how vulnerable she was on the streets. She returned the monks' robes to their hidden store and went to tell their secret guests that no more would be moved that night. She met Culloch on the stairs; he had let himself in through the back door and smelt of drink.

"Hello my pretty one. I just saw you with your boyfriends on the street. Aren't we good enough for you? Why don't we take a walk together and see what friends we can become?"

He pressed himself close to her and Marion squashed back against the wall to keep her face away from his.

"Just what do you think you're doing?" a voice boomed out behind him, and Culloch was almost lifted off his feet by a hand that grabbed the back of his jacket and pulled him away from her.

"Sorry, miss, high spirits, he's a lad away from home and knows no better," said the sergeant who had removed Culloch and given him a boot up the stairs. "He'll not bother you again, I'll make sure of that."

Marion had had enough. She went down the stairs, along the corridor to the nurses' quarters and to her room. She slammed the door and shut out the world. This had to stop.

Marion updated Edith the next morning and told her of the plans to move the last men that night. They were interrupted by information that Edith had a visitor and they went together to the hall to meet him. He told them his name was Georges Quien and said he was a French soldier who needed to get back to his regiment.

"Why would you come here?" Edith said. "We are a clinic, not a railway station."

"I've heard that you can provide help."

"We provide medical help to our patients, that is all. You must leave."

"But I met someone who said you could help."

"You must be mistaken."

"It was Culloch, Private Culloch, he told me to come."

Marion tensed at the name. The sham of their defence was over.

"You know him?" The man pressed his advantage.

"Come to my study," Edith said. "Continue with your work, nurse," and she departed up the stairs with the Frenchman in tow.

When Edith questioned Culloch later, he said he had met Quien in a bar. Despite the curfew Culloch had taken to roaming the streets at night and frequenting the bars used by the locals. Culloch, prematurely aged by drink and poor living, could pass for a much older man. His clothes were nondescript as was his height, light brown hair, and thin face. He fitted in well on the streets and became immediately forgettable. What he did not tell Edith was about the cigarettes the man had given him, nor the drinks he had been bought. He could not remember what he had told the man, but as he lived his life constantly guarded against attack he couldn't imagine he had said much. Quien must have followed him back to the clinic. Culloch didn't trust the man, he never trusted any stranger who bought him drinks. There was always an angle behind it. But he did not tell her that either.

"He's a soldier and he told me he needed help," was all that he said, and Quien was let in.

Culloch could always smell a player and knew Quien was one, but he did not care what the man was about. Culloch had his own plans to leave the clinic that week. He was going to head for Holland, but had no intention of continuing back to England. The Army would only turn him around and ship him back to France with a new rifle and kitbag. He intended to find work somewhere, perhaps on a fishing boat; he had always fancied a life at sea. Or if not work, then he knew he'd find or steal the means to survive. He wouldn't mind a taste of that Nurse Drake before he left, in fact he would have left days before if the smell of her had not got under his skin. Perhaps if he went along when the rest of the group were moved, he would find his chance.

None of the other soldiers paid him any attention. It was clear they did not like him; people rarely did. He was never one of a pack; his feral nature held him separate, and he was often mistrusted. People seemed to instinctively watch their backs when he was around. His winter sojourn in the Mormal forest had been one of his happiest times. He would have preferred more drink and food and greater comfort from the cold, but he had survived. He had befriended one of the stray dogs from a nearby village and they became constant companions, until the morning he woke to find it stiff and cold next to him. For the first time he could remember he had shed a tear. It was boredom more than necessity that had driven him out. He had dodged the Germans at every turn and stolen from huts and houses at will, surprised at the naïve trust of country folk. If it was there for the taking, then he took it.

He had been watching the de Croy's chateau for some days before he saw his opportunity to approach them and ask for help to get out of the area. They had put him in the tower, along with the two other soldiers he had watched arrive the night before. The soldiers had not been on the run for long. They had found themselves on the wrong side of the line after the battle of Neuve Chapelle and were determined to get back into the fight as soon as they could. They assumed he had the same intent.

Culloch had feigned interest in Baxter and the men when he told the princess of his winter in the woods. She had not questioned Culloch's rejection of the plan to surrender. She understood in war it was every man for himself, and Baxter's men had taken an enormous risk to give themselves up in Bavay. The mayor had lost his life but Baxter and the men had survived their capture and had been taken to a prisoner of war camp in Germany, she did not say where. Isabelle had returned to teaching in Lille. Culloch had been relieved that she was not around for him to bump into; she would have turned the princess against him. He liked having a clean slate with her and was truly grateful for the guided passage she and her brother secured for him to Brussels. They had been generous with a gift of cash too, and he had helped himself to a pair of candlesticks, which he hoped to sell. He was still looking for the right place to take them in Brussels. It had taken a week to reach the capital, mostly walking at night. He thought his guide had been over-cautious. He would have taken far more risks, but he had spent his life sailing close to the wind; he found it exhilarating. At the clinic he was under no one's command; he came and went as he pleased and plotted his future each night as he drank.

Marion was on duty with a complex delivery for the whole of the day. Sister Wilkins had supervised her and had been pleased with the way she handled the birth, but both were tired by the evening. Edith told Marion that she must rest and that she would move the men but Marion insisted that she took them. They had been notified of a rendezvous near a café in a rough part of the city and Edith was uncomfortable about it. The soldiers were joining a group of workers who were heading north. There could be safety in numbers. Big, brave, and bold, and right under the noses of the Germans, the last place they would expect to look for escapees.

Culloch was undecided. He was inclined to leave Brussels with the other men, and he had heard they were leaving that evening, but he was determined to catch Nurse Drake on her own, and the best opportunity for this would be on her way back to the clinic. He had sold the candlesticks earlier that day. Quien had come in useful with a contact and they had fetched a good sum. He packed up his things and gathered alongside the other men at the hour they were due to leave. Quien was there, but Culloch could not see Nurse Drake. He kept a look-out for her, but as they all stepped out of the building, she was not to be seen.

"Are you looking for someone?" Quien said as he got into step beside Culloch.

"I wanted to say goodbye to the other nurse."

"Which one is that? What's her name?"

Culloch immediately smelt a trap.

"The pretty one, that's her name, the pretty one."

It was not going to be his night to have her, but he was not going to make it easy for someone else to either. They all slipped out of the back of the building and into the dark shadows on the street, and there she was, waiting for them. She started off ahead of them and the sergeant at the front of the group kept a distance between her and the men.

Culloch kept a close eye on Quien and on whether they were followed. He could not be sure, but he thought he kept seeing a man slipping into the shadows behind them. Probably his imagination. They made their way out of the smart residential part of the city to the narrower streets with alleyways that criss-crossed them. It actually pleased him to think that he would be accompanying Nurse Drake on her return; he didn't want to think of her walking these streets on her own. She was for him. He saw her stop in front of a café where some working men were gathered outside. She went in. She was only gone a few minutes when a man came out and beckoned for all the men to follow him. Culloch watched Quien. He half expected him to slip away from the group but he did not and what now looked like a work party set off, Quien with them. But not Culloch. He stepped back into the shadows and waited. Marion came out minutes later and started to retrace her steps. Culloch knew he had to act soon, before the alleyways ended and the streets broadened. He was light on his feet and kept up close behind her. He looked back once when he heard a footfall behind him, but could not see anyone and it prompted him to act. He saw that she was going to pass the entrance to an alleyway within a few paces, so he ran towards her and grabbed her as she began to turn her head and pushed her into the darkened passageway. His hand was over her mouth to stifle the scream that she now had no time to make. She was taller than him but he had the advantage of surprise and strength and he easily pushed her to the ground. He was on top, pressing down on her as she lay on her front. He just needed to turn her over, when suddenly he felt a kick in his side, followed by another. He gasped with the sharpness of the pain and released his hold on Marion. The next kick almost lifted him off her and he found it difficult to draw in a breath.

"Marion, move, quickly, move."

Culloch heard a man's voice call her name and felt Nurse Drake struggle to her feet.

"Russell?"

Culloch did not hear any more, he was retching into the gutter.

23rd April 1915
Brussels
Russell

"Can you walk?" Russell put his arm around her and pulled her into the street.

"Yes," Marion gasped. "I think so."

"Hurry then, let's get away from here." They could hear retching coming from the alleyway. He kept her tucked into his side and they moved as quickly as they could. He only allowed their pace to slow when they reached the broad avenues and he was convinced her attacker had not followed them. They stopped to catch their breath and Marion brushed down her uniform to remove the grime. She was shaking all over.

"Are you hurt?" Russell asked.

"No, just a bit battered and baffled."

"Thank goodness I was there. I dread to think what would have happened."

"Yes," said Marion, "but what were you doing there? You're a long way from the embassy. It's not your part of town."

"Nor yours Marion, and who were those men? What on earth were you doing with them?"

"Come on, we must keep walking and watch the time." Marion turned and started along the avenue with Russell in step.

"Marion, that man was attacking you. Who was he? Do you know him?"

"I was taking the men to join a work party."

"Why? Who are they?"

"Calm down, Russell, and I'll tell you."

"Calm down! If I hadn't been there you could be dead in a gutter by now."

"You're right, I was in trouble. You saved me."

Those were the words that Russell wanted to hear, but he gained no satisfaction as she conveyed no gratitude in her tone.

"The men are refugees. We have been looking after them at the clinic. They don't have papers so it's dangerous for them to be on the streets, but we heard of a man who could take them north for work. I needed to make the introduction."

"You had to! Why you? It's obviously not safe."

"I didn't want Edith to do it."

"This isn't something for women to be involved in. It's far too dangerous."

"I've had a long tough day, Russell, which hasn't ended well, and I am in no mood for a lecture."

"Well, someone needs to talk some sense into you, it seems. Just imagine what your father would say."

"My father is a minister. He helps people all the time."

"But not taking risks like this, Marion."

"Nothing has gone wrong before."

"Before! You've done this before? Marion, what is going on?"

"Nothing, well not any more, that's the last of them, the refugees."

"Well, thank goodness for that."

"We have maternity cases to deal with now. Another legacy from the Germans."

Russell and Marion had reached the steps of the clinic.

"Thank you, Russell. I am truly grateful for your help this evening. I am tired and am going to go straight to bed."

"And no more evening sojourns, like this, promise me?"

"I promise. Really, I do."

"And you can tell me more about what you have been doing when we are next together."

"I don't have to give an account of myself to you, Russell. Or perhaps you can explain why you were following me, when we next meet."

Without a further word Marion climbed the steps and entered the house. Russell felt wrong-footed again.

Russell had been inspired, when he first assisted Hugh and Mr Whitlock, by how assiduously they wrote their journals. He was aping them with a volume of his own and with their discipline of sitting and writing an entry before bedtime each evening. None of them always managed such a tight routine, but the contents definitely suffered the longer the gap between event and notation. On each fresh page Russell first drew a margin down both sides of the paper. The date typically went into the left hand margin and into the space on the right he noted his assignations with Marion and a few key words to capture the essence of their time together, or their conversation.

Café, 2 hours,
laughed but M worried,
What about?

On some days, in the bureaucratic jungle of his work, Russell was completely lost and could not see the wood for the trees, but he forced himself to put down at least one piece of information each day. It delighted him when he looked back over the months of entries and realized just how much he had done and what had been achieved. The work of the commission had settled into a well-run machine, not without its hitches, but that was to be expected; his latest problem had been the refusal of passes for his new auditors. The Germans had taken exception to the number of changeovers and had refused his requests. He was actually of the same mind as them; his life would be far easier if, once trained, the interns had stayed for the duration, but they were volunteers and he had to accept their terms and timetables. It had taken a letter from Hoover himself to push the German administrators to comply.

Russell had returned to the embassy and was sitting in his room with his journal in front of him. The entry Russell had made the day before in the right-hand margin was a heart with an arrow through it and the letters RC L MD. Juvenile, but he was still smitten, even though she had caused him so much anxiety of late. He had begun to suspect that she was seeing someone else, with her lack of availability and frequent change of plans, and she often seemed distracted when they were together. He no longer asked for an explanation as this inevitably created a reaction from her that was hard to recover from in the limited and always public time they had together.

He had tracked their relationship through his journal and on recent review had challenged himself as to whether the relationship only existed as his fantasy and all they really enjoyed was a friendship, so detached had she seemed. Perhaps he needed to prepare himself to face the truth that she did not love him and was too polite in her British way to tell him; it was, after all, always him that initiated their meetings and she that cancelled.

He picked up his journal and flicked back through the pages. He was still moved to tears when he recalled the thanks the people of the city had expressed to them at the legation at New Year and in such a way that the Germans could do nothing to stop them. He flicked back through the pages and reread his entry for the 1st January 1915.

> *All day long people from the city poured through the doors of the lega-*
> *tion. They had set up a book that they took turns to sign, or place*
> *their visiting cards. Some left flowers, roses and orchids, all gestures of*
> *thanks, for without us they knew they would have starved. Thousands*
> *visited, but always in small clusters. The Germans could never claim*
> *there was a public gathering, so there was no trouble. The gratitude*
> *pervaded all classes, and children too, although I think they had been*
> *more excited about the Rockefeller toys that had arrived at Christmas*
> *than the food. I have never felt more proud of my country ….*

And in the margin:
M distracted.
Not sure she
happy with me.

He had forgotten his concerns went that far back. He picked up his pen to record the evening's events.

> *Marion cancelled our arrangements so I decided on a walk. Fresh air is*
> *always welcome on a pleasant evening and after long winter months.*

> *Walked for half an hour and found myself at Marion's lodgings.*
> *I hadn't paid attention to my route.*

He underlined the word "*hadn't*". There had been no forethought behind his actions that evening.

> *I wondered if I would be making a nuisance of myself if I called*
> *for her. Thought of pretending I hadn't received her note cancelling our*
> *evening. Perhaps someone would tell me what she did on the evenings*
> *she didn't see me, she is always so evasive when I ask. I chickened out*
> *and was moving on around the corner, when I heard the door opening.*
> *It was then that I spotted you.*

Russell had to stop writing and scrub out "*you*" and replace it with "*her*". He grimaced as he realized he was rehearsing his explanation to Marion as he wrote.

> *She was standing on the pavement looking in the other direction*
> *down the street. She didn't see me and I pulled back behind a tree and*
> *watched her.*

Even as he wrote he felt uncomfortable about this.

> *I wanted to know what she was doing and where she was going, and*
> *who with. I didn't have long to wait. About a dozen ragged looking*
> *men walked out of a passageway that appeared to run along the back*
> *of the clinic. Marion set off down the road and, at a distance, the men*
> *followed. They looked like a crew of labourers, but they were all silent.*
> *Twice I thought the man at the rear of the group had spotted me.*
> *He looked around a lot. I wondered how Marion knew her way around*
> *this part of the city. This didn't feel right. The houses became more*
> *run down and the smells were bad. There was garbage everywhere.*
> *I turned a corner just in time to see Marion enter a café. The men stood*
> *together in a group outside, and there were a few other men waiting*
> *on the street too. A man came out of the café and signalled them all to*
> *follow, which they did, apart from one. The man who had been looking*
> *behind him had slipped away from the group.*

Russell remembered seeing him standing beside the arched entrance to a church.

> *I wondered if he was waiting to escort Marion back to the clinic.*
> *Marion left the café and walked back down the road and the*
> *man moved away from the arch and followed behind her. His move-*
> *ments looked furtive as he crept along. It was clear he didn't want*
> *Marion to know he was there as he held back several times when she*

279

turned her head to cross roads. All of a sudden the man started to sprint towards Marion and pounced and in the blink of an eye they had disappeared. I ran along the pavement and into the passage that Marion had been pushed into and almost fell over them. They were both on the ground, the man on top of Marion, so I kicked out as hard as I could. I heard a groan as my foot made contact, so kicked again as hard as I could, and again. My last kick dislodged the man off Marion and I shouted at her to move. She recognized my voice and I helped her away. Thank goodness I was there.

Russell put down his pen. Thank goodness he was there, but the events of the evening had not pulled Marion and him closer to each other. At their parting she had been cordial at best and showed no gratitude for his assistance. Helping refugees? What was she doing out on the streets with them? If they did not have papers she should not be involved. If she won't listen to me, Russell thought, he would ask Hugh to talk some sense into her. The last thing he was going to do when he saw her next was defend why he was on the same street as her. If she could be evasive, then so could he.

26th April 1915
Brussels
Therese

Therese finished her prayers and stood up. The chapel was empty, the way she had wanted it for these final private moments. Today was the day Sister Paul had decided she was to travel to Brussels; the bishop had arranged transport and the necessary passes, so her path had been eased. Therese had grown large in the last few weeks and it was this that had prompted her departure a few weeks ahead of when the baby was due, just in case it arrived early.

She was to be admitted to a private clinic in Rue de la Culture, in the Ixelles region of the city. She had never been to Brussels and was quite keen to see it, but she would have preferred different circumstances. The thought of leaving the convent had created a mixed reaction: sometimes it was panic and other times a feeling of excitement. Nothing had felt the same after she had realized she was pregnant. Since then she had been increasingly aware of herself and that was counter to the self-denial she had been disciplined in for years. She had kept her own counsel on this and had worked out a way to accommodate the needs of the baby while she ignored her own. The mental separation worked in all things; she ate her normal portion of food for herself and then more for the baby; she had her usual rest period and then allowed more when the baby demanded it. Although it was an inner game she played with herself, it enabled her to maintain her sense of self-discipline while not treating her uninvited guest harshly. She would deny her baby nothing.

Sister Paul waited for her to say her goodbyes. They had discussed all the arrangements and Therese was clear on what was to happen and exactly what was expected of her. She had acquiesced to all but the request that she leave her habits behind and travel in clothes that had been provided. To lose her habit felt like a betrayal, both ways. Either she was denying God in her life, or it was symbolic of His separation from her, and she wanted neither.

"It's the bishop's express wish," Sister Paul had repeated against her resistance. "He doesn't want people to see the Church so compromised. You really must make sure you are not seen in this condition."

Therese's will had prevailed even though Sister Paul's lips now pursed every time she saw her. Stubbornness was a sin, but Therese felt no guilt. This experience was hers and she would only accept the terms they dictated when they did not infringe her sense of what was right. Therese had felt Sister Paul's withdrawal after their very first conversation about her pregnancy, when she had expressed no shame and had voiced delight at the thought of hosting a life. Sister Paul's outrage and repugnance had been strong, but Therese had not been cowed.

She collected her bag. Although small, it was weighty, containing her notebooks of the dramas experienced by the refugees. She went through the cloisters to the entrance. It was late evening, part of their plan for her to travel unnoticed, but disappointing, as she would have loved to have passed through the countryside and taken in the views.

"God be with you, Therese." Sister Paul was alone at the entrance.

"And with you, Sister Paul."

"You are not to worry about anything. All the arrangements are in place. The Church will collect the child and the nurses will take care of it until that happens. Once through the ordeal of the birth, all these troubles will be behind us. The Order will welcome you when you are discharged from the clinic. All will be well."

282

Therese smiled her thanks, bent to pick up her bag, and walked through the door. It clanged shut behind her. The door of a motor car was open in front of her and she climbed in. The driver closed the door and then cranked the handle until the engine rumbled into life. Therese felt herself shake when the vehicle started to vibrate. She slid back against the seat and put her hands protectively over her belly and prayed as the car eased forward and then lurched through the streets of Leuven towards Brussels. They were stopped more than a dozen times at roadblocks, and each time their journey was approved by the pass the driver handed over. Therese was more relieved than worried by these stops. They gave her an opportunity to adjust her seat and take some deep breaths. This, her first ride in a motorized vehicle, dominated the experience of being out of the convent, and she did not enjoy it. She became thankful that it was dark. It was better not to see the speed at which they travelled with the countryside rushing past. She had just started to feel nauseous when the lights of Brussels appeared.

Marion's day had been busy and she was on her way back to her room when Edith had caught her on the stairs.

"The special guest I want you to attend to will arrive this evening, Marion. Are you sure you're happy to stay on duty to meet her and settle her in?"

"Yes, a room is ready for her and I'll make sure I'm in reception after supper. Do we know yet what the secrecy is about?"

"Yes, I do, but I'll let you make your own discovery if she wishes to reveal it."

"Well, we're used to secrecy now, aren't we?" Marion replied.

Marion did not push Edith to share her knowledge; they had learnt to trust each other and Marion immediately respected her silence on the matter of their guest. It had been a few days earlier that Edith had described the need for them to provide a private confinement, and Marion had prepared a room away from the other wards.

Marion sat in the reception hall after supper. She was uncertain about the exact time of arrival for their guest. Fourteen babies had been born since they had opened their doors for maternity cases, and Marion now felt confident attending a birth. An administrator from the general hospital had visited them recently to warn them to expect and prepare for an influx of girls who would be due to give birth within the next six weeks. These girls had been raped at the outset of war and many were in a sorry state.

Marion had suffered her own nightmares since the attack on her in the alleyway, and yet she had been saved from any real assault. She could not imagine what the last months had been like for these victims, with the constant reminder growing within them. Marion was convinced her assailant was Culloch. The smell of the man's breath and the wiry body she had felt on top of her had made her think of him. It would have been easy for him to wait back and not follow along with the other men. She had felt his menace whenever their paths had crossed, and he had obviously waited for his chance. She still shuddered at the thought of what would have happened if Russell hadn't rescued her, but she was also angry with him for being there. He had followed her, that was clear, and that thought added to her discomfort. So did the realization that she had not really expressed much gratitude to him and her parting words, in the circumstances, were ungrateful and rude. No wonder she had not heard from him since, and it really was her that had the explaining to do. This time it was her apology that should reach him first.

Marion missed the relaxed freedoms she and Russell had enjoyed at the start of their relationship and wanted them to return. She knew it was her that had introduced the tension and that some contrition on her part was needed. She had to learn to overcome the rebelliousness that burst through every time she felt he wanted to control what she did. Always so headstrong, she could hear her mother's frequent complaint about her. Maybe she would never be ready to "love, honour, and obey". She hoped Edith could withstand the requests and not take in any more soldiers. She wanted to put the pressures behind her and start to relax with Russell. She wanted no more lies between them.

Marion jumped up when she heard a motor car as it turned the corner into their street and slowly progressed as if searching for a particular house. She opened the door and the light from the hall flooded onto the steps as the car came to a stop. The driver alighted and opened the back door. Marion gasped as she watched Therese emerge from the vehicle. She could not actually believe her eyes. A heavily pregnant nun walked slowly towards her and up the stairs.

Therese was relieved when the car stopped and then somewhat shocked when the door immediately opened and she was expected to get out. She struggled with her bag, and the driver reached in and took it from her. She stood on the pavement and put her hands on the roof of the vehicle to help her gain her balance and then turned and walked up the steps to an open door and an open-mouthed nurse.

"Hello, I'm Sister Therese."

Marion quickly tried to gather herself but the surprise, and her embarrassment at revealing it, meant that her French vocabulary escaped her and she stood mute in front of Therese. The driver broke the silence when he delivered Therese's bag at her feet and Marion instinctively bent to retrieve it. She beckoned for Therese to follow her inside and closed the door behind them.

Marion, with Therese behind her, walked slowly as she crossed the hall and up two flights of stairs, pausing to allow Therese to catch her breath, then along some corridors and into a room that was neatly ordered with a bed, small cabinet, chair, and a window. She put down Therese's bag and returned to the door to close it whilst all the time attempting to regain her professional composure. She fixed a smile and turned to welcome Therese.

"You must be tired after your journey. Do sit down and take the weight off your feet. I'm Marion Drake, and I am to be the nurse who will attend you. Please relax and know that you are in safe hands."

Therese was still breathless from climbing the stairs. She sat herself in the chair and looked around. The room was not much larger than her own at the convent, but it had a paper covering on the walls with faded flowers, a much larger bed and window, a mirror on the wall, and a knotted rug on the floor. She looked at the rug and tried to pick out original colours in the rags, but too many years on the floor had dulled these beyond recognition. Marion was standing and looking at her as if waiting for her to speak.

"I am sorry to have shocked you. It's my fault. I was too stubborn. Sister Paul wanted me not to wear my habit, but I insisted. I was only thinking of myself."

"I'm always messing things up by wanting my way. It's my biggest flaw, according to my mother," Marion said as she sat on the corner of the bed.

"Mine was always wanting to pray, according to my mother."

"Mothers are always difficult to please. Shall I help you unpack?" Marion asked.

"No, thank you," Therese said quite abruptly. "I can easily manage. I haven't brought much with me."

"There's a gown on the bed for you to use, and a set of drawers for you to put your things in."

"Thank you. It's good to sit and be still after that journey. My first in a motor," she added by way of explanation. "I think my baby is still jumping around," and she put a protective hand onto the front of her habit. "I should have worn normal clothes. I can see by your reaction they were right. I hadn't appreciated how much my appearance would shock; I must look a strange sight."

"A sight that makes my blood boil. The cruelty seems even more marked against you. You'd think they would at least respect the Church."

"Some did," and Therese told Marion about the two soldiers that acted as their guardians and kept the mob away from them when the rampages started.

"As my mother loves to say, let's be thankful for small mercies," Marion said as she rose and lifted Therese's bag onto the bed.

"Let me leave you to unpack while I go and fetch some refreshments for you. Are you hungry? Will bread and cheese and a hot drink suffice?"

"A little of whatever you have would be fine."

Marion could see the fatigue that was behind Therese's smile.

"I will be quick. Your bathroom is just next door, this way." Marion pointed to the right as she left Therese.

Therese slept well that night. She had not expected to as her surroundings were so new to her, and after such a momentous journey. She was surprised at how refreshed she felt when she awoke the next morning. She could tell that the baby was still asleep so she lay quietly and drifted into her morning meditations; she felt at peace. There was something about this place that made her feel safe. She was unprepared for this. The convent was her place of sanctuary, despite the attack; but here she found she was even more relaxed. As she focused on her meditation she saw a picture from the biblical story of Moses when he was hidden in the bulrushes to escape the putting to death of baby boys that the pharoah had commanded. She watched herself enter the scene and place her baby in the bulrushes, next to Moses. When she came out of the meditation she understood her feeling of well-being. Her baby was going to be safe. He would not be taken by the Church.

A knock on the door was followed by Marion, walking in with a breakfast tray. She placed it on the cabinet.

"Good morning, sister, I hope you slept well."

"Please, do call me Therese, and yes I did, thank you."

"I'll leave you to your breakfast and ablutions, and will return in about an hour to go through our admittance procedures. Will that be all right with you?"

"Whatever is needed is all right with me."

"I'll have to examine you, so you might not want to dress until that's over; no under- garments is what I need."

"Oh, of course." Therese had not anticipated such attentions. "I'll be ready."

And she was when Marion returned with clipboard and medical paraphernalia in hand.

"Let me take your pulse while you are in the chair, and then I'll ask you to lie on the bed."

Marion put her fingers on Therese's wrist, moving them around until she found the radial beat and looked at the pocket watch she had brought into the room with her and counted. She made a note on a sheet under Therese's name. "The beat is really good. I'd expected it to be faster. You've had a great deal going on in the last 24 hours."

"I slept well, but I have just seen myself in a mirror for the first time in years, so I'm surprised it's not faster too. Do you have a cloth that I can cover the mirror with?"

"Seriously? Why would you want to do that, you look lovely?"

Therese's face was framed by fair hair that she usually had scraped back beneath her veil. Her eyes, Marion would call them violet, had dark lashes and the size of them were accentuated by the natural arch of her eyebrows. Her skin was pale but she exuded a healthy glow, even though she had not been in the sun.

"Yes please. It's not our way to see ourselves."

"Of course, I'll arrange that for you. Now do you know which week you are in?"

"From the night it happened, its 35 weeks."

Marion made notes as she continued the physical examination. The baby was in a good position but still had some weeks to grow, so Therese was in for a long confinement. Marion conveyed every piece of information with explanations when required and she could see that Therese picked up on things quickly.

"Your ankles are slightly swollen, so you must have bed rest during the day."

"You don't mean all day, do you?"

"No, not at all, just after lunch for an hour, and feet up in the evening."

Marion placed a trumpet tube onto Therese's navel, put her ear to it and moved it around until she located the heartbeat.

"That's a strong heartbeat I can hear."

Tears ran down Therese's face.

"I'm sorry, that was thoughtless of me. This must be such an ordeal for you. I'm sorry I can't say it will be over soon. Babies arrive when the baby decides."

"This baby is God's gift, Nurse Drake, it's not an ordeal for me; I feel honoured to host this life."

"Really? Can you feel that kindly after being attacked? When I think what those animals did, I can't even imagine the type of beasts they are to do this to you, a nun. Edith told me about the circumstances. Nothing is sacred to them; and you are so sanguine about it."

"Your disgust at my acceptance reminds me of Sister Paul; she was of the same mind as you."

"I am so sorry, Therese. As ever my mouth has run away with me, but I'm so angry with all the German impositions, and to see you like this is the absolute limit. And it's Marion, by the way, please call me Marion."

"I don't harbour hatred in my heart. I love this baby and I want the best for him." As she said this a cloud passed across Therese's face.

"What is it?" Marion asked.

"I'm troubled by the arrangements for my baby; the Church plan to take him to an orphanage. They consider him, like you do, to be the spawn of the Devil. What life will that be for him? His conception is history; it's his life that concerns me. I'm pleased he's not due for a while. I have much to resolve in my mind, for him."

"You seem sure the baby is a boy."

"Of that I have no doubt."

28th April 1915
Brussels
Marion

Edith and Marion were together in Edith's office. They were in celebratory mood.

"The men have crossed the border and are on their way to England," Edith said.

"That's wonderful news. Did they run into any trouble?" Marion asked.

"Apparently not. In fact it was so straightforward, the guide found it hard to believe. He said their individual papers were hardly checked, they passed through as one work group."

"No barbed wire this time. To think of all those nights he has spent dodging spotlights and machine gun fire in the past. Did he still claim his fee?" Marion asked.

"Oh yes, he took his envelope straight away, and he said he did have one problem to deal with."

"What was that?"

"You mean, who? It was Culloch."

"Culloch? What do you mean, what happened?"

"Apparently Culloch was in a fight with someone. He was kicked around a bit. The group thought they'd lost him, and he was in a bit of a state when he caught up with them, but he didn't say what had happened. Kept himself to himself and then he disappeared again after they crossed the border."

"You're sure it was after they crossed the border. He has gone hasn't he?"

"That's what the guide said. They were all safely across when Culloch and the Frenchman, Quien, disappeared. They both slipped away. Had their own plans it seems."

"As long as he *has* gone," Marion said.

Marion had told Edith nothing of the attack. She had not wanted to worry her and there seemed nothing to gain from it. She was relieved to hear that Culloch was across the border. Perhaps she could sleep more easily now she knew he was not roaming the streets waiting for her to step outside. Today she would take her note to Russell at the embassy.

"I'm so pleased they are gone, and the de Croys know we can't take any more," Edith said. "I feel exhausted, and I can see how tired you look. It's good that we can have a break from the pressure."

"I totally agree, no more worries. If the Germans come stamping through the place they'll just have babies to contend with."

"Sister Wilkins said you managed a difficult birth very well the other day."

"She helped me with it. I couldn't have done it on my own. She is always so calm; I can still feel panicked."

"We all can at times, and each birth is different, you never know what to expect."

"I look forward to more. It will be good to be kept on my toes after the tensions of the last months."

"You have handled everything very well, Marion. We've travelled quite a road together and many soldiers have been kept safe because of us. We can proudly say we played our part."

"Not that we can say that to anyone. It's the secrecy that has been the hardest part. I shall be pleased not to have anything to hide from Russell now. I know he has wondered what has been going on with me at times. He's been very patient."

"He is a lucky man if he has you to count on, don't ever forget that, and I am sure he won't."

"Thank you, Edith. I have a break to my schedule after lunch and I plan to go and see him. I'm hoping he can take a walk in the park with me. I'll enjoy some fresh air. I feel as if the winter is really behind us now, and thank goodness after such a long and cold one."

"That sounds like a good idea. I would even be tempted to join you but I have a lot of work to catch up on. I've had to keep two sets of accounts to cover all the additional costs for the soldiers and I need to make sure the records are straight for Dr Depage. Not my favourite task. How is your patient settling in, Sister Therese?"

"Quite well considering how strange everything is for her. Sometimes I can get no conversation out of her at all, but other times she will talk. Amazingly she seems to have accepted what has happened to her, even talks about it being the will of God."

"Extraordinary," Edith said. "How wonderful her faith is so strong."

"It makes her easy to look after. She keeps her own spirits up. Some of the girls are very downcast."

"Yes, we'll be in for some difficult births, I'm sure. Time for your walk, Marion."

Marion and Edith parted, more relaxed than they had felt in a long time.

Marion was sitting in the reception hall at the embassy, waiting for Russell. He was able to join her for a walk, but needed another half an hour first. She was happy to wait. She felt the note in her pocket that she had written to him, but she preferred to be able to talk and was pleased that he had seemed keen to join her. The minutes passed quickly and they were soon arm in arm, matching each other's steps as they strode along the avenue towards the park.

"Thank you for calling round," Russell said. "How are you feeling? Are you recovered from your ordeal? I have been worried about you."

"Yes, I'm fine, really I am. I've had a few sleepless moments in the dead of night, but I'm fine. And I want to thank you, properly thank you. You were an absolute trooper. Thank goodness you were there. You really did save me."

"I would have called round to see how you were, but I had to go to one of the eastern regions to settle in two new administrators. They change so often."

"And I was rude and ungrateful at the time. I'm sorry. Whatever your reason for being there doesn't need to be said."

"Oh, but I …"

"No, Russell, there is no need. Let's both just be thankful that you were there."

"But what are you involved in, Marion? Will you tell me that?"

"Yes, of course. We had been helping some refugees at the clinic and we heard of a working party that they could join …"

"You said this the other evening, Marion," Russell interrupted, "but why were you taking them, and to such a rough part of town? It doesn't make sense."

"I hadn't thought of it as being dangerous."

"He was one of them, you know, the man that attacked you. I saw him hang back. I thought he was going to escort you home. It took me a while to realize he had other ideas."

"It shouldn't surprise me. One of them had been pestering me a bit."

"So you know who it was? We can get the authorities onto him. He won't get away with this."

"He has already got away, Russell. The work party has gone over the border to work in Holland. He's gone. I'm safe, so let's put it all behind us."

"How do you know he's gone? He could still be here? He might try again."

"We heard back that they were all through the border."

"Are you still involved with these people? You said that was the last. Can you promise me that, Marion?"

"Yes, Russell, I can promise you that. There will be no more refugees at the clinic. Edith has said we can't afford it, and anyway we have enough patients to deal with. I have been working on maternity cases."

Marion felt relieved to know that all the subterfuge was behind her, and them. She felt more relaxed than she could remember for a long time and she could tell that she was conveying this to Russell. She kept glancing at him as they walked side by side and smiled every time he caught her eye.

"You certainly seem fine to me. You have quite a spring in your step. It's been a while since I've seen that. Having babies obviously suits you."

"Not having babies, assisting with the births."

"I know, I know. Whatever it is, it's suiting you. Shall we go in here?" Russell had stopped in front of a café.

"I'd rather carry on walking. A circuit of the park would do me good, if that's all right?"

"Yes, me too. I spend far to much time sitting at a desk."

"The girls are so vulnerable, the ones at the clinic, my heart goes out to them. Two have had premature stillbirths and I'm sure they willed their babies to die, or maybe they were just malnourished. It has been a tough winter for so many. When will those Germans pack up and go home?"

"Doesn't look like they have any intention of doing that. All the troops have dug in along the battle line apparently. Hugh and the minister were at a dinner hosted by von Below yesterday. Hugh was telling me about it this morning. Von Below has been called back to Berlin again. I'm not sure who is taking over the administration from him."

"They dined with the Germans?"

"Yes. A few generals and quite a few officers were there too. Hugh said they seemed fine fellows, the sort we would all get along with."

"Get along with? What is he thinking? Look at all the bad things they've done. He should come and meet these girls and their bastard babies."

"As people he meant, not as soldiers. He said they were fine people: educated, well-travelled, well-mannered."

"But they are soldiers. Enemy soldiers."

"They are not my enemy, Marion. The British and the Belgians, yes, but not of the US."

"Are you all hiding behind your political neutrality again? Don't forget how upset you were when they burnt the library at Leuven."

"Yes, that was unspeakable."

"When something is wrong, it's wrong, Russell, and they are the perpetrators."

"I know, but I have to work alongside them and most of the time they don't cause me any problems. They certainly haven't disrupted the distribution of food. Some of the soldiers I've spoken to just want to get back home to their own families. They don't want to be here."

"They should go then. If the soldiers left, there would be no war."

"They shoot deserters and make quite an example of them to deter the rest."

"They'd butcher anyone. I hate them."

"That's because they are a faceless enemy for you, Marion. If you met them in normal circumstances, you would probably like them."

Marion remembered the two officers she had met and found that she could agree with Russell, but by now she was not in the mood to concede to his view.

"We're not going to agree on this, Russell. I've seen too much suffering to forgive them."

"I'm not blind to the difficulties, Marion."

"But you haven't been touched by them, Russell, that's the difference, and until you are you just won't understand, you won't feel it."

"I don't want to feel hatred."

"Not hatred, feel others' hurt, then you can be passionate, then you'll know what's right. Not because of what's in your head, because of what's in your heart."

"You make me sound heartless, Marion, and I'm not. I feel. I feel for you. I would have killed for you the other night."

"My knight in shining armour."

"Don't mock me."

"I'm sorry, I wasn't mocking you. I am deeply grateful to you." Marion squeezed his arm.

"Why does it feel as if we are always fighting, Marion?"

"Does it? Is that what we're doing?"

"We used to have more fun together?"

"These are serious times."

"There you go again, Marion. You keep taking the moral high ground, and that keeps pushing me down."

"Sorry, sorry, you're right. I don't mean to push you down, and I don't want to be serious all the time either. We should feel we can escape when we are together. It's just that we are experiencing very different wars." Marion pulled Russell to sit beside her on a bench seat in the park.

"Or perhaps we are more different from each other than we thought. You're all heart and I'm all head," Russell said.

"I have a good head on my shoulders too," Marion retorted.

"And I have a good heart too, but you seem to doubt that."

"I don't doubt that, Russell. I wouldn't be walking out with you if I did and my father wouldn't have told me to give you a chance if he hadn't felt that. He doesn't miss much about people. But that's why my father said I was to give you a chance. He was telling me to curb my feisty nature. I can be very judgmental and too intolerant of others' opinions when they are counter to mine. I won't kowtow to another's view."

"And I adore that about you, Miss Headstrong Drake and wouldn't want you to be any other way. Shall we head back?"

"Yes. That means we will have disagreements, Russell. Are you prepared to accept that?"

Russell looked at Marion. Her tone had softened and she was smiling at him.

"As long as you can accept that perceptions and opinions will differ," Russell said.

"What you're saying is, I can't always be the one that is right."

"It takes someone to think they're right for an argument to start."

"That sounds clever."

"I am clever. Clever to have found you."

"I thought I found you."

"Do you ever let someone else have the last word?" Russell asked.

"Not very often, but I am one of three sisters and we all liked to hold our ground."

"And they both married military men?"

"Yes, and both husbands are very dashing."

"I was thinking less of their uniforms and more of their skill in giving orders. Perhaps they can teach me."

"Perhaps we can teach each other," Marion said.

"Perhaps we can. Come on, let's liven up a bit, and I insist on walking you back to the clinic," Russell said as he headed them both out of the park.

2nd May 1915
Brussels
Marion

After a few days of looking after Therese, Marion realized that the nun found the constraints of remaining in her room during confinement overbearing. It had been impressed upon her by Edith that Therese was not to be seen outside the clinic, so they had worked out a route along the corridors for her to gain some exercise. It would have been easier if Therese would wear normal clothes, but on this point she was adamant.

"But we could even take a stroll in the park if you didn't wear your habit," Marion said.

"I know I exasperate you, but I need you to understand: this is who I am. My habit is like my outer skin. Take this away and I'm nothing; in God's eyes I won't exist."

"Of course you will, you'll still be you; it's only cloth."

"It is more than that to me. I donned this when I gave my life and myself over to the service of God and since then my daily battle has been to ignore my wants and follow His call. If I strip this away for greater comfort then I place myself before His will. Believe me, I need God on my side to get through this and He hasn't deserted me yet."

"Not even when you were attacked, where was God then?"

"Holding my soul in the palm of His hand."

"Beautiful words," Marion said, "but not much help."

"What happens to the flesh is of little matter; the only affront was to that inner voice that holds myself in such high esteem. There was nothing about me in the attack. I was in the wrong place, in your way of thinking, but in mine I was where God had placed me, and I will follow His path."

Marion found this denial of Therese's concern for anything about herself to be remarkable, and yet from Therese's mouth it did not sound trite or sanctimonious, just matter of fact; that was the way it was for her. To hold such views when in the sanctified world of a convent was one thing, but to be tested in a way that was so abhorrent to any woman, and still accept it as God's will, made Marion's own Sunday faith feel inadequate and superficial.

As each day passed and Therese adjusted to her new surroundings the two women spent more time together and their conversations became more frequent. Therese became more open to Marion's questioning and Marion found herself looking forward to their exchanges.

"How do you know what God's will is for you? How did you know you were to become a nun? Do you hear voices?" Marion asked one morning.

"How did you know to become a nurse? Did you hear voices?"

"No, of course I didn't; it just felt like the right thing to do and offered me a way out of my mother's clutches."

"It was no different for me. Perhaps I've learnt to listen to my inner voice more than you, but to feel what is right is to know what is right for you. Some use this guidance to serve themselves, some, like you, to nurse others, and for myself to serve God."

"Did you just wake up one day and know that you had to become a nun?"

"One day God showed me where He wanted me to be, and that was in a particular convent. I saw this shaft of sunlight and knew I had to go to the place where it settled."

"Like the end of your own rainbow."

"Yes, that was how Sister Paul saw it too; and I've been there ever since. This is my first time away from the convent in over ten years."

"Ten years. That's a lifetime. I can't imagine being shut away like that. You must have missed things. What did you miss?"

"Not much. Nothing that I can really think of."

"But what about your family and friends? You must have thought of them."

"I didn't have any friends. I preferred my own company and I was solitary within my family. I was closest to my brother, but we had nothing in common. None of them shared my love for God. For me it's liberating to give my time and prayers to God."

"You must miss the other sisters. Will anyone come and visit you?"

"None of them know I am here. Only Sister Paul, Mother Superior and the bishop know of my circumstances. I am a blot on their landscape and they want rid of this baby, but I don't want my child put away into an institution. He must be in the world, that is where God wants him, of that I am sure."

"Can't the Church make different arrangements for you?"

"No. They have made their position clear all along and I have no say in this. I think it will be down to me to create a different future for my child and this is what I need to think about."

"Well, you have time on your hands. I'm sure you'll think of something."

"Yes, I have too much time on my hands. How can I be of use to you here? Is there some sewing I can do, or perhaps making bandages? Please make me useful."

"Thank you for the offer. There's always sewing to be done. We need to turn rags into trousers and jackets. I'll bring some along and see how you get on. I have to go now and admit three young girls, all in your condition; they and their village were attacked the week before you. I wish they had your faith. One is in a terrible state and it appears never speaks."

"I remember a girl like that at the convent: she couldn't come out of her shock. I wrote it all down; I have notebooks full of stories. I want them to be used the day these Germans are brought to justice."

Marion did not have the heart to tell her that the inquiry had been held and that the Germans had wriggled out of any punishment. The rules of war had changed. Justice was defined by the victor.

"Who are these clothes for?" Therese handed over a pile of jackets she had spent hours mending.

"Whoever has need of them. We like to have spare clothes for any soldiers or for refugees. I've lost count of the number of soldiers that have passed through here; it was wonderful to help them, but it's too dangerous now. Edith thinks we've started to be followed by the Germans, so she's sent word that no more can come here. I don't know what they'll do without our help. I shall miss them, but it's just as well there's less work. We have six girls here, not counting you, waiting to give birth."

Marion had spent one evening with Therese and had told her of their secret work with the British soldiers. Marion was not a Catholic, but the conversation was how she imagined a confessional would be. But instead of penance being meted out, Therese praised her for her selfless efforts. What she did not realize were the seeds her revelations had sown in Therese's mind.

"Do you think it would be possible for me to go to one of your safe houses, with my baby, when he's born?" Therese asked one day.

"What do you mean? There's nothing there to see, they're just humble homes; the soldiers have all left," said Marion.

"No, I mean for me to stay there."

"But you can stay here, for as long as you need to. We won't ask you to leave."

"But the Church will take my baby and put him into an orphanage and I'm not going to let that happen. Perhaps if I just disappeared they would forget all about me and my child."

"Therese, this needs some careful thought. Where would you live? How would you look after yourself and the baby? A nun and a child is a strange combination: you'd stand out anywhere. People have so little for themselves at the moment, it would be hard for anyone to help you, even if they wanted to."

"I could concoct a story about an abandoned child given into my care. If it's as chaotic out there as you imply, I'm sure I could go unnoticed."

"You could if you wore normal clothes. You could pass as any other refugee, and goodness knows there are hundreds of them; but I'm not sure you can bridge both worlds as a nun, Therese. Perhaps the Church is right on this. It has to be one or the other."

Therese looked pained and Marion felt remorse at not offering more support.

"Look, it's not for me to say it won't work and of course I'll support you. I'll ask a couple of the places if they would be prepared to give you shelter while you think about where you go next. I won't say anything to Edith. She's not good at lying; the less she knows the better for when your Church people come and ask questions. Do you have any family you could live with?"

"I do have family, but not that I could live with. Thank you for your help. I'll give this further thought and prayer. I must be sure of God's will and not give in to my own nature."

"How can you tell the difference?"

"When it's God's will, it's not about me. I'll ask Him to show me what He wants for my baby and how I fit in. I'll feel at peace when His way is clear. There'll be less for me to sort out, and more that will just happen, that's how I know."

"You're lucky, I make decisions and jump in with both feet and then have to live with the consequences. My mother always said it would be my undoing."

"But you seem very happy, you never look troubled by anything."

"You're meeting me at a good time. I've made up with Russell, Mr Clarke, the American gentleman friend I have from the embassy, and the tension has gone after all the subterfuge of the last months. I was always on edge when the soldiers were here."

"That must have been difficult to deal with."

"And keeping it secret was the worst. I've kept the truth from Russell for so long, it almost feels strange not to have something to hide."

"I have truths that I want to share. My notebooks; they'll make good witness statements. Would you be able to give them to your American friend to keep for the trials?"

"I can ask him."

But Russell was not keen to be involved when she met him the next day.

"Sister Therese sounds a very down-to-earth person to me. You should tell her that the inquiry is over and judgments made. It's too late for her work to make any difference."

"I could say that," Marion said to Russell, "or I could take you to meet Therese and she could hand the notebooks to you for safe-keeping. That way she doesn't have to face the futility of her

303

efforts and she can believe that these victims will be heard one day. She has enough to deal with without having man's inhumanity to man further rubbed in her face. Would you do this? For me if not for her."

Marion used to despise girls who used coquettishness to charm men, but now admitted to herself that it was jolly useful at times. She had let her look linger on Russell and watched his cheeks flush; he had to clear his throat before he replied.

"Perhaps if you bring them to me I can hand them to Hugh and he can have them filed with all the court papers. Would that do?"

"I'd prefer it if you collected them from Therese. She doesn't need to know it's not in an official capacity. And anyway, I'd like you to meet her."

"You certainly seem more relaxed this week, more like your old self; perhaps I should meet her and see what she's doing to you."

"Oh, that's not because of Therese ..." Marion interrupted herself. She'd been about to reveal the reason for the drop in tension, but that secret had to remain. "It's, um, because I've had more sleep. Mind you that might change soon: we have several babies due over the coming weeks."

"All right, I'll do it. I'll send Pierre around with a note when I can visit. That will make it seem official."

Marion told Therese that evening.

"Mr Clarke said that he will visit and take a briefing and the notebooks from you. I don't know when but he'll send a note when he is on his way."

"And this is your young man? I am pleased he is coming."

"And I'm pleased he will be meeting you," Marion said.

Their conversation was interrupted by a knock on the door and Marion was called away to attend one of the young girls who had started her labour. Therese lay down on her bed and closed her eyes, a much loved new posture for prayer and meditation. She made her request, "Show me Thy will for this baby and for my service to You," and drifted into a light afternoon sleep. When she awoke she had her answer and a lot more besides.

Marion and the young girl were struggling. The baby's head was engaged and she was well-dilated but after hours of effort from both of them, the birth seemed no nearer. The girl was taut and Marion feared her rigidity would hinder the birth. Marion had just asked for the assisting nurse to fetch some hot drinks for them, when she heard the door to the ward open and saw Therese enter. The lights were dim in the room apart from a beam that shone onto the bed. Therese kept to the shadows and pulled up a chair near the girl's head. She refolded the damp cloth that Marion had placed on her forehead and kept her hand on it as she spoke to the girl.

"This is not your battle to fight. You fought when the soldiers came. You have hated this baby every week that it has grown within you and now you are fighting not to let it enter the world. This contest will kill you both. You are not giving in to them if you let this baby live. This is a God-given soul. Allow God's child to live and you will be filled with His love and blessings. Let this child out. Let this child breathe."

As Therese spoke, the girl started to take deep breaths and relaxed her arched back onto the bed. Marion suddenly had lots to attend to as the head of the baby started to appear. When the assisting nurse returned with the drinks she was just in time to swing the baby to catch its first breath. Marion saw that Therese had left the ward. The girl cried and cried and Marion could see the tension leave her limbs with every sob. Marion herself cried when the girl accepted the blanketed baby and kissed the newborn's forehead.

"How did you know to come? How did you know what to say? You saved them both you know. I was about to send for the doctor."

Marion was exhausted but had called in to see Therese on her way back to her own room.

"Mother and baby are fine now. You were like an angel in the shadows. That's what the girl called you, her angel."

Therese said nothing, but smiled and Marion noticed a radiance that she had not seen before.

"I'm sorry to disturb you, but thought you'd like to have the news."

"It's wonderful news, thank you, now you must go and have some rest."

"I won't argue about that, and you must rest too. I've just picked up a note from reception that Russell, Mr Clarke, will visit tomorrow at 11 o'clock. I'll bring him up to you and then leave you to talk. Is that the best way to organize things?"

"Yes, thank you. Good night and God's blessings."

The next day Russell followed Marion up the stairs from reception and along the corridors until she stopped outside Therese's door.

"This is it."

Marion was slightly breathless. She had tried to tell Russell about the birth the evening before while she led the way to Therese's room. He had been unable to grasp all she had said and was feeling slightly bewildered with the mentions of angels and miracles, which had all come out in a rush.

"You'll have to tell me all that again. I couldn't really catch what you were saying. Are you free for lunch when I've finished here?"

"Yes."

"How will I find you?"

"Ring the bell in reception and we'll take it from there. I have to go out, but I'll be back within half an hour. Now in you go."

Russell knocked and entered the room.

Nothing had prepared him for the shock when he saw Therese. He had not doubted Marion's words, but it was only actually having a nun standing before him, pregnant, that he really believed the Germans had done this. They really had.

"You have the look of doubting Thomas about you," Therese said with a laugh.

Russell tried to recover himself and Therese continued.

"You know the story of the disciple. It didn't matter how many people told him they had seen Jesus alive, it was only when he saw the holes of the nails in Jesus's hands that he believed it for himself. Seeing is believing."

"I must apologize. Marion had told me of your condition, but I must admit it's a shock to meet you and I find myself stumbling for words."

"Well, take a seat and take your time."

Russell sat in the chair and Therese perched on the edge of the bed. She had a pile of notebooks beside her.

"Are you comfortable there, would you prefer this chair?" Russell asked as he stood up, preparing to change places with her.

"No, this is fine for me, thank you, and thank you for coming. I understand you are extremely busy finding food for us. I mustn't keep you from your work."

"No, really, my time is yours. I'm not the one finding the food. I'm just an administrator counting the stocks, but it is quite an operation I can tell you."

"Where is the food coming from?"

"All over the world. North and South America, the southern tip of Africa, India and Australasia, and countries in Europe. The commission has raised funds and gathered foodstuffs from all over. It's quite incredible."

"To think all of these countries know about us and our troubles."

"And they want to help. The money is pouring in. The same help is going to the occupied areas of France as well. We are feeding almost nine million people in all."

"It is good to know that kindness thrives against this deadly foe."

"Yes, a lot of people are being very generous."

"Well, it is very kind of you to see me. Marion told you what it is about?"

"She said you have some records, victim statements, to be used as evidence when the Germans are brought to account."

"Yes, these are what I wanted to show you, and have you take away." Therese picked up one of the books, "But I'm too late with them, aren't I?"

"Too late? What do you mean?"

"The day in court is done, isn't it?"

"I don't know what you mean." Russell felt his face colour a little, and wondered how Therese had heard about the inquiry. Surely Marion had not told her.

"I collected these stories and brought them with me because I thought they would make a difference. I thought that telling the truth would mean something, but I realize now that was a faint hope."

"I don't know what you are saying. I can take the books for you."

"Yes, but to be put in a drawer. Not to bring people to justice."

Russell started to speak but Therese raised her hand to silence him.

"In my meditation I saw a set of scales with a German soldier's belt buckle on one side with the words *Gott mit uns* (God with us) engraved on it, and my notebooks on the other. And then I watched as a black cloth was draped over the side of the scales that carried the notebooks. It smothered and silenced them and left the other side exposed for all to see. The review in court has happened and the German view prevailed. Tell me, Mr Clarke, am I wrong?"

Russell hung his head.

"We wanted to spare you this disappointment, that was all. Your notebooks were to be filed with all the other reports. They would have been safe."

"But the voice of these people, the details of all they suffered will not be heard," Therese said.

"Many witnesses testified. I understand there was no shortage of truth," Russell said, "but this is war and the Germans, it seems, are rewriting the rules."

"Perhaps if I had walked into the courtroom, the Germans would have been silenced."

From the sensation Russell had experienced, he did not doubt that this would have been true.

"I am sure they would. I still find it hard to believe, and you're sitting in front of me."

"We Belgians will stay cowed beneath this black blanket for generations. This truth will stay silenced and it will burden the nation."

"There will be other opportunities, I am sure. When the fighting is over. I can keep the notebooks for you at the embassy."

"Where they'll be lost on a dusty shelf. Perhaps if you heard their voices, you would never forget, and you'll make sure they are heard, sometime."

"I can read them. Be sure that I will."

"Would you listen while I read some pages to you now? Then I'll know they'll be in your heart."

"Has Marion spoken about me then? She doesn't seem to think I have any heart in this matter."

"And do you?"

"To be honest with you, not in the same way that Marion does. She can care for strangers in a way that I never will. But if something happened to my family, or friends, or Marion, I would do all I could

308

to protect and support them. I'd fight for them. Does that sound selfish? Perhaps it is."

"Nameless victims are harder to love," Therese said.

"And nameless soldiers are easier to hate," Russell added.

"Shall I read?" Therese asked.

Russell gave a silent nod.

Russell sat in reception on his own. He had not rung the bell to have someone find Marion. When he left Therese he was too choked to speak and wanted to sit quietly and absorb all he had heard. It had been one shocking experience after another.

"They ran her through with a sabre."

"My baby was shot."

"They set fire to my neighbour's house and shot each one of them as they tried to escape the flames. They laughed as each one fell."

"I heard the girls screaming as they were taken away by the soldiers."

He heard the innocence in the victims' words in the passages Therese read out; it was clear how traumatized and bewildered the speakers had been. Nothing here was manufactured to feed public opinion; the brutality of the soldiers was evident in every case. And the attacks felt so personal with people dragged out of their homes, villagers lined up and shot, and the rapes. How could individuals recover from such devastation? Families were broken beyond repair. But the story that had truly reached him was Therese's own. She had not spared him from any of the detail. She had paused every time he had looked away, and waited until he dragged his eyes back to her face. He shuddered at the picture of Marion or his mother being harmed in such a way and tears had stung his eyes.

Marion found Russell in the hall and saw how pale he looked.

"Are you all right? You look a bit peaky."

"Yes, no, not ill, just sick, sick to my stomach. I've heard some dreadful things. She knew, you know, she knew about the inquiry. How did she know?"

"Russell, what's happened? What did she know? You're not making any sense. Come on. Let's take a walk. It looks as if you could do with some fresh air. I'll go and fetch my coat."

Russell had gathered himself together a little more by the time Marion returned. They did not talk as they walked, but he enjoyed the comfort of Marion on his arm and her very obvious concern. She waited for him to talk and did not rush him, and for once he was truly lost for words. He felt lost. He thought he knew the unwritten rules that governed people, the values that were instilled in human beings, but the butchery he had heard of today made him despair and doubt his fellow man. The attacks had seemed so personal. Soldiers had made individual choices about how far they went. This had not been a battlefield where their actions were governed and they acted as one. They must have known what they did was wrong. "Why didn't they stop themselves?"

"I beg your pardon? What did you say?" Marion asked.

"I'm sorry, I didn't think I'd spoken out loud."

Russell squeezed Marion's hand.

"Thank you for your patience with me. I'm still reeling from meeting Therese. Let's go into this café and I'll tell you all about it."

Russell retold all that had been said.

"She gave me the notebooks and I'll hold onto them until after the war. She doesn't seem to think their stories will ever be told, but I'll make sure that they are, if there is any way that I can. She told me about her attack. She said she had told no one before and she would never describe it again. What an ordeal, for her and so many. She's a remarkable woman. Promise me you'll keep yourself safe, Marion."

"I will, I promise. I can see that she made an impression on you. Did she tell you that she might go into hiding from the Church and keep the baby?"

"No, she didn't tell me that, but I don't think that she will. I can't imagine her leaving the Church, nor should she."

"But what about the baby? How can she stop the Church taking it into an orphanage?" Marion asked.

"What if you tell them it died? They'll go away empty-handed."

"Tell them he died. Of course, that's a brilliant idea, why didn't I think of that before?"

Russell walked Marion back to the clinic. Their goodbye was interrupted by a member of staff who had been on the look-out for her:

"Madam Cavell has asked for you to attend to your guest, Marion. She is having contractions."

Russell turned to leave as Marion ran for the stairs. And who will be left holding the baby, he said to himself as he walked back to the embassy, I wonder?

7th May 1915
Brussels
Therese

It had been a false alarm. Marion had found Therese in quite an agitated state in her room, but the contractions came to nothing. They were mild and soon stopped after her arrival.

"I think it was reliving the attack that started them," Therese told her.

"I'm not surprised," Marion said. "Your story had shaken Russell too. Contractions sometimes happen in the weeks before the birth. It's nothing to worry about, but do try and settle yourself."

But today was different. Marion could tell the minute she walked into Therese's room with her breakfast. She was pacing the floor of her room wearing a nightgown that Marion had given her. They met in the middle of the room and Therese gripped Marion's arms as a wave of contractions washed through her body. When Marion felt the grip soften, she steered Therese to the bed to conduct a quick examination.

"He's on his way this time. You are dilated. When did your waters break?"

"Not long ago. I was dressed. That's why I'm back in this nightgown."

"Don't worry. Your habit can go into the laundry and the nightgown is what you need to be wearing. I would like to take you to the delivery ward. Can you manage the walk? We can stop whenever you need to."

"Yes, I'm sure I can. I want to keep moving."

Marion helped to manoeuvre Therese off the bed, out of the room, and along the corridor. Luckily the delivery ward was on the same floor so they had no stairs to climb. They stopped twice when the contractions gripped and made walking impossible. Marion was relieved to arrive at the ward and had just settled Therese onto the bed when another contraction arrived.

"They're coming fast, Therese, but I don't want you to push. The head needs more room to come through. I need you to slow things down and try and relax. Go into one of your meditations. Just give this baby a bit more time."

"It feels as if he has made his mind up to come now."

"No, your body is trying to expel him, but you're not ready yet. You mustn't push when you have a contraction."

"That's like telling someone not to feel hungry. I have to push."

"Concentrate on your breathing. Count your breaths in and out. I'll do it with you, but no pushing."

Another contraction seized Therese and sweat broke out on her face.

"That's better, don't give into it, hold onto your baby, he needs you for a while longer."

It was seven hours later before Marion allowed Therese to push, and by then both were exhausted.

"The baby's head is coming through, Therese, and he's big. This is going to hurt you and I'll need some help. Excuse the bell." Marion rang a handbell to attract the attention of a nurse who was attending a girl whose baby had been born earlier in the day.

Marion felt more confident with another pair of hands available. She did all that she could to manipulate the baby out as gently as possible but Therese was torn and she could feel her tense against the pain.

"You can push all you want now, Therese, and here he comes."

Marion caught the baby as he slithered across the mat that was placed on the sheets. She cut the cord as the nurse with her cleaned the baby's mouth and face. It was a boy.

"Can you look after him while I attend to Therese? Is he all right?"

"Of course. He's going pink, this one is fine. My patient's baby was stillborn, but it was rape, so she didn't care. What times we live in."

"This one is a little early, but he looks large, doesn't he?" Marion said to the nurse who was cleaning him.

"Yes, he's bonny. Nothing wrong with this one."

Marion was relieved after the problem births they had had. She diverted her attentions back to Therese who needed her ministrations. She kneaded Therese's abdomen and had her concentrate on some more pushing for the afterbirth.

"You are badly torn, Therese, and need some stitches. This is going to be very sore and you will need to rest afterwards. I'll be as quick as I can, but you are bleeding quite a lot and that makes it slippery work."

"How is Alain? How is the baby?" Therese's voice was faint.

"He's bonny, he'll come to you soon, after he's been cleaned up. That's his name is it? Alain, I like it."

"I'm glad you like it. I feel tired now, can you see to him for me."

"I'd like you to hold him, Therese, and see if he wants some milk."

"No, Marion. I can't."

"Don't worry, we'll take care of him. You have some sleep. I've nearly finished here. There's nothing to worry about now, Therese. I've found somewhere you can both go, so rest easy."

"I can't take him, Marion, that's not the way it's to be. He and I are to part."

"Oh. No. We won't let the Church take him. I have an idea about that."

"I knew you would," were Therese's final words as she drifted into sleep.

Marion sat with Alain nestled in her arms. He was sleeping soundly, fed by the young mother whose baby had died. She had been leaking milk and it had made them both more comfortable. Marion had sat with her while she fed him and it seemed as if by holding the baby, Maria had lost something of the haunted look she had had before.

"This is what a baby is supposed to feel like," she had said to Marion, "not the monster they seeded in me."

She told Marion of her rape and the murder of her father and brother and that she was glad her baby had died. She had no love for it. It just made her think of all that she had lost.

"When I feel strong again I can put all this behind me. It's been like a bad dream. I want no more reminders and no extra mouth to feed."

Marion's mild fantasy that this girl, Maria, would take Therese's baby to replace her dead child and give it a home were quashed by her every sentence. Such a neat solution was not to be found here. Marion herself was still wedded to the thought that Therese would keep the baby, and the safe house was ready to receive her. Marion had visited Madame Francoise when Russell had been meeting with Therese. Although it had all been straightforward the visit had left her with some unease. It was only when she returned to the clinic that Marion realized how careless she had been. She remembered her visit.

Days before, after Marion had closed the door on Russell and Therese, she had left the clinic. She had her coat on over her uniform and made her way through the streets to the house where on several occasions she had led soldiers. Today it felt good to enjoy the walk. She was relaxed and, with no cargo to deliver, she had no need to feel wary at every street corner.

Madame Francoise had looked shocked to see her at her door and had hurried her inside.

"Did anyone see you?" she enquired as soon as the door was shut. Marion was quite startled by her anxiety.

"No, I don't think so. I didn't see anyone, but I didn't look. We're safe. There are no soldiers here, there's no danger now. I'm not here about soldiers."

Marion's words rushed out, but she saw no change in Madame Francoise's demean our.

"What have you come about? You shouldn't have come."

Marion explained Therese's situation and Madame Francoise started to thaw.

"The Church is all rules and no kindness. It shouldn't be embarrassed by her; it should embarrass the Germans with her. They have no shame, they strut about our streets as if they own the place."

Marion interrupted before Madame Francoise's rant continued for too long.

"So you would take her in until Therese planned where she goes next?"

"Of course, no one should turn their backs on a nun, nor any women in need. But she'll have no money for her upkeep, will she?"

"No, she has nothing. But she sews well. Perhaps she can repay you in kind."

"She will repay me by ensuring God smiles sweetly on my house. Now you must leave, but go out of the back door. You shouldn't have come in daylight, it's not good for you to be seen here."

Marion was more on her guard when she left the house and walked along the little street at the back. It was empty but she was aware of men on the opposite side of the road as she turned onto the main avenue. They dispersed as she passed, but her return to the clinic was not relaxed as her earlier walk had been. She kept glancing behind her when she heard footsteps, but she could not tell if they were from the same person. Because this mission had been tame and nothing to do with the Germans, or soldiers, she had not given it the usual consideration, but now she could understand Madame Francoise's concerns. Marion had established a connection between herself, the clinic, and one of the safe houses: if anyone was watching, she had just brought together links in a chain. But her worries for herself had evaporated the minute she saw Russell in the hall, looking so out of sorts.

The ward was in darkness but Therese was awake. Marion was sitting in the chair beside the bed and they were talking in whispers.

"It's best that you stay on the ward for a few days. I should want you here if any bleeding started and we need to watch for infection. Maria, a young girl will wet-nurse Alain. "The safe house is ready for you, should you want to go with Alain. I hadn't had a chance to tell you before, but Madame Francoise will help you."

"Thank you Marion, but I can't go. I can't separate myself from the Church; I belong in a convent, in prayer, and that's where I must return. To go into hiding would remove me from the shaft of sunlight that is my communion with God. That's the reason I breathe. I saw this very clearly."

"Well, that's you sorted then," Marion said, "but what about Alain? Have you given up on him? Is he going to an orphanage after all?"

"No, his path is also clear. He's to go to a family, and Marion, it's one that you will provide."

"You're asking me to find a family for him. That's not an easy task. It would be easier if I was at home in England. But here? Russell was right. He didn't think you would be able to leave the Church."

"He's a fine man, Marion."

"He came up with the idea that we tell the Church your baby died. A problem removed for them in an instant."

"I don't want you to tell a lie, Marion, not on my behalf. But he's right, it would solve the problem."

"I could just say, when they come, there is no baby here for them to take. They can draw their own conclusions. I'm sure they'll be satisfied. They want rid of him and this makes it easy for them."

"Yes, I can see it might work."

"But where am I going to find a family that wants to take on another mouth to feed at this difficult time? And it can't just be any family; it needs to be a family that will love and cherish him and give him everything he needs. That's quite a job."

"But one you're prepared to take on? For Alain?"

"Yes of course I will, Therese. I'll do my best for him. Now I have to collect him from his feed. Maria is so helpful with her milk, and yours never arrived, funny that." Marion went to bathe and change Alain; he really did feel special to her.

Therese rested in bed, pleased to be back in her own room. She was incredibly sore, even more so than after the attack. Every shift of her body caused razor sharp pain to shoot through her. When Marion had shown her Alain the pain made sense. He was large. No wonder she was torn to shreds. She had no desire to hold him; she knew that her job was done. What she craved more than anything now was solitude and silence. Too much had happened that disrupted her communion with God. She was ready to return to her sanctuary and stay open only to Him. She craved the intimacy she enjoyed with God, and was tired of so many intrusions. But first she had to recover.

Therese was pleased with the conversation she and Marion had had about Alain. The change to her plan to take off with Alain had been clearly communicated to her in one of her meditations. She still had not told Marion the full story. She did not dare. It was enough for Marion to be asked to find a family for Alain and to know that Therese was to return to the convent. Therese was unclear how the rest of her meditation would unfold.

In her meditation, Therese had seen Marion get on a boat with Alain and a man; they were on their way to England. Marion was hugging Alain close to her chest against the sea air, and telling him everything was going to be all right; she would look after him. Therese had expected the man to be Russell, but having met him, he was not the man on the boat. It was hard for her to see, with the way the tapestry was currently woven, how the threads would create the scene on the boat. Without a doubt she knew that Marion would be a wonderful parent for Alain, but such a thought would not have entered Marion's head. For a young lady to arrive home from abroad, with no husband and a baby, would certainly make society tongues wag. However charitable the background, people would talk. Despite the dilemma to be faced, Therese knew she needn't worry; she didn't know how, but she felt certain that everything would work out.

The Church officials arrived when Alain was three weeks old.

8th May 1915
Brussels
Russell

Russell was interrupted midway through the morning by Hugh who, flustered, had rushed into the office.

"They've sunk the *Lusitania*. We might as well start to pack. We'll be in this war by the end of the month."

"What, what do you mean? What's happened?" Russell asked.

"Torpedoed. She was on her way from America, had reached close to the coast of Ireland when she was sunk by a German submarine. There were hundreds on board, women and children too."

"What a murderous thing to do. No doubt the Germans will have their defence ready. They'll say there were soldiers or munitions on board," Russell said.

"Yes, it was always a risky endeavour to travel on her. Passengers had been warned, but I guess some just wouldn't be deterred. But I'm sure no one imagined this would happen. Over 100 people have been lost," Hugh declared.

"What will we do? Was she under our flag?"

"Yes, and that's what we'll have to wait and see. The wires are buzzing."

"But we've so much to do here, we can't up and leave."

"Business as usual until we receive any instruction, and not a word about our potential departure, to anyone." Hugh tapped the side of his nose twice, and he left the room.

If they had to leave, would it be that bad? Russell walked to the window and pondered the consequences. He had to admit that the challenges of his role were quite mundane, a matter of positioning the right person in the right place with the right documents and brief them about what they were to do. The book-keeping was formulaic and, once set up, did not take his intellect to master. At one level it was work that demanded little intelligence; all the problems stemmed from the people involved. It was attitudes that caused friction and faults. His diplomatic skills were evolving and he could better judge how and when to intervene in fractious situations, but his easy manner and expectation that everyone could get along could appear over-casual in some circles. He was enthralled to watch how Hugh pacified and controlled situations with such a light touch, and without fail remaining mannered and circumspect.

"It's a skill that's as important as the cerebral," Hugh had said after Russell had complimented him one day.

Cerebral. That was what Russell missed, the cerebral challenge of his studies, the banter and debate with fellow students. The exploration of new ideas always stimulated him. If they left Brussels he could return to Oxford and immerse himself once more. But could he? Could he turn his back on all the hardships contained in this war and indulge his forays into the rarified world of academia and continue to find meaning in abstractions from the past? With such pig-headedness on display in the world at large, who would ever listen to a learned voice again? It was might, not majesty, that dominated now. His future, which he had loosely mapped out in his mind, had been interrupted by such tumultuous events he doubted it could ever be restored and certainly not with the same enthusiasm.

Despite the daily challenge of applying himself to the administrative nature of his chores, he knew his contribution mattered. His efforts made a difference to the lives of others, and he found this intoxicating. Marion would understand if he told her. He was sure she experienced the same through her work, but there was a difference between them. For him scale mattered. Marion was thrilled when she touched one person's life, or one person at a time through her individual attentions, but he wanted more. He wanted a community, even a country to flourish. Russell started to mock himself for his grandiose thoughts. But as he reflected he saw he was realizing something new about himself. To continue his historical pursuits was no longer enough to satisfy him. Spending time in the past was only of value when the principles he unearthed could be applied to governance and the policies that shaped life now. That was it, his scholarly endeavour redefined. And how sad. If the embassy closed down he would be separated from such a rich vein of experience. And from Marion.

Russell's initial thoughts had not turned to Marion as he mused about his potential relocation, and this realization startled him. Would their relationship survive a separation or was it a shared location that kept them together? Of late they had been closer and he had enjoyed more of the warmth of their early days, but he still pondered on what had created such a distance between them over the previous months? Russell had wanted answers, but was scared of what he might discover. Instead, his patient acceptance had kept their courtship on course this far. Although she had explained the tensions around the refugees, he did not feel she was telling him everything. He was sure she was holding something back. He had no intention of precipitating a crisis by forcing a confession, or her rejection of him, if that was behind it; but he often wondered if she had another suitor.

He found it difficult to reconcile the Marion of the preceding months with the person she had been since the attack. He now felt he had her full attention when they were together. She was relaxed, fun, and now he thought about it, loving too. There was none of the edginess he had become accustomed to and he had not once felt as if he was treading on eggshells if he enquired into what she had been doing. She had been most enthusiastic when she told him about the babies that had been born, particularly Alain. It was the way she had opened up to him and shared her thoughts and feelings about what she had been doing that was different. That was what he had missed for so long. He had felt on the periphery of her life, distant from what mattered to her. Now she was letting him in again, just when he had something to keep hidden from her.

Dinner that evening was a grim affair. Russell had been invited to join an informal gathering with the minister, Hugh, and a few people who were new to him. The German newspaper was passed around while they were served their aperitifs and it was the headline news that generated rage and indignation in all: *"Ozeandampfer Lusitania Torpediert."*

"They will blame it on the English for carrying munitions," Hugh said.

"And the Americans for selling them," Minister Whitlock continued.

"And the passengers for not heeding their warnings not to travel by sea," another guest added.

"What will happen now?" Russell asked.

"We wait and see, and meanwhile keep our flag flying on the embassy. We've heard nothing from Washington, but we must make our preparations. I'll have Hugh travel to Antwerp. We need to transfer all our official documents there. And I expect you'll be busy, Russell. I anticipate that Hoover will want to load in as much food through Rotterdam as possible, in case we are pulled out."

"I was speaking to Prince de Ligne today. He was expressing his condolences for the loss of American life and he was in two minds as to what he wanted to happen," Hugh said.

"Whether he wanted America to set themselves against Germany, or stay neutral and keep the food coming. Am I correct?" the minister asked.

"To the letter," Hugh replied.

"I expect a visit from von Bissing soon. He will have orders to establish our support and sympathy behind this military action. They seem to be increasingly impatient with our neutrality. If we're not for them, they seem to view us as against them."

"And aren't we?" Russell asked. "Aren't we against them?"

"Politically we have no comment, despite how our morals might govern us. And there is no appetite back home to enter into a war so far from our shores. President Wilson won't baulk against public opinion, that's a sure way to lose his franchise," the minister explained.

"You can feel their frustration increasing. The Germans I mean. They've just fined the city another sack load of cents for refusing to mend the main road to Malines. The cannons they dragged along it have ruined the road, but the civic authorities are refusing to act. They'll make an example of someone over this," Hugh said.

"Yes, and they decided on three months in jail for Madame Carton de Wiart. She's the wife of the justice minister," the minister added for Russell's benefit. "She was caught carrying letters across the border and they tried her as a spy."

"The war isn't going their way. They've made no progress towards Paris. It's stubbornness not strategy that's keeping them on the offensive," Hugh said.

"I saw another copy of *La Libre Belgique* last week," Russell offered, to keep in the conversation. "It's still being printed despite all the raids."

"Yes, it makes their blood boil that they can't find the press for that one. It keeps the local spirits up when each edition hits the streets,"the minister replied.

The conversation continued to jump around different topics throughout the meal. No one appeared to have the energy to engage in a debate about anything other than the news of the *Lusitania* and the potential upheaval this represented for each of them. The tone of these exchanges was subdued. Their dining time was cut short by the announcement of two titled visitors requesting the opportunity to pass on their condolences to the minister and all seemed relieved to move from the table.

Russell joined Hugh as he stood on the verandah enjoying a cigar.

"Would you join up, if America joined the fighting?" Russell asked Hugh.

"I don't know that I see myself with a gun in my hand, but I would certainly want to make myself available to support the war effort. No, I don't think a soldier's life is for me. There would be other ways I could be useful. I speak German and French: that has to be of use to someone. What about you?"

"I think I'd feel duty bound to volunteer," Russell said, "but I hadn't really thought about it until I asked you."

"You stay with the brain work and leave the fighting to the brawn."

"Sometimes it feels difficult to be standing on the sidelines. I want more action," Russell said.

"I've seen action from the embassy motor car when I've been out to the battle scenes. That's close enough for me. It all looked scrappy, nothing like the battle strategies neatly mapped out in the history

325

books we've read. And the bangs are deafening. I'd think long and hard before making any decision to fight."

"You're probably right. But it does have a ring of adventure."

"An adventure that might be short-lived if you took a bullet," Hugh said.

"I think the British and the French will expect something of us now. My sample of one, Nurse Drake, is very disparaging about our silence on German actions. She'll expect words of condemnation, as well as our army, to arrive."

"I'm sure many Americans will speak out and will want to avenge the *Lusitania*, but we'll have to wait and see what the official response is. But", Hugh added, "we need to ready ourselves in case our departure is imminent. I need you to help me sort out and pack our papers tomorrow. Can you set aside some time for this?"

"Sure I can. I wouldn't mind the trip to Antwerp with you either."

"Yes, I'd like that too, but I think the minister will want you here. He's anticipating an influx of foodstuffs. His guess is they'll want to start stockpiling, so I think you're going to be busy."

"It can feel a bit mundane at times, all the paperwork. I enjoy my field visits. I like being out and about."

"I know what you mean. This war has brought a lot of work with it. I never had more than a couple of hours' occupation a day before."

"What did you do with yourself?"

"Pretty much whatever I wanted. A lot of golf and tennis, drives into the countryside, walks. It had been a very social time; dinner out most nights with one host or another. The food is grim now compared to what we were used to."

"And we have it good compared to many. Marion says that some days her meal makes her think of the gruel that was served in workhouses. They are now eating what they used to feed to the poor who came to the clinic."

"Yes, Germany is running low on food too. The British naval blockade is stopping food getting into the country. There'll be some fights over this year's harvest here. Not that much has been cultivated."

"Do you think this war can go on for much longer?"

"I know a lot of talking is going on behind the scenes, and President Wilson is involved, but right now politicians seem better at creating rifts than mending them. There is more than language that divides these nations; there are generations of hostilities behind the posturing."

"So much for civilized nations."

"There will always be a fight to be top dog."

27th May 1915
Brussels
Marion

Marion decided to tell Edith about the plans for Therese and Alain, and to ask for help.

"I know this must sound rash to you. I should have told you right at the beginning, but I thought I could manage everything. This is proving harder than I thought."

Marion was in Edith's office describing her search for a family for Alain.

"I wondered whether any of the ladies in the Hospital Committee would be able to assist. They might know of some family circumstances where Alain would fit in."

"You've taken me by surprise. And just in time," Edith said. "I've had a letter from the bishop's office to say that the clinic will be visited and the child taken tomorrow. So what do you propose we say to them?"

"That the child is no longer with us."

"What is that supposed to convey? That the child died or has gone elsewhere?"

"Personally, I'm comfortable telling them that he was stillborn. It's Therese who doesn't want me to lie. She seems to think they'll be satisfied with the outcome, regardless of the reason, and that they won't ask questions."

"I hope they don't ask questions. We won't have a death certificate to show them."

"I'm sure we could borrow one of those if needed," Marion said.

"You are becoming a little too comfortable with intrigue, my girl. Thank goodness we've stopped our secret guests. I'm quite worn out by it all, and now you want to deceive the Church."

"I'm sure they mean well, but it's Therese's express wish that Alain doesn't go into an orphanage. She's very much led by what she sees as God's will and on this she has been adamant, even to the extent that she would break her vows and look after him herself if necessary."

"But that won't be necessary because you are going to find a family for him?"

"Well, yes, I hope to."

"And if you don't, then whose responsibility does he become? Have you thought of that?"

No. Marion had not.

The next day two men arrived to meet Therese. They were priests from the bishop's office. They left a woman with a pram in reception and followed Marion to Therese's room. Marion knocked and showed the priests in. They had been expected and Therese was up and fully dressed in her habit and veil. She looked much older to Marion when only her face was visible underneath her headgear, and she was still pale. Marion went to fetch an extra chair, and it seemed from the way the silence hung that nothing had been said in her absence. She was about to withdraw, but Therese broke the silence and asked her to stay. The priests positioned their chairs so that they could see Therese and Marion.

"Dear sister," the eldest priest addressed Therese, "we have details with us of your onward arrangements. They're all written here. We just need to know when you will be ready to travel."

Therese looked to Marion.

"How long is the journey?" Marion asked.

"About 20 miles, manageable in two days. The bishop no longer has his car so it will be horse and trap."

"That will be exhausting," Marion said. "Another six weeks at least, I would say."

"Oh surely not," Therese interjected, "two at most. I am quite well recovered."

Marion and Therese looked at each other and the priests said nothing. Marion wanted Therese at the clinic with Alain for as long as possible. She still hoped that Therese would leave the Church and look after him herself.

"I will be ready in two weeks," Therese repeated.

"Very well," Marion said. "Let's say two weeks tomorrow."

The two priests nodded to each other.

"We will have transport here by ten o'clock on that day and the Order will expect you."

"Thank you," Therese said.

"I have come equipped to take the sacrament with you. It is some time since you last partook," the older of the two priests continued.

"And I can see to the other business," said the younger priest. "Are you the nurse to assist me?"

"Yes I am." Marion stood. "Do come with me," and she led him from the room.

"Where is Sister Therese going?" Marion asked the priest as they walked along the corridor to the stairs.

"The Order is a closed one, about seven miles south of Leuven."

"What's a closed order?" Marion asked.

"It's when the nuns are totally enclosed, they have no contact with the outside world; a contemplative order and I think largely silent."

"And that's where you plan to hide her away," Marion stated rather than asked.

"Not at all, this is entirely her wish."

They had reached the reception hall and the lady with the pram.

"The pram won't be needed," Marion said, and in answer to the priest's quizzical look "The baby is no longer with us." She finished her sentence and drew the sign of the cross on the front of her uniform and cast her eyes to the ground.

"Oh, I see," the priest said. "At least I think I do."

"Many babies of war", Marion said, "are stillborn."

"Yes, yes, of course," said the priest. "We hadn't heard. You didn't need to come," he said to the woman with the pram, and as if by explanation to her, "We didn't know."

"We didn't know who to tell," Marion said.

"Indeed," the priest said. "Indeed."

"Is there anything else you need from me?" Marion asked.

"No, no thank you. I'll wait here for Father Tomas."

Marion left the priest, the pram, and the nameless woman and ran back up the stairs to the ward where Alain lay in his cot. She lifted him up and hugged him to her.

"Well, young man, you no longer exist, so let's see who you are to become."

He clutched her little finger in his fist and fed it into his mouth, looking as if he had not a care in the world.

Therese was in a good frame of mind after the visit of the priests. The ritual of the sacrament had settled her. She began to feel rooted again with the experience of childbirth behind her. She had been disorientated from the moment she left the convent, but now she knew she would soon be within the sanctuary of a confined order, she could feel her balance return.

She was exhausted by all the interactions that were required to navigate through a day at the clinic. Everyone moved in different directions, criss-crossing one another's paths. There was always noise at an intersection when people paused and exchanged news and the gossip of the day. It seemed they all had so much to share, and yet to Therese's ears nothing to say. For her there was only one conversation that mattered and that was her communion with God.

The pain and discomfort had been intense after Alain's birth, but Therese had been surprised at how quickly the swelling had reduced and how soon she was able to move around with ease; Marion's salt baths had no doubt helped this process. Therese had kept the water cold, not quite able to allow herself to luxuriate in a warm, relaxed soak. She would not permit herself to get used to physical comforts; it was too easy for them to distract her from her true mission, of prayer.

"Must you go, so soon?" Marion asked a few days later. It was the first day of June and Therese would be gone in ten days' time. "Are you sure you're making the right choice to return?"

"I have a job to do, Marion. I must return. I long to return."

"This may sound stupid. I know you're a nun, but a job? What is your job?"

"Keeping the channels with God open, through prayer, for the benefit of all."

"I sometimes doubt that He's around at all," Marion said. "How can He be and let these Germans do all these dreadful things? And they say He is on their side."

"We have to trust that somewhere inside them, however deeply hidden, they know that what they do is bad. One day, in some way they will have to account for themselves, each one of them."

"The Day of Judgment," Marion gently mocked.

"The day when their conscience asks to be examined, and like it or not, that day comes to us all, God or no God."

Therese was aware that Marion was under pressure. She knew that she spent a lot of time with Alain and was determined to deliver her promise to her to find him a good family, but it was proving to be difficult. Marion had rejected the one possible home that had presented so far, but if he was to be settled before Therese left, time was now running short.

"They were nice people and they seemed kind, but their home was unkempt and dirty,"

Marion had reported back to Therese after her visit. Therese still held onto the picture of Marion travelling to England with Alain, but this solution still seemed to be no more than a fantasy.

"It's as you say, Therese," Marion said, "I'll know when it's the right place for him. Don't be concerned yet; there are some good and kind people out there and I have another family to visit later this week. It's a family known to one of the Ladies' Committee. He will be fine."

"I have no doubt of that," Therese had replied.

Marion was out on that visit now, with Alain, and a planned walk to the park. Therese had declined the invitation to meet her there: an afternoon of quiet contemplation held more appeal. Until the soldiers arrived. Therese was jolted by the sound of German voices. There was no revelry to their tone, more like instructions being barked out. She looked out of the window of her bedroom and saw two army vehicles parked outside. Soldiers were climbing out. They were armed and moved in groups to cover the three front entrances to the clinic. No doubt some had gone to the back as well, Therese thought. This was no casual visit. They thumped on the main door to announce their arrival and Therese watched the street empty as troops climbed the steps and disappeared into the building and out of view. She started to shake and her instinct was to barricade the door to her room. She looked around; the only thing she could use was her bed. If she pushed it against the door it would make it harder for them to get in, but it would not stop them. She slumped down and felt defeated. What could she do to protect herself? She immediately pictured herself kneeling in prayer in a shaft of sunlight and was in this position when two soldiers knocked rather politely on her door and walked in. They took the room in with a glance, bowed their heads and left, closing the door behind them. She almost laughed, so palpable was her relief.

She knew that she was entirely incidental to their visit, but her body held its own memory of their proximity and it remained tense. She assumed their search was for British soldiers, and she also knew they would find none, thank goodness. She felt reassured by this thought and the orderliness of the search party as she listened to their progress along the corridor. Although significantly recovered from her own ordeal she had surprised herself by the strength of her physical reaction to the intrusion. She longed now for the cloisters.

It must have been an hour later that she heard the soldiers on the street. They had left the building in dribs and drabs, with nothing apparent to show for their exertions, but Therese was gasping moments later as she saw Madame Cavell, and Sister Wilkins, being escorted to the front vehicle. Edith turned and stared up at the building and Therese felt that she looked straight at her, their eyes locked in silent communication. The two nurses had clearly been arrested. Therese was shocked and felt a sudden surge of fear for Marion. She watched the vehicles drive away and then made her way to the reception hall where staff and nurses stood in small groups talking in hushed voices. She soon learned that the premises had been searched from basement to attic and that, indeed, arrests had been made. Two soldiers remained in the hall; they had lists of names in their hands, and were verifying who people were with two of the staff members. There was no sign of Marion. It was clear that they were still looking for others and Therese felt sure that Marion's involvement had been exposed in some way. She nodded to two of the nurses she recognized and left the building. She turned in the direction that Marion had taken, just a few hours earlier, and stopped the first person she saw to ask for directions to the Central Park.

Therese did not have the energy for a brisk walk. Her years of confinement and recent inactivity and wounds made this exertion, with its necessary urgency, uncomfortable for her so she was soon quite breathless and hot. This was how Marion found her as they met, rather abruptly, on a street corner.

"Therese, what are you doing here? I didn't think you wanted a walk, are you all right? You look quite flustered. Lean against this wall and catch your breath. How funny to bump into you."

Therese heard the tumble of words from Marion, but it took her time to catch her breath to respond.

"Thank goodness I found you. Thank goodness I found you."

"What's the matter, Therese? What is it? Has something happened? Are you hurt?"

Therese raised her hand to silence the barrage of questions that poured out from Marion and then put her hand on Marion's arm to pull her close.

"The Germans have come and have taken Madame Cavell and Sister Wilkins, and I think they are looking for you too. Where can we move off the street? I'll tell you what happened."

Therese could see that Marion was shocked and frozen to the spot.

"It will be better if we walk. Turn the pram and push it alongside me. We won't be noticed then."

Therese nudged Marion and the pram around and walked them away from the clinic and back towards the park.

They stopped at the first bench and Therese described all that had happened.

"How do you know they are looking for me?" Marion asked.

"They left two soldiers behind and they seemed to be examining lists of names and checking off staff and nurses. You were involved, along with Edith, so it makes sense they'll want you too."

"Does it? How do they know that any of us were involved? And if they found no soldiers, they have no proof of anything. This will all blow over, I'm sure."

"Edith looked very serious as she left, Marion. I don't think it's safe for you to return, at least not until Madame Cavell comes back. You need to go somewhere else."

"To the safe house, I could go to the safe house. It's where I was going to take you and Alain. Madame Francoise will take me in for a few days."

"I'll walk there with you now."

"Is it that urgent?"

"Yes, I fear it is."

"It's quite close, but are you sure you want to walk any further. You've had quite a lot of exercise already."

"If we walk at a slower pace I'll be fine." Now that she had found Marion and the immediate tension had gone, Therese found it easier to move and breathe.

Alain was asleep. Therese looked at him as they walked. She had kept herself away from him and had left him in Marion's care, but he was still her son. She looked at his sleeping form and felt that she knew him. She had to fight the almost magnetic pull she felt to pick him up and hold him to her, and then she stumbled. She had knocked into Marion who had come to a sudden stop and started to reverse her step. Therese was caught by surprise. She was watching Alain stretch his neck, instead of paying attention to where she walked.

"Ssh," Marion said, "move, quick, turn around," and with a few deft movements they retraced their steps.

Therese looked at Marion and saw that she was shaking. She had a firm grip of the handlebar of the pram, but Therese could see the judder through her elbows.

"Did you see them? The Germans? They were there, at the safe house, the safe house. How did they know of it? Oh no, please don't say they followed me. Please don't say I took them there. Madame Francoise, what will she do? Will they arrest her too? You're right, it's not safe. I'm not safe. What do I do? Therese, what do I do?"

"What about the Americans? Could you go to the Americans, to your American friend? They'll help you."

"Yes, yes, of course they will, and I'll tell them about Edith. They might be able to help her too. Oh Therese, I never thought this would happen. Helping them, the soldiers, seemed the right thing to do. We knew it wasn't allowed, but I didn't ever think we would be in trouble. I'm scared, truly scared."

"You will be all right, Marion. You weren't there and they didn't take you. The Americans will keep you safe and get you back to England."

"Back to England. England! I can't leave here. I can't leave Edith, my job, my training, Russell, you. Alain."

Therese could hardly make out the final words that Marion said as she had started to sob.

Marion stopped to blow her nose and regain some self-control, and after some deep breaths they continued to walk.

"I'm sorry, Therese, it was a shock to see the Germans at the safe house. I'm sure this trouble will all blow over; but I will go to Russell and see if he can give me quarter whilst I keep my head down for a few days. Can you take Alain, Therese? Hand him to one of the nurses, perhaps Sophie, to look after him until I return."

"No," Therese said, "Alain stays with you, of that I am sure."

"Well, it's just for a few days."

"Perhaps," said Therese. "But he must stay with you."

"The couple today weren't right for him. There wasn't a reading book in the house. But I have another address to go to. I can go in a couple of days when this has all settled down. I want you to know where he is going to live before you leave."

"As long as he is with you, that's all the comfort I need," Therese said.

"Yes, I'll keep him with me for now. Now let me show you the way back to the clinic. I'll be going in the other direction to the embassy."

"No, you go straight there. The sooner you are off the streets, the better. I can ask for directions. Just point me in the right general direction."

"Thank you so much for coming to find me, Therese. You kept me out of some hot water."

"Thank goodness I found you. Now you must go."

"Yes. You're sure you can find your way?"

"I'm sure I can. I might actually sit and enjoy the park for a moment before I set off. You're right, I should have come out more."

"Perhaps we can meet in the park, tomorrow, or the next day?" Marion suggested.

"Let's see what happens. It's more important that you keep safe. Now go."

"Goodbye, for now," Marion said.

"Goodbye Alain, goodbye Marion. *Pax vobiscum.*"

"Come on then, young man," Marion said to Alain as she turned the pram around, and started off down the path. She turned twice to wave to Therese who watched her until she was out of sight.

Marion felt calmer by the time she had walked to the American legation, introduced herself at reception and was sitting waiting for Russell's return from a field trip he was on. It was Hugh who found her first.

"Nurse Drake, how lovely to see you and how unexpected. Mr Clarke, Russell, is out and about today, conducting one of his audits. He won't be back until late. I hope my staff didn't suggest you wait. I'm just returned from Antwerp."

It was at this moment that Alain decided to wake and to announce this with a cry for attention.

"And who is this in your charge, Nurse Drake? I can see he's a very young patient." Hugh smiled at Alain in the pram.

"He's not a patient, it was his mother, she was the patient. Well not a patient, in confinement, with us, at the clinic. Mothers have been coming to us to have their babies; this is one. His name is Alain. Alain this is Mr Gibson."

Alain continued to cry until Marion picked him up and let him suck on her little finger.

"I don't have any provisions with me, he finished his bottle earlier. Would it be possible to trouble your kitchens for some milk?"

"Is it that urgent? Won't the walk back to the clinic lull him back to sleep?"

"A baby never sleeps on an empty stomach, and anyway, I can't go back to the clinic, not just yet. In fact, not for a while, probably. Oh Mr Gibson, Edith, Madame Cavell is in trouble. She's been arrested by the Germans, and I think they're looking for me too. I have nowhere else to go which is why I've come here."

"I don't understand what you're telling me, but I won't keep you talking in the hall. Come through to my office. I'll order some milk on the way. Shall I push?"

Marion carried Alain, who had quietened in her arms, and followed Hugh as he pushed the pram along the corridor to his office; it faced the gardens on the ground floor. Hugh disappeared with the empty bottle and instructions for it to be made warm and watery; unsurprisingly they had no formula mixture on the premises, but for one feed this would suffice. While she waited, Marion started to create a list of all the things she needed from the clinic. Arriving ill-equipped on their doorstep had begun to look more of a significant imposition than she had first thought. She had almost convinced herself that she and Therese had panicked unnecessarily when Hugh returned and she busied herself with feeding Alain. Once settled, she could delay her story no longer, and told Hugh of everything that she and Edith had been doing to assist British soldiers and of Edith's arrest. It was when she told him of the Germans at the safe house that her tears began to fall.

"I feel so guilty. I think it was me that took the Germans to Madame Francoise's house. They must have followed me the day I went to make arrangements for Therese."

"Therese? Who's Therese? And I'm sure you didn't lead them to the safe house, they've probably been watching it for a time. But the safe house might have led them to you; you are right to be wary. It's best that you stay away from the clinic until we know what's happening. It might all blow over in a few hours. You say there were no British soldiers on the premises?"

"No, and haven't been for weeks. We've been too busy with all the confinements and births. They are all rapes, you know, from the start of the war, poor things, some of them are so young."

"And Therese? Was she one of them? What did she want with a safe house?"

"There were special circumstances with Therese." Marion was suddenly distracted. "I think he's soiled and I need to clean him. Can I use the bathroom? I do have some clean napkins with me in the pram."

"Yes of course, go ahead. I'll start making a few enquiries and see what sort of trouble you ladies might have created for yourselves."

Marion was just returning Alain to his pram when Hugh returned. The baby was contented and gave out such a big sigh that, despite the tension, they both had to smile.

"What have you found out? Are they all right? Elizabeth and Edith I mean, are they all right?"

"I've found out very little, so far. I spoke to von Bissing's assistant under the guise of having information that two British subjects had been arrested. He said he knew nothing of it, and would look into it for me. He's a decent enough fellow, but he did say he knew several raids had been planned that day. He was delighted to inform me that a group of Belgian rebels had been infiltrated and arrested for helping soldiers return to the front and that an example was to be made of them. If your clinic is associated with this band of brothers, then we could be in some significantly stormy waters."

Marion slumped into a chair and then jumped upright as the telephone rang. Hugh answered it, nodded to Marion and then started to make notes as he listened to the call.

Marion only heard one side of the conversation and held her breath until Hugh replaced the handset into its cradle.

"What did he say? What did he tell you?"

"He confirmed the arrests of Madames Cavell and Wilkins on the suspicion of their involvement with a chain of conspirators who have been assisting soldiers to return to their troops to fight against the German Army. He was reading out a statement to me. He said this had been expressly forbidden. All soldiers were to have reported to local German commands as prisoners of war. He reminded me of a recent pronouncement that anyone involved in such activity would face the death penalty, and some have been shot over the past months."

Marion, who was rarely light-headed felt herself start to swoon. To hold herself steady she grabbed hold of the edge of Hugh's desk.

"They may have suspicions, but that doesn't mean proof, does it?" Marion was conscious she was grasping at straws as well as the desk.

"He gave me some good news. Sister Wilkins has been released and is apparently on her way back to the clinic."

"Released, that's wonderful." Marion rose to her feet, almost as if she was heading to the door for a reunion.

"But Madame Cavell hasn't," Hugh added.

"Hasn't? Not released? Why not?"

"Because she has confessed."

Marion heard no more. She had collapsed in a faint.

4th June 1915
Brussels
Russell

Russell walked into Hugh's office and was startled by the tableau in front of him. Hugh was kneeling on the floor with Marion in his arms. She was leaning back against him. Russell was frozen to the spot and failing to make sense of what was in front of him. His fists clenched at his side and his jaw was instantly so taut it made it difficult for him to speak. When his words came out he was shouting.

"Marion, Hugh, what's going on?"

"Russell, thank goodness you're here. Marion has fainted, come and help me."

"Fainted, what do you mean? What have you done to her?"

"I haven't done anything to her. She's coming round," Hugh said, "thank goodness for that. I was about to call for a doctor. Come over here. You hold her."

Hugh moved to one side while he still supported her head, and Russell moved to take his place on the floor and pulled her towards him.

"Marion, Marion," he whispered, and he felt her stir. "Marion, it's all right. It's Russell, I'm here. Easy, easy, stay still, take your time."

Marion was struggling to sit up, so Russell and Hugh helped her to her feet and then onto a chair. She was pale and a slight sweat had appeared on her face. Russell was concerned. He had no idea what he had walked into and it took all the self-restraint he could muster not to blurt out another demand for an explanation. It was then that he saw the pram and the baby.

"I'll go and fetch some brandy." Hugh left the room and Marion immediately threw her arms around Russell and burst into tears. He held her and soothed her, pressed his lips to her hair and still he wondered what was going on. Hugh returned before either of them had spoken.

"Sip this, Marion." Russell passed on the glass Hugh had handed him. Her hand shook as she took it and she choked as the alcohol hit the back of her throat, colour immediately returning to her cheeks. She pressed the back of her hand to her face and wiped the tears away that had clung to her cheeks and chin. Russell offered her his handkerchief and she turned away as she blew her nose.

"I need to go and brief the minister," Hugh said. "I suggest you bring Russell up to date, Marion, and then we'll make some plans. I'll ask Pierre to fetch some milk powder for the baby. Do you need some more napkins too?"

"That's very kind, yes please, more would be helpful." Hugh nodded to Russell and left the room.

"Are you ready to talk, Marion? I feel as if I've walked into something big here. What's going on?"

Marion looked at Russell; she knew she owed him the truth, the total truth. She had no choice now anyway: circumstances made it unavoidable. She took his hand and gave him a weak smile.

Russell could feel the tension in her.

"I've lied to you, Russell, and not just once, many, many times, but today I promise to tell you the truth. You have been a true friend to me and I've betrayed the trust we shared. I'm sorry."

Russell began to tremble.

"What is it, Marion? What are you saying to me? Is it you and Hugh? Are you having a relationship with Hugh? Is that what's been going on all these months? Is that your lie?"

Russell felt anger rise within him. All those times he had wondered at her evasiveness; those evenings when she was not available to see him, for no good reason. In an instant all his doubts and all the mysteries collided. His two friends? Behind his back? He pulled his hand away from hers and went to stand up, but she pressed her hand on his arm.

"Listen to me, Russell. It will take a while, but I'll tell you everything."

"All right, talk. You might remember that I've asked you to many times before, but now it suits you to tell me. Go ahead, talk."

"My deceit started the day we had our first argument. Do you remember? You'd only been back in Brussels a few weeks and we argued. I left the café without you and then you came around to the clinic with flowers and a note of apology. You found me at the door. I was going out when you arrived."

"Yes, I remember. It was your friend Hugh who sent me round with the apology: what irony is that?"

"Russell, you will have every right to be angry with me when you hear what I have to tell you, but it's not about Hugh. I am not having a relationship with Hugh."

"Not Hugh?" Then who?, he thought. "Marion, what is this about?"

"That day, when you arrived with the flowers, I was on my way to bring a note to you. I'd written an apology and in my letter I'd explained to you what I had been doing, why I was on edge, and to ask for your support. But when you arrived, with your own apology, I was pleased to accept it and let you carry the responsibility for our upset. You had been insufferable, but in truth I knew our argument was my fault."

"What's that to do with us here today and you in Hugh's arms?"

Russell had yet to erase that image from his mind, and divest the thought that her lies were about Hugh.

"I'm about to tell you. It all started the day I heard you had returned to Brussels. It had been quiet for some weeks and to be honest, after the drama of the Germans' arrival, time had begun to drag and I was, frankly, quite bored. That evening I had supper with Edith and Elizabeth and we were interrupted by a visit from a Belgian man, known to Dr Depage. He asked us to hide and nurse two British soldiers. They arrived later that evening and stayed with us for some weeks. One had been badly injured."

Russell looked as if he was about to speak but Marion continued.

343

"I know, before you say it, how foolish it was, and how dangerous. I had seen the posters and knew of the penalties, but I, we, felt safe and secure within the clinic. The Red Cross seemed to give us immunity; at least, that was how it felt. But I was on edge and I know you picked up on this and I never had an explanation for you.

"That day we argued, I'd had very little sleep for three nights. I was anxious about what we were doing. I wanted to be able to tell you what was going on, why I was tired. And I felt important too. You weren't the only one doing something worthwhile in this dreadful war. But I could say nothing. And then more soldiers came, my secret life continued, and the lies between us grew."

"So it really is nothing to do with Hugh?" Russell believed it for himself this time.

"No, nothing, and he knew nothing about all this until I came here to find you today."

"To find me? I thought you were here with Hugh."

"He found me waiting for you. He has been really kind. He's a true friend and a gentleman, Russell. I only hope he can help Edith now."

"Edith? What's happened to her? I still don't understand all this."

"There's more to tell."

Marion told him her story, right up to the last moment she could remember before she fainted, Edith's confession.

"They obviously believed her, because they released Elizabeth, and she never had anything to do with the soldiers. In fact she has no idea how many passed through, it was all done by Edith and myself."

"Edith wouldn't tell them about you, surely she wouldn't. Why would she confess?" Russell said.

"I am sure she wouldn't, but I think I've been followed and someone has seen me go into the safe house. I can't go back to the clinic. I don't know what I'm going to do. It's all such a mess, and what is going to happen to Edith?"

"We'll see what Hugh comes back with. But Marion, you have been playing with fire. You're the one that's always said how terrible the Germans are, and now you've really crossed them.

This is serious stuff you've told me. How could you put yourself in such danger?"

"I knew you'd be angry, and I knew you'd want me to stop if I'd told you before, but I couldn't. I would do the same again. At least I know whose side I'm on," Marion said as she held his look, and then softened her response with, "I had to help the men."

Russell was not going to be distracted by yet another of her digs at America's neutrality.

"So the one that attacked you was a soldier, not a refugee?"

"Yes, he was a Scotsman. A horrible man. He had been at the clinic for a few weeks. He gave me the creeps."

"And you were out on the streets on your own with him. I don't know what to make of all this. I thought I knew you, Marion, and now you tell me this."

"It's quite a mess isn't it? I am so worried for Edith."

"I can imagine you are. It's a shame you didn't think of the consequences and keep clear of such matters."

"A lecture is unwelcome, Russell."

"But she will have no defence. Especially if she's confessed."

"If she has confessed. We don't know for sure," Marion said, and held her head in her hands. "What have we done?"

"A stupid thing," Russell said, and before Marion could retort, "and a loyal thing too. I'm not blaming you, Marion. I don't see how you could have refused. I just wish you hadn't been involved."

"No, I couldn't have done any different and the men were so grateful."

"Not all of them."

"No, not all of them. Culloch was dreadful and there was a Frenchman, Quien. He made me feel uncomfortable too. But he was only with us for a couple of days."

"Oh Marion, the risks you've taken. No wonder you've been withdrawn."

"So now you know that you can't trust me. What sort of relationship is that? I'm sorry for the lies."

"I don't think you've lied to me, you just haven't told me the truth. And look at all the worry you've spared me. I would have been far too anxious to let you help them."

"I knew you'd want to stop me."

"So there you are, I brought it on myself. I gave you no choice. If you could've trusted me to respect your decisions instead of anticipating a barrel load of my worries dumped on you, perhaps you would have been more open. I'm not sure I could have lived with knowing what you were doing. We might have fallen out over it."

"I'm sorry, Russell, to dump all this on you, and Hugh."

"Thank goodness you did. You're so feisty I could imagine you marching up to the governor general and demanding he release Edith."

"Would that work, would he listen?"

"No, he wouldn't, Marion. He'd have locked you up with Edith."

"She must be so worried. I hope they treat her well. Can we visit her? Take her some food?"

"You can do no such thing. You have to remain hidden to avoid arrest. One step at a time. We need to find out where they have her and whether they will be making charges. Let's leave all that to Hugh."

"If she's confessed, of course they'll make charges."

"If, Marion, if. Let's wait and see." Russell gave Marion a reassuring hug, but she pulled away.

"So you can come clean now too," Marion said.

"What about? What do you mean?"

"With whatever it is you have been keeping from me over the last few weeks, and why you were following me the night I was attacked."

"Oh."

"Which one first?"

"Well, I …"

"Let me help you. You have been keeping from me the fact that the Americans might join the war and you and Hugh would have to leave Brussels. Am I right?"

"How did you know?"

"I knew you were holding something back from me and I guessed what it was. The Americans leaving Brussels has been the talk of the town. Everyone's waiting to see what will happen."

"We are waiting too. We've heard nothing yet. I was sworn to secrecy."

"As I was about the soldiers."

"Touché."

"And following me?"

"I was feeling uneasy. I guess we can read each other well. I didn't know what you were being cagey about. I didn't set out to follow you. I just saw you on the street and stayed with you. And that's a decision I will never regret."

"You were my guardian angel that night."

"You've been talking to Therese too much."

Russell was being rewarded with a kiss when Hugh walked back into the room and covered his embarrassment with a cough.

"I see you've caught up then," Hugh said.

Russell and Marion drew apart.

"We need to organize ourselves, and as you, Marion, can't leave our premises at the moment, Russell and I need to work on your behalf. Time for some lists, I think."

They gathered together at the desk and thought through the logistics of how to collect items from the clinic for Marion and the baby.

"I need to speak with Sister Wilkins to find out what I can about her situation and the attitude of the Germans. Even if they do watch the clinic, my visit would be an expected outcome of her arrest. Russell can accompany me and meet with Therese, is that the right name? And have her pack Marion's things; Pierre can collect them this evening. I'm travelling to London the day after tomorrow and have a tight schedule tomorrow, so now is the best time to attend to this. Russell, why don't you show Marion to one of the guest rooms and she can settle herself and the baby while we go out. I'll meet you downstairs in ten minutes."

Hugh and Russell found Sister Wilkins pale and trembling. She was pleased and relieved to see them.

"Is Marion with you, at the embassy? Is she safe?"

"Yes, Nurse Drake and the baby are safe."

"Thank goodness for that. They would have taken her if she had been here when they came. They were looking for her and took me instead."

"Where did they take you?" Hugh asked.

"To the German headquarters. They separated Edith and me and I didn't know what they were talking about. They fired questions at me, names, dates: they knew a lot, but I didn't know anything. I think they were realizing that when a man walked in and looked at me, shook his head, and left. They released me soon after that."

"Did you know the man?" Russell asked.

"No. Edith had kept me ignorant of all her goings-on, and I'm thankful that she did. My disposition isn't suited to intrigue. But Marion, Marion is in danger. They are looking for her, well, for someone. They know she has dark hair and is English, like me, but they don't know her name. Edith won't give her up, of that I'm sure."

"But we were told Edith confessed. Why would she do that?"

"They didn't need a confession. They knew just where to look when they searched the clinic. They found two small wards behind wardrobes and a corridor that I'd forgotten about that had been made into a room. Edith told them they were to isolate patients with fevers and I must have looked so confused they never pressed me. Someone had told them where to look."

"There are spies everywhere in the city," Hugh said.

"There may be, but not in here. Our staff members are loyal," Sister Wilkins said.

"Well someone did the dirty," said Russell, "if they knew so much."

"Edith mumbled something about Quien, but I don't know what she meant, she was talking to herself by then, not to me."

"Marion mentioned that name to me, but I can't remember what she said. I'll ask her when we return to the embassy."

"I am so relieved to know she is with you. Sister Therese has been very concerned. I must tell her."

"It was Sister Therese who found Marion and warned her," Russell said.

"Yes, she told me. She is still recovering from her exertions."

"Is she in her room?" Russell asked, "I'd like to see her, and we need to collect Marion's belongings and some items for the baby. Marion is fine with looking after him for the time being. It's good that she has him to keep her occupied. Edith's arrest is sitting very heavily with her. She is very worried."

"We all are. The Germans seem very serious about this. I haven't stopped shaking."

"Do you mind if I ask you a few more questions?" Hugh asked. "Perhaps while Russell sees Sister Therese."

"Yes, that's fine. Your questions are gently asked, unlike—oh, dear, I don't like to think of it."

Russell excused himself and as he left the room he heard Hugh ask more about the attitude of the Germans and whether it was true that Edith had confessed. He left before the answer and was soon completely lost amid the staircases and corridors. It had seemed so straightforward when he had followed Marion on his last visit. He came across some shattered wood at the end of one corridor which looked like the shards of wood from a wardrobe, and behind it he could see some mattresses; one of the secret dens. He went cold when he looked at the evidence the Germans had exposed.

Russell retraced his steps and eventually found his way back to the main staircase and was saved any further difficulty by an orderly who escorted him to Therese's room.

Therese was delighted when Russell knocked and entered her room. She knew this meant Marion was safe. She was ready for him and there were two packed bags for Marion and Alain behind her door.

"I don't know how you'll get the suitcases out. The clinic is watched all the time. Look across the street, the man without a hat, they change over every four hours."

"Hugh, Mr Gibson, will have an idea, I'm sure. Thank you for your efficiency, that's saved us a lot of time."

"It was Sister Wilkins who asked one of the nurses to collect Marion's things, and some items for Alain. I have been tired this afternoon."

"I can't thank you enough for going out to find Marion. You saved her from being arrested."

"How is she?"

"Very upset to learn they have kept Edith in custody, and scared. Scared for herself too."

"Now she's with you at the embassy, she will be safe, until she returns to England. I've written a letter for Marion. Will you give it to her for me? It's to say goodbye."

"Goodbye? Where are you going? What about Alain? You can't just leave."

"It is Marion who will be leaving."

"Marion's not going anywhere. It's not safe for her to leave the embassy. She can stay with us."

"For how long, Mr Clarke? When will you Americans be leaving?"

"We have no plan to leave, nor to enter this war. We can do more by bringing humanitarian help, and some sense into the negotiating rooms, than firing more guns at people."

"Very sensibly spoken, Mr Clarke, but Marion will be going to England and taking Alain with her. I didn't know how this would come about, but I can see it will happen quickly now."

"What?" Russell exploded. "She can't leave with a baby. It's not hers. And her mother? Her mother would take to her bed. You have no idea what you are saying. This is preposterous. You can't ruin Marion's life in this way. It's too much."

"You're right, Mr Clarke. It is too much to ask that Marion keeps Alain, but in my letter I've asked that she find a family for him in England, away from this war. I don't think that is too much to ask."

"But Marion isn't going to England. She just needs to stay safe, until all's gone quiet. She'll be here, she can't leave."

"It's not safe for her here, you have to face this. She has to leave and will only do this if you encourage her to go."

Russell slumped into the chair and put his head in his hands.

"I only came back because of her. I was flattered to be asked, who wouldn't be, but it was being near to Marion that made me say yes. I will miss her so much."

"And she will miss you. You are going to have time apart, but there'll always be a bond between the two of you. Your love is like a river with stepping stones across it. Sometimes you'll stand together on the same stone, sometimes one will be leading the other, and some-times one will be waiting for the other to catch up. The water of the river is your love for each other and it's deep. It will never run dry."

"Fine words, but if I'm not there with her, she might turn to another."

"Marion will never be distracted by another, Russell. You fill up a space in her that is open to no other, just as she does for you."

"How do you know these things? And who says they're true?"

"Would you feel better if you believed them?"

"Of course, much better. I would never have to doubt her again."

"Then hold that belief and enjoy the life it creates for you."

"You mean just tell myself that's the way it is, and live as if it's true."

"Yes, hold this truth within you and it will set the path for both of you."

"It sounds so simple the way you say it. If only it were that easy."

"It is that easy. With your determination you can manage it."

"You teach well, but you never sound religious."

"I'm delighted to hear that. Religion captures and contains, but truths are a source of energy that is boundless, as is love."

"You're a wise one, Therese."

"And yet I've lived so little. Yes, I know people think that of the religious orders. It's not my wisdom, Russell, it's our wisdom; I only lift a veil for you to see what's already within you. Trust the truths within you and your life will be rich."

They were interrupted by a knock on the door and Hugh was ushered in by an orderly.

"Excuse me, I'm looking for Therese."

"Yes," said Russell who had taken in the look of surprise on Hugh's face. "This is Sister Therese."

"But, you're a nun. I thought you were a nursing sister. How did, how could …?"

Hugh was unable to string a sentence together and looked very perplexed.

"I must apologize," Hugh said. "I thought Marion said Therese was the mother of Alain, but I must have remembered that incorrectly."

"No, you are quite correct," Therese said.

"Mr Gibson, it's Mr Gibson from the embassy," Russell intervened with a proper introduction.

"Mr Gibson," Therese said as she nodded her greeting. "Thank you for the help you are extending to Marion. I am confident you will keep her safe."

"Thank you. Yes, but it sounds like your early warning is what saved her. We have a lot to thank you for," Hugh said as he recovered his composure.

"My debt to you will be the greater Mr Gibson."

"I must apologize for being so abrupt, but if you will excuse us, we must leave now."

"Everything was packed and ready," Russell told Hugh.

"That's an excellent help. We'll put the cases in the hall for Pierre to collect later. Sister Therese, we must say goodbye, and I am saddened by your circumstances." Hugh stepped forward to shake her hand, but Therese had pressed her palms together and bowed her head to him instead.

"God's blessings go with you."

Russell felt moved as he left the room. Her earlier words had touched him and he looked forward to telling Marion of their river of love.

"It's worse than I thought," Hugh said to Russell as they walked back to the legation. "The Germans have arrested a whole organization of people who have been transporting Belgian, French, and British soldiers back to their regiments or to England. Edith and Marion at the clinic were one link in a very long chain. This is serious and I would prefer that Marion was safely away before I become embroiled in it."

"Why did Edith confess? Did Sister Wilkins know?"

"Apparently they trapped her with some accusations that she was profiteering from her involvement and she was incensed and trapped herself with her replies. She hasn't said much as yet, but with their techniques they will run rings around her and will have what they want before too long. Sister Wilkins only had a little time with her before she was released, but she said that Edith seemed resigned and even a little relieved. She'd lived with the anxiety of discovery for so long, she was quite worn out."

"What happens now? What about Marion?"

"She must leave with me for London, the day after tomorrow. I'll apply for her travel pass tomorrow."

"But that isn't straightforward, is it. Who will you say she is and why she needs to travel? They don't hand these passes out easily, do they?"

"No, you're right. We'll need to think of a story that I can take to the kommandant. I wish von Below was still here; von Bissing is a very difficult man. This timing is bad. Perhaps you and Marion can help me with some fabrication this evening."

"That's if Marion can be convinced to leave. She can be stubborn you know."

"What woman isn't?" They both tried to laugh to break the tension.

"And don't forget you'll need two passes," Russell said.

"Two? I wouldn't like to think you're leaving too. You're too important here."

"No, not for me, for the baby. Alain has to leave too."

"Yes, I can understand why his mother can't keep him. That was something of a shock. I would have liked to have seen Therese in the witness stand. She alone would have defeated the German defence at the inquiry last year."

"She has given me notebooks full of victim's statements. Perhaps there'll be another chance to hold the Germans to account."

"That, my friend, depends on who wins this war."

For the remainder of their journey Russell described to Hugh the attack that Therese suffered.

"A remarkable woman," said Hugh. "We must make sure her son stays safe."

4th June 1915
Brussels
Russell and Marion

"You need to leave."

These were almost the first words Russell said to Marion when he returned to her at the legation.

"Oh, I see. I know it's been an imposition for me to come here, but I thought …"

"No, not leave the embassy," Russell cut across her, "well, yes you do need to leave here, but I mean you need to leave Brussels, Belgium. We need to get you back to England."

"What? Why? What's happened, what do you mean? I'm not going anywhere." Resistance edged every word.

Russell sat with her and told her all that Hugh had gleaned from Sister Wilkins.

"It's more serious than we thought, isn't it?" Marion said.

Russell could see that she was shaken.

"So many people arrested. I dread to think what will happen to them. Shouldn't I stay and help them?"

"Marion, there isn't anything you can do, and it won't help anyone if you are arrested too."

"Is it possible that I can get away? The escape line has been broken."

Russell took Marion's questions as acceptance that she had to leave. Relieved that she needed no further convincing, Russell told her of Hugh's plans to take her to England and to apply for her travel authorization the next day.

"He needs some help concocting a story to justify your pass."

"That's easy," Marion said, "but how easy will it be to secure a pass? I thought it was impossible."

"Next to impossible," said Russell, "but the American flag still carries some weight around here. So do you have some ideas of what he can say?"

"Yes, but Russell …"

"Yes I know," Russell interrupted her once again. "You'll need to take Alain with you."

"How did you know?"

"Let's just say, I spent half an hour with Therese. She sends her love and this note. Her final words were, 'It's him. It's Mr Gibson.' She said you would understand."

"I keep telling you, Russell, there is nothing between Hugh and myself. You must believe this."

"I do, truly I do. Therese meant you would understand when you read her letter."

Russell handed the envelope to Marion.

"Your bags will arrive soon; Pierre has gone to collect them. The Germans have someone watching the clinic all the time. You can't go back. Sister Wilkins said Edith mentioned the name Quien. She thinks he was the spy that exposed you all."

"I thought there was something strange about that one. It was Culloch who brought him in. He told us he was a French soldier."

"You were lucky to have got away with it all for so long," Russell said.

"That's why the last group got across the border so easily. It was the escape line they were after, not the soldiers. This all feels so strange and sudden, I feel quite sick. I won't be able to say good-bye to Therese or Sister Wilkins, or any of the girls. And Edith, what about Edith? I can't just abandon her. I hate to be running away."

"They all want you safe, more than anything else, and so do I. But are you sure you should be taking Alain with you? Isn't he best left here for the authorities to deal with?"

"Unless Therese has written something to the contrary, he's coming with me."

"But isn't it going to be complicated for you, arriving home with a baby?"

"With an orphan, Russell. He's an orphan."

"Yes, I know, but I'm sure people will gossip, and it is such a responsibility to find a home for him. Surely he should be left here."

"I feel so awful leaving Edith. The least I can do is fulfil my commitment to Therese."

"No one will think badly of you for leaving him at the clinic. These are unexpected circumstances that change everything."

"It will be easier for me to find a family for him through the Church at home, and better to get him away from this war."

"If you're sure?"

"Yes, I am."

Marion was meeting Hugh and Russell for dinner. Pierre had delivered her suitcases and Marion was grateful for the thoughtful packing that had been done for her. She could change for dinner and had all the necessary paraphernalia to look after Alain. Marion had held Alain in her arms as she read Therese's letter. She sat motionless for a long time afterwards, lost in her thoughts, as he drifted off to sleep.

In her letter Therese described her vision of Marion on a ship to England with Alain and a man. That man was Hugh. Therese had known it was not Russell, but knew of no other until Hugh had walked into her room. That was what her words meant; she would be travelling with Hugh. Therese wanted her to take Alain and secure the best care for him in England. Marion's commitment to Alain was unswerving, but her confidence was some distance behind. She had been adamant with Russell about taking him, but as she looked at him in her arms the magnitude of the step she was taking hit her. Circumstances were dictating so much and Marion felt out of control.

Marion preferred to think of her life as determined by herself. Goodness knows the number of battles she had fought to make sure her wishes had not been subsumed; and then someone like Therese comes along, and with certitude seems to know what is going to happen. Marion could make no sense of it, but Therese held a conviction

357

that was difficult to ignore. And now it looked as if she had no choice anyway, the way the situation had developed. But would Hugh be able to secure the travel passes? If she believed Therese, he would.

"So what you are suggesting", Hugh said at the dinner table, "is that I take von Bissing to one side and request he hears me on a delicate matter. I tell him that my fiancée is due to arrive in Brussels and that I have to remove my mistress and love child to London immediately. If my fiancée catches a whiff of my liaison, the wedding would be off and it would cause a dreadful scandal. Appeal to him man-to-man, and he will come up trumps with the travel pass. That's quite a story."

Russell was open-mouthed in admiration as Marion outlined her idea.

"It's brilliant," Russell said. "I really think that could work. How did you think of it, Marion?"

"It's a good story," Hugh said, "apart from two things. I don't have a fiancée and von Bissing will assume I'm a man of low morals, and in this war morals are the only thing I'm able to represent with any consistency. I'm not sure that I'm prepared to lose my reputation over this. Do excuse me for putting my reputation first, Marion."

"No, I see that entirely, it's too big a price to pay. It was a silly idea."

"Not at all. I think it has great merit. We just need to think our way around it. I'm sure we can use it but we need perhaps to change the players, that's all."

During dinner they worked over the idea until they had a version that did not compromise Hugh. Instead it compromised Russell, but as a more junior member of staff, this carried less significance. Armed for his meeting the next day, Hugh withdrew and left Marion and Russell on their own, but Marion also rose from the table.

"I've left Alain for too long. I need to check on him."

"You would have been informed if he was in any distress, but nonetheless, I'll come with you." Russell escorted Marion to her room.

Assured that he was settled, and not in need of a feed, they faced each other across his makeshift cradle, and both watched him as he slept.

"Such innocence," they both said at the same time and then looked at each other, in a way that conveyed such strength of feeling that they were both transfixed. Marion broke the spell.

"Therese has given him over to my care. She asked me to find a family for him in England; she wants him away from this war. He's to be known as an orphan; nothing of his parentage is to be told to him. She wants him freed from the violence of his conception and the heartache of his birth. She says I'll know the right family and I am to keep him until that time. And she says goodbye. To me and to her son."

A tear fell from Marion as she said these final words.

"That's all very well, Therese saying what she wants, but what about you? Are you ready to take on this responsibility, even for a short while? You have your career to think of, your training. You'll want to pick that up again in England, won't you?"

"Of course I will, but only after Alain is settled. He knows me, he recognizes my voice; I'm the one that can comfort him. I'm not going to abandon him or we might as well have let the Church take him in the first place; he needs loving care."

"We all need that," Russell walked around the cradle and pulled her to him.

"Marion, I love you so much I can't bear the thought of you leaving, but I love you so much I can't bear the thought of you staying and being unsafe, or arrested."

"Why don't you come back too? Then we could be together."

"And be a family." Russell finished the sentence for her.

"And what's wrong with that thought?"

"Nothing, my darling, nothing at all. But I can't leave my post, not now. This war is entrenched. The Germans are here for the long haul and the Belgian struggle has only just started. I really am needed here and in all conscience I can't turn my back on my duty."

"Not like I am, you mean, running away."

Marion tried to pull herself out of his arms but he held her fast.

"Marion, you know that isn't how it is. You've taken more risks than most and saved many lives, of that I am sure. But no one wants you to lose your life or your liberty. We must leave that to the soldiers, God rest their souls, but I want you safe."

"When it's over, this war, will we be together? Can you see us still together?"

"Marion, I can't imagine my life without you. I'll always want to be with you. Will you wait for me?"

"Yes, I'll wait."

"That will mean withstanding all those introductions your mother will present you with."

"I'll have my father on my side."

"No more misunderstandings." Russell kissed her.

"No more deceits," Marion returned his kiss, "apart from one."

"What's that?"

"Can you mess your bed to make it look as if you've slept in it and then spend the night here with me?"

Russell was gone before she had a moment to change her mind.

Hugh waited in the anteroom to von Bissing's office. His presence had been announced and he knew that protocol would demand he be kept waiting at least 20 minutes before he was admitted: the grandiose bluster of one with the upper hand. Politics was full of such behaviour and Hugh had long since stopped taking any of it personally. It particularly suited him to accept his place today, so he waited patiently and ran through the prepared script in his mind. In the event, it did not go to plan.

"Good morning, Herr Gibson."

"Good morning, Herr Bissing. Thank you for meeting me at short notice. I need to travel to London and have an additional person travelling with me. I am here to ask you for suitable authorizations. A senior signature always seems to make the passage trouble free. My passenger is a woman and her baby. She is the friend of one of my junior colleagues."

"London, um, when will you be back?"

"It's a quick trip for me. I'll return in three days."

"And you'll have your driver and car?"

"Yes, and this woman and her baby."

"Will they come back?"

"No, they will stay in England."

"But you will return?"

"Yes."

"And the minister will be here?"

"Yes. No one else from the legation is travelling. Its just me that has been called to London."

"Do you have the forms?"

"Yes, they're here."

"The baby is young for such a journey?"

360

"Yes, but he's healthy, and hopefully the journey will be straightforward."

"I can't guarantee that, but you will be allowed to pass. Make sure your flag is flying at all times, and do not let your passengers leave the vehicle."

"No, of course not."

Hugh was astounded at how easy it had been; in fact it felt too easy. His carefully prepared story was redundant. However, as he gathered together the now signed papers, the tone of von Bissing changed.

"I have given you an easy time today, Herr Gibson. A gift, you should view this pass as a gift, and perhaps you could return from London with a gift for me."

"I have no reason to ask for special dispensations. This woman's reason for travel is legitimate."

"But the baby is illegitimate, an embarrassment to someone, or do I assume incorrectly?"

"The parentage of the child is irrelevant. I will not enter into deals with you and I've no intention of bringing you a gift from London."

"So it's of no personal matter to you if this woman travels or not?."

"Professional, yes, personal, no. You've signed the passes, but do you want to think again?" Hugh offered the papers back to him.

"No, Herr Gibson, von Below told me you are a man of honour and I respect that, but should you stumble across the works of Dickens when you are in London, I would love to borrow them from you on your return. I appreciate that this might not be possible."

"You want books? Is that the gift you want from London?"

"Yes it is. I like to read in English."

"Let it not be said that war made beasts of us entirely. We are civilized beings after all. I'll return with the books you've asked for, but as a gift, not in exchange for a travel pass. I hope you understand that."

"Of course, Herr Gibson, of course. I wish you a straightforward journey."

Russell was wide-eyed and wide-awake, despite no sleep. What a night it had been. He and Marion had lain together and talked and made love and touched and made love again; she was perfect. He

361

had not wanted the intimacy of their endearments and embraces to end; their union felt complete. He was humbled by her trust in him. They shed tears at the thought of time apart. He had described the picture of their river of love that Therese had given to him. They had held each other, and despite the turmoil of her impending departure had felt a sense of peace; though sleep had eluded them both.

He had a busy work day ahead. Marion was attending to Alain when he left her, early, before the embassy staff stirred. He hoped that she was able to catch up on some lost hours of sleep, but he doubted she would. She was fretting about Edith, and she herself was not yet safe. Her world had turned upside down, and she now faced the reality of returning home, unannounced and with a child. Not hers, but people would talk: they always did. She had come to Brussels to escape the suffocating expectations of her mother. No wonder she dreaded going back, but there really was no choice. He could not begin to comprehend their separation, but that was tomorrow's challenge. Today he had to induct two new auditors and he was actually pleased to be busy. He finished dressing, and set off to find some breakfast.

Marion tried to enjoy a languorous stretch but her legs were caught in the tangled sheets, and she let out a deep sigh instead. She felt featherweight as she floated in and out of light dozing. She was in a dream-like state, relaxed, and the only thing she wanted to do was purr. No wonder her sisters looked so smug on their return from their honeymoons. She now shared their secret.

She knew it was time to stir herself, wash, dress, and breakfast. Russell had suggested she take Alain into the gardens. They were secluded at the back of the legation building and were quite a sun trap. There was very little for her to do and she was concerned that time would hang. Not used to idleness, she had to find some purpose in the day. She would write some letters, to Edith, Elizabeth, and Therese. Therese, what would she write to Therese? There was nothing left to say. It was clear from her letter that she yearned solitude, so further words from Marion might just be received as noise, but she wanted to thank her for her escape from the Germans. Most importantly, Therese trusted her with Alain and that was all both of them needed to know. Marion pushed herself up and out of the bed. Time to get on with the day, her last in Brussels.

Dinner was a sombre affair after Hugh delivered the news that their travel authorizations were secure.

"It wasn't a problem at all. Bissing seemed more concerned to know that I was going to return than about my departure. Perhaps he thought I was the start of a surreptitious American evacuation. By the way your reputation remains intact, Russell, I didn't have to mention you by name."

The news was bittersweet for Marion and Russell but they were both chilled when Hugh announced they were to start their journey at midnight. Marion and Russell locked eyes and a silent conversation passed between them. Shock at the suddenness of the departure, sadness that they would not share another night together, something they had both anticipated throughout the day. Each soaked in the sight of the other and stocked their memory banks. Hugh had to repeat himself to ensure he had been heard.

"I've always had easier passages at night. There is less army traffic on the roads and no pedestrians."

"But what about the curfew?" Russell asked.

"Our passes are for travel at any time, and the sentries hardly examine the passes at night. They don't want their rest disturbed. I want you out of here and across that border as soon as we can manage it, Marion."

"I am so sorry for causing all this trouble. You really are being so kind-hearted to me and Alain. Was there any news of Edith today?"

"Yes, the minister was informed that Edith had been transferred to the prison and charges had been made against her and several of the others who had been arrested on the same day. I have sent a note around to Sister Wilkins so that she can arrange to take some provisions to Edith."

"Oh, the poor thing. She must be so frightened for Edith. And I can't bear to think of Edith in a prison cell," Marion said.

"I will give a full briefing to your ministers when I am in London and Villobar, the Spanish minister, will visit Edith in my absence, and reassure her that we will be petitioning on her behalf."

"Does Sister Wilkins know this? It will give her such peace of mind."

"Yes, I put that in my note too."

"And I will visit her on my return from London, perhaps with some assurances from your government too." Or perhaps not, thought Hugh, but he kept these sentiments to himself. He felt on edge about the whole business. Edith had been caught breaking the rules and the penalties were clearly known. It was hard to see on what her defence could be based, or why the British government would choose to get involved.

"I suggest you have some rest after dinner. The journey will feel arduous without sleep. What about Alain? Can you manage with him on the move, overnight?"

"Yes, yes, of course. He'll be asleep. As long as he's fed and warm, he doesn't seem to mind where he is."

"As long as you're close to him," Russell said, "that's what settles him."

"He can lie in a basket on the seat between us," Hugh said. "Pierre thinks his pram can fit on the back; he has some straps. I suggest we adjourn and meet at the back entrance just before midnight. Until then I'll leave you two in peace. Put your bags in the corridor and Pierre can pack the car for us while we rest."

Hugh left the table and the room, and within seconds of his departure Russell had Marion in his arms. They released hold of each other to walk along the corridors to her room. Alain was asleep. Russell put her suitcases outside the door before he locked it on their final private moments.

They were a few minutes late to the car, but Hugh was going through papers with the driver and seemed not to notice. Alain was asleep in his basket and had not stirred when Russell positioned him on the back seat. With one last look that lingered between them Marion had climbed in the car and put her hand in the basket. She found comfort in the human touch as Alain curled his hand around her little finger. She had given her letters to Russell and received his promise to deliver them when he considered it safe. They had hardly spoken in their last hour together, satisfied to breathe each other in, with the gentlest of touches.

"I love you, Nurse Drake."

"I love you, Mr Clarke."

"My darling Marion."

"My precious Russell."

"Are we ready then?" Hugh was oblivious to the endearments he was interrupting, and he sat himself the other side of Alain.

"Until the next time, Marion." Russell closed her door.

"Until the next time," Marion said to herself as she turned to take in the last look of him before the car turned out of the gate and he was out of sight.

Marion closed her eyes and rested her head back against the seat. Hugh appreciated this was not the best time to talk. Was this the end or the beginning of their love story, he wondered? Who could tell, these days, who could tell? Perhaps next spring would bring back blue days and fair.

FIVE YEARS LATER, 1920

LONDON

17th March 1920
London, England
Postscript

Marion gasped as the cloth was pulled away to reveal the statue of Edith Cavell. Here she was, a VIP on the steps of St. Martin in the Fields church, to the side of Trafalgar Square, among royalty and robed dignitaries. Heads craned to look at Edith's likeness, her face high above the crowd, and her words immortalized on the facia of the plinth: *"Patriotism is not enough, I must have no hatred or bitterness for anyone."*

Marion felt hatred and bitterness towards the Germans, who had judged and shot Edith, another victim of the war. Marion was swamped by a feeling of sadness and remorse, every time she gave thanks for her own escape. She had been unable to save Edith.

With the speeches over, the last hands shaken and the final note played, Marion walked slowly around the statue. She read the inscribed words aloud: *"humanity, devotion, fortitude, sacrifice"*, and each word was echoed by the child who was holding her hand.

They remained, on their own with Edith, long after the crowd had dispersed.

AUTHORS' ACKNOWLEDGEMENTS:
FICTION FROM FACT

We are storytellers, but the stories are not of our making, they were there for us to find. This novel is largely and at times loosely based on research into the life of Edith Cavell, matron of a nurses' training school and clinic in Brussels and real and imagined characters in the military, political and civilian worlds of British, Belgian and Americans caught up within a war zone and occupied territory at the start of the First World War.

Within the context of mass slaughter and the trench warfare to come, the number of Belgian civilian casualties from the occupation of their country was relatively small. Nevertheless, the ruthlessness of the German Army resulted in mindless destruction, the deaths of men, women, and children and the removal of able-bodied men to work in Germany. It is a matter of debate how much this was due to a paranoia of resistance in their newly occupied territory, primed by experiences from the 1870–71 Franco-Prussian War, and how much of the cause was due to a calculated and premeditated intention to intimidate a smaller nation, and thereby complete its capitulation. Whatever the reason, the Belgian people found themselves the unfortunate victims of a type of warfare thought to belong to less civilized times in Europe.

The events, circumstances, and organizations featured in the book were real, and mostly located at the time, and in the places shown. Fictitious names are given to main characters such as Marion, Therese, Russell, Privates Culloch and Elliott, Isabelle and Lieutenant Baxter, but each is a composite representation of people active at that time. For example, the character Isabelle was inspired by the war hero, Louise Thuliez. All named officials in Brussels and London were real. Colonel Beecham's real name was Boger. One date is out by a few weeks. Edith Cavell was actually arrested in August 1915, not June; creative licence has been taken here. In essence these, or lives such as these, were lived and impacted by the war in the ways described, and the source of their experiences has often been through their diaries and records, in particular those of Hugh Gibson, secretary to the American legation in Brussels, Brand Whitlock, American minister to Belgium, and Princess Marie de Croy, and a selection of regimental war diaries. No facts of any significance have been meddled with, but many personal experiences and conversations rather than official events are imagined.

Trained as a biographer, Lorraine is led to step into the footsteps of people's lives and during her research was stunned by a sentence written by Brand Whitlock in his journal, eight months after the start of the war: *At a certain maternity home extensive preparations were being made to receive nuns from the convents in the eastern provinces of Belgium, victims of German soldiers; their hour was approaching.* In a journal of two volumes and some 1000 pages, this was the only statement of fact offered about the atrocities that the Belgians suffered from the advancing German armies; all other references were prefaced with "alleged" and "reportedly"; Mr. Whitlock was governed by the neutrality of the politics he represented. In this one sentence he revealed a truth that was not even exposed during the Belgian Commission of Enquiry into the German contraventions of the Hague Conventions of War, held in Belgium in November 1914.

The German field marshal and military strategist Alfred von Schlieffen died in 1913 but his name lives on as a principal actor in the tragedy that became the First World War. The *Schlieffen Plan* envisaged a German victory over France in not much more than a month, speed being of the essence so that German forces could be turned around to face Russia, which was expected to be much slower to mobilize. The neutrality of Belgium was not allowed to disrupt the grand Prussian plan. Among the many commentaries and theories as to why the plan failed there is consistent agreement that the unexpected resistance of the relatively tiny Belgian Army was an important factor. Another was the arrival of the British Expeditionary Force (BEF), or the "Old Contemptibles" as the men were proud to be known. The outnumbered BEF fought valiantly against superior odds at Mons. Circumstances meant that the subsequent withdrawal and fighting retreat was not a particularly orderly affair and men frequently found themselves cut off from their units. Many benefitted from the selfless generosity of the Belgian populace, the goodwill continuing even after it became clear that punishment for such assistance included execution. The soldiers kept turning up months after their initial separation from their colleagues, their objective being to reach the Dutch border. The stories of furtive travel, forged papers, hide-outs, civilian disguises, and escape routes provide a harbinger for the more familiar escape narratives of World War II.

There remains controversy among historians and commentators as to whether atrocities took place in Belgium at the hands of the Germans in 1914. The popularly held view is that all references to difficulties were part of a propaganda machine designed to encourage more young men to join Kitchener's volunteer army. Unfortunately the truth was belied by the wild stories repeated in the media of German soldiers bayonetting babies and chopping off the hands of children, events for which no witnesses could be found and were thereafter discredited.

Together with first hand accounts researched by us, recent academic publications by Horne & Kramer, Lipkes, and Zuckerman gave access, through their in-depth researches, to the actions of the German armies during the early weeks of the hostilities; we hope this novel extends the reach of their work and adds our voices to the injustices they report. Like these authors we do not project responsibility for these crimes onto German nationals today; but as members of a global and increasingly psychologically mature society we recognize that an acknowledgement of injustice is the key ingredient to heal hurt. Our hope is to give each soul rest and that readers will offer an apology for these misjudged actions of the past.

Our thanks and acknowledgements go to the London Library, the National Archives at Kew, Times Online, and Abe Books for access to invaluable material currently out of print and archived files; and to the writings of Brand Whitlock, Hugh Gibson, Princess Marie de Croy, and a selection of biographers of Edith Cavell.

A book is always a collaborative effort and thanks are hereby extended to Voula Greenfield, who tutored the authors through the creative and writing process, for Yvonne Bond's entrée to publisher, Oliver Rathbone and for all the professional support through Karnac Books, including Kate Pearce and editor James Darley. Friends and family have provided support and encouragement throughout this endeavour, and a significant number made direct contributions through their review of early drafts. Our thanks in particular go to Sandy, Liz, Gill, CJ, Nick, Yvonne, David, Marion, Teresa, Morag, and Jenny.

We have been honoured to represent the people whose stories are in this book, and on behalf of those who lost their lives and their innocence in World War I,

we remember them

A donation from the profits of each book sold by the authors will go to the War Memorial Trust (www.warmemorials.org).

ABOUT THE AUTHORS

Lorraine Bateman was born in Suffolk and now divides her time between Buckinghamshire and the Isle of Wight. After a corporate career in human resources, Lorraine studied for a master's degree in biography at the University of Buckingham. She now combines work in the field of executive development with writing biographically based historic fiction. She has a keen interest in the First World War, in particular how this affected and influenced the lives of civilians. *At Midnight in a Flaming Town* is her debut novel.

Paul Cole was born in Sussex and now lives in Buckinghamshire with his two sons. After an early career as a City shipbroker followed by sales and marketing work in the healthcare industry, Paul now largely concentrates his time on research and writing. He has a keen interest in military history and a desire to make the stories of the past approachable for new generations of readers. He enjoys unearthing little-known historic facts and features and weaving them into accessible and entertaining narrative. His collaboration on *At Midnight in a Flaming Town* is his debut novel.